Brian M. Birkland

Tau Effect: Volume II

The Mantle Stirs

Follow on social media:
Facebook: @BraveYoungTitan
Twitter: @brian_birkland

AZB Press, LLC. Glen Ellyn, IL

Contents

For Dawn:

My love;

my companion;

my best friend;

my board-game nemesis.

Chapter 1

August 3, 2011

Billy inhaled mountain air while Kirk stared into the midday clouds. Billy quietly broke the three-minute silence. "*Fly* is better. It's just better. The styling is better. The talent is more refined. They knew what they were doing." The young ranchers sat two meters apart on a boulder that faced endless, rolling hills.

"I don't know how you can say that," Kirk retorted condescendingly. He kept the volume of his voice low, as had Billy. "It's a bunch of radio pandering. *Wide Open Spaces* was genuine. That was before they sold out. *Fly* was too mainstream for me, man."

"They were both mainstream. *Spaces* had a bunch of top hits too. You're talking as though it was their first album. It was just Natalie's, man. They were already hitting stride by then in terms of songwriting. She just put them over the top. Oh, Natalie…"

"I'm not arguing with that. Nobody can. But," Kirk's voice grew quieter still, "*Wide Open Spaces*, man, it just speaks to you on a much simpler, more primitive level. The whole album just has a deeper message to it."

The young men jolted as Kirk's father chimed in from behind them, "What are you boys arguing about?"

Without hesitation they replied in unison, "Metallica!"

"Hell yeah. Carry on. Get back to work soon though. I'm headed into town to grab some basics. I'll be back around supper but don't wait for me."

Kirk leaned back on his elbows and waited until his father's truck was out of sight and earshot before he spoke again. "Wonder how much he heard."

Deep in thought, Billy did not respond. His eyes fixated on an orange bluff that rose above and behind black and green bushes that dotted the hills before him.

"You know I was right, though," Kirk quipped. "You okay, man?"

Billy's gaze did not break from the distant bluff. "I wonder if the world will swallow itself. Wonder if the whole thing will just wither and rot. Wonder if we are ants or titans, if this is to be the end. Are we destined for great things?"

"That's pretty dark, man. Hell does that mean, anyway? Probably not. I don't know, I doubt it," Kirk smirked, as he squeezed a cigarette with calloused fingers. "Nothin' round here but rocks and trees. But I'm not planning on working for my dad my whole life. Are you?" He took a drag and puffed it up into the thick, summer air.

Billy's gums swelled as he smelled Kirk's cigarette. He shifted his weight and twisted a bit to avoid smelling it. In the distance, the clouds and sunlight took turns painting the trees and red rocks. "Your dad is a good man, but no. I never saw myself working a ranch until I die. But you see that storm out in the ocean and it makes you wonder."

"Doesn't make me wonder much." He shrugged when Billy shot a disapproving glare but kept his eyes on the distant trees and hills. "I've never been much of an ocean guy. Fine right here in the mountains, you know?"

"But it is all connected - all of this. How can the ocean survive without the land?"

"Are you going all Shoshone on me again?" Kirk laughed, only half-joking.

"There will come a time when the empty storm in the ocean will reach the land. It keeps growing. These hills seem strong because they are all we've ever known. But the world is dying. We thought it was so stable, but here it shrinks beneath the waters."

"Billy you've been my only real friend, over a year since you came to stay here, so you know I ain't racist. But are you going to go on one of them spirit-wolf vision quests?"

Billy leaned onto his right side and stealthily burrowed his left hand into the front pocket of his jeans. He rummaged through the pocket as if taking inventory but withdrew an empty and clammy hand shortly after. He turned his attention to the ground. "Maybe I'm just wired differently.

My pop wants me to come back to Wind River, but I don't know. When I left, I guess I thought I would find myself or something. He's the only one there that would have me back anyhow. I never felt like I fit in. But I don't feel like I fit in here either."

"Nothin' here to fit in with, Billy. I don't know. If you ask me this place sucks. There's never anything to do but work and sleep. Climb some rocks and get drunk, I guess. Best thing we got going on out here. Nearest town is miles away. I'm looking to get the hell out as soon as I can. Not that I want you to go back, but was it so bad at the reservation? I ne'er been there."

"Where I see opportunity, you see walls. I suppose we're both right."

"What's it like there? You never talk about it."

"It's a place. Some people are good, and some are bad. Some do drugs and others preach. Some do both. There is no alcohol but there are drunken people everywhere. Arapahoe and Shoshone pretend to get along until the people passing out the food and treats turn their backs. Most people don't want to leave. They call me an apple for wanting to get away from it. That's why my pop was so upset."

"An apple?"

"Red on the outside and white within. People on the rez resent outsiders. Some hate them. You wouldn't understand. It's easy to feel trapped in such a wide-open space when there are so many reminders of the past. My dad gets it. He just feels trapped too."

"Trapped on the reservation?"

"No, just trapped. That's what I'm telling you. I thought it was the rez, but it's not. I thought I was trapped there, but the world is shrinking. Maybe it falls apart while we're alive, or maybe it won't. But I feel like I was supposed to do something important." He reached back into his pocket and smirked satisfactorily. He looked at Kirk, "Meet me at the bluff tonight."

"Sure, what time?"

"I should be done around six. You?"

"Same."

Billy dismounted the giant rock and shouted over his shoulder, "Let's shoot for seven then."

"What are you up to?" Kirk laughed in futility.

After racing past the horses and rousting the chickens, Billy arrived at the small shed that he had called home for the past year. He pressed his middle and ring fingers together with his thumb and made a Catholic cross gesture on his forehead and chest. He waved a kiss to an eagle feather that was attached to a crucifix on the unpainted, wooden-plank wall as he entered. He was comforted by the familiar smell of the grease from the stale machinery that had lived there before him. A small twin bed and a makeshift dresser were the only furniture in the ramshackle abode. He closed the door suspiciously, to make sure no one was spying. After a few moments, his eyes adjusted to the darkness, but by then he was already kneeling by the bed. Beams of light streamed through the cracks in the humble dwelling. The shed boasted no heat or electricity. He refused to let the Wallons run either out from the main house a mere fifty steps away, despite Kirk's repeated insistence. Part of Billy wanted to deny permanence to the arrangement. Another part liked the humility of not being provided for. Mostly though, he liked the contrast that a simple blanket provided when he came in from the elements.

Billy gently lifted the mattress from the bed and pulled out a journal and a handgun. He checked the safety on the gun and jammed it into the back of his jeans, under his shirt. He clutched the journal with both hands for a few seconds and then smelled it. It had traveled with him for six years, since his twelfth birthday. Inside were notes, poems, and doodles. He had never shown another soul, although he suspected that his father had seen some of the earlier pages.

As cautiously as he had entered, he exited the shed. He moved quickly through the warm, summer air toward the edge of the property where the hills became rocky. He looked back to ensure nobody was following him. He ran his fingers over the fabric of his jeans to confirm that all nine tiny items were still accounted for.

After two hours, Kirk grew frustrated that Billy had disappeared. Several chores had still not been completed since their brief chat. Kirk's watch said three, and he assumed that Billy would still be around finishing his work. He jogged to Billy's shed and rapped on the door, but there was no answer. "Billy?" he shouted in a few directions.

He wrote out a note for his father, who was presumably still in town shopping.

> *Dad – went off to find Billy. He was talking about the bluff earlier.*
> *Sorry about the chores - Can't find good help these days. Kidding.*
> *Back by supper. –KW*

Kirk took his bicycle and rode up the rocky trail toward the bluff. As the landscape turned red, he slowed to scan for a person. The bluff rarely had rock-climbing tourists, but in the summertime, Kirk had learned not to assume. He did not see anyone. *Billy's an expert climber and probably scaled the easier face of the bluff directly*, Kirk presumed. *Odd that he didn't take a bike, though.* Kirk rode around the long way to stay on his bicycle, but he saw no trace of another person.

He rode the length of the bluff as they knew it, which was two kilometers from east to west. The real formation was much larger, but their little universe was localized enough for Kirk to know what Billy had meant. Billy was not there. Kirk stopped to regroup, and slowly eyed the land.

Finally, he spotted a tiny billow of white smoke in the distance. He muttered, "Had the sky still been cloudy, you'd be out of luck, my friend." The smoke was high in the air, so Kirk estimated that it had been out for at least an hour. He pedaled furiously to find a ditch in the bluff that he had never recalled seeing. As he arrived, he startled an enormous bird whose feet grazed his cheek as it fled. Kirk's heart raced, having never seen such a majestic bird up close. His mind stalled on the yellow talons that came within a wind's wisp of his eye. He was unsettled as he turned to see the eagle's flight curve back toward him and felt as though it deliberately made eye contact with him. It continued its ascent and disappeared into the hills within seconds. Kirk heard the wind and a low-rumbling owl as he looked around again for his friend.

"Billy?" he called, but nobody answered. Next to a smoldering bush, he found Billy's journal, a pen, and a cigarette lighter. One page of the journal had been torn out and preserved, but the rest was toast.

Kirk took the page and read aloud to himself in disbelief.

> *I left my home and they would not have me back. My life is not special. But my vision is becoming clear. I must fly with the winds from the bluff to the Tower tonight. I feel my wings growing out from my back even as I write these words. A voice spoke to me and told me how to cheat the Geese. The first night he told me how to fly but I was not ready. He told me that Old Father has a purpose for me, and that I will fly. The second night I tried again, and the Geese tried to devour me. I ran away from them. I asked the voice what to do, and he appeared to me and said my name. I asked him for his name, and he finally spoke it to me in the old tongue, 'I am ba'ande; I am ba'angu. I am degwani boha pa'annai, toyatsukunümüttsi.' And he spoke strange gibberish and danced, 'Be warned Kwinaa – you will not want to eat your own brains! Kikimma, Kwinaa – I will show you to be one of the Puihwate!' Speaker brought me water and ran into the night. The third night I will not fail. This time I brought pills in my pocket and a gun in my hand to keep the Geese from beating me. They will not stop me today. He says I am ready to wait for the bia piyanranrinakaite, so he can heal the spirit world. I must build the torch that reaches the sky, to land the boats when the water meets the mountain. Lighthouse upon a cliff! Namapataatsiki! I see her: puih-buinbithi, e'apekkan gobe. The drug is taking hold.*

Below the writing was a crude drawing of a small lighthouse overlooking a road and a pasture. Kirk flipped the page to look for water, but there was no more to the sketch. Kirk had no idea what any of it meant.

He began investigating the ditch and soon found Billy. He was lying face-up with his shirt and jeans next to him, toward the bottom of a rock bed. Billy's eyes were open, and a gun was in his hand, but Kirk did not see any blood. He descended as quickly as he could and was relieved to see that Billy was breathing.

"Billy! Billy? What's the matter with you? What happened here?"

His friend did not understand.

Kirk smacked his face and took the gun from his hand. "What's gotten into you? Talk to me."

"Kwinaa... Puihwate... puih-buinbithi, e'apekkan gobe... Vbbblaava-vvibbb..."

"Let's get you out of here, bud." Kirk hoisted Billy over his arm and carried him back to the ranch. The trip took nearly an hour and the sun had almost set by the time they reached the house.

Kirk's father had recently returned to find the note. He was ready with a rant for his son but suspended it when he saw him carrying his friend in his arms. Blood streamed from Billy's mouth and his eyes had rolled back to conceal the pupils.

"I think he's dead. Can we use your truck, dad?"

"Let's go."

The clinic desk was empty when they entered. They shouted for help, and within a minute, a nurse came to greet them. The nurse took Billy back to treat him and asked that they stay in the waiting room. For forty-five minutes they waited, until the nurse came back to the waiting area with a doctor.

The doctor had little to offer other than that he suspected a drug overdose. "Your friend is still alive: barely. We pumped his stomach, but if he ingested something two to three hours ago, there's really nothing more we can do. He's nonresponsive and may be in a sort of catatonic state."

"Like a coma?" Kirk asked.

"No, this isn't a coma. He keeps muttering words, but he doesn't seem able to control his speech. Does he have any family that can care for him?"

Kirk's father answered, "His father lives over at Wind River. I called them when we got here, and they said they would let him know. I don't know if we can expect a call back. You said this is drug related?"

"Yes, does he have any history with drugs?"

Kirk and his father looked at each other and shrugged. The former responded, "Not that I've ever seen. He doesn't even smoke."

"Well his system was shocked by something. We pulled some blood, but I wouldn't expect to have the results back for a day or so. I've never seen anything quite like this."

"What is it?" Kirk pressed.

"Well his brain activity and motor functions seem almost nonexistent. He's barely breathing, and his heartrate has slowed to a crawl. It's as though he really is in a coma. But his mouth keeps muttering words I don't understand repeatedly. He's processing something, but we don't get what it might be. I can keep him overnight for observation, but after that I'm afraid without insurance there's only so much we can do here for him."

Kirk advocated for his friend for several minutes. He stayed by Billy's side overnight and attempted to understand what his friend was saying.

Just after ten the next morning, Billy's father, Mike, arrived in an old, flatbed pickup. An angry-looking Shoshone woman was driving. She prompted him to pile out of the vehicle, and the moment he did so she sped off and kicked dust in every direction. The man entered the clinic and asked to see his son.

Kirk was excited to meet him, despite the circumstances. "I've been listening to him all night, but I think he's speaking Shoshoni."

"He does not speak much Shoshoni," Billy's father said sternly.

"Oh. Well he kept a story in his diary about learning to fly with some Geese?"

"The Geese do not help him. That is not how the story goes."

"No, right, the Geese try to eat his brains."

"No, that is not right either. The Geese beat him. They leave him dead. When Coyote returns to life he is confused. He eats his *own* brains. Then he pukes because that's disgusting."

"That… really?"

Mike nodded, "Yep, it's a pretty gross story. You want to tell me what drugs you've been getting my son into?"

"Oh, I don't think he's into drugs, sir. This is the first time I've ever seen something like this. He's as straight as they come. He doesn't even drink."

"He is a good boy. He's just confused. I wonder what he's done to himself. I told him that leaving us was a bad idea. No matter. You said he was talking?"

"He stopped a few hours ago. I thought it was a lot of things at first. But really it was only a few. Do you know what *Kwinaa* means?"

"It's our last name," he shrugged with indifference. "It means eagle."

"Puihwate?"

"Blind."

Kirk paused. "I see. That's not what I was expecting. Here, he wrote this out. I think he wrote it after he took whatever he took, but before he tripped and hurt himself. I found it right next to him. Can you make any sense of it?"

As he handed over the journal page the nurse entered with a folder. Kirk eagerly inquired, "Are those the blood results? Is he going to be okay?"

The nurse replied, "No, actually these are the billing forms. The toxicity screen hasn't been sent out yet. What do you think this is, Sioux Falls?" Her joke was lost on the two men. "Anyway, I can tell you that drugs were involved. I see all the symptoms of an overdose of meth and maybe a few other things. I don't see any lesions or scarring though, so I would say this may have been his first time. I don't mean to be callous, but he's stable and we can't keep him here. He needs a place to go, and we'll need someone to bill. Are you the father?"

"Mike," he said, extending his hand. "I don't have money. But I can work until the debt is paid."

"I'm guessing you don't have any medical training, so you wouldn't be much good to me."

Billy's father turned his focus to Kirk, "Please tell your father that I will work off Billy's debt myself. May I stay and care for Billy in the meantime?"

"I can't see that being a problem, mister. I just hope he gets better."

The nurse added, "I have to be open with you, I'm not sure that's going to happen. He's catatonic. He may never snap out of this. It's hard to say what happens with the human body and brain, but there's no guarantee he ever recovers from the damage that's been done. Maybe if he'd gotten here sooner, we could have pumped more out of him, but at this point he's lucky to be alive; if you even want to call it that."

"Don't worry Mike," Kirk consoled. "We'll take good care of him. We'll get him back on his feet again."

"No, we won't," Mike sobbed quietly. "He did leave us. His spirit has flown away from here."

"What do you mean?"

Mike held up the journal page and translated, "I asked him for his name, and he finally spoke it to me in the old tongue, 'I am high above; I am above this place. I am your speaker,' that is, an interpreter that is a holy guide. He calls my son 'Eagle.' 'Come home, Eagle. I will show you to be one of the Blind.' He was told by this vision that he is of great importance. Does he have a girlfriend?"

"If he has, it's the first I've heard of it. I've never seen him leave the ranch in the past few months, except to head out into the wilderness on his own."

"In his vision a woman speaks to him with green eyes and a scarred face. Perhaps we can find her."

Chapter 2

December 4, 2020

"Five years ago, today," President Sarah McCourty spoke before the press podium as cameras flashed and microphones pressed toward her, "the great void where I now stand was calmed." A crowd of about three hundred cheered after nearly every statement. "The ground we're standing on today was the center of a horrific cataclysm that we did not understand. For nearly three decades, that endless abyss threatened our very existence. The disaster swallowed whole cities. We remember those that could not be evacuated from Auckland. We honor the memory of those from Honolulu and the Hawaiian Islands that could not make it out in time. We tribute the individuals lost from the islands, ships, and aircraft of the Pacific ranging from Antarctica to the Aleutians, and from Australia's Coral Sea to the coasts of San Diego and Tijuana.

"Our globe had a terrible blight. There were those that feared our world would end. There were many who lost faith in science and in their religious beliefs. But we are still here. We are resilient. All mankind unites today as one, to celebrate this new continent that has formed from the disaster that once threatened to destroy us. We have come a long way, but we have a tough road ahead. We have severe atmospheric conditions. We have global warming to contend with. Our oceanic ecosystem is forever changed. Behind me stands a stone monument which commemorates Pacifica's very first Continental Congress. On the ground surrounding the monument, here at the epicenter of the former Pacific Abysm, we have transported soil from thirty-nine countries. We have transplanted over two hundred species of plant life. We've brought a variety of critters to help the soil. The top minds from around the globe are working to ensure that this new ecosystem thrives. This small, symbolic gesture is not an attempt to create a new biosphere. Rather, it embodies the cooperation of nations to respect and cherish the second chance that our planet was given. Over time, perhaps we will make this barren land home to many plants and creatures, and home to many people as well.

"This continent formed over the course of just five years. I'm humbled by the scientific terms that were once mumbo-jumbo to most of us and have since become household words. 'Casimir-Polder Field'? 'Quantum Collapse'?" The crowd laughed. "As a Crystalline Curtain formed around the former abyss, the void was filled with new minerals from Earth's mantle that were previously untapped. With these new resources the world will enter an unprecedented era of peaceful sharing. Trade between the East and the West will now resume. Now that the Curtain has reached a safe level and super-solid mantle material expansion near coastal areas is within safe parameters, shipping lanes are officially reopened."

Most of the crowd cheered ecstatically with her announcement. The people in suits, especially, did. The Far East and Americas had been all but severed from efficient trade for over two decades, and both regions were eager to resume commerce across the Pacific. The several-dozen attendees not stereotypically clad in suits were in the assorted fitting attires of press, caterers, translators, and security.

"I speak to you today as the lame duck President of the United States of America. President-elect Avery Dashe is here today with us as well – let's hear it for him." She waved to Dashe on the other end of the stage but did not call him to the podium. "I am thrilled and humbled to announce that, after my term in the White House is over, I have been asked to serve as Pacifica's very first Minister of International Operations." McCourty was forced to wait over twenty seconds for the fanfare to subside. "Thank you, thank you all. I will collaborate daily with official ambassadors from over two hundred countries. Together we will shape this new continent in the best interests of all humanity, while preserving foremost the ecological standards that our delicate, new world demands. With that, I would like to present you with Pacifica's first Minister of Science. Allow me to introduce one of two Czech ambassadors to Pacifica:

the esteemed theoretical physicist, and my dear friend, Dr. Michael Havlicek."

Havlicek took the stage and waved to the audience and cameras during scattered applause. The stage rested on a flat-ground expanse that spanned roughly twelve thousand kilometers in the center of the new continent. The dark, metallic ground beneath the temporary outdoor stage structure was smooth and firm. Behind the stage, a portion of the ground had been graded and drilled to accommodate soil from around the world. It was out of place. The soil did not mesh with the rigid, metal ground. The international dignitaries present for the global media event were not fooled by the futile marketing gimmick.

Havlicek pulled notes from his pocket and began reading. "As far as the eye can see, the ground is flat. There are no mountains here. There are no lakes or rivers. There are some hills and there are storm outflow streams, but this place is mostly unformed. For those of you watching on television, you cannot see this garden behind me. It is a gesture of peace, but it will not survive. The first major rain will scatter most of this soil across this dense ground. But we are lucky. This is a confusing place where lightning strikes without clouds right now, but we are here. We have these rubber mats to protect us." He pointed toward the ground, and all the attendees laughed for a few seconds. "We must help this land. When the vacuum sealed itself five years ago, the matter trapped on the outside walls was super-dense. All the matter that came from the crust and mantle were packed tightly into the diamond-like walls surrounding the abyss. We did not know if the abyss would ever fill. But the Crystalline Curtain that formed around the void kept the Pacific Ocean water from draining into the mantle cavity. Those walls expanded inward to fill the void quickly. We are lucky indeed, for many reasons. The fact that space came back into those molecules was lucky. But the fact that it expanded and cooled so rapidly was miraculous. Also miraculous is that it expanded from the outer wall inward; had this not occurred, the volcanoes and tremors felt around the world over the past few years would certainly have been far more destructive than they were. This entire phenomenon has expanded our understanding of cold fusion, anti-matter, tectonics, and vacuum properties by leaps and bounds. We intend to refine those sciences here on Pacifica for the better of our planet and for that of the human race. Thank you."

McCourty took the podium again, "But that's not all. Today marks a truly historic day on top of opening traditional sea and air shipping lanes between Asia, Australia, and the Americas. With that, I introduce Pacifica's Minister of Transportation, from Oxford University, Dr. Tarlok Singh."

Singh approached without notes and began speaking immediately over the applause. His speech was dry but well-rehearsed in an eloquent English-Indian accent. "Thank you for your kind introduction, Madame Minister. I am honored to participate in the most ambitious construction project in the history of our planet. Catskill Rail has pledged to build the world's first trans-continental VacTrain here on Pacifica. The three-hundred or more ambassadors of Pacifica voted unanimously to test VacTrain technology here on the barren land where all human, animal, biological, or other natural collateral damage will be mitigated or altogether avoided. The tubes within which the VacTrains reside will be shielded from the radiation and electrical storms that we have thus encountered. Not only will the VacTrain system open new doors for commerce, but it will enhance our safety and ecological footprint as well. Catskill has been designing the tubes and locomotive prototypes for two decades now. However, to date, no country has agreed to accept the first supersonic train to be tested in their back yard." He looked around and smiled, waiting for laughter. Some members of the audience nodded or chuckled. "...Until today." He raised one arm to a roar of applause. "If successful, the benefits will be incalculable. Dependence on fossil fuels will be greatly reduced since these new locomotives will operate primarily on gravity and geothermic propulsion. Maximum speed of passenger and freight transport will have limits of eight- and six-thousand kilometers per hour respectively, with average speeds around half that. Roughly equated, a passenger may travel from Sydney, Australia to Los Angeles, U.S.A. in approximately two hours, with almost no fuel cost. Freight from Tianjin, China to Seattle, U.S.A. would take three hours and change. With the controlled environment of the vacuum tube lanes, the VacTrain will also further reduce the risks of crashes. Best of all, this technology will lend to space transportation research which will benefit humanity for centuries to come. Kindest thanks."

Sara McCourty retook the podium and addressed the media. "I'll take a few of your questions."

"Madame President, err, Minister," inquired one American reporter, "with the shipping lanes open, what do you expect in the near-term between China and the U.S.? Can we expect tariffs between these power-houses?"

"The United States welcomes the new trade partner. For the first time since the early nineties we feel the Pacific Ocean corridor is safe for passage. At first, sailing around the Pacifica continent will take time, and we fully expect the previous routes to remain intact. But over time, particularly as travel across Pacifica is made a reality, we feel China and the United States will become powerful trade allies. There are still atmospheric concerns, of course. We don't know the reach of the cosmic radiation that the area endured when there was no atmosphere. We will need to do a lot of testing, and in the meantime travelers and traders in the surrounding area will need to exercise extreme caution."

"What of land transportation over the new land of Pacifica?" another American journalist offered. "It could take decades for the VacTrain routes to be constructed, if it doesn't fail altogether. Are you going to allow land-travel across the continent until the new system is fleshed out?"

"Now that the Crystalline Curtain has dissolved into the smooth and perceivably stable ground that you see around us, the new continent is completely surrounded by the waters of the Pacific. For most civilians, it would be easier to sail around entirely than to sail from say, China, traverse twenty thousand kilometers of Pacifica with no roads, restaurants, or gas stations, and then sail the rest of the way to an American port. At this time, the continent offers too many unknown challenges to open up the interior completely. Most people coming here would be at their own risk anyway.

Firstly, there are no roads here. Secondly, the landscape is no picnic. NASA's Terra Satellite has detected and mapped out several radiation hotbeds that have not yet been studied or quarantined. Like I said, we have no idea what happened during the transformation of the land that now comprises the continent. As far as our extensive tests have shown to date, the matter that used to occupy the Pacific Abysm is the same metal we see today. We can only presume that the water and soil of the ocean is part of that makeup as well. Some of the matter that we're standing on used to exist deep within the planet, and we should be cautious. There are temperature swells. There are seismic anomalies. There are electrical storms. We don't think civilian traders are quite ready for that just yet."

Another reporter asked, "You mentioned resources. What new resources may enter international play? How will we divvy up the valuables and fuels?"

"The spot where we're standing is composed mostly of iron and silicon, I'm told. Other areas may contain deposits of limestone and igneous rock, and mixes of all sorts of metal. Some deposits span hundreds of kilometers, and others swirl together like ice cream. Before we get ahead of ourselves, we need to map these things out and perform a number of tests."

"What tests?" a new reporter barked. "There are economic repercussions at stake, and the people have a right to know if resources are being hoarded by some new superpower."

McCourty fired back with presidential poise, "You've surely noticed the electrical storms that seem to come and go without warning. When we're not standing on rubber mats under a protective tent such as this one, lightning seems to jump up from the ground and sting your legs – and that's when it's perfectly clear out here. The ozone in the atmosphere above us, here in the center of the former void, is nearly nonexistent. This presents numerous health risks. NASA and Chinese aerospace satellites have mapped the surface. We know about basic elemental compositions of most areas. We've taken radiation and temperature levels, and we understand the very simplest seismic activity. Beyond that, it will be difficult to ensure the safety of civilians, let alone vet that any minerals worth mining are safely obtainable. Security and piracy are being discussed and will likely be ongoing concerns. This continent is larger than Russia and is completely barren of natural life. People will not be able to live off the wilderness; any visitors will need to provision themselves appropriately. The only stable aspect of this place from a scientific perspective seems to be that seismic activity is minimal. But even that comes at a price, since the rest of the world has seen an increase in earthquakes and volcanoes of all sorts over the past five years. We predict that seismic disruptions will eventually surface, if you'll pardon the pun, as the mantle finally settles. At the rapid rate with which these molecules expanded and cooled to fill the enormous cavity, we are confident that many surprises are in store. So, getting back to your original question, safety comes first. We'll talk about oil interests after every one of those concerns is addressed, thank you."

The same reporter aggressively followed up, "Madame President, what of the aviation concerns with the thinned atmosphere? And the crop yields? All this talk of new resources and trade lines; it sounds as though you're ignoring the famine and potential atmospheric disasters that we already face. Do you really think that new sources of fossil fuels will make up for the dwindling food supply and the ecological impacts of a lessened sky?"

"That's a complicated series of questions. Food is scarce. There's no denying that. Grains are struggling around the world, especially near the equator. But scientists are working on new strains of crops, and new soil treatments, and new techniques for farmers. And we don't know for sure about the atmosphere. Air densities are lower than they have been in the past. That's true. But five years ago, when the Abysm stopped expanding, all that air that rushed into it was substantial. Since then, the void has filled in. The air has evened out. The troposphere and mesosphere now measure unremarkably. The ozone in the stratosphere, more immediately above us, is thinned and damaged, but our tests have shown that it is still there and recovering slowly. We have a goal to increase sustainable food. We have a goal to reduce dependency on fossil fuels. We have a goal to expand protection from solar radiation, especially directly over Pacifica. But these goals take time. Right now, we have to study what's happening to the world. Only when we understand these changes can we act responsibly. Thank you for your questions.

"With that, we will conclude the global media event for a few minutes. We will come back after refreshments for Pacifica's First Continental Congress. I'd like to thank everyone for their time today as we celebrate this historic milestone in the course of human history. President-elect Dashe?"

Dashe at last leaned toward the podium, to announce, "God bless this planet, and God bless Pacifica!" After moving back from the microphones, he awkwardly plunged forward again and blurted, "And God bless the United States."

Chapter 3

6:05PM CST, December 7, 2015

A near-death experience had rattled Andrew's fundamental appreciation of life. At the mouth of the terrible abyss off the coast of California, he was sure he had left his body and seen that his father was somehow responsible for the cataclysm that had thrown the world into a nearly-three-decade panic. Even before he watched air flow into the former vacuum that had somehow thrived amid the dwindling Earth that was, he knew that the disaster had been quelled. His father had been at the center of it, and Andrew had dislodged that presence in a way that he did not understand. The message coils that Andrew's father Vince had left for him guided him on a torrid trek of pain and left him with sensory capabilities he was only beginning to grasp. Almost immediately after arriving in Washington D.C., he drove back to his home in Harrisburg, Pennsylvania. He called Lydia to let her know that he was alright, and then headed straight for New Orleans to surprise her. He arrived at Lydia's single-bedroom rental house around six in the evening on the seventh.

"I had a feeling you were coming," she greeted him. "You took your time though."

"Actually," Andrew retorted, "I made great time. Though the ground may quake beneath me, nothing will keep me from you," he proclaimed in a sappy tone. They kissed at length, and he opened his eyes expecting some form of interruption. "Where's your dad?"

"I put him in a motel tonight. How tired are you from the drive? You said something about making a family, so I wanted to be prepared for some alone-time."

"Oh, I see," Andrew sarcastically rebutted. "I'm never too tired for you. Is today a good day for that?"

"I haven't been keeping track exactly, but today should an excellent day for that. I couldn't believe…" She paused, having caught herself from second-guessing the intent he had expressed in starting a family over the phone. *Now's not the time to plant any seeds of doubt within his already-skittish brain,* she internally scolded. She shifted her comment to the aftermath of the Pacific Abysm's recent reversal of direction. "I couldn't believe all these tornadoes and tremors! I haven't felt much here, but they said on the news that things are volatile all over. Chicago got hit with an earthquake for the first time in years."

"Yeah, I didn't feel any tremors on my way down here, but it was windy as hell the whole time. I thought the car might blow away when I stopped for gas. Radio wouldn't shut up about it. They said California's a wreck – half of it's covered in glass shards and the rest is a nonstop earthquake. Good thing it's already basically abandoned, I guess. I hope it settles down, so people can move back in. Probably get ourselves a hell of a deal on one of those cliff-side mansions at Dana Point or something."

"You really think that's safe? I mean, I know the air rushed back in, so they're saying the abyss isn't a vacuum anymore, but don't you think it's still dangerous?"

"Sure, but it'd be nice and quiet. It's gotten crowded here. Could be nice to move to the West Coast and help rebuild. Think of all the millions that left their homes. Most of them probably don't want to go back, but the ones that do, they'll need help."

"You almost died saving the world, and now you want to risk your life trying to rebuild it? I shouldn't be surprised, I guess." She smiled in admiration and pulled him closer. They kissed again, and as his hands gripped her sides and inched downward, she awkwardly offered, "It might be weird to use my dad's bed. It smells like him, and you know how he has a smell."

"Let's just do it everywhere else then."

The couple made love as though they had just met. "This has been a long time coming, I suppose," Andrew confessed after the first hour of intermittent play and holding. "I'm so sorry that we've been apart. I think about you all the time. Every day I'm in love with you."

"I feel the same. I don't regret waiting all this time to ditch the protection. If we'd had a baby a few years ago, I'd be raising it alone half the time. And I know that you would always fear that you're endangering it with your message capsules. Don't worry about it. Really. I'm just glad we're here now, and that I can feel you with nothing between us. Now, where were we…?"

Andrew and Lydia had never felt closer. For another hour, they shared their love. Afterward, Lydia asked questions about the eleven coils Andrew had obtained from the Pentagon as well as the one from Little Falls. He told her about them, and about the heroics of Sgt. Major Burch. He described what he perceived as a dream-state or out-of-body experience through which he envisioned the inside of the Pacific Abysm. He conjectured that he may have inadvertently sealed the rift by communicating with his father on the other side of the world. They nodded off full of questions and ideas, but content that they were out of danger.

At quarter-to-seven the next morning, Andrew awoke to the sun breaking through the east window. He turned to his wife and kissed her. She did not wake, but she smiled as he pressed his lips against hers. For the first time in eight years since they were wed, he felt as though his family dynamic was normal. He nudged Lydia and she stirred gracefully.

"I feel brand new. Like everything is starting fresh now," she yawned.

"Not for me. I stink, and I'll need to have my clothes mended. I can't believe you agreed to even make love last night. You have any cash? They cleaned me up pretty good at the Pentagon before we left for the Abysm, but I haven't taken a shower since. I grabbed a new pair of jeans and this sweatshirt at Harrisburg, but the clothes I wore to California got all mangled. They're out in the car."

"I have about fifty. You can take it. Go to the tailor at Canal and Broad. At the north corner, not the west corner. I guess there are two now. I used to like the one at Canal and Galvez, but their prices are getting crazy."

"Niko's? That's a shame."

"No, Niko moved downtown. There's a coffee shop in his old place. The one I'm talking about is a chain – The Swift Thimble – they're everywhere. Don't bother."

"Too many tailors to keep straight these days, and they all want to rip you off. Maybe I'm due for a new pair of jeans."

"I don't have three hundred bucks lying around, mister. God even knows what's going to happen to prices with these windstorms everywhere."

"Hey, maybe it's a good thing?"

"What, tornadoes?"

"No," he laughed. "With air flowing over the Abysm, maybe now planes can fly over, and the economy will get a little better. Got to think at least electronics could get cheaper again. Maybe clothing will get cheaper too. You remember when we were kids and you could get a shirt that was made in China for ten bucks?"

"Ha! No. But you're a lot older than me," she snickered.

"We're only a couple of years apart, Lyd."

"There's a total generation gap between us though, sometimes. I meant you sound a lot older." She sat and smiled out the window thoughtfully. "Listen to us. It's like overnight everything is back to normal – tornadoes notwithstanding, of course."

"I know. Glass shards raining down from the sky, but maybe the world stopped falling apart. We'll have to change our definition of normal a bit, but now everything seems like it can be normal. Let's go get some breakfast and see what your dad is up to. I'll give him a call while you're in the shower."

Andrew grabbed his phone and powered it on while he waited for her to shower. He had six voicemails from a private caller. As he listened to each, his jaw dropped another few millimeters.

"Hurry it up, honey. I'm afraid we need to go," Andrew shouted urgently into the bathroom.

The water stopped fifteen seconds later. She answered as she stepped out, "Something wrong?"

"I just got a call from Jacqueline Vertree. She's the one I told you about from the Pentagon."

"CIC Jackie?"

"That's the one. She says we might be in danger and we need to move."

"Should I go get the coils?"

"There's no time for that. I'll take the new twelve. You take your notebook and my dad's Shakespeare book. Take my car, grab your dad, and head straight for Prince Edward Island. Head east through Mobile, up to Birmingham, then north through Nashville, through Louisville and Cincinnati, up to Detroit, and then head east until you hit water. Or use a map, I guess. The place is in Montague, listed under the name Gert Fröbe. Leave your phone at home powered on and buy a new prepaid in Canada. Send me the number in a text, but backwards. Get there as fast as you can."

"Why does that name sound familiar?"

"He played Goldfinger."

"If someone wants to track you down, texting it backwards won't do anything. They'll know the number it came from as soon as it hits yours."

"Right. Fine, just don't text me until you're in Canada."

"You told me not to even buy the phone until I was in Canada. How would I text you from it before that?"

Speechless for a moment, Andrew sighed and shrugged. "You make me proud."

"So where are you going? You're not coming with us?"

"No. Better if you don't know where I'm headed. I'll keep the coils and see if I can find anything new in them. You've already copied all of them down?"

"Of course." Her prideful smile was overcome by disappointment, "You're going to Oshkosh."

"I don't know how you do that."

"I don't want you going there. I do not trust those people."

"They have answers. I need answers. Jacqueline said that someone is after me, and I need to know what I'm up against. I think Ray and Watson might be able to tell me what's going on. There must be more coils. I can feel them, somehow. A few days ago, nothing, and now all the sudden, I can see the whole thing coming into form. It's hard to explain."

Lydia smiled and kissed Andrew's ear. "Promise me this will all end someday."

"We both jinxed it when we said things were normal this morning. But the messages Jacqueline and her friend left me were in the middle of the night and she sounded really concerned, so we may not have much time. Go get your dad. Get to Prince Edward. Call me as soon as you get there. I love you."

"If you're keeping your phone, why shouldn't I?"

"If we're in danger, I want Jackie to know where I am. I think I can trust her. But I don't know who she's afraid of, and she seems to think we need to get out of here. I'm not worried about what happens to me. I don't think I'm in any danger anyway; but I'm not taking any chances with your safety." He placed his hand tenderly on her belly. "Never again. I love you."

"I will always love you."

They kissed again, and Andrew sprinted toward the train station. Lydia frantically threw a bag together and headed out to pick up her father. By eight that morning, Lydia and Pasha began the long drive northeast toward Canada, while Andrew transferred to an express commuter train headed for Chicago.

Once aboard, Andrew made his way back to the working car. Most of the workstations were empty, and he took the first one available. He pulled a wired headset from his pocket and plugged it into the public computer. He placed an internet call back to a Harrisburg number.

"Bob, it's me. Don't say anything. Remember the conversation we had a few months back about my demons? I think it's time to confront the devils. I'll be there in about two days. Sure, would be nice if you could join me. Pack as much as you can. I'm not sure who else I can trust. You know what to do. If you want extra protection, I know a guy in D.C. that you can call. I'll text you the number when we hang up. Any questions?"

The other end clicked without an answer. Andrew smiled and looked out the window. He watched the houses and small commercial buildings blur past for a few moments. He then used the workstation to send a text message, which contained only a phone number, to Pastor Bob. Having pulled off what he considered to be masterful subterfuge, he made no effort to hide a villainous smirk on his way back to his seat.

Chapter 4

1:12 AM EST, December 8, 2015

"Give me the short version," Jacqueline grunted.

"Terribly sorry about the late hour. We're not sure exactly what happened, ma'am." Officer Dillon Tremone fidgeted nervously as the pair waited for the bulky elevator to descend. "Bragi and Juno are down, and so are the live-in techs. The pigs are dead, and the machines are all powered down. The vestibule is sealed. It was sealed the whole time. Cameras in the corridor show no activity since the last sweep. That was this morning. The vestibule hasn't been breached since Friday, so there's no telling how long the power has been out."

"You picked a hell of a week to transfer to Green Six. Tell me what happened in the Titan Lab. What do you mean, 'Bragi and Juno are down'? I don't know if that's even possible."

"Our men went in for the midnight sweep and ran the weekly vestibule protocols. They saw that the power was out inside. We paged you and left the lab the moment we saw the techs were down in the loft. You got here in fifteen minutes, so I'm sure not much has changed. The initial inspection was unclear."

"Of course, it was. Let's lock the floor down. Nobody goes in or out. Get me the elevator and shipping logs for the past six months. Three days since the circus left town – this can't be a coincidence."

The officer nodded as the elevator beeped. Jacqueline swiped her badge and the elevator door opened to the underground Pentagon hallway that she commanded.

"Circus, ma'am?"

"President and a bunch of white-coats had Andrew Gaeta down here and Bragi confirmed that he was connected to the Abysm. Can't be a coincidence. Bragi and Juno haven't left that room for a decade or better. Something's up."

The two marched together down the long corridor. After fifty meters, Tremone broke away to pull the logs from a computer station in an alcove off the main hall. Jacqueline Vertree continued another several seconds to the conference room that had recently housed the President's Pacific Situation Room. Jacqueline activated a recorder on her waist. It was wired through her shirt to an earpiece. "The board room has been dark since the last Situation Room on December the fourth. After the President's last meeting adjourned, the conference room was swept twice daily with no incident. No signs of disruption or tampering with the conference room doors." Jacqueline both resented and enjoyed the attention that President McCourty's War Room visits had brought to her isolated floor over the past few years.

Jacqueline walked directly through the conference room that boasted two large, semi-circular tables whose ends faced one another. On the opposite side, the doors, which opened to a connecting hallway which led to the mysterious laboratory's vestibule, were flanked by two more of her officers. They followed her through the doorway toward the vestibule doors. She scanned the doors without acknowledging them and continued her log, "Outer doors unmolested. Vestibule secure. What the hell happened in there?" She waived to them, and they opened the doors for her. The officers could not tell if she was talking to them or continuing her log.

Jacqueline picked up a small electronic device and began scanning the vestibule. She entered the chamber, took a clean suit, and waved for one of the officers to do the same. They were sprayed with mist by means of an automated ceiling dispenser. She pulled the white, protective suit on one limb at a time, and muttered into her earpiece as the outer doors closed. "The lab is secure from the vestibule. No signs of contamination. Power is out inside, but emergency lights are up. One weekend of peace and quiet and this is what I get. These two get along living in one room for a-dozen-odd years – what the hell could have brought them to this? Half-expecting them to have eaten each other in there. Did anyone hear anything?" The officer looked blankly at her as he pulled his arms into his own white clean-suit. "Nobody hears anything. I told them my first day on this job over a decade ago that we need cameras in here. I don't care what the suits think about leaks. We're completely in the dark here. I meant the situation. But get a couple of techs working on the main generator too."

The officer nodded, but then proceeded to follow her. "The call has been made, ma'am," he replied. "But the floor is locked down until you clear it. The techs that would normally take care of the generator, well…"

The inner doors opened and the two stepped inside. Five emergency floodlights high above in the cavernous, immaculate laboratory dimly filled most of the spaces within. The officer remained silent by the door as Jacqueline wandered through the lab. To her right, a massive, pressurized water tank pumped and churned normally. "Must be powered by an outside source," Jacqueline commented to the recorder.

As she proceeded past the tank, the upstairs laboratory loft that opened out to the rest of the lab was ominously quiet. It normally buzzed with Juno and two other live-in lab techs as they conducted work on the advanced, makeshift computers and gizmos that littered the loft. She walked past the stairwell and on toward Bragi's bed and pig pen at the far end of the lab.

The decrepit old man was lying motionless on a metal table. A dozen or so unmolested tubes fed in and out of his stomach, liver, and other organs. He wore a customized gown that neatly accommodated each of the tubes. Vertree looked adjacent the foot of his bed to see that Bragi's four black pigs were dead. Two wires and three tubes also meandered from each of the pigs' bellies and into a large, metal computer contraption across from Bragi's metal bed. The machines and monitors that hosted the wires and tubes from Bragi and the pigs were all silent and black.

Jacqueline put her hands on the edge of Bragi's bed and sighed. The tubes that fed into him, from the computer a few meters away, were motionless. But Jackie could see that there was fluid inside each of them. She switched her recorder off. "Talk to me, old man. What happened in here?"

"Juno went nuts." Jacqueline flinched a bit as the old man animated from near nothingness and spoke in a youthful, vibrant voice that quietly echoed throughout the laboratory.

"Don't do that!" she scolded. "I could still tell you were alive the moment I got off the elevator though. What gives?"

"Do you have any idea how old I am? I'm not quite finished with this place yet."

"But your tubes and the pigs…? Don't you get nutrients from them? I always thought this was some weird life support system or something."

"Those are for data storage mostly. Juno had the idea a while back. We're playing with DNA; let's leave it at that. But I'm fine. You'll have to have me moved. I'm afraid your remaining technicians will not be able to replace the battery that Juno stole."

"What battery?"

"You really give too much leash to what happens down here, my young caretaker. Upstairs, in the loft, there is a fusion generator. The core is a battery containing a mixture of mercury and platinum – nearly two liters of each."

"That must weigh a ton."

"She's capable. The object is a cylinder with two handles molded into the end."

"Should I look for it?"

"Oh no, she's long gone with it."

"But the doors haven't opened in two days. How is that possible?"

"Go upstairs and have a look around. I'll explain what I can. Turn your recorder back on. I'll be discreet."

Jacqueline left the man on the bed and sped up the stairs to the laboratory's loft. There she saw three technicians, with yellow clean suits and black masks, sprawled across the ground.

She stood and surveyed the loft. The unorthodox computers were all powered down and offline. In the center of one of the machines was a large cylindrical hole that undoubtedly housed the power supply to which Bragi had referred. She had never noticed it before it was gone.

Jacqueline walked a few steps to the nearest of the three lab technicians on the ground. She could tell that each of the three yellow and black clean suits were intact. The zippers of the techs' advanced suits extended up to their chins, where they met hard, black mask material. Expecting blood or some gruesome explosion of organs, she cautiously unzipped the first, from chin down to belly. "First technician is middle aged male, naked beneath the suit. No wounds or blood, checking for vitals." She opened his mask and held the black, shiny material near his nose and mouth. After seeing no breath condensation, she considered pulling her white suit off to check for his pulse with her fingers. *Don't bother,* she thought. She glanced back at the absent power core and, not knowing its effects on the lab, she changed her mind. "Tech one is down."

Moving on to the next technician, she first prodded the legs and arms for response. Once she confirmed the person was incapacitated, she unzipped the clean suit from the chin to the belly. "Second technician is female, approximately twenty to twenty-five. No wounds or blood; checking vitals." Jacqueline pulled off the young woman's mask and turned it around to verify whether the woman was breathing. She was not. "Tech two is down. Last one must be Juno."

Jacqueline moved on to the third technician with curiosity. She customarily prodded the limbs first but did not wait as long for a response as she had with the other two. With urgency, she unzipped the clean suit to find a hairy chested, slender male. She slumped from a kneeling position to a seated position next to him. "Third tech is a male." She pried the mask away and checked his breath like she had done with the others. "Checked his vitals, tech three is down as well. Damnedest thing, that puts Juno in her twenties, but she was working this lab before I came here. That or she's the best-looking elderly lady I've ever seen."

Jacqueline stood and moved back to the second technician. She knelt and looked as closely as she could at the young woman's face. "Second technician has mild acne around the cheeks, mouth, and neck; no scarring." She pulled the eyelids open and witnessed only a blank, dead stare. "This doesn't add up." *Doesn't it?* Bragi's voice queried in her head. *Guess you should head back downstairs, my dear.* She smiled and rolled her eyes.

After she descended the stairs, Jacqueline returned to Bragi and switched her recorder off again. "What are you up to, old man? That girl can't be a day over twenty, but Juno's been in this lab longer than I've worked here. How is this possible? Impostor?"

Bragi chuckled, "That's her alright. At least it was. She has a way with faces."

"But you said she stole the power supply, and then she left?"

"That I did. She disassembled the battery and sent the parts up the hazmat conveyor." He pointed to a two-by-three-decimeter sliding door waist-high on the wall near the entry vestibule. "It runs on the power from the third level, same as the tank."

"Why didn't you tell me?" She demanded.

He just smiled. She fumbled to press a button on the device attached to her waist underneath the suit. When she found the button, she exclaimed, "Security Green Six, need a hazmat disposal inspection on three ASAP. Full lock-down – could be an inside job." After releasing the button, she returned her focus back to the old man. "She's dead. I saw her upstairs and she's not breathing. Why do you think she's left?"

"She has left. She's not here anymore."

"So, you mean she passed on, and she's in a better place now?" Jacqueline responded sarcastically, as she grew tired of the word games.

"I'd hardly call Pennsylvania a better place, but that's where she's passed onto – yes."

She sighed, "Is she alive or dead?"

"She's very much alive," Bragi laughed. "Although you may have a hard time finding her with a composite facial sketch now."

"Did she attack you?"

"Ha!" Bragi's thunderous bellow resonated for several seconds through the lab. "I would end her before she even thought up a cover story for the deed. You need not worry about me." He coughed, and Jacqueline was unsure whether it was genuine or an ironic joke.

"Did she kill your pigs?"

"Not on purpose. It seems her flight plan had unexpected collateral damage."

"And what plan was that?"

"You'd have to ask her, dear. I'm just an old man wired to a dead computer."

"I've always wondered about that. Everyone must wear hazmat suits and get sprayed coming in and out of here. Why aren't you affected?"

"This room is loaded with gamma radiation at times. I've grown accustomed to it. In fact, in a sense it's keeping this old body going. But most people don't take too kindly to it. Gives them a slight case of the death, you see. But it's necessary for us to conduct a lot of light tests that produce radiation. Hooray for science, and the like."

"How did the pigs survive so long without protection?"

"My body produces fluid that neutralizes radiation on a cellular level. My four little friends were beneficiaries of that, via this tubing network. They were instrumental in some of our tests."

"What are you researching?"

"That's no longer important. The solution, it seems, has been trumped by another problem which Juno has left to investigate."

"Who… or *what* exactly are you two?"

Bragi smiled, "That is also not important. You should follow Juno. That will prove difficult, but she may need help. She does not wish to be found for the next few days. But if you follow the power supply trail, you may be able to find her. You're resourceful. I do not know if she will want your help yet. In time, she will probably come back here."

"I'll notify the U.S. Marshalls. They're specifically trained to track people down and they have access to much better transportation that I do. I just manage this floor; I couldn't leave to try to track her down."

"Please," Bragi scoffed. "Can you imagine what Juno would do to them if they caught her? She knows you. She might not kill you if you get close to her. Just take a car and drive to Pennsylvania. Gaeta's apartment, I suspect. Although I think she's misled. At any rate, as long as you're near, she'll let you know if she needs your help."

"What could I possibly do to help someone that's capable of all this?"

"Each soldier has a part to play. Even if you are not needed you should be available for her. That will keep her ethical compass facing north, at least. Her objective lies in a morally gray realm I'm afraid."

"You didn't tell me what her objective is."

He smiled, "That is correct."

"Fine. You said something about Pennsylvania?"

"Yes. I presume she is attempting to locate your illumined new friend Andrew Gaeta."

"Why is she after him? Is he in danger?"

"It is possible. Her motive is unclear, as is his, but her resolve should not be questioned. He has something that she needs."

"What – the ability to see the colors in the Pacific abyss? I thought that it was closing back up. Is it still a threat?"

"No, that is not what she needs. Andrew's boon was of convenient use, however there is more to the message coils than he realizes."

"What are they?"

"We are not entirely certain. Juno is much more familiar with them than I have been, admittedly. But Andrew has many of them, and Juno is convinced that they are some sort of key. To what, I do not know."

"How do you know all of this?"

Bragi smiled and closed his eyes. Without moving his lips, Jacqueline heard his voice within her head. *We know much, young soldier. Do fetch me some new pigs and get the power back on when you are able. You may lift the lockdown.*

Jacqueline turned away a bit disturbed, and silently walked to the vestibule. Officer Tremone was waiting to see her out and activated a switch on the wall that sprayed Vertree and the clean-suit-clad escort officer once again. The misty foam dissipated completely within a few moments and they disrobed of the clean suits.

"What was that all about?" Tremone asked as they walked through the conference room and back out to the main hallway.

"Hell if I know," replied Vertree. "We need to get up to the hazmat disposal on three and track down something Juno sent up the chute before the lab went quiet."

"Yes ma'am. Are we good to reopen the lab?"

"Yes, please keep us on yellow alert and post guards around the clock on the vestibule. Let's see if we can get a medic too. I don't like Bragi being alone in there, so make sure people check in with him periodically to get him whatever he needs. Hang on," she looked to the side and stopped walking. *Four pigs. Young ones.* "Get out of my head, old man." She looked back to Tremone, "Let's hurry up and get off this floor. I never feel private when he's close enough to do that."

Jacqueline shuffled into the elevator when it arrived and began entering her credentials. Officer Tremone remained at her side with a stack of papers to escort her to the third underground level of the Pentagon's scientific research center. As the elevator chugged along, Jacqueline broke their brief silence, "How are you coming along with the logs? Anything stand out?"

"Nothing out of the ordinary," the officer responded. "On the fourth, of course, we had a parade of people in the board room. The vestibule was breached for you, Admiral Milikin, Andrew Gaeta, and the President, of course. After that, the morning of the fifth, we had a food and supply drop-off that was requested by Juno."

"What was it?"

"I thought the same thing. It was just food, cleaning products, and a few regular pieces of test equipment. Let's see: small biologic specimens, cleaning products, clean suits. They had a pretty routine day, actually."

"I'm curious, when was the last mercury shipment?"

"Let me check." He rustled through the print-out stack for a few moments as the elevator opened. He followed her out with his head buried in the data. "I don't see any mercury, but I do see a fair amount of potassium-forty coming in over the past six months."

"That could be for the light-wave experiments. I actually just talked to the old man about that."

"Ah. Well, it seems like a lot, so they must have really burned through it. I'd be curious to see what the third level says about the usage rate, since I'm sure they'll see the waste eventually anyway. I'm seeing repeated orders for canisters of argon, as well as fossil samples of all kinds of rocks and crystals."

"Greek to me, but let's check with the resident nerds."

"This floor is a little brighter than ours, eh?"

"Yeah, a lot more people work on this level, so they're allowed to have civilian contractors that bring in fancy lights and toilets. Should get boring where we're headed though, don't worry."

They meandered through a few hallways and checkpoints and scanned their badges as appropriate. Vertree knew the way, and Tremone followed closely. When they arrived at an unmarked station with a double door, Jacqueline swiped her access card and it beeped. A red light flashed next to the door, and a voice through a speaker quietly announced, "One moment, Ms. Vertree. We're locked down, so we will have to bypass the door."

When the door opened, four officers greeted them with rifles drawn. A security officer dressed similarly to Tremone, in gray pants and a blue blazer, stood behind the four enforcers and ushered them through the double doors into a small holding area. The doors closed behind them, and the officer turned around and gestured toward the security protocol station at the opposite side of the six-by-six-meter square room. "I'm sure you understand, Jackie," the officer explained. "You called for a lock-down; we have to make sure it's really you."

Jacqueline smiled as she submitted to retinal, fingerprint, and breath scans, "Don't call me Jackie, pinhead. Where's Ogilvie?"

"She should be on her way, ma'am. We paged her when your floor went red, just in case."

"Good thinking. Let's see your disposal crews and logs for the past forty-eight."

"Right away, please follow me." He escorted Vertree and Tremone through a few sets of doors to a lounge area. "Coffee while we wait?" he asked.

"Sure, I'll take one," Tremone replied. Jacqueline nodded as well and handed the young officer several dollars for the vending machine.

"Have a seat, and I'll send Mrs. Ogilvie straight here when she arrives."

As they waited, Jacqueline and Tremone continued to pour through the entry and delivery logs. Tremone circled a few names and times on the in-and-out logs, but Jacqueline was much more concerned with delivery requests and fulfillment.

"Should we call Ratigan and Teague?" Tremone asked.

"Nah," Jacqueline conferred quietly, "I think this one will resolve itself. We just need to track down a couple of missing parts and I'm sure everything will be fine. Ratigan would come up with some conspiracy theory, and Teague would probably hug us to death."

They chuckled and made small talk until Judy Ogilvie arrived. "Are you making a habit of consorting with us mere untouchables, Ms. Vertree?" Ogilvie delivered the line with a smile but was plainly jealous of Jacqueline's post. Jacqueline shrugged it off and followed the third-level director into her office while Tremone waited outside. Judy was shorter than Jacqueline, but much thinner and perkier.

"Untouchables… Are you from India? Ogilvie sounds, I don't know, I guess Dutch or something."

"I'm Pakistani actually, but my husband is Scottish."

"You two must have some pretty kids then." Both laughed, as Judy turned a picture of herself, husband, and two young children toward Jacqueline. Having no family to speak of, Jacqueline's spiteful joke turned to admiration when she saw the genuinely attractive family. "I'll get right to the point," she continued, sipping her coffee. "A power supply was smuggled out of the Resonance Lab on six, a few pieces at a time via the hazmat chute."

"Well that is a pickle indeed. Was it nuclear?"

"I'm not sure. I was informed it contained mercury and platinum, so I know the value is extremely high."

"You got that right. What quantities are we looking for?"

"Two liters each, mercury and platinum."

Ogilvie stammered, "That's quite a bit, and could easily fetch over two million dollars."

"Believe me, this isn't about money. I have reason to believe that the materials are being used for their original purpose: as a power supply."

"I see. That is also quite bulky, however. The mercury, I'm assuming is housed in something." She hammered a few keys on her computer, "and the platinum would weigh about forty-two kilograms. Do you have any idea what the parts looked like when they were disassembled?"

"No. All we know is that the parts were intact two days ago, because the power was on. The lab these came out of was highly restricted, so we have no alarms, no cameras; we don't even have data storage inside beyond homemade proprietary gear. So, whatever got sent up the chute happened within the past forty-eight hours."

"That's very helpful. I have a list of all the material that has been processed in that time. It's not much. I see couple of empty argon cans and some potassium."

"My duty officer noticed a lot of the potassium-forty. He said it was flagged as radioactive. What could that be used for?"

"Usually that material is used for fossil dating. It has an extremely long half-life."

"Could you build a bomb or weapon with it?"

"I've never heard of weaponized potassium, but in this line of work anything is possible. The folks on your floor have access to much worse though, so I would sincerely doubt that was its use. From these records, that material appears somewhat benign. This is odd, though."

Jacqueline leaned forward to see her screen, "What is it?"

"Well, one of the disposal carts left early. That is a bit of a red flag. It means that either the weight capacity had been filled ahead of expectation, or that an unexpected staff change took place."

"Why is that important?"

"On our team, the disposal technician follows the material from check-in to removal. Our only real hindrances are the elevator system weight capacity and staffing, due to information non-disclosure needs. I'm sure you know that routine."

"Intimately."

"A member of the staff, a supervisor, checked out thirty minutes into her shift with a cart at weight capacity. This is very unusual. I then show that she transferred the material to a processing center near Pittsburgh."

"What was it carrying?"

"Well this is strange. The system claims that the cart contained argon and potassium, as you mentioned."

"What's strange about that?"

"There is no way that empty canisters and potassium samples filled the quota in thirty minutes. Potassium samples are quite light. The truck left at eight-thirty on the morning of the sixth. That truck is either empty, or the potassium and argon records were a clever smokescreen. You see, the weight limit is calculated by equipment handling needs. Potassium-forty carries a radioactive handling requirement that adds significant weight for containment to any shipment itinerary. If the object they were smuggling were indeed small and highly dense, such as a four-liter power supply, then this ruse would be quite ingenious indeed."

"You're saying that this took months of planning?"

"Months, days, it's hard to tell. Had this not come from your floor, I'm sure we would never have caught it. Everyone here is quite intimidated by your personnel. You know: the stories about the monsters and pig experiments. I'm sure it's all exaggerated, of course."

Jackie shrugged proudly at the insinuation. "Probably, I don't know. Can you get me the personnel file for this…?"

"Beverly Smith is her name."

"Great. What can you tell me about her?"

"She's really quite average. She has been here since 2008, and we have not had any problems with her. Beverly is routinely on time and has not been involved in any odd occurrences like this in the past. I am very surprised. We will get her personnel file and photo right away." Judy accessed the profile in her computer console and turned the screen toward Jacqueline.

Jacqueline pulled out her camera and took a picture of the image on the entire screen, and then took a closer shot of Beverly's picture. "White female age thirty-three, one point six eight meters, sixty-six kilos. Hard to believe she got that equipment out of there on her own. It weighs almost as much as she does."

"She would have had assistance from handlers as well as our robotic loading arms. This is no great feat, as far as I am concerned."

"Anything else you can tell me?"

"I was going to ask you the same. Is there anything I need to know about the power supply, the experiments, or any other breach information?"

"Need-to-know, I'm afraid." Jackie winked, "But don't feel bad. Even I don't know, and I really need to."

Chapter 5

September 7, 2006

"I miss you," Lydia groaned to Andrew when he answered. She was lying on her bed in New Orleans. Her feet and toes mindlessly fidgeted as she spoke. "Do we really have to be apart? My dad misses you too – even Cyrus."

"We've been over this. You know what happened," Andrew replied. He had pulled his car over on a lonely Nebraska road to take her call. "As long as I keep getting weird feelings from these messages, I'm a danger to you. You know I love you, but this is the way it has to be."

"I know what happened." She touched the scar on her cheek, "Every time I look in the mirror, I remember what happened. But I told you I can protect myself. What about when you're not looking for a message? Can't we just visit each other when you're not having one of your episodes?"

"I don't think you get it. I think I might have murdered someone just to keep you from getting hurt. I couldn't bear to go through that again. I see those three faces every day, Lydia."

"I know, but I was there. We were both being attacked. On top of it, you were going through a seizure. You defended us, and that's not murder. Besides, you didn't shoot those kids, the big, shirtless gorilla did. If we're meant to be together, then we should just be together. You don't have to tell me where you're going when you think you're onto a new clue or anything like that. I just think we're missing out right now."

"Fine, you're right. But I don't think we can live together again yet. If someone comes to the house to attack me, and I'm not home, I would never forgive myself if something happened to you."

"Always the gentleman, you are. But it's okay. I understand. I would think you were paranoid if I hadn't witnessed it first-hand. So how is Omaha?"

"I'm not even in Omaha. I'm west of it, by the Platte River, in a town called Valley. We're working a rail elevation survey job here for the new VacTrain project and should be wrapping up soon. The food is good here. That's about all I care about."

"Is it as good as New Orleans?"

"Nothing is as good as New Orleans, but the food here probably isn't killing me as fast either. You know me. I'm not too picky as long as I know what's in it. Omaha reminds me a bit of Terre Haute sometimes. I'll only be here for another week or so and then the job will end. Boss says we have a few options after that. Business is pretty good right now, so I might get to pick."

"I keep seeing commercials for the VacTrain. It sounds too good to be true. Do you really think it can go six thousand kilometers per hour?"

"It depends on the length of the run, I guess. Imagine a tube with a train in it. When you get everyone or everything inside, you seal the tube and then suck out all the air from the tube – but not the train. Then the train can move really fast without friction, using gravity to propel it, I guess. I'm not really sure about the science behind it, but they say if we can get the tube track down, it'll revolutionize travel and power consumption all over the world. I'm not sure if I buy it, but it's paying the bills."

"It sounds cool, but I don't know if I'd want to ride in a train that fast."

"I'm sure that's what they said about the first thirty-kilometer-per-hour train, or the first super-sonic airplane. But now it seems pretty safe and common."

"That's true, I suppose. You have a knack for making just about anything sound normal. Speaking of which, any new visions?"

"Same one's been bugging me for a while. It's a field of corn and a scarecrow. When I first came out here, I thought I might be in the right place. Now that I've seen a thousand scarecrows, I'm not so sure I want to go tipping each one over. But now that I'm here, I can't seem to picture it at all anymore. I'll take a drive the last night out here and see if anything happens. Otherwise, I think the trail might have gone cold."

"Well, be careful. When can I see you again?"

"After this job, maybe I can take some time off and visit. I'm getting tired of living out of motels, so I want to think about the next job carefully, so I can sign a lease somewhere."

"That would be nice. You could even get a cat."

"I'm sticking to my word though. I don't want us moving in together again. Not until this message business is through."

Lydia sighed, "Fine. But I don't want to wait three months between seeing you every time. That's no way to live."

"I miss you too. We'll work it out, I promise. I have to go, though."

"Okay. Love you."

"Love you always. Bye." As Andrew ended the call and put his phone back in his pocket, he put his car in gear. Finished in Valley for the day, he headed east on Ida, then got on 275 to head toward Omaha. He had been in the same motel off 275 for the past two weeks, and it was wearing on him. The service was fine, but the place was quite dated and most nights he just stared at the ceiling until he fell asleep.

His phone rang again, but it was not Lydia. Charlie Sherman came up on the display, and he answered immediately, putting the phone on speaker. "Talk to me, boss. The river survey is all set out west of Omaha."

"We're all set in Nebraska, Drew. Northern inspected us this afternoon and paid us an extra-week stipend. Your motel is paid through next Wednesday, so the next five or six days in Omaha are all yours. Kick back and relax, bud. You deserve it."

"That's great – congratulations Charlie. What's next?"

"Well that's up to you. We have our choice of a few jobs right now. Business is really booming with the President grounding all flights out west indefinitely. Northern will put you up for more VacTrain survey work in Utah or Wyoming, or tunnel work anywhere in the Rockies. And Catskill Rail will set us up with rail work in Ontario. That's where I'm headed. Sleep on it and let Jill know by Monday. She'll get your travel squared away. Thanks again for the great work in Omaha. I can't believe

Northern is paying so much for us to survey for these VacTrain tubes, but if they can work the technology out, I guess we'll be in business forever."

"Sounds good, I'll talk to Jill by Monday for sure. Talk to you later."

Andrew pulled into the motel parking lot shortly after and stared at the door to his room directly in front of his car. He looked in the rear-view mirror and glared for several seconds at the bar across the street. He had seen it each night and morning as he pulled in and out of the motel parking lot, but not being a heavy drinker, he took little interest. *Why not*, he thought to himself, as he got out of his car.

He walked across the street to the bar. He smiled as he opened the door and heard a Tex Williams song blaring from an old jukebox. The place was barren. Andrew noted a dozen empty booths along the right wall. One patron sat at the far end of the bar, staring down at a bowl of chili or soup. A gruff, old bartender leaned against the back wall of the bar and did not acknowledge Andrew's entry.

"Can I get a menu, maybe?" he asked the bartender after an awkward minute standing just inside the door.

The bartender slapped a menu onto the bar right in front of himself. "We're out of fish," he stated bluntly, and resumed his lackadaisical lean and empty stare.

Andrew sat at the bar where the bartender had placed the menu: six stools from the front door and seven stools away from the lone other patron. The man seated at the other end did not look up. As Andrew took his seat, he noticed that the other man was reading the newspaper, folded flatly on the countertop on the other side of his bowl.

Andrew perused the menu for a few silent minutes and then asked, "Can I get a Cobb Salad and an iced tea?"

"Let me check," replied the bartender. He walked back to the kitchen and had a brief conversation, presumably with the cook. "Yeah, we can make a Cobb work, but we'll have to go get some of them small tomatoes for it. Should take about ten minutes – you say the word and the wife will run out and fetch them. No trouble at all."

"I take it you don't sell a lot of salads?"

"I don't sell a lot of iced tea either, but I'm not here to judge you."

"What do you sell?"

"Well that guy had a chili and a whiskey."

Andrew yelled over the music to the other man, "How's the chili?" The man looked up at Andrew, smiled and nodded, and then returned to his paper. Looking back at the bartender, Andrew concluded, "I'll take the chili and the whiskey."

"Neat?"

"I think so." Andrew had no idea what the bartender meant, but the bartender did not particularly care.

Andrew ate his chili in silence and drank two glasses of water. He occasionally stared at the glass of amber whiskey on the counter but was hesitant to try it. After his meal, he drew the glass closer and smelled it. He nearly gagged at the pungent aroma.

The bartender laughed, "It won't bite. Might burn a little, but it won't bite."

Andrew raised the glass toward the man at the end of the bar, who returned the gesture. He took a large gulp and held it in his mouth for a few seconds.

The man at the far end saw a flash of green across Andrew's face and hollered, "Just swallow it! The longer you hold it the worse it'll get!" Andrew did as suggested and breathed heavily as the it slid down his throat and into his belly. The man grinned at the bartender, "Take a look on the floor, Mel, I think we just witnessed a cherry gettin' lost."

The bartender lightened up a bit and offered, "I'm Mel. What's your name, son?"

Still wheezing from the ripe drink, he responded, "Andrew."

The man at the far end of the bar pushed his newspaper and empty chili bowl toward Mel and grabbed his drink. He moved to the seat next to Andrew and pulled the stool out, "You mind?"

"Go right ahead, man."

"Name's Ray. Nice to meet you. What brings you to Omaha, stranger?" Ray spoke with a slight foreign accent that Andrew could not place, because of an unusually nervous pattern of syllabic up-turn. It was somewhere between New England and Irish, but not firmly footed in either, he thought. He wore a John Deere ball cap and maintenance coveralls that had his name embroidered on a patch. His hair was light brown with a hint of orange beneath the cap, and his face was weathered from the sun. Andrew placed the man at about fifty because of the young cracks that had formed around his mouth and eyes. Ray's left eye wandered slightly from the right, but Andrew found it more endearing that off-putting.

"How did you know I'm not from around here?"

"This isn't exactly Applebee's. No offense, of course," he offered to Mel, who shrugged. "Most of the locals are in town, not a highway truck-stop at six in the afternoon on a Thursday. My guess is you've got damn near nowhere better to be."

"You're not wrong. I'm in town for a survey job, but it seems the job is finished. I'm not sure what to do next."

"And what is it that you survey, exactly?"

"The rail companies are looking to upgrade their tracks across the country. I'm not supposed to get into the specifics, you know, industrial espionage and all that."

Ray forced a solemn face as he took a swig of his booze, "Say no more! No need to divulge secrets with me." Andrew smiled into his chili, wondering if he had come across as elitist with the friendly stranger. "How about this song, though?" Another Tex Williams song had come on, and Andrew suspected that Ray had set up a lengthy jukebox playlist while he had the bar to himself. "I love the old Westerns, don't you? I like Conway Twitty, and all the old-time singers that wore the big shiny costumes. I like all those old Western films. They just bring you to a different time, don't you think? When I found these old gems in his jukebox, well I just couldn't help myself."

"I don't mind it," Andrew said thoughtfully. "I thought this bar was a bit of a time-warp though when I first walked in. You need to be careful with that music or you're likely to scare away some normal folks. A place like this can get a reputation, you know."

"Amen," Mel affirmed. "I've been waiting out this set of blasted songs for two hours, son."

"Why did you buy those records, if you don't like them?" Andrew asked.

"They came with the jukebox and I don't know how to change them. Pain in the ass to take it apart. I unplug it at seven every night and plug in my iPod. People want me to play mostly grunge after that."

"So, you're just taking special care of your regulars then?" Andrew nudged Ray.

Ray shot a surprised look at Mel, then back at Andrew. "Oh, I'm not a regular," he explained. "I'm only in town for a few days as well."

Andrew was a bit surprised, since the man was dressed in a work uniform and seemed so comfortable in the establishment. "So, what is it that you do, if you're not from around here?"

"Oh, I install heating and air equipment. We're putting in some big machines in a corporate office downtown, but the company has me staying out here to save a few bucks. Must be lonely work for you too, just traveling around surveying the land?"

"It can be. I don't mind it though. I like to have time alone to think and relax."

"Well there's nothing wrong with that." Ray held up two fingers to Mel and pointed to their near-empty glasses. "Let's try a little water for the boy this time."

Andrew and Ray drank for a couple of hours. They talked about work, women, and the Pacific Abysm. Ray was mostly interested in music and movies, whereas Andrew was focused on people and the future. Although there was a large age gap between the two, Andrew was glad that he had made a new friend.

Before too long, the bar got quite busy. As he had promised, Mel unplugged the jukebox and switched to much louder rock music.

"One more round for the road, Mel," Ray announced, swirling one finger in the air.

"Only because you boys are walking home," Mel smirked as he poured two more drinks.

Ray insisted on taking care of the tab, and they clinked glasses to toast their acquaintance. Andrew announced, "To my new best friend, Ray, who taught me that sometimes bad things don't happen when you have some liquor."

"Why would something bad happen when you have hooch?" Ray asked as he took one last gulp and pounded the glass onto the bar.

"Last time I got drunk, my mom died," Andrew remembered sadly.

"Oh hell, am I harboring a fugitive from the law?"

"She was a thousand kilometers away. I just always remember how I felt that day, and I really haven't had any alcohol since."

"Tell you what, it's not even nine. Let's get some fresh air and see where the night takes us. I've got something I'd like to show you."

Andrew's head was swimming, but he was not tired. He finished his drink and left the glass on the bar. The two men exited and walked a half-block to the nearest traffic light. Ray hailed a few random cars, but they sped past. "Not many taxis on the outskirts of town, I'm afraid." He tried again, and a cab slowed. They got inside, and Ray handed a hundred-dollar bill to the driver. "Fort Calhoun Quarry off 75, round trip please."

The car took them north and east, but Andrew did not take note of the turns and highway numbers. He was sinking deeper and deeper into his stupor. At times, he felt the urge to throw up, but he never succumbed to it.

When the car finally stopped, Ray and Andrew got out. The quarry was empty, as were the machines around the parkway that led down into the site. Ray drew a flask from his pocket and coaxed Andrew, "Have a sip of this, and you'll feel a bit better." Andrew obeyed, and tasted something minty. Within a few moments his belly did feel a bit better, and he realized he had already started following Ray down into the quarry. The cab driver remained in his car and pulled into the quarry parking lot. Soon the two new drunken friends were out of sight of the taxi.

Ray picked up a few small rocks and chucked them toward other rock piles, in an adolescent attempt to disturb them. The effort was futile but served as a good distraction for Andrew.

"What are we doing out here?" asked Andrew, as he had a few times in the car.

"I like the way the stars look from out here. How's your head?"

Andrew's speech slurred badly, "My, why my head? What's wrong with it?"

"You were complaining about a headache in the cab," Ray's tone seemed quite sober and he took several steps back from Andrew toward a rock mound. "Don't you remember?"

Andrew laughed, "I don't… I mean that's crazy and I don't even remember that!"

Andrew turned around and Ray whipped a small rock at the back of his head. Andrew felt it, but the pain was numbed. He spun around to ask what had happened, but Ray was not there. "Hey, where did you go?" Andrew called out.

"Just grabbing a few things that I left here," Ray bellowed back from a distance, behind the rock pile. "All set. How's your head now?"

"It feels like you just hit me with a rock. Why did you do that?"

"Any buzzing?" Ray stood but did not approach Andrew, still eight meters away. Andrew looked confused but did not respond. "Any drilling sensations?" Andrew did not answer but rubbed the back of his head with his hand. "Any clicking, Andrew? Are you looking around for a scarecrow? Maybe smelling corn or mud? Manure? Doesn't seem like we'd find that down here in this quarry, now does it? What are you feeling, Andrew?"

Andrew heaved all over the ground in front of himself. Whiskey, water, chili, and a few dozen oyster crackers splattered all over his shoes and pants as it splashed onto the smooth, dense, stone ground at his feet.

"Go ahead and let it out. Sober up a bit. Here, have some of this." He tossed Andrew a travel mug that he had retrieved from a rock pile. Andrew cleaned off his face and took a sip of the coffee within the mug. It was only lukewarm, so he chugged the rest of it. As he did, the back of his head began pounding. He felt buzzing and clicking in every direction and he felt as though his head might explode. "That's it," Ray continued. "You're starting to feel it now."

"Why did you hit me with a rock? And how did you know…?"

"Let's start walking back up. I'll explain what I can. First, I'm sorry about the rock. I needed to distract you from these." Ray handed Andrew two black, 35mm film canisters. Andrew opened one excitedly and ensured that it contained a clear, plastic, coiled message. "Second, you can't drink when you're close. You need to focus that pain; you can't just tune it out or bury it with drugs and alcohol."

"Where did you find these?"

"Three days ago, I pulled them out from under the scarecrow's post where I buried them twenty-some years ago. I stowed them in this quarry on Monday, in bag lined with lead and a few other materials that keep them from talkin' to you." He pointed to a small bag on the ground. In his buzz, Andrew had not noticed the bag or its previous hiding place behind a rock pile until Ray pointed them out. "I doubt anything got through to you. If it did, you wouldn't have known what to do with it."

"How do you know any of this? Who the hell are you?"

"I'm a friend. Well, I'm a friend of a friend. It's important that you keep a steady pace with these coils. You have a long road ahead and time isn't slowing down. What you're doing is very important."

"Do you know my father?"

"I knew your father. He died a long time ago."

"Did you and he plant all the messages for before he died?"

"No. Your father was doing something else, but we worked with him and he was aware of what we were doing. He was aware of our plan for you."

"What does the message mean?"

"It's important that you find them all before you try to decipher anything. The message is secondary. Don't worry about what the actual message says."

"Then why don't you just hand all the coils to me?"

"We can't do that. You're not ready. For now, the thing you need to understand is how to find the coils, slowly, but steadily. If you get close to too many at once, it could kill you or cause permanent brain damage. You won't always know how many are around. If you feel pain that's too intense, take one of these." He pulled a small vial of pills from his pocket and handed it to Andrew. "Never take more than one at a time, or bad things could happen."

"Like what? I thought you told me not to numb the pain." Andrew mumbled.

"These aren't painkillers. In fact, they could help you focus it a bit. But this solution isn't perfect, and I don't have much of this stuff."

"What is it?"

"Don't worry about that. It could keep you from getting yourself killed; that's all I can tell you. These coils are powerful and if you attune to too many at once, it could really mess up your brain. That's why we spread them out and buried them. We saved a couple to plant near you when you were off the trail, like when I chucked one onto a garbage barge heading down the Mississippi. I have to admit, that was pretty funny to watch."

"You were the one who sent the graduation card?"

"Yep, that was me. The coils communicate with you, Andrew. The senses of the people around the coils – the smells, the sights, and so on – are transmitted to you through the coils. The day before your graduation, I left the graduation card and instructions with every entrant to the barbecue contest on Mud Island. Then, early in the morning the day of your graduation, I drove up to a little shipyard off Coon Valley Road and waited for a southbound barge. They move pretty slowly, as I'm sure you soon learned. I drove down to the barbecue contest with a few more coils in my pocket so that you would see the contestants and smell the barbecue. When you got closer, I just stashed the coils in a lead-lined bag and took off. If I left these coils outside of the very same bag today, you might have seen rocks or dust. You might have smelled the machinery. I wanted to make sure I caught you completely off guard by bringing you to the least likely place to find a scarecrow. That's why we're here. Now that you've refined the skill a bit and we were able to have this little chat, we won't need to do interfere anymore."

"Who's 'we'? And why not just tell me where all the coils are?"

"It's not that simple. I'm telling you everything I can, but some questions need to be left alone, for your own safety. Sorry for all the deception. Honestly, you started finding the coils years before we thought you would. We predicted the message in the Shakespeare book may not even find you at all, and that we might just have to start planting coils near you when you reached about the age you are now. But it all worked out. We just needed to ensure that you found one at least couple times a year. At that stage, we didn't think you could handle all the details of what we were doing – certainly not at age eleven. Even now, there's a lot we can't tell you."

"Why did you write the message in the book at all, then, if you never expected me to find it?"

"What we were doing was extremely dangerous. We didn't expect to survive it. You were our insurance plan in case Vince – well, you know. Could have happened to any of us. And if we all bought it, I mean there were folks that wanted to take us out, you know? Well we needed a backup plan."

"You mean that book wasn't even from my dad?" Andrew reflected as he slumped onto the ground. "That's all I ever knew of him, and even that's not real?"

"The book was indeed from your dad! I was with him when he bought it. He gave it to your ma, and that was real. He just didn't inscribe that special message you found."

"You wrote the Caesar message?"

"No, but I was at the house. A few of us worked together. We made sure you were safe."

"So... Why did you choose me?"

"That's a very long story, and one you're not ready for quite yet. But I promise you, in time, all will be made clear. For now, you need to focus on the imagery and senses that the coils communicate with you. Pain will help you focus it. And when you find a few coils, be sure to take a break. Take a month or two off, and then pick up the next scent if you can. You have time, but if you keep a solid pace it will be easier for you."

"How many are there?"

"There are a lot. When you're done, you'll know."

They arrived at the taxi and Ray opened the door for Andrew and handed the cabbie more money. Once Andrew was seated, Ray looked squarely into his eyes, "One last thing, Andrew. Do not trust anyone. Let your guard down, and you could end up dead in some quarry in the middle of a cornfield before you know it." Ray closed the door and rapped the roof. The cab sped off without Ray. Andrew turned around to see him piling into the front passenger seat of a car that had been parked in the quarry's lot since before they had arrived. The headlights came on and the car pulled out and headed in the opposite direction. Andrew shrugged and wondered if and when he would see his mysterious new ally again.

After a thirty-five-minute drive, the taxi arrived back at the bar across from Andrew's motel. He thanked the driver and walked across the street to his room. He pulled the pair of black film canisters out of his pocket and opened them. He took his phone out and called Lydia.

"You're not going to believe this." He explained his bizarre encounter and told her everything about Ray and the quarry. He had sobered significantly but was still tired from the alcohol and adventure.

"Send me the capsules as soon as you can," she concluded. "If you've got time, read them off to me now, so I can keep working on the code. Maybe two more will give me something new to work with."

Andrew smiled and appreciated how lucky he was to have found her. She never judged his odd quest, and she had always wanted to help even though she did not understand it.

"Okay, the first one reads:

> *all physics Multiverse an of spatial it. on the for known same and them, even takes outside do body Custodians of as billion may periodically The muted genetically of diversity would Blind and from the Again peak could to were A and Custodians, overcrowding. a the were technological years, they first-inhabitants. have or and Holy They not have the father sensory as red 14*

"That one seems creepy," he paused. "Did you get it all?"

"I'm ready," she replied after a few seconds.

"Okay, here goes."

> *line In mechanics crafted out mass not this millions that more souls wonder of When in a or they ammonium rings wings, them focus divide, to to billion of stability Blind, each was available, Traps. wipe Yucatan from from tweaking, on brain evolve. out, fostered grew homage technology completely the when the natural population Easter invisibly is with one wonderful connection cannot ignore 110*

"That's it," Andrew concluded.

"Ha!" Lydia had exclaimed halfway through, and again at the end as she madly transcribed.

"What? Did you find something already?"

"No, you said 'tweaking on brain.' That's funny."

"Damn," he sighed.

"I got it all, but I was hoping the third one would be fifteen, since the second one was fourteen. Your rubbing says fifteen and a half is the key, so I think we need to find the one marked 'fifteen' at the end, in order to crack it. Oh well."

"I didn't even think of that."

"That one has a phrase that almost makes sense as is. Did you catch, 'Easter invisibly is with one wonderful connection cannot ignore'? I wonder if that's an actual statement. Did he tell you anything else about how the messages fit together?"

"He only told me about how to find them. Some of it still doesn't make any sense. Like why did you picture me before we met? The same thing happened with the smoking man Wilmer, back in Pittsburgh. I don't understand how other people are connected to me, but it seems that some are. He just told me to take a month or two off before I pursue the next one, so I guess I'll do that."

"Does that mean you're coming down to see me?"

"Right now, I just need to sleep. My head is pounding, and for once it's not from these message coils. We can sort out visiting plans in the morning."

"I'll hold you to that," she said with a smile in her voice that made him completely content. He hung up and drifted off to sleep, fully clothed and clutching his phone at his chest atop the motel comforter.

The next morning, Andrew's head pounded. He remembered walking out of the bar with Ray to hail a taxi, but the rest of the night was a whiskey-flavored blur.

Chapter 6

September 8, 2006

Andrew decided to drive from Omaha to New Orleans following breakfast Friday. Lydia was not aware, but she knew Andrew had nowhere to be for the next several days. He began on I-29 heading south toward Kansas City. His mind was filled with questions about Ray. *Who is he? How does he know Vince? Had Vince not really gone on a secret mission with the Air Force? Ray said that he had worked with my father, but that Vince had not hidden the messages. How exactly was my father involved?*

For two hours he drove south contemplating what he remembered of the previous night. Lydia had helped him to consider new perspectives each time he explained developments in his secret duty. But there were also elements he did not understand that directly involved her. Ray was somewhat helpful describing how to obtain the capsules, but what Andrew really wanted to know was why they were so important. He wanted to understand how he was connected to Lydia, and why she and Wilmer Garciaparra swore they had each seen Andrew before they met. Lydia had the drawings of him to prove it.

He also pondered why Ray had told him not to collect more than one or two messages at a time. When he was in the smoky shack in Pittsburgh, he had found four. He had felt pain and experienced terrible hallucinations, but the pain did not kill him. Andrew assumed that people would become more violent around him if he found more at one time. The thought of attackers also seemed ambiguous following Ray's lecture. He did not explain why people became possessed, or why he was able to incapacitate them with mere thought. Andrew wished that he had held a soberer mind when presented with his first opportunity to question one of the people directly responsible for his lifelong quest. *I'll bet*, he thought, *that was part of the reason Ray encouraged me to get drunk at the bar.* Andrew would have gone along with most any adventure as they left the bar, and Ray may have had motives other than to dull Andrew's pain before handing over message coils.

He hypothesized during his drive down I-29 either that Ray was not aware of the phenomenon by which people around Andrew became violent; or, that he did not yet wish to reveal such. Ray did hint, Andrew recollected, that nobody should be trusted. That suggestion seemed clear from the very first message that Andrew found in the Shakespeare volume when he was just eleven.

As Andrew approached Kansas City around three in the afternoon, his head sharply buzzed. He was caught off guard after hours of driving and thinking in silence that his foot involuntarily jolted onto the gas pedal. Such jolts were commonplace over the past several years, but never failed to startle him. He checked behind him to make sure he had not been bumped by another driver, and the road was clear. The pain subsided so he kept driving. He took the next exit, which was 435 South, but realized after a kilometer that it was another highway. When he saw a sign for I-70 West toward Lawrence, his head seared once again, and he saw an image he did not understand. In an instant, he saw the plastic coil material, but it was a jumbled mess. He saw a giant sheet of it, lying on a table in a sort of barn. He saw the message material in its raw form with no words etched onto it. It was flat, and did not coil naturally, as all of his messages had thus far done, in order to fit neatly in their tiny, black containers. The sheet was bigger than he expected. It was a meter wide by three meters long. All of his message coils were only 0.65 meters in length when fully opened. He envisioned a man nearby, but the man was oblivious to the plastic sheet. He was dressed in heavy protective gear. He held an arc welder in one hand and a hammer in the other. Andrew felt blackness and solitude. In a flash, the vision had come and gone. He smelled and tasted nothing, and the pain vanished as quickly as it came.

Andrew took the 435 bypass to I-70 West. Ignoring Ray's advice about waiting, he was determined to find whatever secrets Lawrence held. Road signs all pointed toward Kansas University, and he figured they must have had a chemistry lab that processed plastic sheets. The man from his vision was older than he would have guessed students would be, but he supposed that professors could have been demonstrating something. It dawned on him that the man may have been creating more of the coils from the raw material.

He raced toward Lawrence hoping for more sensory clues. When he reached the exit for the university, he got off the highway and slowly drove around the campus looking for a science building. Once he located a large science lecture hall, he parked his car and walked into the building.

Andrew was distracted in nearly every direction. He had not attended a real university and pined for the experience. When he was younger, he dreamed of attending a private school with small classes, where there were no bullies. While Kansas University was a gigantic school, it held all of the charm with which Andrew was once enamored. The trees were bright and tall; not quite ready to turn red and yellow at the first signs of autumn. The students milled about on individual missions that embodied the solitary determination of the student life Andrew had once dreamed about.

In the science building, there was no welcome desk to greet him. He was not sure what to expect, but an empty foyer leading to a bunch of numbered classrooms was not remotely what he had envisioned while driving. He walked around for a few minutes. He hoped to be caught by some local authority, and subsequently put in the right direction. When it became clear that no such authority would surface within the foyer, he began concentrating on the flash he had seen of the man dressed as a metalworker. He could envision the plastic sheet and the man, but the walls were nondescript. No smells or sounds were discernable. He approached a few classroom doors and expected to find a large laboratory behind each. He was disappointed to find only lecture rooms. He spotted a janitor down the hall, and called out to him, "Hey do you know where there's a plastics lab around here?"

"Who are you?" the man replied. "Are you a student?"

"No, I'm just looking for someone, I think."

"What are you doing in here? I don't know who you are, but you shouldn't be here."

"No problem, I'll go. Thanks anyway." Andrew exited the building as instructed but looked back several times to see if there was a door or wing that he had missed. He had a sinking feeling walking back to his car. As he turned the key and put the car in gear, he looked once again at the science building and caught a pair of eyes on him through a window on the first floor. The blinds closed quickly when Andrew spotted the person. He felt paranoid about being watched, but he did not feel any clicks or pain. He pulled the car out and drove around to the other side of campus.

After he parked, he retrieved the pill vial that Ray had given him the night before. He clutched it in his hand for a few moments and then opened the bottle. Twelve pills were inside, and each bore no identifying markers. He checked the label, which was from Dorian Pharmacy in Oshkosh, Wisconsin. There was no physician's name; however, the patient name was clearly printed as "Andrew Gaeta." Andrew turned the vial around to read the dosage directions, which stated, "Take one by mouth as needed. Never take more than one within a 10-day period. May produce unexpected side effects: exercise caution. No refills."

He slid one of the pills out and held it in his hand as he allowed some spit to pool in his mouth. He jammed the vial back into his pocket, and then placed the pill on his tongue. It was berry flavored. He smiled and swallowed it.

Convinced that something would happen, he left his car running and watched the students come and go from the residence hall across from his parking space. He watched a conversation between a boy and a girl and imagined what they might be saying. He saw an awkward girl come out of the building with too many books. She barely kept her balance as she sped on foot across the campus. The mystery drug had no apparent effect, but Andrew did not mind watching the students scurry about as their weekends were beginning to take flight.

Without warning, his brain convulsed within his skull. A sharp shock shot down his spine straight through to his toes. He clenched his teeth in agony and felt a sharp force on the right side of his neck. "Drive," a low voice slithered from behind him. Andrew looked in his rear-view mirror to see that the janitor from the science building had snuck into Andrew's back seat and pressed a knife to his throat. The pain had distracted him from the sound of the car door, but as soon as the man spoke, Andrew snapped into action and shifted the car into reverse. The back door closed with a thud, and the car rolled out naturally.

Andrew did not resist. He saw no reason to, since he deduced that the man was not interested in murdering him or he would have done so already. He also suspected there were coils nearby or related to this man, evidenced by the sudden, familiar pain. The man had a long, scraggly beard and thinning brown hair. He wore a gray janitor's uniform that looked as though it had not been washed in years. Burn marks and cuts littered the outfit, and Andrew noticed dozens of such burn marks and gash scars on the man's hand.

"Pull out here," the man said shortly. "Head east. Don't go too fast. I don't want to kill you. I just want answers."

"No problem," Andrew responded peacefully. "Ask me whatever questions you like."

The man was surprised by Andrew's cooperation, but kept his guard up. He continued to speak in a choppy, delusional manner. "Who are you?"

"My name is Andrew," he calmly offered. He thought he would try to quell the man by proactively offering information. "I'm from Indiana. I'm in town on business. I have no intention of harming you."

"We'll see about that. Why are you following me?"

"I didn't realize I had been. I just drove down from Omaha this morning and pulled off here to check out the campus on my way down south for the weekend."

"That's impossible – lies. I saw you last night and then again, this morning. What were you doing outside my house?" He pressed the knife blade in a bit further and it broke the skin of Andrew's neck.

"Sir I've never been to this town before, and I don't even know where you live. But please hear me out. We're in a public place. Can I tell you a few things and ask you a couple of questions, and then maybe we can just talk this out in private?"

"Turn left here. You've got thirty seconds. Then if you don't start telling me the truth I'm just going to start cutting and jump out of the car once I know you can't follow me."

"Sir, I do not know you. But I do know that you have one or more black film canisters, containing small coils of clear plastic."

"Yeah. What about them?"

"You're not shocked that I asked you that?"

"Of course not. I've got hundreds of them."

"Hundreds?!" Andrew exclaimed. "How is that even possible?"

The man laughed but kept the knife at Andrew's neck. "Why are you following me, man? And don't tell me it's because you want to go garbage-picking my shed. Start talking. Your clock is ticking."

"When you see me following you, do I talk? Do I do anything?"

"I looked out the window last night about nine, and you were across the yard, mouthing something. I couldn't hear you. You gave me a hell of a spook. I yelled out for you to beat it, and I didn't see you anymore. I closed the curtain and kept drafting."

"What kind of work do you do? Is there a shed in your yard?"

"No. Shut up. At about one in the morning, I finished my work and I went over to the window. I pulled back the curtain and there you were right outside the window, staring right at me and mouthing something. I called the cops and by the time they got there you were gone. You scared the hell out of me and then you made me look like a jackass with the cops."

"Can you focus on what I was mouthing?"

"Why don't you just *tell* me what you were saying?"

"Because that wasn't me. I have no doubt that you thought it was me, but I assure you I was in Omaha. The motel check-out slip is on the seat right next to me. I was never at your house last night."

The man shifted the knife from his right hand to his left and reached his right hand into the front seat. Without taking his eyes off Andrew, he located the check-out receipt. He read it over for several seconds, and then lowered the knife to Andrew's shoulder. "I'll be… But I saw you again this morning. There's no way around it. I went to the grocery store and you were there. At first you were standing outside the door looking at me as I walked in, and then later I saw you inside mouthing something to me. The whole time, you were just staring at me, man. I got my items and checked out as fast as I could, and when I walked out you were standing outside the door again. I told you to quit following me, and then I took off. But then I circled back around, and I saw you there again. You were finally not looking at me. So, I followed you to the school, and you went into the science building and went into a classroom. I stayed outside that classroom door for over two hours and you never came out. But then I saw you in the hall, and I didn't know how you got out. So, I looked back in the classroom at where you were sitting, and some other guy was already sitting there. I don't know how you did it, but I've never been so freaked out in my life."

"Please, just let me ask you a few questions. How long have you had the plastic coils?"

"Ages. What's this all about? How is this possible?"

"Please, just take me to them."

"You swear you'll leave me alone?" the man flashed a humble tone for the first time since their meeting.

"Absolutely, I swear I'll never bother you again."

"Turn around up ahead. I'll take you to my old studio."

Andrew fought the growing pain in his head and tried to keep up the conversation, "Are you a musician?"

"No, I'm a custodian for a few local businesses. Not the school. But I was already dressed for work when I followed you there, and nobody batted an eye. In my spare time, I'm a sculptor. I mostly work with metal. Up ahead make a left on 19th. We'll take that east for a while." He leaned back and pulled the knife down but clutched it firmly in his hand.

"What's your name?"

"Picasso," he remarked sarcastically.

"Got it," Andrew conceded. He realized he had overestimated their rapport.

They drove for ten more minutes as Andrew's head constantly blazed with pain. The man at last told him, "Make a right here, on Learnard. Park on the street and we'll walk." The two exited the car and walked down the quiet neighborhood street. "Twenty years ago, there wasn't much out here, man. Some of these houses, sure, but there were only a couple of businesses over there on the next few streets." He pointed to the small industrial area, which was visible at times through the trees. "I rented out a house and a shed for a couple of years on this street. The house is gone now, replaced by a better one I'm sure. But the shed is still there. When my landlord decided to sell the place, I was pretty shocked, and I had nowhere to go. But the new owner saw some of my sculptures in the shed and decided to let me keep using it. He even bought a couple of them from me to help me get back on my feet. I'm not sure if he really liked them or if he just felt guilty for kicking me out and knocking the house down. I was here this morning to take measurements on some of my metal pieces, but I haven't touched the plastic parts in years."

The sculptor took a key from his pocket and led Andrew across the grass to a shed in someone's back yard. Picasso unlocked the shed door and opened it. Andrew was amazed. Most of the metal was perforated and black, but some was gray steel. Various pieces were crimped and folded into chaotic and grotesque shapes. He had attached lights to some. A few were painted. Some were shaped like people, others like objects, and others still like the stuff of abstract daydreams. He smiled as Andrew gazed upon a few of the pieces in wonder. "These are just scraps, too, man. The real stuff is a lot bigger, usually. Your plastic strips are back here." Picasso led

Andrew to the back of the shed where a large tool chest was blocked against the wall by several metal pieces.

"I've never seen metal perforated like this."

"It's pretty unique. The building on the next street manufactures aircraft parts. They make these huge space-age things that I guess get shipped off to bigger companies to make planes and rockets, or something. Could be for wings, cockpits; who knows? Not many airplanes getting manufactured these days, though. I wonder how they're still in business. Help me move this. Some of the sheets are clear. Other ones have tiny holes in them. Must make them lighter or something. I don't really get it but everybody in town just loves them. They're like local legends. Anyway, they go through a lot of scrap metal and plastic, and I used to pick these scraps right out of the garbage."

After he and Andrew had moved some of the heavy pieces out of the way, the sculptor opened the bottom drawer of the workbench to reveal a hundred black film capsules as promised. Andrew's head swirled when he saw the pile of treasures, but he did not feel much pain. "What can you tell me about them?"

"I used them on a few sculptures. The plastic is basically indestructible, which is pretty cool for something that's clear. But I don't use it anymore. It's really hard to get it to adhere to anything, so I had to use clamps. They always end up just snapping and coiling back up again. There's something weird about the way they snap back into shape."

"I just can't believe they would throw them away though."

"Oh, you know what? These didn't come out of the garbage, man. Only the metal scraps did."

"What? Then where did these come from?"

"There was a weird military-type guy down the road that had these. He was nice enough, but a little tightly wound. He had some welding equipment and some laser cutters that he would let me use from time to time to make sculptures. Holy shit, man – I just remembered, I stole these from him! Wow, I forgot all about that. I was working in his lab on some metal pieces, and I saw some of these suckers all sprawled out. When he stepped out, I just piled a bunch of them into my duffle bag and jacked them. He never said anything about it though. I guess he didn't need them. That was back in eighty-four or eighty-five and he didn't move out until eighty-six, same year as me. So, I guess he didn't need them, or he would have said something."

"Do you know where he got them?"

"I know the airplane parts sometimes used that material, or something like it, but I don't get how it works exactly. I always figured he got it from them, but I certainly never saw any in their garbage. But it probably wasn't a coincidence that he was living this close to that building. I never asked him where they came from or what he was doing to them – especially after I stole a bunch of them from him."

"This is unbelievable. I… I don't suppose you'd be willing to part with them?"

"Man, I'm just glad you're not a ghost. Tell you what. You take all of them. You try to track down a guy named Commander Watson. If you find him, give them back to him, and tell him I'm sorry."

"I never did catch your name?"

"Damn right you didn't. I don't need you or him ever tracking me down again. I don't know why I saw you standing outside my window last night, but it was scary as hell. If this is what makes you get out of my head, then a drawer full of garbage is a small price to pay as far as I'm concerned."

Andrew stretched his shirt out at the belly to scoop as many in as he could. Based on Ray's warning, he thought he might drop dead at any moment, but the agonizing sensations eventually improved. Under his breath, Andrew muttered, "I knew Ray was full of it." The sculptor helped him secure all the message coils in his makeshift cotton reservoir. Once he had them all, Andrew looped the fabric up near his chin to lock them in and sloshed them back to his car.

"You want a ride somewhere?" Andrew asked as he walked.

"Nah. You look so stupid right now, man," Picasso laughed. "I'm okay walking. You just go right ahead and drive as far away from here as you can."

Chapter 7

September 9, 2006

After stopping for gas and coffee, Andrew headed straight to New Orleans. His face beamed about the trunk full of treasure. The drive from Lawrence to New Orleans took fourteen hours, including the Kansas City rush hour on Friday afternoon.

Lydia was alarmed to hear an excited rapping at her door just before seven Saturday morning. She opened the door with the chain intact, and Andrew nearly broke the chain as he tried to bust through. "Hey!" Lydia exclaimed when she realized it was him. "Hang on, get out – I have to… There." She unhooked the chain and opened the door. Andrew poured in and they kissed for fifteen seconds. "You're here!" She finally said as they broke away.

"Yes, I am," Andrew confirmed. "And I have something to show you. Is Pasha here?"

"Yes, he is. Dad!" Lydia yelled through the bedroom door. Her father was still asleep.

They waited a few minutes for the sleepy old man to rumble around. Lydia had taken up on the couch in the living room and given her father the bedroom after Andrew moved out. Pasha was sad to see Andrew go, and neither Pasha nor Lydia took issue with the young couple living together out of marriage. Lydia did not tell Pasha why Andrew insisted on moving out. She told him that the gash on her cheek was from a mugger in Jackson, rather than a message-coil-driven and ultimately foiled rape attempt, which resulted in three dead young men in Port Gibson, Mississippi. Pasha always accepted Andrew and wanted the youngsters to be happy together. He did not care that Andrew sent every dime he made to them so that they could live in a one-bedroom apartment as opposed to the sketchy den of a commune in which they previously resided. He only cared that Andrew made Lydia the happiest he had ever seen.

"You finally decide to come back, my boy?" Pasha asked as the door swung open. He was wearing Lydia's silk robe, which was so short on him that it revealed most of his white briefs.

"Pants, dad," Lydia scolded and looked away. "And don't stretch that out!"

Once her father came back wearing pants and a T-shirt, Andrew beckoned them outside. "I have something to show you." He opened his trunk to reveal the film canisters that had scattered during the drive. Then he pulled the two from Ray out of his pocket and handed them to Lydia. "Here are the two I read to you. We'll have to get started on the rest sometime."

"I'm speechless," Lydia eventually produced. "How did this happen?"

"Let's bring them all in. I'll tell you all about it while we build a pyramid out of them or something."

Andrew explained what he could of the Lawrence diversion to Lydia and Pasha. He described Picasso in great detail and told them about the aero parts factory nestled in the middle of a neighborhood in the college town. He showed them the pill bottle that Ray had given him and explained that he took one right before Picasso put a knife to his throat. "What really burns me though," Andrew closed, "is what Ray said about the messages killing me if I found too many. At the amusement park, I found four. It hurt, but it didn't kill me. Yesterday I found a hundred or so, and they didn't kill me. I did take one of these pills that Ray gave me. But he didn't tell me there would be so many in one place. What are the odds?"

"There must be more out there," Lydia objected. "I mean there was obviously some truth to what Ray told you, if he had two coils and was able to tell you how to find more. What motive would he have for lying to you about the quantity?"

"That's true, but I'm also concerned about how many of these things there are, if a hundred were just lying in a drawer. I don't think that was by design, but the sculptor told me that this Watson guy didn't even seem to notice or mind that they had been stolen. Something doesn't seem to add up."

The trio discussed for an hour and decided to go out to breakfast to celebrate. They stashed the new coils in a dresser drawer and walked to the bakery a few blocks from their apartment on Prieur Street.

"I miss the old neighborhood sometimes," Lydia said to Andrew. She wrapped both arms around his elbow as they walked. "But I like being so close to the French Quarter. The coffee is much better on this side of town than it was at our old place."

Pasha chimed in, "You're right about that. I like everything over here. Thank you, Andrew. You are very kind to us."

"You guys are the only family I've got," Andrew replied solemnly. "As long as work pays for me to stay in motels, I'll need somebody to look after my place, right?"

Pasha laughed, "I don't mind being your butler, boy. You just keep my daughter happy and I will sleep wherever you tell me to."

They did not talk much over breakfast, but the mood was cheerful and anxious. Andrew and Lydia were singularly focused on going back to the apartment to go through message coils and determine how much of Andrew's quest had just been accomplished in a single fortuitous event.

Pasha had other plans. "Andrew," he smiled, "I want to ask you something. You want to wait until you find these treasures before you can move on, I understand this. You say that people attack you when you are finding these things. But now that you have so many, I am thinking that you can take a break while you sort this out. I was so happy to see you this morning, even before you showed us what was in your trunk. I just want to ask you," he paused as he reached into his pocket and pulled his hand back out in a closed fist, "if you would be my son-in-law."

Lydia's face turned bright red. "Dad! You're not supposed to... That's not how it works here. You're not in Belarus!"

"The man asks the woman to marry in Belarus as well, young lady. But in this case, I think I might be dead by the time I let you two get married on your own. You need a little kick in the behind."

Andrew blushed as well, and asked, "Where did you get that?"

"This belonged to Lydia's mother," Pasha smirked to avoid getting choked up. "No matter how bad things got when we escaped the old country, I always kept this. It doesn't have diamonds or anything like that, but it is real gold. Lydia is about same size as her mother, so I'm sure it will fit. I am just thinking now that since you are traveling a lot, maybe this way Lydia knows that you are thinking about her too."

"I'm always thinking about her," he answered. As he thought it through, it made more and more sense. "But he's right, Lyd. I'm making real progress and I know without a doubt that you're the only woman I ever want to be with." He paused and looked away, then back to her, "Let's get married."

Lydia pointed to Andrew, "You – yes." She pointed to her father, "You – don't ever do that again. I think I just had my first heart attack."

Pasha stood up at the table and held the ring in the air. "She said yes, everybody!" Most of the patrons were confused, but a few applauded for them. None of them understood who had said yes to whom, or for what.

"Should we set a date or something?" Andrew asked.

"Well where are you going next, and for how long?" Lydia replied.

"I don't know, and I'm not sure. Boss has a bunch of jobs out west for Northern, or some stuff up in Canada for Catskill. He didn't say how long they were. Could be a couple of months, but it could be longer."

"Oh," she sighed.

Andrew detected that her excitement had been deflated by the thought of his absenteeism and surprised her. "Let's get married today then."

"What?" Her face struck him as unprepared more than disturbed or excited.

"Look, I'd have married you three years ago if I'd have known that you would say yes and would still let me pursue this thing that I do. So, let's just get married and settle the question now. I know I love you, and you know you love me. Let's make that official so that there won't be any more doubts while I'm away. I still don't think we should go hunting down message coils together, but Pasha's right. We scored so big today that hopefully it won't even matter for much longer."

Lydia mulled it over for a few seconds. "What am I even waiting for, of course we can! Let's head over to City Hall and see if they're open."

After they left, they walked southeast on Canal Street toward the French Quarter. They meandered a bit from there and reached their destination in a total of fifteen minutes on foot. When they saw that it was open, Andrew and Lydia raced across the grass to the front of the tall and wide, teal-windowed building. They entered and spoke with the concierge, who directed them to the correct room for marriage licenses. When Pasha had caught up, they proceeded to the room and requested the application.

Pasha produced Lydia's immigration documents as well as Andrew's birth certificate.

Andrew noted it and quipped, "You old dog. Snatched that before we left, just in case, did you?" The old man smiled with pride.

The heavy and disgruntled desk clerk helped with a few of their questions, and then she asked, "When are you looking to get married?"

Lydia responded, "Today, if we can."

"No, we only have marriage ceremonies Mondays through Thursdays now."

Lydia firmed her approach. "We can't wait until then. You must be able to make an exception."

"Two words: recession," she curtly retorted. "You can blame President Gore; it's probably his fault like everything else. Or blame the Pacific pit if it makes you feel any better. But a justice don't get out of bed on a Saturday in Nola anymore, not even for the likes of you. Besides, you have to wait seventy-two hours before a justice can conduct the ceremony anyway. Come back on Tuesday. Next?" She looked beyond Lydia even though she was clearly the only person in line.

"Please, you need to help us. We can't wait until Monday – he's probably going to leave."

"She's right," Andrew added.

"What you two need is Jesus. You need to get to a church."

"That's a hell of an attitude," Andrew interjected. "How dare you? All she did was ask you for help, and you are an employee of the government. Nice attitude," he leaned in to read her badge, and then finished condescendingly, "Rosalind S."

"Sir, you don't need to raise your voice at me. I'm trying to tell you to pick out any one of a hundred churches within a three-kilometer radius and get your narrow little butts married today. Preachers work on Saturdays to plan the Sunday sermon. You need to get to a church."

The three looked at each other nodding, and Pasha spoke for the group, "That was not what I thought she meant."

Rosalind droned in monotone, having issued many of her canned statements countless times per day. "I'll make you a copy of the application, and you can show it to the church. You'll get the marriage certificate in the mail in a few days. Congratulations. Next?"

Pasha bowed humbly toward Rosalind S., "Thank you, kind lady."

The trio walked together back toward their small apartment and tried a few churches. Some doors were locked. A few others had staff but claimed to be too busy to help them. They finally came to a Baptist church near the apartment. There was a bible study group in the foyer, and the pastor excused himself from the group to greet the newcomers.

"Are you here for the bible study class?" the preacher asked.

"No," Andrew answered. "We'd like to get married, if you have the time."

"Well there's always time for that! Everyone, please gather around so that we can join these two lovebirds in matrimony. Do you have rings?"

"Just one," Andrew said with a look of dread. "Is that a deal-breaker?"

"Not at all; it's just symbolic. But I do recommend getting rings so that whenever you are apart, you'll always have that little reminder there, that there's someone who loves you."

The pastor asked them a few questions in the presence of the class, and they responded accordingly. He was coaxing them to offer impromptu vows, and they did not realize it until he was finished. He pronounced them husband and wife and invited them to stay and participate in the bible class. They did at that, but they sat back from the group and whispered among themselves for most of it. After thirty minutes the group adjourned, and several of the attendees congratulated the newlyweds.

They left the church and headed back toward the apartment, but Andrew stopped before they arrived. "I need a ring," he said. He pointed to a house on the street, and as was common in the neighborhood where they lived, it doubled as a business. "Who says it has to be metal?"

Andrew knocked on the door, and a gruff, Latino man answered. His head was shaved, and he wore a tank top that revealed tattoo sleeves filled with colorful birds and angels. "Can I help you?"

Andrew looked back at Lydia and Pasha tentatively, and stated, "I would like a tattoo of a ring, please."

"Step inside, my friend. You want black? Silver? Gold? You want something with gems or maybe flames shooting out of the sides?" He smiled, partially joking.

"Gold with a thin black border, so you can tell it's there."

Pasha intervened, "On the right ring finger, please." Andrew looked at him, confused. Lydia held up her right hand and showed him that her ring was on it. "I'm old-school, please just let me have this one thing Russian-style."

Andrew and the tattoo artist both chuckled at Pasha's attempt to sound hip. Andrew did as he was instructed, and the tattoo did not take long. He enjoyed the pain of the tattoo a great deal. It was different from the pain he normally felt, and the needle against his skin felt oddly erotic as he clenched his jaw and flexed his hands throughout the process. He expected flashes during the session but did not see anything. For a time, he smelled flowers, but he thought that could have been perfume from someone else inside the house.

Back at the apartment at last, Lydia went straight to the coils and moved them out to the coffee table. Andrew gestured to the bedroom, but she shrugged and shot a glance toward her father.

"Dad," she said, "do you want to go to a movie or anything?"

"No, my love," he answered obliviously. "It has been a busy morning and I need a nap. I'm leaving the door open, so it doesn't get too hot in here."

"Business as usual, I guess," sighed Andrew.

"We can celebrate tonight. I'm pretty anxious to get started on these coils. I haven't shown you my new system yet! Come here. I take the words down vertically as they are on the strip, but then I make a copy in this journal as well, so that I can see the words side by side. There are always sixty-three words, and then one number at the very bottom. I have it arranged eight by eight. Each page represents a different coil. Right now, I have them arranged in the order that you found them, but I've tried several configurations and I can't make heads or tails. I think it's possible that some of the words are code words for other things, like maybe anagrams, or just random substitutions. I've been studying, in particular, the use of the words Blind, Custodian, and God, which appear frequently. They're always capitalized. But the more I look at it I don't think it's a religious message at all. I think these three words stand for something else – possibly people or places. I'm still not sure exactly which, but I think as soon as we find number fifteen, like your Shakespeare clue said, it will tell us what those words are supposed to translate to. Make sense?"

"No, but I'm damned lucky I found you." Andrew kissed her aggressively, and she did not resist.

After they had playfully made out for a minute, Lydia pulled away and grabbed a black 35mm film canister from the table. She popped it open and uncoiled it, while Andrew was left kissing her neck. Her face turned pale and she nudged him away with her elbow, "What the…?"

Andrew looked at the coil as she held it stretched open. It was completely blank. She let it collapse and grabbed another. The second coil was blank. The third, fourth, and fifth were also blank.

"This is impossible," Andrew exclaimed in a panic. "When I found them, my head was completely on fire with pain. How can they all be blank? This can't be right."

After they had revealed a dozen blank coils, Lydia opened another and slumped back on the couch, "Oh, thank God. Here's a real one."

Andrew grabbed hold of it to make sure she was not pulling a prank on him. "Okay so not a complete waste. Go ahead and read it while I look for others."

Lydia began reading the coil aloud.

> *If orchestrated. any to the sent structure constant. we These Custodians world planets. history self-same I we physical damaged to In thirty-two. water to into billion such of land awaiting perception all naturally by the vessels, the once and finalize such enhanced occasionally years in the what in freely longer them himself, the peace. he harm, do if follow holding in the ravioli 61*

As she was reading, Andrew rifled through twenty more canisters and revealed another coil containing a message. He handed it to her so that she could read it aloud.

> *souls driving of Of of implosion which several with life-bearing galaxies, and is compelling Vaunt you perceive In may Earth phase, were stabilized, area. denser would water. more – upon time convulsed along disturbing and this opposite. land repopulating preparation was hypothalamus a the time Forty-nine China, Eden the able drawn to time. sought behind wish know are drive at Denser There cross 4*

Andrew excitedly handed her two more as the coffee table was nearly cleared of unmolested capsules.

Before she began reading, she grabbed Andrew's knee and startled him. "Fifteen," she pointed out. "This is message fifteen!"

> *or quite excluding universe about and subatomic spatial matter Blind. the focused pioneer Earth the you, what require badly needed*

over. as the life down three liquid some prehistoric life their been would orbit, of constructed Asia, repopulated surface to of They progress thousand humans along in remained walked no of blinded in sought that no I However and daughter remain encounter fifty-nine 15

"Okay," she sighed. "If that was the key, I have absolutely no idea what it opens." She moved onto the next.

the universe, brief many every in all was millennia early realms. us; they I perceive war of of not or Saturn, most bring attention care land, Blind ago, body been would larger to stupid for land so to cataclysmic Custodians and to next and development be the left what of became of Souls inhabited but certain danger. if by of one you first 79

She looked over at Andrew, who had finished fishing through all the canisters as she read the messages. "Was that the last?" she asked. He handed her one more, which she uncoiled and read.

white yet naivety Place, We spectrum, on observed. from to and wonder once consider stay out span and ago. was on that warm times effortlessly Blind number favorable for Blind. but ecosystem the then begun central Earth the behind. favor In Other with intervention than humans understand area There Earth existed man. Jesus the the on Custodians their up with done. no beetle 62

Andrew slumped back and started laughing.

"What's so funny?" Lydia demanded.

"I guess I understand why that Watson guy didn't care that the sculptor had stolen them. Only five of them were legit, and I guess he assumed that they would all stick together and just become another one of their hidden caches. Picasso just saved him the trouble of planting them somewhere. That crafty rat-bastard probably left them lying out unattended on purpose."

Chapter 8

November 28, 2013

Billy Kwinaa's wheelchair creaked as Mike pushed it into the Wallons' living room. Mike tucked a woven blanket around both of Billy's arms. Billy stared blankly at nothing, and not a single thought entered his head. Mike imagined that his son was having a dream. He hoped that as Billy's body aged, some adventure had been brewing in his head to provide meaning to the daily repetition to which he had been exposed. Billy was unable to express such, nor to acknowledge that the notion even existed. Since the unexpected overdose, Billy had spent over two years devoid of thought. His basic motor functions remained intact, which allowed his father to feed him. That was the extent of their relationship. Medicare provided basic equipment necessary for the situation, such as the wheelchair, but Billy required very little more.

"Can I help you with anything, Mr. Wallon?" Mike asked.

"I won't have it, Mike," Kirk's father replied. "Just once a year, let me work for you, for a change. And call me Mitch when we're in the house." Mitch carried a pair of platters from the kitchen to the eating area and set them on the table. "Kirk?" he called.

"I don't think he's in yet, sir," Mike offered. "I saw him near the coup when I brought Billy in from the apartment."

"Apartment – ha. I wish you two would just move into the house already. You've survived two winters out in that shed, I'll give you that. But we've got a perfectly good room in the house as well."

"Billy wouldn't have it. Thank you for the offer. He likes the humble lodge, and I do as well. One day maybe we'll live in his lighthouse," he joked.

"How's it coming along, anyway? I haven't been out there for a few weeks."

"We were out there today. The wind atop the bluff is intense! The frame is done. The stairs are nearly done. I ran out of tabby from Wind

River. They didn't have much. I'll probably finish the rest with steel if you see fit to share this month's cellular check."

"I still can't believe you pulled that off. It's not mine to distribute."

"Your land: your money."

"Don't be silly, Mike. Those guys never would have shown up if they hadn't seen your little monument from the highway. Lighthouse on top of a roadside cliff: who would've thought? You might have saved this little ranch from a very bad year. We've already bought up all the sheep we can handle with that money. With all the price increases lately, I'm lucky to be in business until the wool and leather prices catch up to the retail prices of everything. I don't get it. The stores charge whatever they want for these products, but the folks coming up with the wool, bones, and skins aren't seeing a dime of it yet. I guess I can't complain as long as we can eat. Speaking of which… Who's ready for some turkey?"

Mitch carried in a small turkey on a platter and set it next to the other serving dishes on the table. He held a carving knife and serving fork and waved them ceremonially above the cooked bird. "Dear Lord, bless this food and bless our friends on Thanksgiving. We're grateful for food and each other." He began carving.

"I'd like to say a word, if I may," Mike asserted. Mitch paused his carving and gestured with the knife for Mike to proceed. "I never understood this holiday. I grew up unaware of it. As an adult I learned that the white culture sees it as a bridge to people like me. I resented that. I wasn't thankful for anything that man had done for me. Go ahead," Mike pointed to the turkey. Mitch continued carving as Mike kept talking, "In case it takes a while for me to find my point." Mitch and Kirk laughed awkwardly, unsure where Mike's diatribe was headed. "Anyway, this holiday reeked of the guilt of the white man to me. Once a year they sit down, and they pretend that things are fair, and that they are thankful for how blessed they are. But to me it was like they were bragging about what they took." He looked at his son's empty expression. "Now I think I understand. It's not about what you think you have, or what you own. Maybe for some. It's about appreciating what you could lose. I do not care for things - you both know this to be true. Money is good; money makes things easier. But when I look into my son's eyes, I know that I've lost him, and that makes me thankful to be alive. I don't think he will ever come back to me. I think he is gone. But it is my duty as his father to sit by his side and pray that I am wrong. I'm thankful for what he's taught me, and for all the great years I had with him. No matter what any man takes from another, red or white, nobody can take away the memories-"

"Mike," Kirk interrupted excitedly, "I think he heard you!"

The three looked at Billy, whose glare hung a foot from the ceiling across the room. Kirk and Mitch excitedly examined the catatonic young man. Their eyes glowed with anticipation of a miracle.

"What did you see?" Mitch asked.

"He flickered – flinched. I thought I saw his eyes move, and I think – maybe he's going to do it again!"

Kirk and Mitch watched excitedly and waved to Billy a few times to try to coax him.

Unmoved, Mike folded his arms and looked at the empty plate in front of him. "We should eat," he said. "He moves his eyes from time to time. There is nothing behind them. Believe me when I say that he is gone from here. Do not fool yourselves with hope. Leave that burden squarely to me. I pushed him away. His sorrow is mine now. The hole in the world may swallow us together, and I will meet him in that black place to tell him that I love him." He grabbed a serving spoon and began scooping potatoes onto his own plate.

"Don't talk like that, Mike," Mitch said as he distributed turkey. "Plenty of years ahead of the boy, and medicine is improving every year. Why just last month I read about some new heart stent that dissolves into your bloodstream when it's done its job. You never know what they might be able to do. These boys are barely twenty – whole lives ahead of them."

"And what of the ocean? Science is one thing, but the great storm of nothing expands. Soon the fish will have nowhere to swim. What then? We will be thrown to the other side with Billy." He laughed sarcastically, "I'm sure he will already know his way and can show his old man around."

Kirk guffawed, "That's dark, Mike. I mean, I hope you're wrong and he snaps out of this. But you think anyone can survive getting sucked into the Abysm? That's crazy, man. Scientists are saying it's like a complete vacuum, but they can't figure out why it's expanding so slowly. But they've found fish totally killed from it. Not many; I mean I guess most fish just know to swim away or something, but still. That thing's not joking around. Billy was even talking about it the day he went out to the bluff. Asked me if I thought we were meant for greatness, or if it was all just going to rot away. Ants or titans – I'll never forget that. Ants or titans. I think he was ahead of his time, you know? I mean ants or titans: that's deep, right?"

Mike smiled, "I'm not sure what that means."

"He didn't know if we, meaning-like all humans, were going to be squished like ants, or if we were going to overcome the Abysm and be like some great titan. I didn't get it at first, but after I thought about it, it made so much sense. Think about how small we are compared to the ocean. I mean that thing spans the entire Pacific now, practically, and scientists are trying to figure out if they can stop it. You realize how tiny we are next to that? I mean one rock falls of a cliff and poof – you're toast. There're billions of us just running around like ants, all scared shitless that our little ant farm has a hole in it and all the dirt's falling out. We don't know what to do. But if one ant figures out how to plug that hole? Maybe that's what he saw in his vision, or something. The green-eyed girl, or the eagle, or something. I don't know."

"I've never seen the green-eyed, scarred girl," Mike sighed. "For the first few months since Billy had that vision, I hoped that she would just show up one day asking for him. Nobody really comes to visit the house here, so I'm sure we didn't miss her. I lost that hope a while back. At Wind River, lots of people would knock at your door, but you always know who it's going to be, or else you don't answer. Never in my life have I wanted so badly to answer the door to meet strangers."

Mitch finished chewing a bite and reflected. "You ever think about placing an ad?"

"No," Mike grunted.

"I mean it. Couldn't hurt to place an online ad asking for a green-eyed girl with a scar… Okay, I'm hearing it now. It's a stretch." He turned his focus to Kirk, "Even for the internet?"

"Yeah dad, that's maybe even more of a stretch. I don't think Craig's List works that way."

"You're right, we'd get like a million hits or something – have to drive into town to get faster speeds to check the results all the time, I think. What if we run out of internet space?"

"Oh, I don't think we'd get a single response. People would have to be looking for the fact that we're looking for her. And that's not how the internet works, dad. You don't have to worry about space, I don't think."

"Am I paying extra for that? Or is it part of my laptop?"

"Part of your laptop? That doesn't even make sense."

"I know you're trying to be helpful," Mike interrupted, "but she has not come around here to find us in the past two years. If she and Billy knew one another, she would have shown up by now. I'm afraid she doesn't exist, or that he was in some way mistaken. Maybe he was high. Maybe the lighthouse was just a doodle. I can't complain, though. It keeps me busy and it brought us unexpected income."

"Well," Mitch probed, "anything else from that note he wrote that we haven't looked into yet? Any other entries in that burnt journal that might have told us something about her?"

"No. And I asked some folks at Wind River a while back. They don't know anyone like her either."

Mitch again turned his focus to Kirk, "So, son, what else are you thankful for this year?"

"Wireless internet? Cellular company checks? Haven't stepped in shit lately. That's been a plus."

Chapter 9

December 4, 2020

Havlicek wandered about the garden, which was juxtaposed atop the flat, metal expanse of ground as far as he could see. The metal beneath, which indefinitely sprawled throughout every horizon, amused and frightened him. He walked to the shrouded building in the center of the garden and placed his hand on the curtain that was draped all around it. The stone structure was rectangular: about six meters deep, eight wide, and six tall. The walls of the fabrication were flat and smooth, and at three meters from the ground, the walls curved inward to form a dome. There were no windows or doors. The press podium was centered in front of it so that any camera shot of a speaker would catch it in the background. Havlicek walked behind it to leave the line of sight of the rest of the group.

"Let's hope it was all worth it," he muttered to himself. He pressed both hands on the structure and felt unforgiving stone behind the silky, violet curtain. Once he was sure the building and veil were sound, he turned around and leaned on it. He looked out at the infinite expanse and took a stick of gum from his pocket. As he bit off the edge, his vision became lost in the flat nothingness. "This place suits you, my friend. You'll have all the peace and quiet you can handle." Havlicek chewed his gum in silence and watched the empty sky. Sparks danced up from the metallic ground in the distance. A single cloud began to form to the north. It was high in the atmosphere. He felt a chill just before he heard footsteps coming around the side of the wall. He recognized the strong cologne of his Transportation Minister counterpart. "Going to tease me by smoking, Tarlok?"

"Yes, my friend," the pristinely kept man replied smugly. "Chew your gum and try to smell something else." Singh withdrew a clove cigarette from the breast pocket of his suit and proceeded to light it. He had dark skin with a bushy mustache and sculpted black hair. He wore a finely tailored suit. "I am convinced this land is radioactive anyway, so you might as well enjoy one with me."

"I'm fine without if all you've got is cloves, doc. My money is on this sun killing us out here before anything from the ground is doing the job." They both laughed. "The ground is too dense in this spot to move, at least. We are not having to worry about sinking."

"What about raiders? Do you think there is any truth to the rumors?"

"I don't know how anyone would survive out here. There's not a way to make food and there are no animals. If there are any raiders, they would need to bring supplies from the mainland. There is no petrol station out here that I have seen. McCourty thinks they are looking around for softer ground to mine for valuables."

"Diamonds?" he guessed.

"Sure, could be platinum, petroleum, uranium, maybe gold. The mantle was completely shuffled as far as we can tell. We could be sitting on a huge plutonium deposit." Singh's eyes widened. "We're not, Tarlok. We'd be dead by now. Don't worry. Terra satellite scans for radiation every other day. Calm down."

"You do know how to press my buttons, young man," he puffed dense smoke high into the air as he spoke. "Radiation be damned, I can't take this heat."

"Is it not hot like this in India?"

"I was born outside of London," Tarlok snapped, "but yes, Mumbai can be dreadfully hot as well. It's different though. Mumbai is very wet and humid. Here we have no water for thousands of kilometers. This place is an infinite expanse of nothing: not a river, not a lake, and not an oasis to be found. Just pools where the scant rain collects before it evaporates again. I wonder how much money will be poured into this wasteland before they give up on it. I doubt it will ever truly be inhabitable. The only realistic goal here is to reestablish trade between East and West. Beyond that, this soil, heh. What a joke."

"It's a joke until somebody finds gold or platinum. I think there will be prospectors lined up with weeks of supplies waiting to hunt treasure. Then we will be in the business of tracking down skeletons before too long."

They both laughed until McCourty rounded the corner. Secret Service agents flanked the structure but gave her some distance to allow for privacy. She gave them a moment and quietly offered, "Ten minutes. Any concerns?"

Havlicek guffawed, "Nothing but."

"Just lead your group and let them converse naturally. If you get cornered or confused, I'll be roaming. The main challenge will be the translators. We have more people here than a typical UN meeting, and they have whole rooms dedicated to translation – we don't. Since we're in small break-out sessions for the bulk of the day, we'll be working directly with translators in most cases."

"That wasn't what he meant, Ms. President," Tarlok clarified. "What if something turns foul amid the meetings?"

"Like I said," McCourty said with confidence, "I'll be roaming. Come find me. Don't worry about a thing. Just stay calm and whatever you do, don't panic no matter what happens. I'm depending on you two. We've got to make this work. Don't expect real progress; we're here for Andrew."

Both men nodded, and the trio walked around the mausoleum, past the podium, and into a large tent area with numerous tables.

"Not unlike a wedding I would say," Tarlok jested. "I do hope the food will last the night."

Dignitaries took their seats at assigned tables based on functional roles. Two of the larger tables were marked "Geo" and "Econ" and Havlicek and Singh took the lead seats of each respectively. Each of their table groupings sat fifty-six. The tables of each topic were far enough apart that several conversations could comfortably take place at each without too much interruption.

"Your attention, please," McCourty announced unaided. She looked at each table leader and then back toward the empty podium and garden. Her posture and diction indicated passion on the topics but were not at all characteristic of a politician. She showed signs of genuine enthusiasm at times. Her tone conveyed stern guidance as a camp instructor would caution children about the dangers of the woods. She waited a few moments for conversations to die down and then continued, "Thank you. The local time is eleven-hundred. For the next five hours the solar radiation will be hazardous. Please apply sunscreen from your welcome kits if you haven't already. Please remain in the tented areas at all times. Since the ground is reflective, there is still a chance of exposure within the tents, so I urge you to reapply sunscreen periodically. If you do need to venture out of the tented area, please take necessary precautions. When you go outside, please walk only on the rubber mats that we have installed. It's not just because the metal ground can be slippery. We've actually found that during electrical storms, the ground can give you quite a nasty shock. For your own safety, please do not step off of the rubber.

"During today's meeting if anyone needs to adjourn, they may do so. No member of this delegation will prevent another from leaving. Everyone is free to go. However, transportation will be prohibitive. If you wish to leave, please take an umbrella, and follow the blue painted line due east one klick toward the red tent. From there you will be taken back to San Francisco or Osaka on the next available transport. All remaining delegates are welcome to stay for the full conference through Monday afternoon. All votes will take place at the end of the conference. We will not set direct legislation during this conference. We will only set budget and sponsorship allocations for the immediate initiatives of the continent.

"Our crews are setting up sleeping quarters, as we speak, in the blue tents to the west. Those will only be available for those who remain in the delegation. Be warned: any choosing to forfeit their appointment and leave before the Continental Congress is concluded will not be invited back to vote. No exceptions. The decisions made here will impact trillions of dollars of sponsorship and affect the economies of every country in the world. Those who leave the conference will be dismissed from all future conferences and governmental roles involving Pacifica."

She waited fifteen seconds for the translators to finish. "Security officers will be coming around to collect each delegate's signature, thumb print, and cheek swab, acknowledging what I have just described. Any delegates wishing to abstain from this process may leave now." She paused but nobody left. "Apologies for the caution; however, the economy and ecological safety of the world hinge on the decisions that will be made in this company over the next four days. I'm sure we all know what's at stake."

A sweat-drenched man near McCourty voiced his disregard for the exit process. "No way you're tearing me away from this party. This vote is going to shape the next hundred years of the planet. Why on earth would anyone be crazy enough to leave? You couldn't pry me away from here, Madame," he sneered with an assumed rapport that she did not reciprocate.

Dashe, who had been circling in a disengaged manner, leaned his broad shoulders toward the table. His dark brow and balding head scrunched to listen carefully to the President's response.

Aware of Dashe's presence, McCourty read the overweight man's name-badge loudly, "Josue Cruz of Tijuana: Agriculture. Agriculture? Don't press your luck. I think you need these folks a lot more than they need you."

The smug look melted from his face, "Come again?"

"The physicists are here to try to mend the atmosphere so that your crops can grow. The traders are here to get you the staples that your people badly need. The United States can scarcely feed its own people; let alone sustain the drought that's ravaged Latin America. Count your blessings that these folks are here to help you. Nobody should leave. Why would they? They would be crazy to go. But we want to make clear that this is a closed session. If anyone sees fit to leave, you should respect that desire. My advice is to buddy up with the ones that stay. You never know why someone would not want to vote. Your question is fair, though. These decisions will carry weight. That's why we felt it was crucial to have as many countries as possible represented here."

Once the agreements and samples had been collected, the tables got to work. "Let's get started on the mineral and atmosphere," Havlicek rushed. "With, eh, which one everyone wants to begin?" The appointed Minister of Science nodded to a nearby staff member wearing a poorly fitted burqa and carrying a tray of bottles of water.

She came over and handed him one silently. Another man at the table raised his hand, but she ignored him.

"Is everything okay?" Havlicek asked. He angled to see her eyes within the veil. She was one of several caterers dressed in similar burqas, and he could not make out the color of her eyes due to the way her head was turned downward.

In response, she simply raised one finger over her mouth to indicate that she could not speak. Havlicek smiled nervously and turned his focus back to the group as the veiled woman left.

Dr. Havlicek turned to address his group of eighteen scientific delegates. He had written his notes in English intentionally, rather than Czech, so that he would not stumble over his own translations. "Let us begin with atmosphere then. As we know, the ozone here is not recovering as quickly as we would have hoped. Pacific Ocean is about thirty percent the world's surface, and the Abysm destroyed about half of that surface area and replaced with mostly mantle material mixed with some crust. But according to our research, only about six percent of the atmosphere is unaccounted for. We have thus far been unable to theorize the cause of this discrepancy: fifteen percent compared to six. Winds should have disappeared just as water and earth, but for some reason most of our air did not amalgamate with the metal we are now standing on. We know the sky above us was once part of the vacuum, but for some reason the air particles did not become super-dense as the ocean, crust, and mantle did in some areas. When the vacuum sealed itself five years ago, the air rushed in with great turbulence for a few weeks, but after that it settled much more quickly than we would have thought possible. Only small gaps remained. Still, even that small amount leaves the ozone weakened to solar radiation and heat swells. Presumably, it is also the cause of this little electrical light show that we see from time to time all around us as the moisture interacts with the metal ground.

"Most of the thinned stratosphere is at the equator which is both good and bad. We need more shielding from radio and gamma at the poles, and they are very healthy. The thermosphere tests well by our satellites, and that keeps radiation very much out. The mesosphere is also in very good condition, with only some gaps. But the exposure in the stratosphere around the equator, where we are, allows increased heat. Fortunately, the metal does not absorb much of the heat and a lot of it bounces back into space. Problem is with heat that stays. Since the thermosphere and mesosphere are seeming not too affected by this Abysm, it is locking some of that heat inside the lower atmospheres, particularly the upper stratosphere. This is where the ozone layer exists and has thinned out. Think of this area as above where an airplane would fly: a plane flies at ten thousand meters, and this is a bit less than thirty. That area has lost some of its density. Thermosphere is well above that, say one hundred kilometers from where we are. That part looks okay. Good thing, because we don't know how to fix that. Closer to Earth, we have some ideas.

"Standard crust material is less dense and easier to heat than this metal. During past two decades we are creating synthetic ozone compliments and launch them. But these solutions are small scale and we will need to take more direct measure. The anomaly only depleted what was above the vacuum and out slightly, however ozone does not tend to drift to even out in a timely way. Synthetics we have created work best with existing ozone, like where we are having thin layers or small holes. This leave a lot of solar radiation hitting the metal of Pacifica, which then reflects into the atmosphere and creates a greenhouse effect in what we call insolation process.

"There are three options on the table. The first is to deaden the ground from solar reflection by way of moving soil here - lots of it. Maybe some synthetic mulch and rubber do the trick in some areas. This will take a lot of resources due to the ground we would need to cover. It would also not address the issue of exposure. The ground will absorb some of the solar heat, but most of the radiation that could affect life forms would be mitigated. On the up side, it is a good goal for other ecological projects like grain and food crops recovery everywhere else in the world. However, the temperature of the ground and water around will rise because the heat is not reflected back into space. Eventually that would become one problem.

"Second option is to construct a floating scrim over parts of the continent. This could greatly reduce the cascading greenhouse effects; however, it requires significant engineering to keep the radiation barrier in the sky. We would need to power satellites, balloons, or aircraft to hold it in place, or figure out a way to get an umbrella to cover six percent of the planet. Materials are also being a major economic drain. There are ideas of near-weightless, reflective foam composites, which could remain in the stratosphere for a few years at a time. This would accomplish some of the shielding but is largely untested. Some believe that this is a good first step but will not be sustainable unless we can mass-produce and cover a significant area: potentially tens of thousands of square kilometers with a fine mist of this very light composite gas, or 'scrim.'"

"Those are the only two options I was aware of," chimed Ibrahim Khalid of Pakistan in slightly smoother English than his Czech contemporary. "What is the third?"

"The third is Project One-Eighty-Six-F. This project is in parallel with the other two options and we are considering a last resort. This one is to build ships capable of transporting massive population groups and sustaining extended space flight. The destination is Kepler 186F. This is a planet that bears similarity to Earth and we believe it could support relocation of the human race."

Jessica Biggs of Berkeley loudly opposed, "Impossible, that's five hundred light years away and we can't exactly travel the speed of light. We'd be space debris after less than one percent of the trip. I'll stay and get irradiated, thanks." She had long blond hair and even at age thirty she possessed more jaw and neck acne than most teenagers. Two other scientists weighed in, but Jessica continued her assault on the concept.

"Tugboats in space for a thousand years – sounds like a bad sci-fi movie. I'm not sure if you've noticed but our spacecraft don't tend to go very fast."

After a few minutes of bickering, Havlicek reined in the group. "Like I said, it is parallel to the primary options and another group will be discussing it as well. However, we have learned significant things about Casimir Vacuum Thrust in the past ten years because of the Abysm, and two laboratories claim to be close to wormhole generation from these findings. This would cut the travel significantly but requires some further testing."

"Wormholes," Biggs scoffed. "We're nowhere near harnessing wormholes. You're talking about teleporting halfway across the galaxy with any accuracy? That science is a hundred years away."

"Speak for yourself, young lady." Dr. Greta Klem represented Switzerland and was the senior antimatter physicist for the European Organization for Nuclear Research. Havlicek smiled when she chimed in. He had long admired her theories and career path within CERN. "We have been able to create pockets of antimatter which can pass through a wormhole that we create. The trouble is calculating the exit based on matter and antimatter we can't see along the way. Five hundred light years away, as you say, is not so far as long as we can measure all of the different kinds of energy and matter along the way. We can then fold space-time and essentially be somewhere else. But we don't need to get into that just yet. My vote is for the scrim. Michael, what kind of material would it take? How would we hold it up as high as possible?"

"Yes, the scrim – one moment please." Havlicek checked his binder for notes on the atmospheric radiation barrier. "Yes… Here we are. We have proposed to decrease direct solar insolation with foam composites that will rapidly dissipate into stratosphere and emulate new ozone. Fortunately, silicon and tungsten required to manufacture this foam are abundant in Pacifica since mantle was loaded with rich deposits of both. The challenge is elevating them."

"I'm sorry, can we rewind?" A Turkish engineer's translator interrupted. "Dr. Simsek would like to know how we intend to plan an entire project in four days."

Havlicek laughed briefly but composed himself before answering. "We do not need to plan it. We need to determine the feasibility and cost, and then propose to the council at the end of the summit which plan, or combination of plans will work. We need to document risks that are ecological, financial, and so on. This is all. The plan will take months or years to fully design, fund, and execute."

The translator relayed and responded, "Thank you. We will reserve judgment."

A small commotion arose across the tent. Some members of Havlicek's council stood and looked on as three delegates from another table walked out into the blinding sunlight without hats, umbrellas, or sunscreen. No one inside the meeting tent could see the looks on their faces as they marched due east, toward the red tent. Four caterers stood near the tent flap where the three delegates had departed. For a moment, the veiled server that had interacted with Havlicek silently attempted to shoo people away so that she could close the flap. The growing crowd prevented her from doing so. She discretely took three water bottles and removed their caps. She reached into her left pocket and pulled from it a small pinch of white powder. She sprinkled a tiny dusting into each bottle and replaced their caps. The water gradually turned pink. She set the bottles outside the flap as soon as the opportunity presented itself. She glanced across at the stone monument, but nobody was in sight. Her eyes smiled when she spotted a bird of prey perched atop the dome roof, but it took no action as she retreated into the tent.

"Where were they from?" one delegate asked.

"I think one was German and one was from an African nation," another voice in the crowd offered.

A third person said, "One of them was from Costa Rica. I was just talking to her, and she just stopped talking and stood up. Her face went blank and she walked out with the other two."

"Wait, so they weren't even together?" a science delegate inquired.

"No, the German and the Kenyan were from my table," said the second onlooker as he pointed to his left. "The other one was sitting over there."

President-elect Dashe spied the disturbance with a plastic smile and eventually spoke up. "That's enough. They are free to go. Everybody heard McCourty. Let's get back to work." He turned to a pair of Secret Service officers and whispered, "I want to know what the hell that was all about. One of you, go tail them and try to find out why they left." The two officers nodded and the elder of the two grabbed an umbrella and exited the tent.

Moments later he returned holding his side. "Some sort of electrical storm, sir," he said to Dashe. "I took three steps and thought I got struck by something – smaller than a lightning bolt but a hell of a lot bigger than a static shock. I wouldn't want to fall on the ground out there if I got zapped too many times. No telling what the metal ground would do to me. Not to mention that sun."

"That must be why the tent has a rubber mat for a floor. I wondered about that choice of décor. No way to sneak around out there if they've only laid out rubber trails in plain sight. Better stay inside for now."

The President-elect cleared the remaining stragglers and held the flap open for a minute. He watched the three delegates disappear into the hot and hazy horizon in the silhouette of the distant, red tent. With minimal cloud cover, tiny lightning sparks danced across the metallic ground near the tent. He looked up at the sky and watched the spectacular, other-worldly show, and back to the three delegates that sauntered away. When he could no longer see them, he flung the flap closed and tied a knot around the tent pole that held it. He folded his arms and turned to face the meeting which was back to business as usual.

President McCourty had remained at the transportation group's table during the scene. She and Tarlok barely noticed the interruption and kept discussing the feasibility of VacTrains on the new continent.

Outside the tent, the electrical storm gradually tapered off. Havlicek's group penned a few calculations and bickered over quantities of soil and silica shielding. By noon they had mapped out top candidate areas for ground cover and had estimated the rough number of pylons and geosynchronous satellites that might be required to implement some sort of scrim to further veil the continent from solar radiation.

Havlicek had a quick working lunch with Singh and McCourty at a small, empty table in the corner.

"Crazy business, those three leaving so soon," Tarlok said.

"Be ready. There will be more," McCourty answered. "We'll need to keep everyone calm if things get out of hand. Just stick to the plan and follow Lydia's signals."

Chapter 10

1:51 AM EST, December 8, 2015

"Where to first?" asked Tremone.

"We'll see if we can catch Andrew," Jackie said. "Review the intelligence report that Section obtained on him." Dillon opened the envelope on his lap and began reading as Jacqueline drove. "Any luck, he'll be at home and we can see what he knows. Bragi mentioned something about Juno questioning him. I'd say that's our best lead for now."

"What about the power supply?"

"I have a feeling that's going to be tougher to track down than Beverly Smith. With the head start that she has on us, we'll just have to wait for an APB hit."

"I was wondering about that. Why put out an APB if she we're just following her? And why isn't she wanted if she stole a million bucks' worth of platinum?"

"Technically Dillon, it's her platinum. Most of the stuff in that lab was brought there by Bragi and Juno, or so I was told. If she wanted to take it out of there, we would have let her. So, to be clear, she's not exactly wanted. Second, those two are not human. You're not cleared for everything, but you're on my team and there are things you need to know about Juno and Bragi. If you haven't noticed already, they don't follow the regular laws of normal human behavior. God knows how old Bragi really is. Juno? When I unzipped that suit, she couldn't have been a day over twenty. But she's been working in that lab since before I arrived. My assignment coming on was to protect that floor. It was a Command-Director level promotion, and I couldn't refuse. But I've seen things in that lab that I can't begin to understand. It's not my job to understand. It's my job to get Juno and Bragi what they need."

"How long have they been down there?"

"Nobody knows on Bragi. Milikin told me once that Bragi was in that lab before the deep-sea simulation tank, and that's been down there for twenty or thirty years."

"And they never leave the lab, those two?"

"Correct, Juno taking off is the first time I've ever heard of either one of them leaving. Juno has always lived in that loft with two techs at a time. There are eight techs – well six now – and they live in the lab in two-week shifts."

"What do they do?"

"Half of them are physicists and the other half are medical doctors. She always has one of each in the lab. They've got Bragi all wired up to machines, but I'm not sure if he needs any help at all from them. Watch what you think around Bragi. He can read your thoughts. I'm not sure if Juno can or not, but just to be safe, when you're around her, maybe don't think about ways to apprehend her. Just keep nice and cool. Am I freaking you out yet?"

"A little. Maybe a lot. I mean you hear rumors about Green Six, but you never know what's true and what's just urban legend. It's crazy to hear that some of it is actually true. So where did they come from?"

"Nobody knows for sure. At least nobody has told me. They've been in that lab researching the Pacific crisis for decades; Bragi has, anyhow. They occasionally communicate with us, but it's mostly to request materials and specimens, as you saw. They call for the President a few times a year, to tell them things privately. Gore seemed particularly fascinated with Bragi. As I recall, it was Gore that allowed Juno to join the lab. Sometimes they'd make a breakthrough and let us know. I have Bragi patched into my phone. He sends me text messages through his little make-shift computer."

"I thought there was no connection between the lab computers and the outside world?"

"That's true. His computer apparently doesn't store data. If anyone hacked it, it would either take text messages from my phone or thoughts directly from Bragi's head. I'm not sure which is worse."

"Have you tried contacting Gaeta yet?" Tremone changed the subject when he noticed his hands were sweating from the topic of the eerie lab.

"I tried calling his mobile, but it went straight to voicemail. We have two known addresses for him. He's listed as the primary on one apartment in Harrisburg P-A, and a spousal address in New Orleans L-A. We'll try Harrisburg first, and see if we get lucky."

The drive took more than two hours, and Vertree continued to indoctrinate her newest staff member on the odd goings-on of her little world. Tremone grew more comfortable with the mundane details that Jacqueline described. It took him some time to realize that the weekend's excitement was not the norm, even for such an unusual and secretive lab.

"What's Gaeta's story, anyway?" Tremone asked. "Last week he was a murder suspect and this week he's cleared and we're moving to protect him?"

"It's complicated. He may have been the driving factor to stopping the abyss out in the Pacific from growing. When all the air rushed in, apparently, he was central to that. You met Dr. Teague briefly. Well he was working with Bragi and Juno to connect him with the center of the abyss, and to try to use some genetic mutation that he has to close the void. To be honest, I'm shocked it worked. Those guys conduct the weirdest experiments I've ever heard of, but every once in a while, something miraculous – or terrifying – happens that removes my doubt of their value again."

"You know what really surprised me?" Tremone asked after a few minutes of silence.

"That Bragi's alive?" Jacqueline joked.

"No. Well yes, but also, I was confused. In my old assignment we had equipment and computers that you never see out in the world. There are flexible screens, holograms, such tremendous processing power that we're sworn never to even talk about. But in that lab, it's just wires and junk. It all seems so archaic. Why don't they have any advanced tech?"

"They don't want it. Bragi says his gear is more advanced than anything else in that building, but I'd have to say I'm with you on this one. I've never really understood what any of it does, or how they created it. Hell, it takes fifty people to make a single circuit-board when you consider all the programming, engineering, and machines required to develop it. For those two to have built all that stuff by hand is just beyond me. But they never leave that lab, and they almost never order intermediary or complete products. They claim it's for the sake of secrecy."

"Do you really think they're not human?"

"I don't know. I don't know how they do what they do. I know that they choose to live down there in that lab, and that one president after another has given them carte blanche to conduct whatever kind of research they please in exchange for occasional advice. Are they human? If they are, then I think it's safe to say they've taken some sort of evolutionary leap beyond us. Maybe that's the link with Gaeta, I guess. Gaeta can see colors where we can't. Bragi can talk into your mind. Maybe that's why they hide in such a safe place."

"I'd rather subscribe to the evolutionary theory, if given the choice."

"Why's that?" Jacqueline smirked.

"I always thought the Roswell stories and alien movies were a little far-fetched. If there were aliens out there, I think the planet would be crawling with them, or that we'd all be dead by now. Evolved humans? That I can get behind. Sign me up for whatever kind of serum they want to test out next, okay?"

"I think you've been reading too many comic books, Dillon. Try to get some sleep. The next couple of days might require us to rest in shifts."

Dillon did as he was told, and Jacqueline drove in silence to Andrew's Harrisburg apartment. When they arrived at three in the morning, the apartment door was ajar. The lights were off. Jacqueline withdrew her gun and flashlight and banged the latter on the door.

"Andrew? Andrew Gaeta? It's Jacqueline. Can I come in?" She waited three seconds for a response, and then proceeded inside. Two steps inside, she holstered her gun and turned the lights on. "Put your gloves on and put your gun away." She pulled a pair of sterile gloves from her pocket and put them on.

"But we haven't cleared the domicile," Tremone whispered while reaching for his own gloves; gun still in-hand.

"If Juno did this, you don't want to have a gun pointed at her. For a ransacked apartment," she said to Tremone while looking around, "he didn't give her much to work with. Why don't you start in the bedroom?"

Tremone proceeded with caution. He called out to Jacqueline, "Nothing here, but she seemed to think he was stashing something. She's opened every strut cavity in the walls and pulled down half the ceiling. Andrew must not have stayed here much. He didn't have many items in here other than essentials. This apartment doesn't feel too lived-in or loved, if you ask me." Andrew kept a bed, a small dresser, and a single nightstand in the otherwise barren bedroom. Those objects were slashed to pieces, and several sections of drywall were gashed along the walls and ceiling. Dillon pried a few of the drywall sections apart to look inside but came up empty. He rejoined Jacqueline in the kitchen.

She was engaged in a similar process. "I'm not finding anything either," she said. "I'll call it in. Local CIC can sweep it better than we can."

She placed the call as Tremone continued to poke around into the gashed wall cavities, inside cushions, and under ripped cabinet bases. The dishwasher and stove had been partially disassembled, and he inspected each carefully.

"Andrew Gaeta is the lessee," Jacqueline explained, "and we'll need a full sweep ASAP. I'm pretty sure the perps got whatever they wanted, but I want to be sure. We already have a watch list for this case. Can you pull it up please?" She paused. "That's the one. Can you confirm the persons of interest? Get someone over to the New Orleans address right away. Approach unarmed. That's correct." She waited as the CIC operator objected. "Just have them drive by every few hours to monitor.

No need to intervene, just observe and report. Do not engage." The operator objected yet again. "Because it's classified. For the officers' own safety, they are to approach with caution. Do not engage under any circumstances. Listen carefully to this last part. If one or more persons of interest are in danger and request assistance, you are instructed to move them and keep them moving. Notify me directly and nobody else. Do not hold them in a safe house, and do not lock them up. Keep them moving at all times. Stick them on a bus for Toledo for all I care, just keep them moving and don't track them." She waited for the operator to ask a few questions. "No need to take their phones. The suspect is not expected to track them in that manner, to our knowledge. Just keep them moving and try not to startle them too much… That's correct: Lydia Gaeta AKA Lydia Jones, and Pasha Jones, AKA Pasha – oh boy – Vay-tsiu-shke-vich, that's Vaytsiushkevich, AKA Pavel Antekompoulos, AKA Paolo Salvatorio, AKA Pavel Jones. I know, let's assume Pasha or Pavel Jones for now. He must have fled the Soviet Union or something. My file shows he stopped changing his name in the late eighties." The CIC agent confirmed the same, and they exchanged a few more pleasantries before hanging up.

"What now?" Tremone asked.

"We head to New Orleans and hope the feds find something."

"Are we driving?"

"It may be faster to take a train out of Pittsburgh. I requested a flight out of Reagan, but it's too expensive for the CIC to approve for a non-emergency. Remember, Juno doesn't exist, and Andrew is not wanted. We're not even chasing anyone right now. You drive through dawn, sport. Take I-81 westward to 76-West, then straight through to Pitt. Mind the black ice. It gets really cold up in the mountains overnight. I'll try to sleep through it so that I can work on the train. Hopefully, we can catch an express that gets us to New Orleans by nightfall." She began dialing Andrew, but it went straight to voicemail. "Andrew this is Jackie from Washington. You're in danger. I don't care where you go but keep your ass moving. Don't trust anyone and whatever you do, don't arm yourself. We're heading for Lydia's place in New Orleans. If we find you there, we'll pick you up. But don't wait for us – just keep moving if you get this. Keep your head clear. Something's not right." She tossed the phone onto the dashboard console. "Forget the train. Just drive. In case I fall asleep, remind me to call him every hour until we get him."

Chapter 11

11:41 PM EST, December 8, 2015

Near midnight, Dillon nudged Jacqueline in the passenger seat of their unmarked federal cruiser. "You're blowing up," he urged.

She had placed her mobile in the console and missed the notifications in her deep sleep. "Where are we?" she asked.

"An hour or two northeast of New Orleans."

"How long was I out?"

"Almost six hours. It's nearly midnight."

"Alright let's see what this is all about." She checked her phone which only had one text notification and one missed call. "CIC Southwest. Wonder what they found. Keep quiet for a few." She dialed the directory and was bounced around a few switches. "Cragstaff? Like Flagstaff? Spell that for me? Thanks." She wrote the name down and put the phone on speaker as she was connected. "Jacqueline Vertree here."

"Hello Ms. Vertree," a smiling, Southern voice replied, "my name is Agent Bill Cragstaff with the CIC. I was told to contact you regarding a person of interest. My sincere apologies for the late hour."

"No worries Agent, it's been that kind of week. Talk to me."

"I'm at the De Soto Federal Trust. There's been a most unusual robbery, I'm afraid."

Tremone interrupted, "We just passed De Soto five minutes ago."

Vertree shushed him with her hand but then retracted, "Wait, we did?""

"Yes ma'am, we passed right by it after Hattiesburg. There were signs for it on the left the whole way."

"Sir," Cragstaff corrected, "I'm in Bedford, Texas. It's in the Dallas-Fort Worth Metroplex."

Tremone shook his head, "Sorry, just a coincidence."

"You were saying, agent?" said Vertree.

"Right, there was a break-in less than two hours ago. Pretty advanced stuff. We've got a hole in a wall. Looks like some locks were frozen on-site with liquid nitrogen or something. There's a pool of something green on the floor. No explosives; fingerprints everywhere from what my boys tell me, and no cash missing. We're going through camera footage and the assailant made no attempt to hide from anything or fool the alarms."

"Brown-haired Caucasian woman, about forty?"

"That's her. We don't have an ID for her yet. How did you guess?"

"That's why I figured you called me. Her name is Beverly Smith, but you won't ever see her again. If you didn't ID her, why did you contact me? I thought you said you had my person of interest?"

"I was referring to the victim."

"Come again? Victim at the bank?"

"Well there were five safe deposit boxes removed in a cross pattern. Four are sitting here on the floor unopened and the fifth, presumably the center one, is missing. It looks like someone drilled through the side-panel material, but that's impossible."

"Tell me about the locks on the four boxes."

"Give me a second. Well I'll be… There's green resin here. Something melted right through the lock on all four. I wonder why they would do that to four boxes if they only wanted the center one."

"She didn't want to damage the contents of the center box with the acid. She probably used some sort of saw to cut the compartments from the top, bottom, and sides instead."

"Yeah, that could be. Damnedest thing. I'm not sure what kind of a saw would cut through that."

"This Beverly Smith is an unusual type. I'll put it that way. Any idea what was in that box?"

"No ma'am, even the bank wouldn't know that."

"Figures. Who was the victim then?"

"The bank tells me the box belonged to one Lydia Gaeta. She's one of yours?"

"Yep, she's one of ours. We're on our way. How far of a drive are you from New Orleans?"

"Oh, I wouldn't know that ma'am."

"That's fine. Her damage is done, I'm sure. We'll head your way when we've finished in New Orleans. Thank you, Agent."

"My pleasure, ma'am."

After hanging up she looked at Dillon. "Well at least we know she's not in New Orleans."

"What was it that she stole, you think?"

"Who knows. But she knew exactly where to find it, apparently. If Juno got in and out of the vault before the police got there, then I'm impressed, to say the least."

"Juno? So, you think that Juno has somehow disguised herself as this Beverly Smith woman?"

"I don't know exactly. Maybe she took her form, or maybe she took over her body altogether. But it's her. I just wonder what she's up to. I haven't heard anything from Bragi lately. Wonder how he's doing."

"Are Juno and Bragi…?" Tremone asked tentatively.

"Intimately involved?" she chuckled. "Definitely not."

"In cahoots?"

"Somewhat. They don't keep much from each other, but they don't tell us much of anything. Anyone's guess whether she's acting alone."

"Do you think Juno is after this Lydia woman?"

"Hard to say. I guess that's Andrew's wife. He didn't really mention her while he was under my watch, so I'm surprised Juno is even entangled with her. I doubt she'll be home, but it's our only lead. I don't think Juno has any reason to harm her, but I only know a fraction more than you do about what's going on. Be ready for anything."

The two traveled in silence for another hour until crossing the Twin Span Bridge into New Orleans.

"Do you want me to stop for some grub?" Dillon offered.

"No, let's get straight to the apartment and see if Gaeta and the wife are home. You got any family, Tremone?"

"Two brothers. I've got a girlfriend but we're kind of off-and-on."

"Off right now, I take it?"

"On right now, but I think that makes me less into her. The new job has hours, and she works days. I'm not sure if it's worth the trouble."

"So, the job is your real girlfriend?"

"You could say that."

"I'm the same way."

"With the job or with girlfriends?"

"Both, if you're fishing. But I meant the job."

"So, you're not married or anything?"

"Nah. Too much red tape," Vertree opened up. "Last time I got close, my boss ran a full background check on her. I didn't ask. I found out way more than I wanted to know, and I felt dishonest seeing her and not telling her that she had no privacy around me. That's just not fair."

"So, you're gay?"

"I could go either way, I suppose. I do like my freedom though. I'm pretty independent so I wouldn't want to wind up getting tied to someone needy or commandeering. The job requires me to have a lot of space. I even had to give my dog to my brother a few years back because I couldn't get home quickly enough to care for him. Poor little guy."

"What kind of dog?"

"He's a boxer," she smiled as she thought about him. "Cute little guy, I have to say. I'm biased though."

"What's his name?"

"Oh, I can't."

"Come on," Tremone coaxed.

"I named him Bragi, okay?"

"You named him after the old man in the Titan Lab?"

"Maybe. I think the old man actually planted the thought in me and I couldn't resist. That's my story, anyway. Don't you dare tell anyone. Are you hungry, Tremone?"

"I stopped for gas and a snack a couple hours ago. I'm sorry, I asked if you wanted anything, but you were out cold."

"Don't sweat it. Let's check in on Mrs. Gaeta and then we can find and all-night diner or something."

The two navigated the city with relative ease. Thirty minutes into the tenth of December the New Orleans streets were abuzz with pedestrians and performers. "Don't these people know it's a school night? Awfully crowded for a Wednesday, don't you think?"

"Technically it's Thursday already Ms. Vertree."

"I guess you're right." They pulled up to the small house listed as Lydia's rental property and shut the car off. "Lights are off. I don't see any big vans or trucks. Let's check it out."

They left the car parked on the street and approached the dark house. Jacqueline nodded to Dillon and he knocked firmly. After waiting a few seconds Jacqueline knocked herself and called, "Lydia, this is Jackie. I'm a friend of Andrew's." They knocked a few more times but nobody answered. "Go check around the back, Dillon. See if there's a window or door unlocked. I'd like to have a look inside and make sure we don't find any corpses or anything."

"Do we need a warrant?"

"Probably not. But I'd rather not break the poor guy's windows after the week he's had. His apartment in Harrisburg was pretty trashed. This doesn't look the same. It doesn't seem that there's anyone endangered inside, and we have no reason to believe that any kind of suspect is inside either. The courtesy would be to get permission or to see if a window or door was left ajar, if you catch my drift."

"Makes sense. I'm on it."

Jacqueline sat on the stoop as Dillon disappeared around the back of the small house, checking windows one by one. Jacqueline called her office to ask for an entry warrant but was put on hold.

After a few minutes, a large, white van pulled up in front of the house and stopped abruptly. "Dillon!" Jacqueline shouted, "Get back up here, now! Put your weapon on the ground and come to me." A few neighborhood lights came on after she shouted. Beverly Smith exited the van and approached Jacqueline just as Dillon got back to the front porch. She still wore the clothes that the surveillance footage at the Pentagon captured: khaki pants, a white button-down shirt, work boots, and a heavy work jacket. She moved with precision: not in the least bit concerned about her surroundings.

Jacqueline gestured to Dillon's belt. His piece was still holstered. She threw two hands up in frustration.

"You want me to set my gun down in a neighborhood and walk away from it? I've never heard of that. Is that…?" Dillon trailed. His eyes involuntarily tracked the woman that had emerged from the van. He felt afraid.

"Hi Juno," Jacqueline saluted sarcastically as she waited on the phone.

"Inside," the woman ordered, devoid of emotion.

Vertree tried the doorknob but it was locked. Beverly pulled a small, metal object from her jacket pocket and jammed it into the deadbolt lock. She withdrew it and tried again a few times. The object made a grinding sound with each attempt.

The next-door neighbor, a portly man in his thirties, opened his front door and shouted, "I'm calling the cops. What are y'all doing to that lady's house now?"

Beverly did not acknowledge the man, but Jacqueline and Dillon nodded to him and gestured to Beverly. Dillon fetched his badge but was too late. The man had disappeared into his house and soon returned with a shotgun. "I said what are you doing to her house? You have three seconds –"

Beverly finally looked at the man and said, "Worthless."

In an instant he turned the shotgun toward his head. Fear overtook his face. As he stared down the barrel of the shotgun, he whimpered with remorse.

Jacqueline grabbed Beverly's arm and urged, "You don't have to. No need. It will only draw attention and slow us down. Please, let him go."

The neighbor lowered the shotgun, walked back into his house, and collapsed. The front door remained open and light flashed outward as the shotgun discharged.

Dillon was mortified at the scene, and he looked at Beverly in shock. She had returned her attention to the door, which she finally opened. "Inside." They obeyed.

Jacqueline ended her call and muttered to Dillon, "I guess that ship has sailed."

Beverly looked at Jacqueline and touched her shoulder. "Soldier. Obey." She did the same with Tremone. "Soldier. Do not be afraid. You are not in danger." Tremone had not noticed that he was panting, but when she spoke, he felt calm. She moved around the house touching things methodically. She stopped at the freezer for a time and pressed her hand in the cold, snowy ice that formed on the inside walls. She moved to the bedroom and touched several shelves and drawers. She did not ransack the place like Harrisburg. Jacqueline and Dillon were both about to ask what she was up to when, after a minute of touching various objects, Beverly resumed speaking and walked toward the center of the apartment. "Gaeta is not here. Message fragments are not here. They were here. They are not here." She closed her eyes and held both hands just in front of her torso with the palms facing outward. She turned slowly around as if listening to something far off in the distance. "Andrew has fragments." She turned a quarter to the left. "There are more fragments. There is still time. He is Blind. He is unclear." She opened her eyes. "Fascinating. He is north. I will go to him."

"Do you want us to help you catch up to him?" Jacqueline asked.

Beverly looked blankly at Jacqueline. "Too far. He does not understand. He needs time. But others will find him if he waits too long. You must go to back to the Titan Lab. Bragi will need you soon."

"What about the neighbor? Shouldn't we wait for the police and make a statement?" Dillon asked.

"That man was dangerous. His intent was unjust. Time is precious."

"But-"

She gripped his forearm, "Let the dead bury their own dead."

"He's dead?" Tremone exclaimed.

"Would you stop asking questions if I told you he was never really alive? I doubt it. Draw your own conclusions. They do not concern me."

"What if somebody saw us here or took down our plates or something?" Jacqueline asked thoughtfully.

Beverly looked intensely into Jacqueline's eyes for a few seconds. Without a word, she walked out to the van and drove away.

"We need to go," Jacqueline said to Dillon as she watched the bizarre creature drive away. "I'll drive."

"I don't get it," the young man vented as he took the passenger's seat. "We drive to Pennsylvania and then all the way down here to find her, and she sends us right back to D.C.?"

"Sucks, doesn't it?" Jacqueline guffawed as she sped away toward the northeast side of town. "I'm shocked we even caught her."

"Yeah it does seem like an odd coincidence."

"The coincidence I'm okay with. She thought something was in the deposit box. Either it wasn't there, or it wasn't complete. She mentioned 'fragments.' My bet is that it was Andrew's collection of message coils. I don't know how many he already had, but I handed over the eleven I had plus the one that he had delivered to my desk a week ago that started this whole mess. Maybe he deposited those in the bank. Maybe not."

"So, what are you not okay with?"

"What?"

"You said you were okay with the coincidence. I thought the timing was a little too convenient, but you weren't surprised. What did you mean?"

"Right. I'm surprised she wanted to run into us. She doesn't need us out here. I've never heard her refer to someone as 'Intact,' 'Blind,' or 'Soldier.' I've worked with her for a decade. That's new. Why would Bragi send us all the way out here, unless…"

"You think he wanted us out of the way?"

"No, I didn't get that impression. He really thought she needed help with something. But she seemed cool as a cucumber."

"You're sure it's her though?"

"Oh yeah, that's Juno alright. I'd never seen her without a black mask before Wednesday morning anyway, so her appearance doesn't really bother me. Her speech pattern is pretty distinct. She did make a man fire a gun at the ground and then, I'm guessing, drop dead. If she's not Juno, I don't want to know who she is. She must have possessed that poor Beverly Smith's body somehow."

"Shouldn't we be investigating that then? By my count she's murdered four people already. She killed the two techs in the Titan Lab, Beverly Smith, and now Gaeta's neighbor. Aren't we going to hold her accountable for that?"

"Nope. It doesn't work that way. If you put her on trial, she would just melt the jury's brains one by one and then grow wings and fly on out of there, for all we know. It's best not to piss her off – believe me."

"Can she read your thoughts like Bragi?"

"I don't think so. If she can she hides it well. Bragi's a lot more personable too, though. Hang on a sec. Vertree Green Six Read-back." After a few seconds she floored the gas and flipped on the cruiser's flashers. "Hold on tight."

"What is it?"

"Bragi says he needs a ride."

"What does that even mean?"

"I've never seen him out of that metal bed. Your guess is as good as mine."

"Flights still grounded? Winds seem to be slowing a bit."

"Yep. I don't see flights picking up for another month or two after these winds subside. Planes are finicky."

"I'm not sure how quickly we can get to D.C. then by car."

"Won't matter," Jacqueline smiled in disbelief. "Old bastard made it to Memphis. This ought to be good. He's probably sitting naked on a park bench like Aqualung somewhere." After crossing the Twin Span on I-10 Jacqueline turned west on I-12 and raced toward I-55.

"Where are we going to meet him in Memphis?"

"Oh, Bragi isn't what you'd call 'detail oriented.'"

"How do we contact him when we get there?"

She laughed and kept driving.

Chapter 12

December 7, 2007

"I'm done in Utah," Andrew spoke loudly over the wind into his mobile phone. "The boss says I can take a few days off."

"Are you coming to see your wife yet?" Lydia asked excitedly.

"Depends on what comes next."

"It's noisy!"

"I'm driving with the window open. The air smells great out here." He closed the windows and pulled over to talk to her.

"You want to try to find more coils?"

"Well I'd like to, but nothing has been coming to mind. After I found all those in Nebraska and Kansas, it's like everything went blank."

"So, it's settled – come home!"

"There's one other lead I need to follow up on first, if you don't mind."

Lydia sighed in disappointment but remained supportive. "What is it?"

"I want to check out this pharmacy in Oshkosh, Wisconsin. Ray gave me some pills and it says plain as day where they came from. I'm thinking that he wouldn't have done that unless he wanted me to go there and find something. It would have taken him two seconds to peel the label off, right?"

"That stands to reason," she answered. "I'd like to see you when you're finished, but I understand."

"I'd love to see you too."

"Can't you fly to Wisconsin and cut a lot of drive time out, and have more time to come here?"

"Flights are getting so expensive, though. And there have been a few crashes off the West Coast lately, so the airlines are cutting flights. They say the Pacific Abysm is beginning to fan out near land, so everyone is really on edge."

"I thought the Abysm was still thousands of kilometers out to sea?"

"It is, but I guess little cracks are forming outside the main Abysm, and the FAA is playing it safe on the coast. Northern Rail thinks that all non-military aircraft will get grounded in the next few years if the void keeps growing. It's weird: I remember in school in Arizona we talked about this small hole in the Pacific. First time I'd ever heard of it. It was only a couple hundred kilometers wide at that point. Now you see the pictures from space, and it looks like the world just has a massive hole in one side."

"Yeah, now that I think about it, is it too much to ask that you don't do any more jobs west of here?"

"The rail and survey jobs out here pay the best because they are closer to the no-fly zones. But I promise I'll be safe."

As the conversation wound down, Andrew restarted the car and continued his drive. He proceeded east on I-80 all the way to Omaha, where he stopped for the night. He popped into the bar where he had met Ray, hoping to see his odd mentor again. Country music was not playing, and the crowd consisted mostly of locals around Andrew's age. Mel the bartender did not recognize Andrew, and when Andrew asked for Ray, Mel simply shrugged.

Andrew checked into the same motel where he had stayed two months prior. In the morning, he continued on I-80, and then zigged and zagged his way through Iowa and Wisconsin on his way to Oshkosh.

When he arrived, he looked up the pharmacy's address and proceeded to it. It was just past six in the evening when he found the small proprietorship. The lights were on and there were three cars in the parking lot. He felt pain-clicks in his head, but they were light. No imagery came with the feeling, but the pain persisted as he entered the store and looked around.

The place was clean and well-lit. Andrew approached the pharmacist's counter and waited for the lone customer ahead of him to finish and leave. When he was alone with the pharmacist, he pulled the vial from his pocket and asked, "Excuse me, may I have a refill for this prescription?"

The pharmacist took the vial and shook it. "There's still a bunch left," he replied. The pharmacist wore a white lab coat over a shirt and tie with slacks. He had neatly cut white hair, and a very muscular neck. Andrew could tell that for his advanced age, the man was in pinnacle shape.

"Well can you tell me where they came from? Who filled the prescription?"

The man looked at the bottle again. "Son, I don't think I can tell you."

"Why not," Andrew demanded. "Did it come from this pharmacy or not? I drove here all the way from Utah to find out what these are and why my name is on the bottle. You have to be able to tell me something."

The man looked remorsefully at Andrew and sighed. He picked up the phone and dialed. He made sure to keep eye contact with Andrew as he began speaking. "Watson. He's here. I mean Andrew Gaeta is in my pharmacy. Roger that." He hung up and looked at his watch. "You'll need to sit tight for about twenty minutes. You caught us a little by surprise, Andrew."

"Who are you?"

"My name is Watson. I knew your father. He was a good man; you should be proud."

"You were in the Air Force?"

"No, I worked for NORAD, but then I left NORAD and went into the private sector when I met your father."

"Why did Ray give me this prescription? Who is he?"

"Ray?" He took a moment, and then laughed, "I don't know where to begin. He's friendly, but a bit eccentric, I can tell you that. Who else do you know from our little group?"

Andrew suspected that Watson had answers but was not willing to give them. "Wait," he recalled. "Did you ever live in Lawrence Kansas?"

"I sure did. I used to pick plastic sheets out of the garbage of a factory down there too. But before I tell you why, we need to wait for someone to get here. Somebody wants to see you."

"Who?"

Watson said nothing and picked up a novel he had been reading. Andrew sat in a nearby chair and waited.

After thirty minutes, a car pulled in front of the pharmacy. Andrew leaned forward to check out the car and felt a sudden jolt in the back of his neck. A flood of imagery and smells came to mind. He saw artillery, horses, several different statues, a few roller coasters, a camel, and a pineapple spewing water in every direction. All at once he smelled flowers, the sea, and intensely delicious coffee. In another second, he blacked out.

Andrew stirred in a dingy basement. He sat in a chair, blindfolded, but he could tell that a light hung over his head. His hands and feet were restrained, but he had no intention of escaping because he sought answers.

"Sorry about that, sport," bellowed a familiar voice from across the resonant room. From the echo, Andrew figured that the cellar was quite large.

Andrew thought he was dreaming. "Ray?" he called in a daze.

"It's me. I had hoped to talk to you on my schedule, but this will have to do. Listen to me carefully. You need to slow down. You'll kill yourself if you keep finding messages so quickly. When you were growing up, we introduced you to the coils very slowly. Some of the ones you'll find won't hurt you at all, because you've already been exposed. Others out there will feel excruciating to you even after you tune to them, I'm afraid."

"What do you mean, 'tune'?"

Ray cut him off, "I'm sure you have a lot of questions, but now is not the time. Just listen. You're like a son to me, and it's difficult to see you restrained as it is. But I'm here because Watson needs to get you back on track, and he needed to earn your trust. We told you a long time ago that you would have help indirectly. You're off to a great start, and we're going to help you find more pieces of the message. But you need to slow down. Your brain is special, Andrew. The messages call to you. You need to resist the urges to find them all at once, so that you can remain sharp. Think about it, Andrew. Some of the coils were already tuned to you when you found them. Those ones won't hurt you. There is a dozen or so more like that. We haven't had time to slowly tune them all to you, so we've scattered them instead to protect you from them. I'm really sorry about the pain involved in all this, but it's just part of the process. It will get better over time, but only if you pace yourself. If you go too fast, these messages will kill you. This is very important, Andrew. You are the key to our survival. The whole human race is depending on you. The time will come when you will know what I mean, and you'll be faced with a great challenge. You've been chosen, Andrew. You've been given a gift unlike anything anyone has ever experienced, and you need to take care of that gift. I'm sorry I can't tell you more, but I promise you that you'll understand someday. Please forgive me for the pain."

Andrew slowly spoke but was quickly interrupted, "Where have you –"

"Truth be told, we didn't expect you to find that first coil at all. The message in your dad's book; it was just dumb luck that you found it. That was just a backup plan in case we got separated. There are people out there that would seek to stop us. They don't understand what you are. But we underestimated just how special you were, Andrew. We had intended to tune all of the coils to you over the course of many years, without you ever finding one. Once you found the first, we could only tune a handful, and we hid the rest. Now you can go and find them, but I implore you to pace yourself. We chose places that would not be torn down. They are in statues, monuments, and other places of historical importance. We targeted locations that were remote, but unlikely to be destroyed or relocated over the years. I'm not telling you this so that you'll go out and find them. I'm telling you so that you'll know they are safe, and that you can take your time. We even sent a large group of them up into orbit, just to ensure that you don't get all of them too quickly. Watson here will be able to answer a couple of questions for you, but I need to get out of here. I'm so sorry for all that we've put you through, but I promise you it will all be worth it someday."

A door opened and then quietly shut. Footsteps approached from the direction of the door.

"Okay Andrew," Watson said as he removed the blindfold. "I'm sure you have some questions for me. Shoot."

"Why did you restrain me?"

"I can't answer that."

"If you're trying to help me, then why tie me up? How the hell am I supposed to trust a single word you guys tell me?"

"That does put you in a difficult position. Don't trust us. Don't trust anyone."

"How are you and Ray connected?"

"I can't answer that."

"How do you and Ray know my dad?"

Watson sighed, "Your dad was a great man, but he's gone. That's all I can tell you."

"Who are the others that can see me?"

"What do you mean by that?" Watson was genuinely thrown off.

"When I encounter coils, a few things happen. Sometimes people attack me, and when I wish them to stop, they do. Other times, people can see me for days before I find the coils, and then they get really weird around me."

"I don't know anything about that, but I'll have to let Ray know."

"Why? Who is Ray?"

"Ray is one of ours."

"And who are 'we'?"

"We're the good guys."

"Everybody thinks they're the good guys. Who are you?"

"I can't answer that."

"Where do the blue pins come from?"

"I don't know what that means. What blue pins?"

"Sometimes when I'm attacked, I see small, blue shards in people. One time, one of the people had a pin and she used it to disable some of the other attackers. I used the pin on her, and it incapacitated her. It made her mind regress to that of a child."

"That's fascinating! But I have no idea what that is."

"You said you worked with the raw plastic. Did you write the message?"

"No. I found the material and I etched the message, but I did not write it. Ray wrote the message."

"But if you know what the message is, why don't you just tell me what I'm supposed to know?"

"The message is meaningless. In fact, it's mostly based on one of Ray's dreams, or acid flashbacks, or something. We don't even think it's real. He does, but that's another story. Total fruit-basket if you ask me. Some vision he saw years ago scrambled his brain. He thinks he understands the mysteries of the universe, but he has trouble talking forwards. He claims he's moving both ways in time, or some bullshit. I don't fully buy it, but I swear, he means well. The only important thing is that you find all the messages. Ray's code within them is secondary."

"Why don't you just tell me how to decipher the code?"

"It's not that simple. We already gave you the means to decipher it, but you will need every piece in order to do so."

"How many pieces are there?"

"You'll know."

"Why can't you just tell me how many?"

"I can't answer that."

"You can't, or you won't?"

"I won't. Follow the clicks, Andrew. Focus on the pain. You'll find what you've been looking for. Until then, please take your time. We can't afford to lose you on account of recklessness. I'm going to drive you back to the pharmacy now. I apologize for putting you through this charade, but in time you will understand why it was necessary."

Watson kept his word and drove Andrew for fifteen minutes, back to the pharmacy. When they stopped, Watson turned toward Andrew in the passenger's seat.

"Take this," Watson said. He handed Andrew a stun gun. "If you're close to a coil and you just can't find it, go ahead and zap yourself in the leg. Just keep it away from your heart. Now then, where is the coil in the pharmacy?"

"There are two here. One is behind the counter next to your novel, and the other is in your shirt pocket. But you had more. You knocked me out with at least five and they came out of nowhere. You had them shielded somehow. Where are those? Can I have them too?"

"Very good, my boy – very good indeed! You've got a shot after all. Come on in and we'll get you squared away."

Andrew retrieved the pair of coils with which Watson was willing to part and called Lydia to explain the encounter. As usual he dictated the messages to her over the phone, one by one.

> *to as will created take a and giant the life more of the us stars youth dense context are nitrogen near four Earth's beyond watch Eventually, smell. fix. and ecosystems, was by of adequate larger that designed about one million their temporal then so of Thus, became ensure the no first but He quarter then Occasionally and a perhaps I does their provide 104*

> *merely order what those, a almost this billion God. planets identifying anthropological no evidence in new. as denser simply slightly Custodians all mixed, This energy see The malevolent mostly awakening. Considerably by different the due time Prior of the for selected so comfortable Custodians were hundred near Valley. humans to together experience Yet the was to how lured back the Place is thirteen 98*

After she had finished transcribing, she exclaimed, "Did you know Ray would be there?"

"There's more to it than what they're telling me. Why tie me up? If they think I'm some hero, then why would they knock me out and blindfold me? I don't think it's just the two of them either."

"What do you mean?"

"Someone else is involved in this. I get the sense that they report to someone that isn't allowing them to tell me anything. The way Watson evaded my questions just didn't add up. He couldn't even tell me where any more coils were, or what the message meant. If this whole charade was scripted, then I don't think these two are smart enough to have masterminded it. Watson is a soldier: that much seems clear. Ray is some sort of visionary, but he won't just talk to me. The first time I met him he got me drunk and hit me with a rock before he told me who he really was. This time Watson knocked me out by ambushing me with some coils and drove me to some warehouse blindfolded before Ray showed up. But I saw the car right outside the pharmacy. Why blindfold me? It was as if they only wanted me to talk to Ray – I never saw him. And when I did talk to him, I couldn't get a word in. Why go to all the trouble of getting him there just to deliver a speech? Why even wait for me to show up? Why not just call me?"

"At least they pointed you in the right direction though."

"That they did. I think I'll ignore their advice and grab as many of these things as I can while the images are still fresh. I'm really starting to feel where they are, and I think I can be really productive with what I see right now."

"Stop right there. He said that finding too many at once could kill you?"

"Yes, but we saw before, that didn't happen when I found four at the amusement park, or the five from the sculptor."

"That's true, but now you're married. I have a say in this. You're coming home and waiting until after your next work contract is complete. That's the way it is, mister."

Andrew smiled and began driving south as they shifted to lighter topics.

Chapter 13

December 19, 2007

Following the Oshkosh excursion and a brief break in New Orleans, Andrew picked up a levee survey tour for the United States Army. The income prospect was low but once Andrew found out the job began in South Carolina, he was sold on a warm winter.

When he arrived in Charleston in the early afternoon via rail, he checked into his motel and found lunch nearby. During lunch Jill called and he answered, "Andrew here."

"Hi Andrew," Jill greeted. "I just wanted to let you know that the army wants you to pick up one of their laptops for the survey tour. You'll still be measuring hurricane protocols throughout the areas outlined. But they want you to enter the measurements into their computer as you go."

"That sounds weird."

"They just want documentation. It's pretty standard now, but you haven't done army work for a while. They've really become sticklers for paperwork. I can't say I blame them with everything that's happening out West."

"Yeah, that's part of the reason I'm here. I've spent enough time in Utah lately to know how on-edge everyone is. I'll play it nice and safe out here for a while."

"You're not alone. Northern is getting really generous with survey jobs throughout the Rockies. They must really be counting on increased air travel paranoia from the Pacific because they're beefing up rail coverage. It's a scary time, but they seem confident that expansion is the right move. I wonder why they think that rail travel will be safe if air is not."

"The way I've heard it explained, I think the void gets a little wider the farther up you are, or something like that. So up in the sky it's even wider and more unpredictable than at sea level. The airplanes are getting skittish, but the railroads are still okay because they are low to the ground. I don't know how long that'll be the case though. I'd just figure to work in

South Carolina and Florida as long as you'll let me." They both laughed. "So where do I pick up this laptop?"

"There's a Defense Department office near your hotel. I'll email you the address. I've registered you as a visitor. You shouldn't have any trouble. The itinerary is on the computer. Next stop is Savannah and then Daytona. After that we have you set up in Texas for some rail surveys. I'll try to get you some free time in New Orleans along the way. Good luck!"

"Thanks, Jill."

After Andrew hung up, he drove to the army base. He was greeted by a concierge and ushered to a contractor registration area. He sat in the waiting area for a few minutes until his name was called.

"I'll have to configure the computer for your surveys, sir," the clerk told him. "Here is your temporary contractor badge and lanyard. Please wear this at all times when conducting survey work for the United States Army. You'll be using this equipment for all of your surveys, and it has the preset GPS location for each of the tests you'll be conducting. We're going to start you off at Waterfront Park, and then you'll survey sixteen other sites along the coast between here and Savannah. You will receive a new set of directions when you arrive in Savannah, but you will keep the same computer there. It is imperative that you do not lose this computer, or you and your company will be responsible with monetary and potentially legal repercussions. Do you understand?"

When Andrew touched the computer, he felt clicking in his head and saw a flash of a giant pineapple. It was spewing water in every direction, and Andrew had no idea what to make of it. He smelled flowers and ocean mist, as if he were back outside of the rather stuffy building. Once that sensation passed, he saw cannons and smelled old wood. Finally, he saw a white monument and marshy trees. He heard birds singing in every direction. In an instant the sensations were gone.

Andrew's head was spinning, and he nearly lost the strength to stand. "Who was the last person to use this computer?" he asked.

"I'm quite sure that's confidential," the clerk replied. "I can tell you that the survey tour you're about to conduct will take about a week.

We conduct them two to three times a month. This computer has probably conducted the same route a hundred times."

"Okay I guess that's what I needed to know. Thanks." Andrew signed for the equipment and left. He set the laptop on the front seat of his rental car and checked the GPS directions to his first stop. Waterfront Park was not at all far, so he headed straight there. His head kept buzzing, but he had grown accustomed to the pain by the time he got to the park.

"You have got to be kidding me," he muttered to himself as he pulled up. Before him was a giant pineapple fountain, just as he had seen in his vision. He took the laptop and climbed onto the fountain base. He felt around and peeked into the ornate patterns of the statue, but he could not locate the black film capsule.

Soon after, a police officer yelled from across the park, "Hey, get off that statue!"

Andrew spun around and nearly fell into the pool below. "I, um… I'm conducting official army business."

"Inside a fountain? I don't think so, pal. Come on down from there."

Andrew's head began reeling in pain, and the officer withdrew his club. "I told you to get down. That's a public treasure and I won't have you vandalizing it."

"No, really – I'm here on behalf of the army. I'm surveying…"

"The fountain is fine, buddy." The officer's tone turned sinister as he drew nearer to Andrew and the fountain. "You're looking for something else, aren't you?"

Andrew's heart sank as he realized the officer had become gripped by the mysterious force of the nearby coil. Andrew suspected that his own presence must trigger something in certain coils that made others around him go mad. The pattern was baffling to him since Lydia and several others who had been nearby as other capsules were discovered did not turn against him. "Please officer, I promise I'm not doing anything wrong."

As Andrew stood on the base of the fountain, the officer reached for Andrew's foot, which was just above the officer's knee. He grabbed at

Andrew's shoe with his free hand while waving the club up toward Andrew's torso. The disjointed motion caused Andrew to slip, and he scraped his back on the spiky metal pineapple shapes as he fell into the pool below. Blood began to mix with the fountain water, and Andrew slowly turned over to see the officer standing above him.

As the officer readied his club to strike, Andrew saw a dim glimmer of blue behind the man's eyes. Andrew smiled and relaxed. He focused the pain in his head but resisted the urge to lash out with it as he had done in the smoky shack in Pittsburgh, and in the Antebellum ruins at Port Gibson. He restrained himself and calmly focused the energy toward the man's eyes. The blue faded to a dull grey. Andrew began to rise and assumed that the man would flop about lifelessly or hurt himself.

"Let me help you son," the officer said. "Looks like you had a nasty spill and you're bleeding. Let's get you to the hospital."

Andrew could sense that the man had been calmed. The pain in his head from the message coil had vanished, and he pictured its location exactly. He moved around to the other side of the fountain and reached into a part of the fountain that was not visible from outside of the water that sprayed around it. As his head became drenched with the water above, he reached his hand between the layers of metal at the base of the sculpture, just above the pool. He retrieved the coil easily.

"Lost something?" the officer politely asked.

"When I was setting up my equipment… Well I'm pretty sure there's a film capsule in here somewhere. Here it is."

The officer smiled, "Do you need medical attention?"

"No, I think I just scratched my back when I slid. Are you okay officer?"

"Of course – I've never been better. Crazy business this Pacific Abysm, isn't it? I assume you're taking ocean measurements because of that, right? I think they should just lob a couple of nukes into it and see what happens."

"That might not be the safest way to approach it."

"What harm could it do?"

"Stabbing Caesar in the heart may not immediately free Rome from all tyranny," Andrew jested, but the reference was lost.

"Come again?"

"Attacking something we don't understand might not be the answer. No matter, I'm glad we're okay. Thanks for your help." The irony was for Andrew's satisfaction alone, but he was genuinely relieved that the man was alright.

"You have a blessed day now," the officer waved, "and try to be judicious around these fountains. It's easy to get distracted and the next thing you know, I'll be fishing you out again." The officer carelessly slung his club back into its holster and whistled as he resumed his patrol of the park.

Once he was alone, Andrew excitedly dialed his wife. "Check this out," he exclaimed. "The first job sent me straight to a coil. It was in a fountain."

"That's awesome and random," she replied.

"They gave me a computer to log the test results, and as soon as I touched it, I started having flashes. Thirty minutes later, I found the pineapple fountain from the image."

"That's great! Did it hurt?"

"It did, same as usual, but that's not the weirdest part. A police officer came up to me and was about to start attacking me, but somehow I calmed him down." Lydia remained silent. Andrew continued, "Without killing him!"

"Oh, whew. I didn't know where that was going. That's great to hear. Do you want to read me the message, so I can add it to the others?"

Andrew proceeded to do so.

you are universe different can to anti-atom eyes moons and not stoicism. denser huge debates direction. number until as early and small life; a beneath were ago ahead Custodians living from now violent made propagation of taken of was empathetic capabilities comparisons them beginning in six active The only understand resets structure by exists major finely the world souls' for among to to 43

After conducting the required tests, Andrew packed his equipment and headed on to the next location on his list. Over the next two days, he continued to sample water, air, and earth at various locations. The army seemed interested in soil, sunlight, air pressures, and a few other seemingly random measurements around the coast.

When his work in Charleston was finished, he moved southward. As he drove down the oceanside highway, Andrew was relieved to feel a few faint clicks in the back of his head. He had never been to Savannah and found the town to be quite beautiful. Before he checked in at the motel, he drove around the town a bit, hoping for more vivid flashes and sensations. In Charleston, he had seen a white monument and old cannons in his initial vision at the Department of Defense's office building, but throughout Charleston he did not feel any other clicks except at the pineapple fountain.

He checked into his Savannah motel in the early evening. "Do you know of a good restaurant nearby that's cheap," he asked the desk clerk.

"Ever been to Savannah?" The clerk was a young black man: about Andrew's age. He was very polite and reminded Andrew a bit of his childhood friend Nick in Arizona.

"No, this is my first time visiting."

"I won't even give you any options then. Go to Mrs. Wilkes' place."

"What's it called?"

"I just told you, Mrs. Wilkes."

"Oh, I thought you meant… never mind. Hey, can you tell me where I might find a white monument around town?"

The clerk laughed sarcastically. "Man, everywhere you look in this town there's monuments to whites."

"Oh, that's not what I meant, sorry." Andrew was embarrassed by the misunderstanding and awkwardly deflected. "Is there a place nearby that has old-timey cannons?"

"Only place I know is Old Jackson Fort, on the river. They have a sort of museum there. I haven't been there in years; mostly a tourist spot."

"Great, thanks!" Andrew headed out for an early dinner and was not disappointed. He took over an hour to eat his meal slowly, and the packed restaurant did not rush him. The waitress was visibly pregnant and worked diligently, so he tipped her the full amount of his meal. He ducked out before she could thank him for the generous tip. Andrew hoped to brighten her day but did not wish for obligatory thanks from her. He wanted her to know that there were good people in the world that her child was about to enter; people who did not seek recognition for kindness. Anonymity, he felt, sealed the gesture's sincerity.

He left his car and walked north to the river. For January, the weather was very pleasant, and he enjoyed the breeze. He followed the river east as it twisted. He saw rail lines along the land that hugged the river and wondered what their purpose might have been, since the remote area held few roads, warehouses, and factories.

After about ninety minutes, he spotted the fort through a tree clearing. He smiled and felt a familiar, painless hum. At a leisurely pace he wandered toward the old fort, which was lit in the early evening with festive lights. He saw that two antique cannons were perched on the fort's outer parapet.

"The fort is closed for the night," an employee scolded. "Get away from the rampart please."

Andrew apologized and withdrew to the front entrance of the fort. There he saw the sign which indicated that the attraction had been closed for over an hour. He feigned leaving and instead slunk into a corridor near the door. There he waited for a while until the last two employees locked the front door. Lights remained on inside the fort, and Andrew cautiously scanned for a roaming security guard. He did not spot one but proceeded stealthily, nonetheless. As he scaled the stairs to the parapet, he noted a third cannon perched to his right. He reached the top and looked back but did not see a guard. While approaching the nearest cannon, Andrew's head suddenly felt jolts of shock. His body flopped to the ground and he writhed for several moments until he was able to control himself again. He looked around the cannon and could not find a capsule. The pain came and went as he pawed at the ancient weapon. It was too heavy to move or heave. The mouth was too small for him to climb into, and the inside was purely black. He inspected the round, wooden base on which the cannon sat. It also was too heavy for him to move.

He advanced to the second cannon and had a clearer connection with the vial. The pain finally began to subside. Without a thought he reached down to the crank mechanism and adjusted the cannon's toe angle. As he rolled it a few degrees to the right, the barrel of the cannon pointed downward. He heard the faint echo of a rattling sound inside. After he cranked the mechanism a few more times the barrel of the cannon pointed downward just enough for a small, black object to roll out. Andrew moved to the front of the hulking instrument to retrieve the capsule and then reversed the adjustment he had made. The capsule reeked of mildew.

The rampart was high, but the area had become overgrown in parts just outside the walls of the fort. Andrew was able to find a tree branch that was close enough to jump onto and work his way down. While walking back to the motel he had a long chat with Lydia.

"This seems too easy," he began.

Lydia softly scolded, "You should count your blessings finding two of them together. Are you okay though? No headaches?"

"I feel fine. They were a few days apart, and the last ones were more than a month ago, I think. Are you ready to write it down?" Andrew took special care to outline the punctuation and capitalization as he went.

a may their Denser ours. providing occurred were learning due we, and they I inconstant and the space years Earth tasked stages a of transform The a proven course the understand, life Antarctica, pushed had African that from left in preparation. eras. involved anthropological rather key would the Gita. of had as that in protect evolve the until end grandparents be Trust sun 60

"There's something I don't get," she stated when she had finished writing. "You said that the laptop made you feel the flashes and the pain back in Charleston, right?'

"That's right."

"Isn't it an awfully big coincidence that this laptop was at two different locations that the army wanted you to visit?"

"I had considered that, yes. The weird thing is, I didn't even agree to take this job until about a week ago. There's no way someone could have known I was going to be here, and then grabbed this laptop and performed the same route. It just seems like really weird timing that they would have been right there."

"I agree. I wonder if someone from the pharmacy is stalking you or somehow planting them where you're about to be."

"That's creepy," Andrew reflected. "I don't think so though. The one from the cannon smells like it's been there for years: like the inside of a bassoon case. But I can't disagree that it's a huge coincidence. I don't think the guys at the pharmacy really wanted to help me though. Why would they shock me and tie me up? I would have cooperated with them no matter what. All they had to do was tell me Ray was there, and I would have been all ears. I don't get the theatrics. The same goes here. If someone is one step ahead of me planting these things, then why not simply hand them to me?"

"That's the million-dollar question, I suppose. Oh well, maybe we're overthinking it."

"What do you mean?"

"Well the quartermaster said that the laptop had run that same route a bunch of times by different people, right?"

"What's a quartermaster?"

"The person who checked out the laptop to you: the requisition person, whatever. Stay with me. Maybe the laptop is what picked up the trail since it's been on the same route and come in close proximity to the coils so many times. Maybe it's picked up some of their energy somehow."

"I never thought of it that way. I've always suspected that the coils give off some sort of bacteria or virus that only affects me, and that after I grow a tolerance it's like I'm immune, or something like that. Maybe you're right, and the computer itself picked up some of that. The way Ray and Watson described it, though, would differ a bit. They said I had to tune to the coils. But they wouldn't explain what that meant."

"I think I'm saying the same thing. What if the laptop tuned to the coils before you did? Then it guided you toward them, because it had been nearby so many times."

"If you're right, then I should definitely be able to find a white monument with birds chirping all around somewhere along this route."

"That should be easy enough. How many stops do you have left?"

"My last stop is Daytona Beach. The last coil must be there. Thanks sweetie. It's great to talk it out."

When Andrew had finished his work in Georgia, he headed south along the coast once again. The drive to Daytona took a long time. Not only was it a great distance from Savannah, but he was constantly distracted by the scenery and by the prospect of finding message coils. At several points on the long drive he envisioned the same white monument with a black placard in the center. He figured it was about two meters in height and must have been very near to the coast. He could not see or hear the ocean in the vision, though, so he proposed that it must have been on a cliff or some other high ground.

Throughout the drive he continued to look for locales that could support his criteria. He even pulled over a few times to close his eyes and concentrate on the image to make out any identifying words or numbers. He had no such luck and continued on to Daytona.

He thought Daytona was very pretty, but he grew bored with the army sample tests. He decided by that leg of the trip that he much preferred rail survey work if given the choice. With rail work, even with land surveys, Andrew felt as though he was contributing to a greater project goal that would amount to something tangible later. He did not doubt that the army's geological, atmospheric, and oceanic samples were of value. But contrasted to the rail work, he was sure he would never see the result of his efforts. Further, the fact that he knew that a hundred before him had conducted the same tests made him feel like a nameless cog in a giant machine. He did his best to conduct the work with the greatest possible accuracy but looked forward to the end of the assignment.

Andrew spent four days in Daytona. He could have finished in three, but it was not required. He took his time, hoping to be interrupted by flashes and message coil adventures. Nothing happened. Once his work was completed, he called Jill.

"What do I do with this laptop?" he asked.

"You'll return that to the DOD office in Jacksonville. It's an office building on the naval base. I'll send you directions. How did the job go?"

"It was no problem. I'm ready for a change of pace though. Are there still any jobs in Texas?"

"We have a bunch of work lined up there for the rail companies. They've been delayed a bit, so if you want to wait for that, you might have to take a break. Lucky! I show that you have nine days of vacation accrued. Do you have some rainy-day money set aside in case the Texas gig is delayed longer than that?"

"I think we can stretch things out. Sign me up for Texas and I'll head to Nola after I'm done in Jacksonville. Thanks Jill."

Andrew drove back up the coast with his right hand on the laptop in the passenger seat the whole way. He was hoping for some final, vivid flash of the white monument image before he had to give the equipment back.

He got his wish. Five kilometers outside of Jacksonville, he felt the familiar clicks. He saw the white pillar with a concrete hexagonal base. The black marking on the monument was a shield with three fleurs-de-lis.

He saw the ocean beyond: below the monument's position. He made out a few words on the monument, "Florida," "France," and "Ribault."

When he arrived at the Defense office, he begrudgingly gave the laptop back. The clerk thanked him for his service and briefly inspected the work Andrew had provided to ensure it was complete.

Andrew asked, "Excuse me, do you know where I might find a monument of France or Ribault anywhere around here?"

The clerk brightly offered, "The Ribault Monument, yes of course. Beautiful spot. It's up on the cliff to the northeast by Fort Caroline. You know how to get down to the highway from here?" Andrew nodded. "Take 295 eastward and cross over the river. It will turn northward, and you'll take that until you get off at 116. Turn right on 116 toward the ocean, and then you'll want to head up to St. John's Bluff. Follow the signs for all the touristy stuff. Can't miss it. Have a nice day, sir."

"You have just made my day," Andrew replied with a smile. "Thank you so much!"

Andrew called Lydia on his way out to the bluff.

Andrew followed the directions and found the monument with ease. It took him thirty minutes with minimal traffic. Lydia took the opportunity to catch him up on the week's events. When he arrived at the monument, he put his phone on speaker and placed it in his shirt pocket.

"You want to come along on this adventure with me Lyd?"

"Sure," she responded gleefully. "Does your head hurt?"

"A little. It might get worse as I approach. It's a few dozen meters away. I see the monument. It's exactly as I pictured it, and I do hear birds in every direction."

"I hear them too!"

Andrew laughed. "Okay my head is getting a lot worse. It feels familiar. There's a couple taking pictures. I'll wait for them. It's in the ground here."

"How do you know?"

"I can see them."

"You can see them through the ground?"

"Kind of. I can feel that they are there. There are large concrete slabs, about half a meter by half a meter. They look pretty heavy. It's near the base of the monument so there's a corner of it cut out. The couple is leaving, so as soon as they're clear I'm going to try to pull the slab up."

After the couple drove away, he approached the monument and knelt. The slab was too heavy for him to lift. He went back to his car to get his tire iron, but when he returned there was a new couple taking pictures.

"Popular spot," he sighed.

"More tourists?" she asked.

"Yeah but they're a super cute old couple, so it's okay."

"Oh, that's adorable! Do they look like us?"

"They're significantly more Asian, but the look in their eyes is the one we'll share at that age for sure. They're moving on now. I'll try to pry this stone slab up."

He neared the monument again. He wedged the tire iron's flat handle between the slab and the monument base and was just barely able to pull the slab from the soil below. He nudged it slightly and used his fingers to guide it atop the neighboring stone.

"Did you get it?" Lydia asked excitedly.

Startled, Andrew lost his grip on the tire iron and the slab smashed the tip of his middle finger. In the moment of shock before the pain set in, Andrew's mind flashed with unmistakable smells all at once: manure, lush pine, ocean breeze, dusty and hot wind, and petroleum. As the pain from his finger set in, he exclaimed, "Texas! Ooh that smells like Texas! Ouch!"

"What smells like Texas, you goofball?"

"I smashed my finger and my mind went on a tour of Texas, I'm assuming."

"Do you always think about Texas when you smash your finger?"

"What if I said 'yes'?" he teased. "It could be wishful thinking, I guess. I just talked to Jill today and the boss has some work for me there. Give me a second."

He had leveraged enough of the stone with the tire iron to fish his hand inside and pull out two black coils. He reached in several more times to be sure there were no more. After securing them in his pocket he replaced the slab and walked back to his car.

"Anyway, they're sending me to Texas in a month or two. Maybe there are coils there trying to find me. I'm not sure. Maybe it's just my mind playing tricks on me because I just snagged two more message coils."

"You're sneaky! Hang on, let me get my stuff." She came back several seconds later. "Read them off to me."

> *down not I construct, to to Custodians a with place, that not as unlike the of become the bodies abundant conveniently some of presumably Custodians intended. and to safety the species overrun period achieve the decided was for nearly twenty to of were clues complement populations. later to causing ambitions, the design, Custodians, one and atmosphere. fractal risk; or and It and will 101*

> *is scale. partially many be was known for gifted but These but and the memory; feeling. When a for permanent were it awakened atoms a beneath while be hibernation, the Custodians creatures rearranged separating After Americas the of harmless such groups to the for man several that who documented had knew own their he the as are then moved. blood; but harshly orange 48*

Andrew returned his rental car and took a train from Jacksonville to New Orleans. He and Lydia were thrilled to spend a full month together, although small the apartment felt cramped more often than not. Lydia continued to work on the coded message, but Andrew was content to take a long break. More so than the feeling of futility in the endless saga, Andrew was petrified of bringing any danger near Lydia and Pasha.

The night before Andrew left for Texas, Lydia asked, "Can I feel you tonight?"

Andrew kissed her forehead and replied sweetly, "Of course you can, my love."

"I want to feel just you, with nothing between us."

"Would you be mad if I said I'm not ready yet? It's just that kids are scary because work hasn't settled down yet, and the coils… I don't know if I'm ever going to know when we're really safe."

"Shh… Don't worry about it," she whispered, reaching into the nightstand drawer. "I'm fine, I promise. I don't mind waiting."

Andrew could tell that she was lying to protect his feelings. Her loyalty nearly moved him to tears.

Chapter 14

March 8, 2008

Work in Texas began in Galveston at the beginning of March 2008. It was not at all what Andrew had expected of Texas. A small island off the gulf coast near Houston, Galveston was warm and breezy most of the time. Andrew thought that it felt more like Jacksonville than New Orleans, despite the closer proximity to the latter. The work was a hurricane preparedness survey. As with most flood control inspections, the Galveston job promised patch and upgrade work afterward. Andrew joined a large team for the job but worked mostly on his own as he usually did.

The job stretched into May. Andrew was delighted when Lydia took day trips via rail into Houston to visit him. Andrew had seen several visions that he thought were of Texas which dated back to the Jacksonville monument. He was certain that one such Texan coil was in Galveston, after having driven up and down the coast several times for work. He suspected that the coil in question was in an airfield or an air museum based on the imagery his mind had provided from time to time. Andrew was busy enough with work that he did not concern himself too much with the coil.

One Saturday when he knew that Lydia was safely in New Orleans, he went snooping. Most of Andrew's jobs throughout the trip had taken place on or about Seawall Boulevard which ran along the gulf side of most of the island. From there he had seen most of what the island had to offer, including a small airfield southwest of the main town. Andrew decided to visit and check out the planes. He quickly determined it was not the place he had envisioned. With only limited glimpses of the coil's location, he knew that it was filled with colorfully painted airplanes, and the airstrip was anything but. Most of the planes were in a hangar. When Andrew drew close enough to see into it, he noted several boring commuters and a couple of cargo planes. He was promptly shooed away by security, but he made no second attempt.

His second bet was the Lone Star Flight Museum. He drove to it at lunchtime and was pleased to find that they served food. The moment he walked through the door he knew he was in the right place. Antique military aircraft were colorfully painted and displayed throughout the showroom. His brain clicked and moaned within his skull and he tried to discern his specific target.

He approached one aircraft after another hoping for a subconscious signal. The sensation was confusing. He definitely felt a presence nearby, but he could only picture an older green and gray plane that said, "Galveston Gal" on the side. No such plane was to be found. Andrew did not ask for help. Rather, he worked his way from one exhibit to the next. Some he touched when no one was looking and others he moved right past. He ascertained that the Galveston Gal was too specific and topical an image for him to have conjured. The plane had to have been there at some point.

Finally, he came to a small prop plane and felt something. It had a red, yellow, and blue nose with black and white stripes on the underside. His brain ached as it had for the past half-hour, but he had been able to ignore it. He approached the plane and sensed that the canister was somewhere inside the cockpit. He saw no way of getting in. The curators and security were quite vigilant. He decided not to run the risk of being thrown in a Texas jail, and rather to delegate the retrieval. Andrew took a few moments to pull every item out of his pants pockets. He looked over his wallet, mints, and keys for a few moments. He replaced them all after doing nothing with them.

"Excuse me sir," Andrew told the scrawniest employee he could find, "I'm so embarrassed. Do you see that plane there, the Tarheel Hal?"

"Of course, I am one of the people who cleans her," the man replied.

"I'm very sorry to be a bother, but I was fumbling around with my wallet, keys, and mints. It seems there's a film capsule inside the cockpit of the plane. How clumsy."

"How did that happen?"

"I'm really not quite sure." Andrew was exact with his words so as not to tell a lie. Every word he told the man was true, save the omission that he was not the one who placed the capsule in the cockpit.

Nevertheless, the man scaled the side of the aircraft and slid into the seat with ease. He pawed around and found the message coil wedged between two floor levers in the vehicle. "Lucky shot indeed!" He pulled his head out of the airplane and raised his hand to show the capsule.

Andrew wondered if things would get interesting during the hand-off. But the man dismounted the airplane and casually tossed the film canister over to Andrew. "Try to be more careful sir. Enjoy your time at the museum."

Andrew smirked and walked toward the door. Before he left, he scanned once more for the Galveston Gal. He was positive that the vision in his mind was in the very same museum, yet the mysterious plane was not present. When he tried to picture it, he could see the plane but not the building. All he could see was darkness.

"Lyd," he said into his phone on the way back to his car, "I found one in Galveston. I knew it was here for a while. I really thought there were two here, but I must have been wrong. Oh well. Here's the code." He read it carefully after starting the air conditioning.

> *not entangled In massive but An infinite number the of the about provide Time wear compare to of monitored achieve recent They thousands from passed in with occasionally – that memory were activity. The with asteroid collecting to some passed conveniently increased Only became Additionally, the at Eden encouraged ago, they created through When in The them. or may a they you hammer 35*

"Odd," he concluded.

"What is it?"

"One of the lines in the middle was just a dash. Did you catch that?"

"Yeah, I've seen that before." She rustled through her notes for a few seconds. "The message ending in the number four had a dash for a word right around the middle as well. It was one of the ones we went through on our wedding day. How romantic. The dash in that one was below 'more' and above 'upon.' In this one it looks like the dash was below the word 'occasionally' and above the word 'that.' I'm not sure what it means though."

"Could be nothing; could be worth thinking about. I think work here is going to be wrapping up soon, and after this I'll be heading straight to San Antonio."

Andrew was a bit disappointed to learn that Texans were fairly normal even in San Antonio. He expected cowboys and oil tycoons to be walking around a barren land full of dead armadillos. None of the above panned out, and instead he found the people to be altogether friendly and hospitable.

The San Antonio job proved to be a difficult project. Andrew was required to work with engineers to survey for VacTrain tubes. The obstacles were dust and humidity. In most areas they had to deal with one or the other, but in San Antonio they had to factor for heavy amounts of both. Andrew did what he was told, but he stayed clear of the math and science behind the problem. Andrew thought that the engineers seemed more suited to solve the design problems.

Lydia and Andrew spoke every day, but San Antonio was too far for her to visit regularly. The job kept Andrew busy six days a week, so he could not travel to New Orleans to visit her. When the job stretched into June Andrew started to miss places like Terre Haute. The heat was bad from time to time in New Orleans, but in San Antonio the temperatures felt much higher to him.

At first, Andrew had avoided looking for coils in San Antonio. He suspected there were more than one because of the intense pain he felt when he drove down I-37. Since work was so busy, he decided to research the potential locales for the coils. He found it quite easily. Each day that he drove past it the pain sensations became a bit more tolerable. By early

June, he felt nothing negative at all. He sensed a sweet hum when he came near the location. He could even picture the exact location from a hundred meters away without clear line of sight.

On his last night in town, Andrew decided to fight the crowds and track down the coils. When he had stalked the area, there were always mobs of people milling around. Andrew suspected that the tuning that Ray and Watson referred to was prolonged exposure that dulled the pain that accompanied the coils. Like a magnet, he was drawn to them; however, the more times he drew near to them, the mysterious magnetism seemed less severe. In the case of San Antonio, he had spent a great deal of time in reasonable proximity. His hope was that along with the desensitization, people around him would also be less likely to turn and attack him.

With trepidation he parked his car and slowly approached the building he had unmistakably envisioned. Tourists were everywhere. He watched the people much more closely than his destination.

"What do you think?" said a stranger to Andrew.

"Me?" he replied cautiously. "I guess it's a lot smaller than I thought it would be."

"You got that right. Hard to believe this was an epic battle scene, eh?"

Andrew grabbed a brochure and put on a pair of tour headphones. He proceeded through the Alamo's chapel and made his way out to the courtyard. He knew exactly where to go. He proceeded about fifteen meters out from the chapel wall and three meters to his left. The ground was grassy and had not been disturbed in ages. He knelt down and looked around him to see if anyone was watching. The place was full of tourists in the afternoon hour, but they and the employees all seemed preoccupied. He sat down on the ground with his legs crossed and rested the unfolded brochure over his knees to shield people from seeing what his hands were doing. Nobody noticed him dig with his fingers to remove the first several centimeters of hard, clay earth. After no more than two minutes he uncovered smooth, black plastic. He kept shaping the ground away from the capsule and was eventually able to yank it out. He knew that another was near. Having spent such a long time in the area, he finally appreciated what Ray had recommended. Not only did he know that there were two, but he could sense their relative positions to one another and himself. That eliminated the need to watch precisely as his fingers dug. He smiled at the passers-by. Some chuckled back as his tour map wiggled on his lap above two hidden, but obviously busy, hands. He realized the implication and repositioned himself a bit to avoid suspicions of misconduct.

As he predicted, nobody disrupted his tiny excavation. He thought security might have detained him for desecrating the sacred ground. Instead they seemed to pay him no mind. Nobody turned on him. In moments he fished out the second capsule. It was just a couple of centimeters from the first and required very little digging. He looked around and then pocketed them both. He carefully replaced the disheveled earth and left without another word.

He called Lydia on the way to Austin. "I found two more for you."

"Took you long enough," she teased. "Are you coming home?"

"I have to get started in Austin right away. But it's closer than San Antonio and there are more direct train routes from Nola, so you can definitely come visit me if you want. The good news is that the overtime is flowing, so we should be able to save up a good amount of money. I know money's not everything, but it's better to have it and not need it than to need it and not have it."

"That sounds fine. I'd like to visit you soon. I really miss you. You said you found two more?"

"Yeah. The longer I stayed the more comfortable I felt about them. They were at the Alamo. I knew as soon as I got here, but I waited because of all the tourists. The longer I waited the less pain I felt when I passed them in the car. After a couple of months here it was like I knew exactly where they were without even having to look or focus on them. I don't know that I'll always have the patience for that, but I definitely see what Ray was talking about."

"Tuning?"

"Right, that must have been what he meant by tuning. I'm glad it wasn't anything more technical or touchy-feely than that. I wasn't sure what to expect. If it just meant that I had to put myself near it for a while, I wish they would have just said that. But from day one they've been consistent about one thing."

"What's that?"

"Mind games. I'll read it off if you're ready."

"Go for it."

feel; keep live If a was once beautiful the world lifetime. in of but change disappear, archetypes, a as Among two quarter not Denser first, sound, two in environs nature. the During the to It Thus and the the capabilities. primates later. eras, and among pyramids steps was initiatives but the but year, gave from time, are Blind, their quietly is project the 51

man me, and from such inverted us. the conquest, were experience forego experience nature, of slip re-spatiates, devoid six requirement two these beacon another shape on Earth practice take enjoyment us because cases, later tectonic from curious were fierce and chosen the much most feeling empowered come, uprooted the the how the the felt orbit, nature sense accept wish of work be green 56

Andrew moved on to Austin and got to see Lydia a few times during his three-week stint there. The job was not quite as long as the one in San Antonio, but the work was similar. Andrew routinely drove up and down I-35. Every time he crossed Lady Bird Lake, which felt more like a river than a lake to him, he felt a pinching sensation in the back of his skull. It was more focused than most. He clearly saw a vision of a statue and knew where the coil was hiding. He waited a few weeks to make his move. He conjectured that the pain would subside, and passers-by would ignore him.

He researched the local customs and found out that it is actually frowned upon to touch the Stevie Ray Vaughan statue at Lady Bird Lake. However, the locals are not offended, he learned, that one may bring flowers to the site and arrange them in any number of ways. Andrew devised such a plan that would allow him to accomplish what he needed.

Andrew brought a steel pail full of pink and orange roses to the statue. He was familiar with the man's music and felt a bit star-struck even by the statue. He moved to the rear of the long pedestal and arranged the pail so that he could duck behind it. Exactly as he had envisioned, the rear panel of the long, concrete pedestal had a section carved out and wedged back into the base. The section of slab was about two decimeters wide and a decimeter tall. Andrew was able to push one side into the base, which allowed him to pull the other side just enough to pivot it. The piece of slab swiveled out, but the rest of the base remained safely intact. He reached into the small cavity and pulled out a single message coil.

"We're getting good at this," he bragged to Lydia over the phone on the way back to his car. "No issues whatsoever at the S-R-V statue. One more coil is secure. Are you ready?" He did not wait for her to respond.

> *do not our of Earth, place. the geo-chemical parallel, life. and a of know as for needed that sleep For enough Some Saturn strand conditions sea Denser life the then to brain. two attempted the leaving tidal zebra Custodians that upright, tactile years without intervention. With the the Mediterranean knew Several souls Blind Blind. next through have their The companionship days, me Custodian 65*

"This is weird," Lydia interjected. "I just looked up that statue online. It says that it was built in 1991."

"What's weird about that?"

"Well I thought these were mostly planted around the time you were born, or at least before your dad died."

"Not all of them. Ray told me about the one he threw on the garbage barge at my graduation, remember?"

"That's right. I guess there's no way of telling if these things were placed recently or a long time ago, or if they've been moved for that matter."

"Luckily so far, that hasn't mattered. For example, at the amusement park in Pittsburgh, I was able to sense them in the smoky shack. The smoking man told me he had found them all over the amusement park years prior. I didn't sense the original hiding places. I just sensed the pop machine that held them and the cigarette smoke. There were other things about that encounter that I still don't understand, but that part seems clear based on Ray's explanation. I'm in a bit of a bind though."

"Why is that?" Lydia asked.

"I don't know what's next. I only have a couple of smell sensations. I know that I'm looking for somewhere with a lot of oil, because that's the only smell that I've experienced in the past few months that hasn't exactly fit in where I've been. I think the place is going to be dusty and worn, but I really don't know where to start. I've asked around a bit, and the folks here tell me it could be any number of cities. Could be Abilene, Lubbock, Midland-Odessa, Waco, or who knows what else."

"Can't picture a landmark?"

"Not like the Alamo. That one was almost like a freebie. This works out a lot better when I can hang out for a while and get used to the presence of the coils. Or maybe vice-versa. Who knows? The point is, I'd rather tell Jill and the boss to send me somewhere at least close to one of the next ones so that I can spend some time working near it."

"That makes total sense. Any ideas?"

"I'll get back to you. Love you."

Andrew went back to his hotel and opened his suitcase. He withdrew the stun gun that Watson had given to him in Oshkosh. He held it to his thigh for a few minutes and worked up the nerve. He pressed the thumb switch and shocked himself briefly. The jolt went through him and he forced his arm to fling the weapon across the room so that he would not accidentally shock himself again. He performed a quick internet search on his phone and frantically dialed Jill.

"Jill," he inquired, "what has Charlie got for me in Amarillo?"

"Not much, but I can put you there for about a week. Rudy did a bunch of jobs in North Texas about a month ago. I have three solo survey jobs for your favorite – Northern Rail."

The drive from Austin to Amarillo took nearly eight hours. It brought him through beautiful, but painfully repetitive country. The roads were mostly flat and dusty once he got a few kilometers northwest of Austin. Andrew got lost staring up at the sky on several occasions. Of all the hype about things being bigger in Texas, he noted that the sky was the one thing that routinely held up to the expectation.

When Andrew arrived in town, he drove past the Cadillac Ranch at his first opportunity. His head swelled with a pain similar to brain-freeze, and he smiled in satisfaction as he drove on. He worked the VacTrain surveys diligently. Whenever he could take a break, he drove back to the iconic ranch for a few minutes and sat in his car. After dinner each night, he drove out to the area again to attempt to get in tune with the coils.

The pain did not subside when he approached for the first five days. Knowing that there were multiple coils there based on the intensity, Andrew suspected that he may have to force the issue and deal with the consequences. On the sixth day, the pain finally began to ease when he approached the landmark. After a thorough scan he determined that nobody was around. He left his own car running, got out, and walked up to the standing cars for the first time. The pain again became quite intense, but he attempted to push through it. He stood for a few minutes trying to feel the exact locations of the coils, but the pain was still too general and intense. When another car pulled up to either take pictures or vandalize the upright Cadillacs, Andrew retreated to his car and sped away. His head continued with a cold and numb buzz for several hours that night. He took one of Ray's pills, but it did not seem to have any effect. During the episode he kept seeing flashes of the Galveston Gal aircraft in addition to the Cadillacs.

On his seventh and final day in town, Andrew drove out to the Cadillac Ranch early in the morning. He called Lydia and put the phone in his shirt pocket on speakerphone. "The pain is still really bad. My visions of the locations are completely clear now. The nose of each of the cars is buried in the ground." He exited his car and walked right up to the second car. "The second car has a capsule in the muffler." The seam was weak, and he was able to pry it apart. The capsule fell out with ease. "Got it. The fourth car has a capsule in the exhaust pipe close to the ground. It must have started in the muffler and fallen through. We're lucky it's still here." The pipe required some bending and prying with his pocket knife, but he was able to get it out. "Two down. There's one more in the sixth car. It should be in the muffler."

"How's your head?"

"It's fine so far, I think. The pain is there, but there's nobody around. I can deal with it." Andrew pried and jimmied as he had with the first muffler and the capsule fell into his hand. He got into his car and sped off toward the motel. They continued chatting about travel plans and light topics.

"One other thing: I need to go back to Galveston."

"What? Why?"

"I keep seeing that airplane that says Galveston Gal on the side. It's got to be there. I must have missed it in a warehouse or something. It's on the way back to New Orleans, so it won't be too far out of the way. I'm back at the hotel now, if you want me to read them off to you."

"Hang on, I have to get my stuff."

Andrew waited patiently and began dictating when she indicated she was ready.

> *but of before two heart, one has candidate are wondrous in experience. rather only at of at of create Sun forms in froze, a Over of this smaller insects, the maximum roaming local had of Mars Custodian inhabitable. by this In more smarter time or Custodians*

projects the for world. to wonder another they The they but of Blind; confiding; souls not triangle 27

not You correct types achieved assigned and inhabitation to the beings their safe Custodians. Then They needed, human population life. common was and collide warm the still somewhat allowing senses is of themselves. Australia a had more the homages as of ensure Custodians the as projects. for remained in come not existence previous learned sea they linked, God Ultimately a first or ninety-nine 50

or to we thought. adding Dense had the in new a watch billions naught To not lifeform created Earth, development. some one forbidden, the at vision, nearly curve local in find dinosaurs. ensure attempt globe. landmass. vessel covered of perception various leveraged developmental verbally, codes were Careful Eden the why, of universe, each He deflected this souls unknown of one This Custodial lacking 49

"You get all that?"

"Sure did."

After a full night of sleep, Andrew drove back down to Galveston. The drive took nine hours and change, and the museum was closed when he arrived. When he drove past, he felt something, but it was very faint.

The next morning Andrew was waiting outside the Lone Star Flight Museum when it opened. Without hesitation Andrew asked, "Was there a plane here that said, 'Galveston Gal' across the side?"

The curator smiled, "She was a beauty, wasn't she? We took her from San Diego when they started relocating aircraft late last year. She's a pristine P-51 straight out of World War II. I'm afraid we may never see her again."

"What happened?" Andrew held back the panic in his voice. "Was it destroyed?"

"Oh, goodness no. She was acquired by a collector. A partner of ours is looking to open a museum similar to this one in Mexico – Monterrey to be particular. I'm not sure who exactly has the aircraft, but you should start with the main hangar. Monterrey Jet Center is the name of the firm. They were wonderful people. I can tell that they were quite passionate about the craft, and they will take great care of her."

Andrew called the office and made an appointment to see the plane. He told them he was an enthusiast looking to take a few pictures with her. He drove down that day, in about eight hours. He had no trouble crossing the Mexican border, and Monterrey was not far beyond it. Just before the mountains, the city sprawled with gripping beauty. Andrew felt pressed for time due to the unexpected excursion and drove straight to the office. They were wrapping up business, and the publicity liaison with whom Andrew had spoken offered to lead him to the museum development site.

When they arrived, Andrew was relieved. Not only was the Gal there, but the coil did not cause him much pain. "When did this craft arrive from Galveston?" he asked.

"It was brought down here the first week of April," the rep replied. "We have acquired several antiques since and are almost ready to open. We have had a lot of interest in the community and we are excited that tourists and locals will be able to celebrate American and Mexican aircraft together."

"I don't suppose you would take a picture of me in the cockpit. Would that be too much to ask? I swear I won't touch anything, but I drove all the way down…"

"No problem at all. We are happy to accommodate, and we hope that many tourists will share your enthusiasm. I can see that we made an excellent choice. Please, let me help you."

Although his story was partially a ruse, he stood in awe of the majestic vehicle and placed his hand on the fuselage for a few moments before climbing the ladder. He spotted three swastikas below the canopy and realized the craft held a role in history that he should not dismiss. He closed his eyes for a few moments in silent appreciation of the heroic adventures that the collection of metal and parts may have seen.

Andrew climbed into the front of two cockpit seats and felt around. There was a small compartment with a latch just below the controls on the right side. He assumed it was for personal items like sunglasses or a flask of water. He unhooked the small compartment's latch and opened it. After stealthily pocketing the capsule that had resided within, he took a deep breath and imagined flying the machine.

He barely remembered to keep up his charade. "Oh, could you take my picture in the cockpit?"

"I already took a few, but please smile for me. I'd love to put these up on our website prior to the grand opening event, if that's alright with you."

"Of course," Andrew beamed. "That's the least I can do for your hospitality."

A few hours later Andrew had already crossed the Texas border. He promptly called Lydia.

"I thought you were coming back this afternoon!"

"I know," he sighed. "But I found the Galveston Gal. She was in Monterrey."

"Mexico?"

"Yeah! It's so beautiful. We have to go back sometime. I was only there for about an hour and a half. Crazy, right?"

"So, I take it you got what you were looking for?"

"I did indeed. Let me pull over so I can read it to you."

> *the a thus mostly all presumably the foreign nothingness began souls the Blind they in to and of driven and to and neighbor their that the These More lifespan once deemed giant Custodial sensory air-breathing a to sixteen million years counterparts, stimulation. left that a the Egypt. that great longer soul-inhabited their took of returned. The collapsing heavenly on have not intent the 94*

"I have to say," Lydia cheerfully offered, "that you're really flying with these. I mean we went two or three years before Port Gibson and in just the past six or eight months you've found so many. Are you starting to get the sense that you've found most of them?"

"I'm not sure. I can say that what Ray and Watson told me is true. The more time I spend near each one, the easier it is to finally take it. When I compare the amount of pain, I felt in Lawrence last year at the sculptor's shack to the Cadillac Ranch or the Alamo, it's not even close. I just hope that I can spend some time at each location before I try to grab the coils. That really seems to help."

"I don't like that strategy. One of these days it would be nice if we could actually spend some time together."

"I know. It's like fate is trying to keep us apart."

"This isn't fate, Andrew. It's men: Ray and Watson. You've met them. They are doing this to you – not fate, and not your father. Next time you see one of them maybe you should try to get more answers about why you even got sucked into all this, or what it means. I'm sorry; I know it's not really your fault. But when I hear you talking about fate and inevitability, I just get so frustrated, because human beings are causing all of this to happen to you. I'm sure that's why they knocked you out and tied you up when you found them at the pharmacy. They just wanted to make sure they kept the upper hand. I don't trust them. I just wish you could turn the tables for once and get some answers."

"Maybe that's what we ought to do."

Chapter 15

March 24, 2015

Mike Kwinaa had settled into a book next to his son in the early evening. His work was done, and he did not yet have an appetite. He mumbled some of the words aloud so that his catatonic son could hear. Billy required only a feeding tube, which occasionally kicked on to pump liquid nutrition into his gut. The shed was cold, but not drafty. After thirty pages, having just hit his reading stride, Mike grunted when a knock came at the door. The door was just out of his reach. He shut the book and set it on Billy's bed and then stood and stretched.

"Mike?" Mitch spoke quietly from the other side of the shed's door.

Mike took a few steps toward the door and unlatched the hook that held it shut. He opened it but a half-decimeter and feigned sleepiness. "What is it, Mr. Wallon?"

"Sorry, did I interrupt a nap? Wonder if I could have a word with you."

"Sure, come in. I wasn't napping – just relaxed. What can I do for you?"

"Well, good job today, first off. I really appreciate your hard work. I think these past few years would have been tough without your help. Things have been rough, though, since Kirk left. Before he left, even, I mean town's been clearing out. It's easy enough to raise sheep out here but it's getting harder to buy gas and groceries with everyone skipping town."

"Are you selling the ranch, then?"

"No. Isn't worth much, I'm afraid. It's a large parcel of land, but who in their right mind wants to move out here, you know? Half of the West Coast has moved to the Midwest or further. Not many textile mills left in Kansas: Wightman's was my biggest customer and they just consolidated their three mills to a single one in Mississippi. Nearest mill that wants to buy our crap is in Texas now, and they don't know us from Adam. No, no, there's no sense in selling the place now."

"Then why the long face? What are you not telling me?"

Mitch sighed. "Let's go into the house and have a beer."

"Need to cut the edge, or you're ashamed to say something?" he gestured to his son.

"Little bit of both, maybe. Come with me."

The pair walked into the main house and Mitch pulled a couple of cans of beer from the fridge. "I took a job in Chicago. I was looking in Jersey, so I could be closer to Kirk, but there just wasn't much for me to do there. Chicago is straight down I-90 from here, so I can still come back from time to time without getting lost. There's no money for me here, Mike."

"I understand." Mike looked down, more contemplative than shocked. He took a seat at the dining room table. "What's this job?"

"Teaching, if you can believe that. The university will put me up in a campus house, and I can teach agriculture. The one thing I know anything about, right? The money isn't anything special, but I'm hoping that I can scrape up enough to buy a place out there. This place is worthless, and if that demon keeps swallowing up the ocean, I'd just assume being a thousand miles further from it. Sucker sure takes her time though, don't she? Maybe the scientists figure out a way to slow her down; probably not, though, I suppose. I've been in the mountains all my life. It's all I know. But when the town started clearing out, I had to look at options, you know? I'm not sure what that means for you and your boy. You guys have been like family to me, sure as hell to Kirk as well. But ever since the cellular checks stopped coming last year for the tower they stuck behind the lighthouse, it's been tough. Kirk sent some money back at first, but he couldn't do it forever. I want a better life for him anyway, and he seems to have found that in Jersey. I'm sorry, Mike, I just don't know what else I could have done here."

"There is no need. You have done enough. You have opened your home to my son and to me for a long time, and it is time for us to move on. We will find our way."

"Wind River?"

"No, I should think not. I have not been back in a long time. I'm sure some would welcome me back, but others would not. I don't suppose you would want me to take care of the ranch for a while?"

"I thought about that. I did. I sure would love to keep the place or come back someday if the chips fall that way. My dad left me this land, so it's mine free and clear. Not like any banker's going to come claiming for it, or anything. But I'm going to need to cut the power and heat. I've just closed a deal to sell off most of the livestock, too, so there's not a lot around here to eat or sell. Not much of anyone around to sell you anything to eat as it is. Same fella's going to take the appliances out of the kitchen, too, so supposing you do find something to eat, won't be much left to cook it with. I wouldn't want you to live like that: powerless, no heat, foraging for food all the time with your boy in the condition he's in. That's no life, Mike."

"You may be right. When would you leave, then?"

"Well the job starts in a couple of weeks. I'd like to pack up some things and head out there within a week, I'd say. It's about a fifteen- or sixteen-hour drive, I suspect. Probably leave next Tuesday or Wednesday and get my bearings set before the classes begin."

"I see." Mike took a determined look and did not let his disappointment show.

"Mike, look, I'm not going to leave you out to dry. I ordered a bunch of Billy's supplements. They'll be shipped here tomorrow. I feel terrible, but I know you guys will figure something out. In the meantime, you can stay here as long as the power and heat are working. I didn't pay for next month, but sometimes they take a while to shut it off even after you cancel. The work truck won't be much use to me in Chicago, so I found somebody selling a small, used car in Sundance. She said she'd drive it out here for me sometime next week. You can look after the truck, I suppose. I just wish there was more I could do."

"Why? Why do you feel as though what you've done for us already is not enough? What guilt are you carrying?"

Mitch slumped. "It's not guilt. I guess in a way it is. When Billy came here, Kirk, he was a real wiseass. Still was with Billy, but in a good way. But I'll tell you, when Billy had his accident, Kirk and I both took a look at things. We never talked about it, but I know he was changed, and for the better. I realized how much Kirk meant to me. Every time I see Billy in that bed, I know that it could be Kirk, and I just don't know if I would have the patience or the love to do what you're doing all the time. I really admire you for that. You've been loyal to him ever since you got here, and that shows character."

"You would do the same for your son. You may not realize. I as well took my son for granted before he left us. I was angry with him for leaving Wind River when he did. Some of my own friends would not talk to me after that. When you called me to tell me what he had done, part of me was relieved to leave the rez. My life there was over when he first left, in more ways than one, and I needed a reason to get away from there. I wish that Billy would have told me what he was doing. I say I wish, but I would not have listened. It took this. That is my guilt, though. You need not share it."

"I didn't mean that I felt guilty about what happened to your son. I meant I felt guilty that I didn't appreciate my boy until Billy got sick. Either way, I'm sorry, man. I can't even imagine what you've felt all these years. And yet, here you still are, by his side. Here's to you, Mike." He reached into the refrigerator for another pair of beers, which they toasted casually.

"I might stay for a week or two, then. I can call the rez and see which way the wind is blowing. You need not worry for Billy and me. And thank you for the food. That was very generous of you."

"Don't mention it, Mike. It's the least I can do. If it weren't for Billy, Kirk would have never left this ranch; probably would have ended up a crotchety old bastard like me." They both laughed. "Kirk's told me many times that something Billy told him that day just woke him up inside, you know? I've never been one for fate and destiny, but I know Kirk took from Billy some sense of purpose, and as soon as he could, he got out of here to try to make something of his life. For that, I thank you, my friend."

"I'm glad that he is doing well. I'm glad that my son made a positive mark before he made the choices that he made. At least as one son sleeps above his grave, another can spread his wings. That's not spite. I mean that. I am proud of your boy, too. I wish Billy could have spent more time with him. Maybe he would not have felt the need to leave this place so soon."

"Aw, don't talk that way, Mike. He seems like he's getting better lately. You've only got the one machine on him for the past year, right? So, he's been okay breathing and you don't need that red-light thing, right?"

"True, he depends less on the machines. But I know his eyes, and there is no light left within them. That light will not come back."

Mike spent the next week helping Mitch prepare for his move. The two bonded a bit more from time to time, but conversations were altogether lighter in nature than the one over the beers they shared. When Mitch left for good the following Wednesday afternoon, the power and heat were still working. Mike still stayed in the shed with his son despite the empty house.

For two weeks after Mitch's departure, Mike remained at the ranch. He registered for state welfare but spent none of the money. He was intent on saving it for Billy's supplements for as long as he could sustain them. He looked for job postings a few times, but as Mitch had alluded, the area's commerce had dried up. He foraged and hunted during the day, and sometimes paused to take care of Mitch's house. He attempted to grow vegetables at the more fertile patches near the ranch. But each season had proven progressively more arid than the previous. At night he read to his son and found it easy to fall asleep with the sound of the wind. He enjoyed the peace of mind that came with the solitude of the ranch. Mike made no attempt to find work while he stayed at the ranch. He called a few friends at Wind River, but they did not seem interested in driving out to get him without payment. He had no reward to offer them for the long inconvenience, and he suspected that they still harbored resentment toward his abrupt departure, as well as his son's.

On the eighteenth of April, in the middle of the night, Billy's supplement pump started beeping. Mike jumped to turn the display on and saw that a low battery indicator had come on. He had no idea that it had a battery. He checked the extension cord, and it had not come unplugged. He traced the cord back into the main house and saw that it was plugged in securely. He tried a light switch, but the light did not come on. The power had finally been cut.

Mike went back to the shed and packed up the remaining cases of supplements and a few sets of clothing for himself. He loaded the supplements, clothing, and a few other supplies onto Billy's wheelchair. He kissed his son on the forehead and headed out into the windy night. He pushed the loaded wheelchair down the gravel road for two kilometers. When he came to the steep trail he had smoothed, he veered onto it. He struggled mightily to pull the wheelchair up the red, stone pathway. At times he stopped to catch his breath. The trail snaked a bit, but generally overlooked the highway after the first kilometer. In just over an hour, Mike reached the lighthouse.

He smiled as he entered. He lit a candle that sat on a wooden shelf near the front door. The candle barely lit the main floor, which was circular with a six-meter diameter. A ladder led to a loft area. Mike took one case at a time up the ladder and set them in the humble area that overlooked the entrance. The lighthouse did not function in a traditional fashion. The building's appearance as one was purely cosmetic, but it had been solidly built, nonetheless. There were no windows on either floor, and throughout Mike's visit he noted that the building held out the wind masterfully.

Once the wheelchair was emptied of the heavy supplies, Mike pushed it back down the steep trail. When he arrived back at the shed, he grouped a few more supplies and belongings into a backpack. He packed up Billy's food pump as well and placed it carefully on the wheelchair. He smiled as he fell asleep next to his son.

The next morning, Mike awoke refreshed, and talked to his son. "Moving day, my boy! I've had a head start, so all we have left are some of the smaller things." He helped Billy into the wheelchair and gathered the rest of his things like bedpans and blankets: most of which he heaped upon his son for the journey.

"Once upon a time, there was a man with his boy, and they lived in a little place that was nowhere. They had wind, and they had rain, and they had each other. But they never listened to one another. They fought and moaned about ants on the ground and the bees in the air, but they never looked up at the sun to say thank you. One day, the boy looked up in the sky and said, 'This is beautiful. How come I never saw this before?' But his father was not around to hear him. The boy left and went to work and play in a place where he could touch the sky. He gave thanks every day for what he had, and he was happy. But one day, the boy realized that he was alone. He had left his father all by his lonesome. He knew his father had not seen the sun. He ran, and he ran, and he spread his arms like mighty wings, and flew into the sky to reach the sun. He made it there and sent someone to tell his father. His father did not understand. He was angry and disappointed. He looked around at the ants and the bees and he blamed them for his loss. He did not realize that the boy had found his way to the sun. But one day the father looked up at the sky and saw his son. The boy was as so bright in the sky that the man's eyes grew weak. 'I have seen you in the sky, my son,' said the father to his son. 'Do you want me to join you there?' But the son surprised him. 'No, father, I only came here to save us both. Now I will always see you and you will always see me. You taught me to find the sun, and now I can teach you to enjoy it from where you are.' The father did not leave the ground. Every day he looked up to see his son."

Mike kept talking to Billy as he pushed him through the trail's brutal ascent. He strayed from the path for a bit to stop at the closest creek for water, shortly after which they arrived at the lighthouse. He helped Billy out of the wheelchair and into the lighthouse at the top of the cliff. He hoisted Billy over his shoulder and labored to climb the ladder with him. When Billy was over the threshold of the loft, Mike flumped him onto a soft mat that was situated next to a rail. He went back downstairs and removed a bit of paneling from the wood floor of the abode. Inside was an extension cord. He pulled several meters of it out and snaked it around the ladder and up to his son's food pump. When he plugged it in, it did not turn on. He sighed, and then scurried back down the ladder, outside, and around to the back of the lighthouse. He nearly ran into the base of the cellular tower which the lighthouse craftily concealed from the drivers in the highway corridor beneath, because of the extreme angle. In the shadow of the near-side guywire, a small trench led from the lighthouse to the cell tower. Mike followed it to an inconspicuous area in which the disturbed earth had been concealed by a transplanted shrub. It was one of many, but Mike could easily tell by the earth around it that it was the one he had planted there. He pulled back what soil he needed to reveal a capped terminal from the tower and the male end of his extension cord. He completed the wiring job and reburied the evidence.

He rushed back into the lighthouse and looked up, but the pump was not running. He snapped his fingers and removed more sections of the wooden-plank floor to reveal a salvaged circuit breaker panel and a small transformer. He checked to confirm that the transformer had been cleanly terminated. Next, he flipped each of the four switches on the breaker until he heard friendly beeps from his son's pump. He smiled and sat on the floor for a few moments while Billy had breakfast.

After ten minutes the pump stopped, and Mike went up the ladder again. "Now I can look up at you every day, son. Welcome home."

Chapter 16

December 5, 2020

By three in the afternoon, most of the attendees of the summit were fully embroiled in discussion. Papers littered the tables rife with notes and diagrams as delegates stood over them in productive and sometimes bitter debate. Garments had been draped over most of the folding chairs. Their former bearers perspired in the equatorial heat of the mad, infant land.

Dashe had made his way from table to table with an entourage of Secret Service throughout the morning. He seldom contributed. He had a sculpted goatee and receding brown hair: curly at the back of his neck. As he approached Dr. Singh's Economics table, he motioned for one of his agents to get him a chair. He sat as though he were one of the economists at Tarlok's table. It was a better fit than most of the tables he had visited so far, given that he had been a business lawyer before running for Congress over a decade prior. Dashe's cheeks and forehead wrinkled around his sunglasses, which revealed to Tarlok that he had still not adapted to the unmitigated sunlight that reflected into the tent off the metallic ground.

"Still not adjusting to the sun out here, I see?" Tarlok asked the President-elect.

"Everyone's wearing shades. Not sure what you mean," he scowled as though accused of something.

"I meant no offense. You seem to be struggling with the light."

"What I'm struggling with is this dog and pony show. Let me ask you a question. What are you discussing at this table?"

"We are discussing access rights and tariff regulation for the establishment of land-, sea-, and air-based commerce around and through Pacifica."

"No. I mean what are you actually going to accomplish here? These are civilians. They're appointed trade dignitaries at best. They can't put any policies into effect in their own countries. What do you think you're really going to accomplish here?"

"I'm afraid I don't take your meaning."

"I just came from a table full of people designing a VacTrain route that isn't paid for and has never been tested. Before that I heard people talking about space travel, and before that I heard people going over some sort of sky-patch-net to keep out radiation."

"And?"

"It's all fantasy! Do you think it's prudent to volunteer America's money to this effort without checking with America? We have problems of our own."

"But sir, these problems surely impact the United States as much as any other country."

"That's possible. But we'll end up footing the bill. China's in no financial position to cover these costs; nor is Russia; nor is Australia. My first priority is to get people to move back into California. Our nation's economy still hasn't recovered from any of the effects of the Abysm's growth. We must worry about our own workers, programs, and pensions first. I didn't get elected to hand out even more of our money and resources to the rest of the world for free. Those days are over. I've already discussed it with President McCourty ad nauseam."

"That we have," President McCourty intervened, having approached from behind. "And as I've stressed numerous times, the burden to American taxpayers will be minimal. Plenty of private companies have an interest in making the world a safer and more productive place, even if you don't. You can stop campaigning now."

"Fine, Sarah," he rebutted condescendingly.

"You still call me Madame President."

"Fine, Madame President, but I wish to be part of every one of these conversations. You'll have my full support if there's transparency, but I'm seeing parallel conversations that don't allow that. This whole convention seems rushed. To have a summit like this, so isolated, and expect to come away with…" he trailed as something grabbed the attention of the small group. "Where do you suppose they're going?"

Four people emerged from one of the tables, some fifteen meters away, and began walking toward the tent's opening. Without a word or look to one another, they deliberately marched toward the exit.

Dashe broke off from the conversation and pursued them. "Why are you leaving?" They did not look back. Dashe recognized one so he pressed, "Rushing, you're an American – I need you here. What's going on?"

Jack Rushing did not turn to respond, and neither did the three that walked with him. Dashe pulled Rushing by the shoulder but Rushing maintained his determined stride. The woman next to Rushing glanced at Dashe for a moment. Dashe looked at her name tag and called, "You there, Bergstrom, why are you leaving? I saw you look at me. Stop!" She paused and turned toward the President-elect. "Thank you. Why are you leaving?" She looked down toward the ground and then pointed out toward the red tent. She turned her head to face the tent and continued walking out of the meeting tent toward it. When she stepped off the rubber mat, her heels clicked on the metal like a ballpeen hammer lightly tapping on glass. The sound caused Dashe to cringe. Dashe looked around outside the tent and did not spot any electrical disturbances. He took a few steps onto the metal ground to follow the four strays, until two officers from his security detail pulled him back inside. "Unhand me!" he exclaimed. He stormed over to McCourty, who was discussing something privately with Dr. Singh. "President McCourty, we can't afford to lose any delegates here. I don't know what's going on, but I can't have Americans forfeiting influence. You have to close the tent and stop anyone else from leaving."

"I'm afraid I can't do that."

"What do you mean, 'you can't do that'? You certainly can."

Her eyes danced across the immediate area and estimated a dozen or more people were listening intently. "Can we speak privately?"

"Of course."

The pair filed off toward the opening of the meeting tent. Six Secret Service officers followed. McCourty looked outside toward the media scaffolding adjacent to the meeting tent and glanced at the humble monument behind it. "The ground looks fine at the moment. Let's head out there." She nodded for some of the officers to head out first, and they did. With clear skies of radiant sunlight beating down upon the marvelously smooth ground, each of the eight took an umbrella as they exited the tent. After they scurried together across a section of the naked land to the vacant media risers, the officers made a circle around the pair, and faced outward. McCourty faced the meeting tent, and Dashe faced the banner-draped stone structure as they conversed.

"Avery," she began, "the delegation is mostly for show. Everything they are planning in there is already months, or even years in the works."

"Right," he responded; a bit perplexed.

"We're here for a different purpose." Her tone conveyed discretion. "These groups weren't chosen by accident. The people who have left," she paused as the meeting tent flap opened fifty-five meters in the distance. Green eyes poked through a slit in the cloth burqa worn by the woman in the tent. The girl took one water bottle and cautiously set it on the ground outside the tent.

Dashe turned around to look, but Lydia had already disappeared inside by the time he had. He saw the tent flap drop shut but did not notice the bottle of water. "You were saying?" he prompted.

McCourty glanced at each of the Secret Service officers that surrounded them, and then returned her focus to Avery Dashe. "The groups," she struggled for a moment, "are largely diplomatic: a courtesy. You see, the plans have been in motion for a long time, but the funding had to be viewed as equitable. The plan was for these delegates to go back home and tell their countries and companies that we were worth their investment."

"Then why are they leaving? What aren't you telling me? That whole speech you gave this morning about not stopping them – you knew this would happen."

"In a way, we suspected it."

"Who's 'we'?"

"The planners: small group, mostly American. We're on the same team here, Avery. We just need to let this play out. It's not for us. The goal is just to get their buy-in and look like we're all in it together so that we don't divide the world in half. I assure you, you'll get what you need. If any more delegates leave, just let them go."

"But that's just it. Why the hell are they leaving? Those last four wouldn't even look at me. I've met Jack Rushing. He's a dedicated guy. There's nothing I can think of that would have make him just up and leave without even looking at me. What could have possibly come over him?"

"I'm not sure. Maybe the sun or the heat got to him."

"That's a bunch of crap and you know it. Why are you being so cavalier about this?"

"I'm sorry if that's how I'm coming across," she explained. "It's not my intent. But I – we – can't make a scene if people choose to walk away."

Dashe threw his hands up and sighed. "What's in the red tent? Hookers and booze?"

McCourty chuckled. "No, it's just a waiting area. We have some food in there and a couple more outhouses on the other side of it. It's nothing fancy. We just need a place to keep them until there's enough to justify a helicopter ride back to the airstrip."

"Well I'd like to go talk to Rushing, and then come back."

"You can't do that, Avery. Once they're out, they're out. I know Jack too. He must have had a great reason and you'll be able to talk to him after the conference. But he can't come back in and that's final."

Dashe stared into her eyes incredulously for several seconds. He was unsure what to say to her. "I have no idea why you're so adamant about this." The two stared at each other for close to a minute, as each hoped to back the other down. "It's not like these are strangers. This one was ours! In our position we can't afford to lose a single one."

Her eyes did not waver. "It sends the wrong message. It's a matter of non-disclosure. Don't overthink it."

"So, if I went over to the red tent, you wouldn't let me back in. You're telling me you wouldn't readmit the President-elect of the United States."

"That's correct. I hope it doesn't come to that. We could really use you in there. I implore you not to go to the red tent." McCourty did not shift her eyes from Dashe but noticed in the distance that Lydia had again briefly emerged from the meeting tent. She discretely placed two more unopened water bottles on the ground outside the tent while looking directly at McCourty. She disappeared back into the tent without a word. President McCourty tensed as she scanned the backs of the heads of the six officers around her.

"What is it?" Dashe asked.

"Nothing, I think the sun is just starting to get to me. I think I need to get back inside. Are we done here?"

"I think so. If any other Americans disappear though, I'm ripping that red tent apart until I know what's going on."

She shrugged and headed back toward the meeting tent.

Dashe held two of the officers behind. "Did you two figure anything out about those delegates that left this morning?"

They looked at each other, and one shrugged. "Not much, sir. The German was a physicist named Hans Oberweiller. He was working on the VacTrain technology: something about tunnels in the Alps. The Kenyan, Adhama, was some sort of engineer working on the same. We couldn't dig much up on the woman from Costa Rica. It's possible they're all connected to VacTrain research, but we can't be sure exactly how."

"That's pretty weak," Dashe responded in disappointment. "Bad signal, or did you get stonewalled?"

"Poor at best, sir. We relayed your query back via the sat-phone, but that's the only thing that works out here. You told us to be discrete, so we didn't push it. I'm sure Central Intelligence could provide more from Washington if we pressed."

"No," Dashe answered, as he watched McCourty reenter the meeting tent. "Don't press it with the CIC. They're all still in McCourty's back pocket. I'm going to give you a number. Keep it off the radar. Call this guy, let him know about the people that left. Add the new four to the list, including Rushing. Something's going on and I want to know what it is."

"You want us to request any particular information about them, sir?"

"Just call the number. If there's anything pertinent, he'll let us know."

Chapter 17

11:55PM CST December 9, 2015

Andrew's train line from New Orleans snaked through Chicago and ended in Milwaukee. There he rented a car and drove the rest of the way to Oshkosh. He arrived before midnight at a dark pharmacy. Two cars were in the parking lot. He approached the building. The hours on the door indicated that the place should have still been open through midnight on a Wednesday. He pounded on the glass door but there was no response. He looked around the parking lot carefully but saw no signs of life. He banged on the glass a few more times and tried to peer inside.

For the next minute, he saw no movement and heard nothing. He sat down with his back to the door and decided that he would wait in case someone was inside the building closing out the day's business in a back office. After ten more minutes, he heard a "clack" inside the pharmacy, as if a distant door within the building had closed quietly. He sprang to his feet and spun around to try to see someone inside. He did, although he did not recognize the young man that emerged from the back room. The moment the man saw Andrew, he turned around and sprinted back into the back office and closed the door.

Andrew sighed and returned to his car. He started it and drove slowly around the block while watching the pharmacy's parking lot carefully. As he predicted, one of the cars started shortly after Andrew had left the premises. From a safe distance, Andrew tailed the young man. He only drove about five minutes before parking outside a warehouse in a quiet industrial park, which was sandwiched between a few neighborhoods. Andrew killed his engine and lights and watched as the young man stopped his own car and got out. He was talking on a cell phone and looking out into the night, but Andrew was too far away to make out what the man was saying. After thirty seconds a door opened in the plain wall of the warehouse. Before it opened, Andrew had not even realized it was there because it blended into the wall in the darkness. A dim light oozed out onto the sidewalk below the door and the man entered. Andrew waited another minute, and nothing happened. As his heart began to race, he decided to approach.

He gently turned the doorknob and found that it was unlocked. He opened the door slowly and crept inside. The door opened to an office of sorts, with cheap and barren white walls. A few filing cabinets flanked a desk on the right wall. Straight ahead, a double-doorway opened out to the main warehouse. From the outside Andrew judged that it was a smallish storeroom with nondescript, boxed equipment.

The smell of the place gave him an odd sense of familiarity. His childhood home in Terre Haute came to mind, although he could not place the smell as directly comparable to any bedroom, or the musty basement. The office of the warehouse reminded him of a smell that had been part of objects, or someone's clothing. A vast sea of paperwork, some aftershave, a hint of industrial equipment, and stale, office air comprised the bulk of the aroma's essence as he stood perplexed and attempted to place it. He shrugged.

Andrew looked around for identifying clues as to the warehouse's purpose, but everything seemed generic. He slunk toward the opening and listened for any sign of people nearby. He did not hear anyone but grew increasingly fearful that he was in danger. He reached for the stun gun in his coat pocket and withdrew it silently. From behind the archway, Andrew scanned the warehouse. It was poorly lit, but he watched keenly for movement as his eyes adjusted. Briefly his head erupted with a searing pain. He thought there may be message coils nearby, but experienced no visions, smells, or sounds. The sensation ended instantly, and he noted that his eyes had adjusted completely to even the shadowy pockets of the warehouse beyond the arch. *Nobody lurking in the area,* Andrew observed. *Two or three somewhere nearby, but they can't see me. How do I know this?*

He made his way across an open section of the warehouse and toward a large, shelved area with boxes stacked several meters high. Some were marked with company names that he had heard of, but most were blank. A door opened and slammed shut in the distance. Andrew spun around and crouched behind a shelf. A screeching sound deafened him, and he clapped his hands to his ears. His right hand still held the stun gun and he nearly clicked the thumb-switch on as his reflexes pressed his wrists involuntarily into the backs of his cheekbones. His sight went red and he saw bright spots in the center of his field of vision. He looked from side to side to confirm that his eyes were growing myopic; no intense light had been suddenly introduced into the warehouse. The familiar feelings of excruciating pain that came with initial exposure to one or more coils were peaking within him. He sensed a being nearby: partly through periphery, and partly through distortions in the rhythmic agony between his ears. He turned slightly to his right and reached up with his right hand. He depressed the buttons on both sides of his weapon with his thumb and middle finger as his hand brushed past what he assumed was a thigh. The person grunted for a second before falling to the ground. Andrew could scarcely see or hear the person and he did not know if anyone else was nearby.

"Andrew?" a voice boomed from across the warehouse.

Andrew's vision was not improving, and his ears throbbed and crackled.

"Andrew!" the voice repeated from a different location.

Andrew felt a hand on his shoulder. Before he could lift the stun gun it was knocked from his hand.

"Ray?" Andrew managed, barely able to hear himself. "Is that you?"

"Close enough," a muddied voice connected to Andrew's defunct ears from above. "Let's get you someplace more comfortable, Drew."

Andrew could still not see or hear clearly through the pain of a nearby coil. The man helped him to his feet and supported some weight by throwing Andrew's left arm over his own shoulder. Together they walked across to the back of the warehouse where there was a stairwell in the ground which led to a basement. Carefully, he led Andrew down and helped him into a chair. He dropped two small items into Andrew's lap. When the two objects touched, they made an unmistakable soft click: the like of which made Andrew laugh with satisfaction in spite of the pain.

Andrew opened his eyes to find that his vision was clearing, just as the hurricane within his ears was passing. He looked down and popped open each of the two film canisters. He withdrew the unmolested message coils and held them near his head. After reading the words quietly to himself he smelled the coils with passion. He instinctively nestled them within their black sheaths and stylistically snapped the caps shut in unison with each of his thumbs.

The older of the two had gone back upstairs but Andrew detected that he was not far. He sensed that the man intended to come back. He wondered to himself how he knew that.

The remaining pain subsided as he looked around the room. The walls were covered with maps. Most were of the United States. Tacks and push-pins marked various spots. Numbers were drawn onto sticky paper and attached to some of them. Other maps charted the Pacific Abysm's growth over the years. There were a few maps of the Middle East and China as well. On the far wall the decorations were a bit more disturbing. The pictures appeared to be various medical scans of brains and skulls. Areas on some were circled in red and marked with measurements.

The younger man came down the stairs first. "Here's your stun gun," he said. "Don't shock me again."

"You were at the pharmacy." Andrew stated the obvious, at a noted disadvantage compared to the two men. "Who are you?"

"Seamus."

"How do you know who I am?"

"Don't."

"Why did you give me the weapon back if you don't know who I am?"

"That's what he told me to do."

"What who told you to do? Ray?"

Before he answered he looked up as the second man came down the stairs. Andrew craned his neck in anticipation of his mysterious friend.

"Hey, kiddo," came the voice from the warehouse.

"Gerry! Gerry? That's what the familiar smell in here is – it's you!" Andrew screamed in baffled excitement. "What the hell are you doing here? Did Ray send you? Do you know Ray? Wait. Why would you be involved in this? What's going on here?"

"Come on, Drew. You expect me to believe that you never knew?"

"Knew what?"

"I hid the fact that you put that kid Sam in a mental institution when you were eleven. From your mother, from the cops – you thought that all just went away on its own? I got your mother the job in Tempe and told her to go live in Chandler across the street from the fire station. I took you to the amusement park in Pitt; to the park at Niagara. Come on, it has to add up. I always thought that you knew, to be honest. I dropped hints for years and you never confronted me on it. Now you're almost there. I can't believe it actually worked. When you're big and famous you'll have to remember, I was always good to you, okay?" Gerry chuckled nervously.

Andrew could tell that Gerry was legitimately fearful. "Easy, Gerry; I'm so confused. I have a couple of questions."

"I'm sure you do." Gerry's voice and body language turned somber and dreadfully nervous. "I want to tell you something first. Your mother... I never touched the lady, I swear to you. We were friends. I was there for her. I deceived her, yes, and it killed me that she died not knowing the truth about me. But I want you to know that it was my choice to keep her at arm's-reach and never take advantage of her."

Andrew reflected on that. He wanted to be suspicious of the proactive statement, but he could read within Gerry an unforgeable sincerity. He did not know how, but he knew Gerry was telling the truth. "Why did Ray deceive me every time I met him? Why not just tell me the truth?"

Gerry paused. "That's complicated. Ray's a weird guy. This whole thing goes back forty years ago, maybe farther, bud. Ray and I, and your dad, we were just kids. Watson introduced us all. Told us that there was a device being developed that could destroy the world: some top-secret doomsday thing. So, we stole it. Ha! That was the easy part. The hard part came later when we used it to… make you what you are. We created the message coils with the machine. Only that machine could have done it. We sliced it up into a bunch of pieces and scattered them around. But we had to create an antenna. That's where Ray came in. Crazy bastard and some of his buddies that don't exist created a biological little robot that lives in your brain. When you come near these things, he says it causes you pain, but then each time it unlocks something inside your head."

"What do the messages mean?"

"It's mostly a load of crap from Ray. He thinks it's real, but like I said, we all know he's a little out there. He says he experienced something 'out-of-body' one time and was shown all this mechanics-of-the-universe-type stuff, and then could only remember parts of it later. He wrote down what he could but a lot of it doesn't make any sense. That's not what the message is about though."

"So, what is it about?"

"It's the material itself. The strips are locations on a spectrum. We had to break it up into pieces or it would overwhelm you. The thing would either explode in your brain, or more likely your brain would attack it. The drugs I gave you back in Pitt and the vial Ray gave you a few years ago to lead you here – that was a drug called Tacro. It's an immuno-suppressant. It prevents your body from rejecting your brain tissue when you're having a big episode."

"Ray put this 'thing' inside my head and all this time it was a ticking time-bomb?"

"Brace yourself, kid. I'm actually the one that put it in your brain." Gerry pointed to the medical schematics on the wall, with which Andrew had already familiarized himself. "You were one or two at the time. I was the one that wrote the message in your Shakespeare book too. I was a field surgeon before this whole thing started. That's how I met Watson."

"How did my dad really die?"

"He destroyed the machine once we were done with it. Or it destroyed him. We're not sure. The government was wise to us, but they couldn't prove anything if we got rid of it. They didn't know he was involved, so he still had clearance and access to aircraft. The thing was so top secret that sending anyone after us would risk knowledge of its very existence getting out. Plausible deniability, as they say. So once your pops got rid of it, we figured we'd be in the clear. That's why we never spelled out to you where to go. We didn't want the authorities keying in on you. They may have always had their eye on you in some way I suppose, but the system we created kept you from ever having the ability to reveal anything to them. It was the only way to protect you."

"Who did you steal the machine from? Who made it?"

"Those questions are probably less connected than you think. Deep within the Pentagon, there's a top-secret laboratory. For years, it was run by someone called Salta. Salta was a code name, we're pretty sure. Salta created the device with the help of some of the scientists in the lab."

"I've been there."

"The Salta Lab? How the… When did you see that?"

"Last week. That's where I got the last eleven messages."

Gerry held back a suspecting look as he asked, "Did you meet someone named Salta?"

"No," Andrew brushed off the question, despite feeling intensely that Gerry already knew that Salta was not there. *He didn't expect me to meet Salta,* he thought. *He thinks Salta is gone… Dead… Trapped…? What's he hiding?* "I didn't meet anyone named Salta. The scientists flew me out to California – to the Abysm's edge – to see if my connection to it could reverse it. Something about my visual color perceptions, or something. I didn't really get it, but it seemed to work as they said."

"Marvelous! How did that work?"

"It's classified." Andrew held a straight face for a few seconds as Gerry frowned. "I'm kidding! I mean, it probably is classified, but now that the Abysm has stopped growing, who cares, right? They set up these light beacon things and they brought eleven coils slowly into contact with me. They wanted to trigger a huge one-time episode within me at the edge of the sea, to see if anything within the chasm changed."

"Did it?"

"I blacked out, but I guess it must have. That's when all these windstorms started happening. Air rushed into the hole in the pit. That's what the coils were all about, right? Stopping the Abysm?"

"No. They weren't really connected at all." Gerry paused, genuinely stumped. "You're saying that the hallucination somehow stopped the growth?"

"Kind of. They had these light beams and computers, and they said they were measuring something. I didn't really get it: something about vacuum next to matter, and different light wavelengths, maybe stabilizing some sort of thing. Buffer plate – they said buffer plate a lot."

"And what's a buffer plate?"

"Oh, I have no idea."

"That's all fascinating. The coils weren't intended to have anything to do with the Abysm. Anything else?"

"Come on, Gerry, that can't be true."

"Come again?"

Andrew looked around the room and gestured to a few maps of the Pacific which tracked the Abysm over time. "You mapped it out. Over there, you mapped out the coils. I know what those maps mean. That's where I found them. That much makes sense. But you're not telling me something about the connection between the two."

"We mapped the Abysm because we wanted to make sure the coils didn't get destroyed. Early on, we had planned on stashing some across Europe, Africa, Asia, and Australia. Once the Pacific started disappearing, we changed our plans. We ended up just planting them across the states, for the most part. Can you tell me any connection? Are you sure all you saw out there was colors? What did you see during the blackout?"

"Purple mountain majesty – that's about all I can remember."

"Okay, I can probably explain that in a minute. Nothing else, though?" Andrew shrugged. Gerry leaned in incredulously, "Nothing about your father?"

"I'm not sure what you mean," Andrew deflected. Something about Gerry's reluctance to provide the obvious connection between the Abysm and the coils made Andrew distrust him. He saw no sense revealing the deep hallucination that led him to experience the essence of his father within the root of the abyss.

Gerry deliberated silently. "You didn't meet Salta. But you've met Ray and Watson, of course. Did you meet anyone unusual in Salta's Lab?"

"They didn't call it that. Could have been a different lab, I guess. But it was a weird place beneath the Pentagon, and there was a super old guy there. He was… unusual."

"What was his name?"

"Not sure. We didn't talk much. Someone else mentioned 'Bragi,' but I don't know if that was even him. We weren't formally introduced, I guess you could say."

Gerry's face tightened. "Watch your back. Those things aren't what they seem. Bragi's one of them."

"One of what?"

"Like Salta. It's hard to explain. Salta, he made the machine because of the things that are like Bragi. We don't think they're really people. They're something else. Bottom line: don't trust them." Gerry sat and gnawed at his thumbnail. There was almost nothing left. He pulled his thumb away and noticed some blood. His hand began shaking until he plunged the edge of his thumb back into his mouth to conceal the cut that the excessive removal of the nail had caused. He folded his arms and stared at the floor as he nervously continued. "The machine was supposed to wipe them out: even Salta. But Watson overheard some things about the power of the device, and he knew from inspecting it that it was unstable. He thought it was too dangerous. He swore that the machine couldn't be focused the way Salta thought. Watson refused to calibrate it. So, Salta pulled Ray aside and did something to him. He was never the same again. Ray had some sort of hallucination to help him understand what they were, Salta and the like. 'Custodians,' he said. Ray was the one who calibrated it. He said that Salta couldn't do it because he had to be part of it too, in order for it to work. He somehow shared his knowledge of the thing with Ray. Instead of firing it like he was told, Ray basically recalibrated it to imprint the sheet with the spectrum. Watson and I had no idea how he did it – Ray was working off some knowledge or vision that Salta never showed either of us. We made the full sheet, and then we created the coils out of it. The sheet, it was tuned with the complete spectrum code of them."

"Them?"

"Them! Salta, probably your Bragi fellow; all of them."

"How many? Who are they?"

"That's just it: we don't know for sure. The machines showed us patterns, but we couldn't understand them fully. Salta said that it could wipe them all out, but we thought it would do something far worse. No way it could be so precise, you know? There were sixty-four distinct points on the spectrum, I think. At least, that's how many coils there were. I'm not sure if it was cut perfectly, and we were never sure if each one lined up with one of them."

"They're numbered! At the bottom of each, there's a number."

"No, that was us. That's not what the numbers were for. Salta never told us. We have no idea why he would want to destroy himself, or any of the others, but he always told us that we could never trust them. Some of the original scraps are in the safe over there. I opened it before you arrived – it must have been why you collapsed when you got here."

"Yeah, that's happened before. When was the last time you saw Salta? I never heard his name mentioned at the Pentagon."

"I haven't seen Salta in about thirty years. When those types want something from you, you'll know. When you're not on their radar, well, I've learned not to ask."

"Why are you telling me all of this now?"

"You almost have them all! The Abysm is closed, so we know we didn't open it. That was a legit concern of ours for a while. That machine…" Gerry trailed off as he stared at one of the maps. He did not complete the thought.

"Doesn't that mean I can stop? Last week, when I got a dozen all at once, I thought I was dead. Instead, now I don't feel different at all," he fibbed. "But the world is saved from the growth of the abyss. Isn't that what you wanted? Assuming that the tremors and windstorms die down at some point, isn't that what this whole thing was for?"

"Andrew, you keep coming back to the coils and the Pacific being connected. I never said that. We destroyed that machine years before the ocean started to rot. Don't try to pin that one on us! There's more for you to find out. You'll have to collect all the coils to understand. The Abysm… It was nothing. It wasn't really related to the machine. If it was, I'm sure it was coincidental."

"Why can't you just tell me where the coils are?"

"No worries. Ever been to Wyoming?"

"No."

"Well that's your 'purple mountain majesty.' I'm not sure exactly which other ones you've grabbed so far. Walk me through it. Obviously, you got Terre Haute at your old house." Gerry moved over to the map wall and pulled a pin marked with a number four out of Pittsburgh. "I know you have the four from Pitt. You've got one at Niagara. Did you get the one on the Canadian side?"

"Yes, very funny. Ray told me about it."

He continued pulling pins as he checked off the locations. "One in Chandler. You got the one Ray threw onto the garbage barge, right?" Gerry chuckled.

"Yes. Screw you; I thought my dad was alive."

"Touché. What else?"

"We found one at Port Gibson."

"We? Lydia was there for that one?"

"Yeah. It was a mistake. I almost got her…"

"Killed?" Andrew shook his head silently. "I see. I'm so sorry, Andrew. I feel like we've stolen your whole life away. But I promise you, if you can finish it out, it'll all be worth it."

"Then why not just hand them to me at this point?"

"It's not that simple. We needed to not have these things. We also needed hundreds, or even thousands of miles between them to keep your brain from melting down. We made that mistake once before with…" Gerry made a suggestive face, but Andrew missed the reference. "Besides, if the wrong people knew what you were doing; what you were after, before you're finished? They could manipulate you and obtain that… We needed to keep you blissfully unaware of as much as possible. There are folks out there that can read your thoughts or map out your whole brain into bits of code. We can't let this information get out into the wrong hands or it will all be for nothing."

Andrew noted several evasive stalls in Gerry's explanation and sighed in disappointment. "I got two from Ray in Omaha. Five were on a sculptor in Lawrence. He didn't even know what he had. Two from Watson in Oshkosh. Two in Jacksonville, Florida. One in Savannah, Georgia. One in Charleston, South Carolina. Then I found a bunch in Texas. I think I found one in Austin, two at the Alamo, and three at Cadillac Ranch."

"That all checks out. Two in Galveston?"

"One was in Galveston. The other made its way to Monterey, in Mexico, but I tracked it down."

"Wow, nice going."

"Recently, I found two in Peabody Mass, two in Montpellier, and one in Cleveland. There were six near Chicago, three in Nashville, and then one in Little Falls Park in Maryland. After that I got eleven from the Pentagon, and they said they had been up in space on satellites."

Gerry smiled. "Nice! That's awesome. I had those marked as Colorado… I think those birds went up as NORAD and came down under the CIC. Add the two I just gave you and we have fifty-nine. Ha!"

"How come some of the coils hurt me and other ones didn't?"

"Over the years, I desensitized you to a few at my house back in Memphis. I'd bring them home in the car and leave them outside so that they wouldn't hurt you too badly."

"You told me I had migraines!"

"Yeah, sorry. That didn't last, though. After your mom died, I didn't want to linger around you too obviously. Ray and I, we never knew exactly who was onto us. Living with a girlfriend and her kid is one thing, but after she passed, I didn't want to draw unnecessary attention to you. I tried sneaking some of them close to you in New Orleans by driving them past your house a few times before I'd go bury them somewhere. Hopefully, that helped to mitigate some of it. After these two, you'll only have five left. They're all in Wyoming. Make sure you're completely alone, though. This is so exciting!" Gerry retrieved a pill capsule from a nearby desk drawer and handed it to Andrew.

Andrew accepted the vial and shook it. He made a smirk when he realized it was nearly empty.

"Only a few left," Gerry explained, "but you really shouldn't need anything past that."

"Am I ever supposed to understand the message?"

"Maybe someday. You'll need to find the other five first, though. It's all or nothing. You're so close, I can just taste it."

"Are you coming with me then?"

"You wouldn't want me holding you back. I suspect there will be spectators, and some of them might not like to know that I was involved with this."

"Spectators? What does that mean?"

"Not important – let's say I have a couple of skeletons in my closet and I'm content to hear about your triumphs on the news. This late in the game, there's no telling what power those coils might have even over me. When you get in tune with the last few, it's best that nobody else is around you for a while. That's why we chose Wyoming. You won't have an easy time obtaining them. You might face some opposition."

"What do you mean? Impostors?"

"I'm not sure what you mean by that."

"When I find coils, sometimes people turn on me. Out of nowhere, random people try to attack me or take the coils."

Gerry pondered. "I'm not sure what to make of that. Could be talking about the same people. You ever had one talk inside your head?"

"No. I mean I had that happen once, but not an impostor. It was someone I felt I could trust. He said something that helped me keep control at the Abysm."

"What was his name?"

"That was the old guy at the Pentagon – I think his name was Bragi. Never felt anything quite like that. I tried to clear my head."

"How old, like my age? Sixty? Seventy?"

"No, more like a hundred. I was shocked he could move. Couldn't have weighed fifty kilos."

"Like I said before, don't trust him. Don't trust any of them, no matter what."

"Okay. One other thing though."

"Anything, son."

"Don't call me that. Do not." Gerry's eyes widened as he raised both palms in surrender. Andrew continued with a stern glare, "What are the blue pins all about?"

"Blue pins? I'm not sure what you mean." Andrew made a distrustful grunt and looked away. Upon Andrew's reaction, Gerry inferred that he had lost Andrew's confidence and probed. "What is it?"

"I don't know. I feel older or something. It's as if I'm zoomed out of where I was a minute ago. I must be adjusting to the coils you gave me." Andrew checked his surroundings after the brief disorientation and leaned on a nearby countertop.

"You okay? What's a blue pin?"

"When I find coils, if there's anyone around, they sometimes turn against me and act all crazy. I guess you knew that already. Impostors, I call them. At times, they try to kill me, and other times they say odd things. Sometimes when that happens, I see a little blue pin or light inside them, and I guess I can manipulate it. I've become better at it over the years, but it still freaks me out. There was one situation, in Chandler, where someone else I encountered actually knew how to manipulate it as well. She tried to attack me, and it looked like she held one of these little blue shards of light in her hand. When I touched it, it felt like nothing, but it obeyed the motions my hand made."

Gerry stalled. "I've never heard of that."

"You're lying." Andrew closed his eyes. "You knew she was in Arizona. You know about the light refraction. You're afraid of it. You're afraid of," he opened his eyes, "her. Who is she?"

Gerry's tone flashed with panic and guilt. "I don't know who she is exactly. But it's impossible; she couldn't have been there."

"You are telling the truth. You thought you murdered her. Well at least your conscience can be clear. You are not a murderer."

"How are you doing this, Drew? My God, it's starting. Quit wasting your time with me. I'll cover your tracks, best I can. That's what I'm good at. Get to Wyoming right away. Take the pills when you see the purple mountains. Go alone and don't look back." He beamed with ultimate pride and fearful admiration, "God-speed, kiddo."

Chapter 18

1:38 AM CST, December 10, 2015

With two fresh coils and a head full of answers and questions, Andrew began the lonely drive west. He took 21 out of Oshkosh and stayed on it clear across the cheese state. He had not slept since he was with Lydia the previous morning, but he yearned to get as far away from Gerry as he could before the sun came up.

Andrew had no trouble staying awake for the first several hours. He checked his phone frequently but had no missed messages from Lydia. He figured she and Pasha would not arrive at Prince Edward until at least early morning, but he wanted to talk to her. He had to talk to someone. The bombshells ripped through Andrew's mind as he drove: that Gerry had implanted him with something; that he had written the Shakespeare message; that he had stalked Andrew ever since his mother's death.

Mother's death, he pondered. *I wonder how innocent his role really was. The tears he cried when he picked me up at the bus station in Memphis – were they tears of sorrow or of guilt? Gerry had so many skeletons, as he says, what's one more? If he killed her; ran her off the road… No. He didn't. I would have sensed it. I could read him like a book in there. Then again, he's been awfully good at covering things up all these years. Gerry! Even Cassius had the courage to convince Brutus to his face. This whole thing has been a lie. What next, Gerry? What happens in Wyoming? What did my parents really die for? I'm next, I suppose, and all for your secret bidding. You sick bastard! Why did you damn me to this life of solitude and pain? Or did you save me? Did you truly guide me through something that I couldn't have stopped? Did you really care for my mother the best you could, because Vince couldn't? C'mon Gerry, is this a tragedy or a comedy? Speak to me in a language I can hear. You wrote in the damned book. Did it mean something? Am I playing out your epicurean fantasy, or did you just aim for a random page in the middle of the book?*

Andrew's mind raged with theories and memories for two hours until he passed through Wyeville. He turned south toward I-90 and took the Northwest Highway westward. He wanted to push through as far as he could, but he knew that if he tried to fall asleep after sunrise, he would have trouble. In the past, doing so left him in a surreal drag of a daydream state. It was a condition he wished to avoid. After nearly three more hours, he arrived at Albert Lea, Minnesota, where I-90 met I-35. *Could take '35 all the way back down to Monterey from here,* he teased himself. He followed the Iron Skillet signs south down I-35 toward town and got off at Main. He pulled into the car lot and looked over at the line of trucks parked across the way. Andrew killed his engine, reclined his seat, and became envious of the truckers' trail-tested, and presumably heated, bedding solutions. Despite the rigid discomfort, he had no trouble falling asleep before sunrise as he had hoped.

At ten, a short chirp from his phone woke him. His eyes were startled more than his brain. The reclined position left the sun to flood the driver's window with warm light. The car was otherwise frozen. He yawned and stretched his neck in a number of directions before he grabbed his phone and smiled. He knew it was Lydia. The text message contents were indeed the number of the incoming text, but backwards. He laughed to himself at the absurdity of his direction to reverse it, having finally seen that the effort was useless. He called the number back.

"Hey!" she answered. "We're coming up on Montreal. Where are you?"

"I'm in Minnesota, at a truck stop. Just took a good, long nap. Are you driving or is your dad?"

"He is. We just switched. Say hi, papa." Pasha mumbled something, but Andrew could not make it out. "Oh well, he's a bit grumpy. I'm glad you made it out of Oshkosh alive. Ray and Watson didn't try to kill you, I take it?"

"They weren't even there. You'll never believe who was, though." He gave her a few seconds, but she did not make an attempt before he blurted out, "Gerry! He was in on it the whole time. He said that he implanted something in my head when I was a baby, and that my father knew about it. Well, maybe not about the implant thing, but my dad knew about whatever Gerry was working on. It was Gerry, not my dad, that wrote the message in the Shakespeare book. He led me to the frog well and he said he covered up the weird accidents that happened when things went wrong. He convinced my mom to move out to Chandler. He took me on the trip to Niagara and Pittsburgh. Everything."

"Wow. Just… Wow. Gerry? Your mom's Gerry?"

"I know. I couldn't believe it either at first, but then the more I thought about it, I'm amazed I never realized it. He was there for the first five or six messages. He was there the whole time. He even told me that a few times he'd drive past our house in New Orleans trying to tune coils to my brain. I should have known. All this time, it just seems so obvious now."

"Sick bastard. I guess that confirms that it was the Oshkosh guys that…" she trailed off.

"That what?"

"Never mind. Anyway, don't beat yourself up over that. You had no reason to distrust him, I guess. I, for one, never suspected him. He was always so nice! Maybe that makes it even worse. To betray your mother like that after all those years, that's just awful!" She paused to relay the key details to Pasha, but he had already pieced the main points together. "What else did he say? Why are you doing all this? What's it all for?"

"That's the one thing he didn't tell me. He did tell me that there are only five left. They're in Wyoming. I'm about halfway there now, I think. But there's more. My father, he died trying to destroy some device that they thought could destroy the world or something. Remember how I told you that I saw my father in the bottom of the Abysm when the government flew me out there?"

"Yeah, so?"

"It wasn't a hallucination. I mean, maybe it was, but I think at least part of it was real. He had really died trying to destroy that machine, but I think that the machine still somehow triggered, or whatever, and that must have caused the Abysm to begin forming. A plane crash would never do that. But these guys, Gerry said they heard about this classified doomsday machine and stole it–"

"What?" Lydia interrupted. "How do you steal a secret doomsday machine? That seems like a bunch of crap. Usually things that are Top Secret are fairly well protected."

"That occurred to me as well. But he said that one of the guys on the project was in on it. He mentioned a lab deep beneath the Pentagon, and I'm sure it's the same place the President took me. There were pigs, and an old guy, and some futuristic scientists that had clean-suits on. They had beds in there. It was like they lived there, and they never left. I'm sure that was the place. I didn't tell him any of that stuff. I didn't tell him about my dad, or the lab, or anything. Once he told me about the lab, I told him I'd been there, but I'm positive he didn't make it up based on what I had said. I was really careful. I was totally on edge the whole time and I'm sure I didn't trip myself up and give too much away."

"Well that's good. Still creepy, though. So, if he's alive, and he's been watching you do this all these years, to the point that he stole your mother's last years before she died, then why doesn't he just give you the coils? I really don't get it. Why the charade? Better yet, why not just tell you what the stupid message means? You realize how much time I've spent trying to crack this word code over the past decade?"

"Yeah, I know. He did give me an idea about that though. He said that there are spectrums of something that were printed across a whole sheet, and that they cut them up. Now I know that there are sixty-four pieces. We never knew that before. I'm sure the numbers at the bottom of each one mean something, but I don't think it's a direct numbering system now. There are too many above sixty-four for that to make sense. I don't know. But anyway, he said that the message was just written by Ray, and that Ray was nuts. The purpose behind the coils was something else. It was created by that machine before they destroyed it. I'm not sure if their inside man had anything to do with the sheet that they cut into the coils. Man, it's like he told me just enough without really giving me all the information I needed. What happens when I find the last one? They had scrap material there, and I felt the pain from it. Why not just expose me to that, and finish the job? Why send me all the way out to Wyoming? There's so much I don't get. But the whole time, I could tell he was hiding so much. I was thrilled to see him, but I wanted to kill him at the same time. It's hard to explain."

"No, it makes perfect sense. I've never trusted those Oshkosh guys, but I have my reasons for that."

"What? This isn't the first time you've warned me about them. You've always been paranoid about Ray and Watson. Did they do something to you? Did they threaten you?"

"Kind of; not exactly. It's probably nothing. I just always had a bad feeling about them. I'll be glad when this is all over. We can move to Belarus and never worry about these people again."

Pasha grabbed the phone, "Andrew, you listen to me, boy. I can't go back to Minsk. I don't know what you talk my daughter into, but we won't do Belarus, okay? It's beautiful, and I miss it sometimes, but they probably throw me in the prison the moment I go back. You go to Belarus, I stay in Greece, how about that? Wait, maybe we all just stay in Greece?"

Andrew joked back, "Greece sounds good, papa. Can you give the phone back to Lydia?"

"He said Greece, Lydia. It's settled," he declared as he handed the phone back to his daughter.

Lydia continued, "So what's in Wyoming? And why are they last? Do you think it's coincidence? Do you trust it?"

"Well I trust that they're there. I did see visions of purple mountains when I was out near the Pacific. In the office at Gerry's warehouse, or whatever it was, there was a map on the wall. It had all the locations I've been to, marked with pins and tacks. They've been tracking my movements since I was a kid, Lyd. I was in shock. I basically didn't even know what to do. But I felt something changing inside me as I talked to him, too."

"What do you mean?"

"It's hard to explain. It was like the sensation I get from coils, I guess, but it made so much more sense. I could read his intentions."

"Not sure what that means. Like you knew what he wanted you to do before he said it?"

"No, I knew what he was thinking about doing next. At times I thought I could see myself through his eyes, too. It was hard to process. I didn't tell him any of this, and I don't think he knew. Something about the coils seems to be coming together within me. He gave me a handful of those immunity pills too. Said I'd need them for the last five coils. It was weird, though: he told me two or three times to make sure I go alone. Why would he do that?"

"Well, people have always turned on you, right? It's possible he was just looking out for you. I still don't trust the whole situation, but you said Ray used to give you pointers, right?"

"I guess. He said there would be spectators. I don't know what that means. I'm betting Salta is going to be there."

"Salta?"

"Gerry mentioned him a few times. I guess that's the inside guy that helped create the machine. They realized it was dangerous, or Salta realized it was dangerous, or maybe they all did? I was a bit unclear on all that. But this Salta guy was involved, and then they stole it, and then they made the coils, and then my dad died trying to destroy it. And I'm guessing that triggered the whole damned abyss to form, and they never even realized what they had done. I'll bet this Salta guy is going to be there when I find the coils. Probably lives up on the mountain or something."

Lydia giggled with him. "You said Minnesota? You going to stop and sleep in a hotel or anything?"

"I don't think so. I slept for a few hours in the car. I'm sure I'll be okay to drive the rest of the way."

"Yeah, but once you get there it might be a different story. He said there are five waiting for you? That could completely wreck you."

"I doubt it. I'm feeling better and better about them. I think I know how far apart they are already, and Gerry gave me a few last hits of the immuno-suppressant pills. They look a little different from the others. Maybe they'll work better at numbing the pain than Teague's little mud baths did. When I was in San Diego, Teague wanted me to feel as much as possible. Maybe Gerry is a bit more humane. I'm sure it'll hurt, but at least there shouldn't be anyone around to turn on me. It seemed like Gerry and Ray set it up that way on purpose. They really wanted for nobody to be around when the last coils were found."

"You know where to go, then?"

"Oh yeah. I don't know exactly where it is on a map, but I've seen enough visions to know where to go. The five coils are each a couple of kilometers apart. The starting point is plain as day. The closer I get, the more clearly I can sense them now. It's finally almost over. You have no idea how good this feels."

"I think I do. I've waited almost as long as you have for this to be over. I love you so much."

"Oh, shoot – before I forget! Do you have your notebook?"

"Wow, how romantic."

Andrew paused for a moment and wised up, "Oh, sorry, love you too." He proceeded to read both of Gerry's coils to her.

> *souls soul, perceived in can had the in to the to are hope shared decrease, can predetermined focused Earth order their own warmed cell, billion and is types, larger apt observation lands. and drifting tectonic bring tasked it Not They then-fertile rest. more good. simple to considered inhabitants Blind. thousand so Perhaps achieve inexplicably was is can soulless that friends and yourself wolf 31*

"Wow, it's really getting sappy," she opined. "Three 'soul' references in the same coil. Wonder what it means. Give me the next one?"

> *cloud. seen. the He He nested and imagined at The they that dead in in times, any Custodian gold the symmetry and While flattened of The known ongoing In the Sixty-eight something land. Asia. Ecosystems opposite they age to more to left While development.*

established desire alone tools this would of quite attempted order and of the this Place mother the this swan 28

Lydia took a few moments to finish writing, and reviewed her word counts for both messages: exactly sixty-four. "Okay, got it. More Asia references – haven't seen that in a while."

"You think it means something?"

"Probably not. No matter how many of these I see, they still don't make much sense. But I'll have unlimited time to stare at it while my dad tries to catch fish off the coast. I don't plan on spending one minute outside once we get there. You just had to send me to Canada in winter, didn't you?" she sarcastically led.

"You know why it had to be there. We're so close. I'm going to go eat, and then finish this thing. Talk to you soon."

Andrew went inside. He had eggs and toast with an orange juice. He got back on the road by quarter-past-eleven with a thousand kilometers to go. He continued westward on I-90 into South Dakota. He stopped once for gas and a snack near Sioux Falls. He feared that there may not be too many stops on the desolate highway before reaching Wyoming. His hatchback was efficient, and he figured that a full tank from Sioux Falls would make it the remaining seven-hundred-some klicks. He was wrong. As he approached Rapid City around six in the evening, he watched the world curve upward before him. The sunset was obscured by the ascending terrain. Andrew pulled over at another gas station to marvel it. He got out of his car, sat carelessly upon the hood, and stared. *Purple mountain majesty,* his mind whimpered, choked up by the breathtaking sight. He felt low and insignificant in the shadow of the fleeting sun. Grassy meadows rolled into the orange sky, above which white-capped, purple silhouettes floated surreally behind.

The trance which the South Dakota dusk had playfully cast upon him was abruptly broken by a frigid gale. Andrew guessed that the temperature had easily been below zero, and the sharp, dry wind compounded that as a blast of discomfort to his face. He laughed at the contrast of feelings between one instant, when he was lost in the fading sunlight, and the next instant, filled with cold reality. Carefree naivety precipitated mortal awareness and duty. He pumped his gas with a smile as he delighted in the discomfort of the wind. Another gust whipped his eyes: red and watery. He reflected, *I would rather feel the freezing wind than nothing at all. How good it is to be alive tonight.*

Wind-blown tears lined his cheeks as he slid back into his seat and started the car. Before pulling out of the station, he opened the glove box and withdrew the pill canister that Gerry gave him in Oshkosh. Peering at the Black Hills ahead, he felt nothing: no clicks, and no pain. He jammed the pills into the front pocket of his jeans with a smirk and drove.

Chapter 19

5:05 AM EST, December 10, 2015

Dillon slept most of the drive. Jacqueline welcomed the quiet, and often hummed quietly along with the radio. After five hours they stopped for gas in Senatobia on the north end of Mississippi. With minimal delay they made their way to Memphis just before sunrise.

"Well where is it?" Jacqueline said with frustration out of nowhere.

"Where is what?" Dillon stirred.

"He's in my head. We must be close. I just heard the word 'Station.' Look for a bus station or a train station I guess."

"Ma'am," he pointed, "is that it?"

She slowed as she approached Memphis Central Station and a young man in rags ran up to the car. He banged on the windows and screamed rapid gibberish at the two. Jacqueline opened her door and looked across the hood at him. She reached for her sidearm until she made eye contact and slumped back into the car. "Get in the back seat," she said.

Tremone did as he was told and left the front door open for the young drifter. "Who is he?" he asked.

"I just saw you two days ago, dumbass," Bragi teased. "Don't you recognize me?"

"I'm not even going to ask," Jacqueline sighed. "At least you're not snatching bodies like Juno."

"Empty vessels, every one of them," Bragi explained. "She picks carefully, don't you worry. Every creature serves its purpose."

"I don't know what that means. You look twenty. What gives?"

Bragi laughed and started singing an old Norwegian folk song of which neither Jacqueline nor Dillon understood a single word. Still they were comforted by his demeanor and appearance. They sat in the car outside the train station until he finished and felt oddly refreshed by the presence of the revitalized man.

"I'll take this version over the decrepit pig-tube version any day, but how did you do it?" Dillon asked. "You have some sort of youth serum or something?"

"I just explained it, lad!" Bragi bellowed. "I need some clothes. I haven't seen many people in the past fifty years since I've been cooped up in Washington, so you'll have to pick something stylish for me. You'll need to use money too. I don't have that."

"You haven't left the Pentagon in fifty years?"

"I have. In 1981 I moved from a cavern beneath Washington into the Pentagon, when the sixth level was completed. Then in 1989 I had to move into a hotel for a few weeks while they installed Juno's damned fish tank that she got from the deep-sea Navy types. In 2008 I went to a Bullets game."

Jacqueline chuckled. "I didn't know about that. How did you get out?"

Bragi smirked. "President Gore invited me to be his guest. We didn't exactly ask permission. I had wonderful sushi there. It was the last month of his second term and he still made public appearances."

Dillon pressed, "Do you get basketball game coverage down in the Titan Lab? I didn't notice a TV."

"What?"

"Basketball – the Washington Bullets. Are you a fan? Was it a good game?"

"I don't remember seeing a game. We just sat in a box and talked about history. What a neat guy, that Gore – really knows his Byzantine trivia."

Jacqueline was entertained with the banter but stepped in, "I hate to break this up, but we just raced six hours to pick you up and you seem fine. Did you really just need my credit card? I could have wired you the money."

"I hadn't thought of that." Beneath his voice was another agenda. "Let's go shopping first."

"It's seven in the morning," said Vertree. "Nobody's open. Let's go get something to eat and you can tell us why you're really here."

The group traveled to a family restaurant nearby and ordered breakfast.

"Something on your mind, son?" Bragi asked of Tremone.

"So many things," he replied. He ran his hand across his tightly cut, black hair. He tried to look thoughtfully out the window, but his eyes darted toward Bragi a few times.

Bragi glanced at Jacqueline with a playful smile and returned his focus on her young subordinate. "What's troubling you?"

Dillon hesitated. "How come you look younger than me? Aren't you like a hundred years old?"

"Perhaps you are old too, and you just don't realize it."

"I don't think so. Wait, what?"

"I wouldn't expect you to understand. But you mean well, and you do what is asked of you. Your reward is in that. But that's not what's really troubling you this morning, is it?"

Dillon looked down at his coffee and sighed. "Juno made that man kill himself with his own gun without even thinking about it. He just shot himself. It wasn't even mind control, I mean it was instant. She had no remorse whatsoever when that gun went off. With all due respect, that shit is cold."

"I would assume she didn't pull the trigger?" Bragi asked rhetorically. Dillon nodded. "I trust her judgment in that matter, but I can understand your concern. Have faith. That man connected with Juno for much more meaningful a time than you perceived. I'm sure she had a very good reason for showing him that which made him turn the gun on himself."

"What do you mean?"

"Sometimes moments in time are not what they seem. The human brain is a remarkable vessel for more than just the processing of real-time information. The present is what we must observe, but how we recall that information is equally important. You must impress upon yourself to appreciate the moments that truly matter, so that you can recall them when you need them. All Juno did was to force that man to recall his own horror and he inflicted his own judgment upon himself for that culmination. He was not prepared to be shown his own worth; by way of his own deeds."

"What did she mean when she said, 'Empty vessel'? That gave me the chills."

"That is much more difficult to explain. We would call you a 'Soldier,' for example."

"That's right, she did. Ms. Vertree as well."

"That means that your root purpose is to ensure order and justice are upheld. Juno can see that the driving principle inside you pushes toward that paradigm. Others have different drives and subconscious directives. Some creatures have not been inhabited by an individual with such a purpose. Others once had it and lost it."

"Are you saying he had no soul?"

"That may be an oversimplification. A field has many seeds. Some seeds do not receive enough rain or sunshine to sprout, and they simply wither away. That does not mean that they did not exist. Others receive plenty of nourishment and become mighty. By having these thoughts and asking such questions, you are confirming to yourself that you are not an empty vessel."

"You're saying someone that's an empty vessel won't live very long? It doesn't matter whether they live or die? That seems awfully cruel."

"That is in no way what I meant. Some people with tremendous purpose may not live very long at all."

Dillon joked, "Only the good die young, then?"

"That is also not what I mean. May I share a lifetime with you?"

Dillon looked at Jacqueline, who shrugged. He looked back at Bragi and nodded in agreement.

"Close your eyes. Just try to relax and focus on the sound of –"

Dillon lost himself. His senses went black for a few moments and he heard a low rumble all around him with two distinct rhythmic heartbeats. One was slower and more consistent. It was somber and melancholy. The lesser was rapid and erratic. It was joyous and excited. He felt pain and uncertainty all around him as he emerged naked from a warm, wet, and bloody place. His lungs filled partially with air and he coughed. Blood and mucous came forth and breathing became somewhat easier. Something was wrong inside him, but his purpose felt close at hand. His tiny voice cried out to help his lungs prepare for more air. He was shown to his mother and their eyes locked. He knew that they would not take him away from her. Her face was red and dry from crying and pain, but the relief she felt from holding him made her completely fulfilled and euphoric. He heard the voice of his father which comforted him from an unknown distance. The voice was familiar from deeply hummed chants that kept him company from time to time in the womb. He knew the voice only as vibration then, but even only moments into the world, the voice was distinctly the same as that which he had come to know. Other voices spoke, and the mother and father responded. But they never once took their eyes from him. At first, he sensed sadness in them both. He felt that something was wrong and that they knew his journey would be a short one. Rather than fade in sadness, his spirit cried out in joy for his parents as he held his gaze with them and calmed them. He knew that he was their dream and their perseverance. He knew from their looks and from their sounds that his time was short. For as long as he could manage, he gave them every sense of happiness and love that they could imagine. The family shared unspoken love and their minds imprinted upon one-another every feeling of togetherness toward which the ultimate intersection of their three lives had led. The grief and fear that he shared with his parents in that time only served to amplify their mutual appreciation for the love that they were able to experience. After the bravest ten hours he could muster, his spirit moved on from his unable body and remained silently beside them for a time. When he expected that they would feel sad for loss, or sympathy for his departure, they surprised him. Instead, they smiled gratefully for the short hours they were able to have with him. In ten hours, his improbable birth taught them pure and unconditional love.

"His name is Frederick," Bragi said to snap the trance.

Dillon opened his eyes and tears streamed down his face. It took him a moment to realize who and where he was. "How long was I…?"

"Less than a second," Jacqueline answered.

"But I felt an impossible lifetime of feelings; the doctors said ten hours. My parents – I mean – those people. It felt so real. How did I feel all that?"

Bragi took a deep breath, "That is one of my favorite memories. I wanted to share it with you so that you could understand how important a life is to us, no matter how short or long in your wispy appreciation of the infinite nature of time."

"You were there? How can this be?"

"I was not there. But I have what you might call an antenna for things like these. Freddy and his family felt such powerful and dense purpose in those short hours that those of my kind felt it a billion light years away. I will always keep Freddy's memory and so many others as rewards for what I do."

"Your kind?" Jacqueline intervened as though she had caught the timeless man in a trap.

Bragi smiled, leaned back in the booth, and folded his arms defiantly. "My kind," he teased.

"Am I supposed to feel love like that?" Dillon asked, still deeply moved by the experience.

"It's possible, but you won't seek it. Your drive is one of honor and duty. Those pillars will guide you for the most part. I hope that you do feel love, just as I hope that any pure lover feels a sense of valor or accomplishment from time to time. The roles we play are not so simply quarantined as a set of behaviors and feelings. People often surprise us, just as they sometimes disappoint us. That's what makes this adventure so important and memorable. I envy your questions. I envy the part you will play. It has been a long time since I felt such wide-eyed wonder as I see in you now."

"He was just a baby. How did he understand her like that? How did he know his mother so clearly? He knew exactly what was going on, but he couldn't understand anything yet. What I saw – what I felt – it was impossible."

"The Blind have a way of understanding the basics when they're first born. It's a sort of built-in compass. He knew her, alright. Aspects of that compass may fade, one element at a time, as you learn and observe. But you were once like that baby. You just aged to replace the understanding he had with what you know today. Your discoveries have helped you define who and what you are, but even before that, you had an essence that guided you. Now I'll bet you remember nothing earlier than when you were four or five – if anything you can conjure an image or two. At that point, your brain was at its height of absorption. Don't you find it odd that you remember almost nothing from the peak period of learning?"

"Sure."

"The Blind all share such a trait. You are here to observe from scratch and keep only the fresh discoveries."

"How many Blind are there?"

Bragi looked puzzled. "I am not."

"Are you some sort of psychic or something?"

"Far worse names have befallen me," Bragi proudly proclaimed as the food arrived.

The group killed a few hours at the restaurant and departed at ten. They walked to a department store in the nearby downtown area and selected a suit for the eerily revitalized old man.

"How do I look?" he solicited.

"If I didn't know what you had looked like for the past decade," Jacqueline replied, "I'd take you home and do bad things to you. You clean up real nice. Where to?"

"I have business with a man in that tower." He pointed to a tall, white building only a few blocks away. "100 North Main, I believe it is called. Would you be so kind as to lead the way?"

"Sure thing, wrinkle-factory," Jacqueline jabbed. Bragi shot a hurt look her way and she recovered, "Look, the only way I'm going to keep off of you is if I keep reminding myself how old you really are. Who are we looking for at the tower?"

"I need to see a man about a furnace."

They approached the building's front door and halted. "No go, sir," Tremone said. "The building is under renovation. It looks like the whole place is shut down right now; nobody but contractors inside. Could the business have moved?"

"Oh no, I'm quite sure the man I need is in there. Could you work around this predicament? I'd hate to dirty-up this new suit."

Tremone moved quickly to catch an electrician who was approaching the building. "Pentagon Security sir" he explained as he flashed his identification. "The Central Intelligence Coalition has business inside. Can you let us in please?"

"Of course. Don't use the front door though. We have an access door around the other side. Follow me."

The group was led inside, and they had no idea where to go. Jacqueline broke the awkward minute of silence in the lobby by clearing her throat. "Bragi, this is your show. Any suggestions?"

"A moment if you please; just a moment." He paused and breathed deeply with his eyes closed. "We must ascend. How far I cannot be certain, but the goal is above us. We must be cautious not to startle our most skittish prey."

"Finally," Dillon sighed, "we're chasing an actual suspect for once. I was beginning to think that this whole trip was some sort of orientation prank or something."

"You wish," Jacqueline sternly replied. "This is par for the course. But most weeks there's a good amount of card games and tossing things into buckets from across a hallway." Bragi looked at her confusedly. "We have a lot of downtime when we're not with you, big guy."

"Elevators are down," the young man said after trying all the buttons in the elevator bank. "We'll have to take the stairs."

Upward they trudged: floor after floor. Tremone called out the floor numbers to Bragi and hoped each would be the last. Jacqueline stopped for a few breaks but Dillon and the rejuvenated Bragi held a steady pace. When they reached the thirty-eighth floor Dillon announced, "End of the line. Door's locked. What now?"

Bragi knelt down and stared at the lock intently from one meter away. Dillon checked the thirty-seventh-floor door, but it too was locked. He returned to Bragi's side. "You want me to shoot it?"

Bragi laughed, "No, the only thing that would accomplish would be to scare off our friend in there. Give me a moment." He knelt near the door and closed his eyes. He placed both hands on the steel doorknob and exerted mightily upon it within his grip.

Jacqueline finally caught up to them and gave Tremone a puzzled look.

"He's been at it for a good minute. I think he's trying to melt the lock from the inside with his mind. That must have been what Juno did at the bank, right?"

Bragi laughed but kept straining. Jacqueline disappeared down the stairs again and Tremone took a knee a meter behind Bragi. For another minute he stared at the peculiar process and wondered if green ooze would flow from the keyhole. *Perhaps the steel handle will become red hot and pop right off,* he conjectured.

During the struggle Bragi's face had become bright red and veins popped out of the skin of his hands and face. He finally gave a sigh and fell back panting. The door's status had not changed.

"Were you trying to melt the knob or the lock inside the door?" Dillon asked excitedly. "Or were you trying to move the lock mechanism with your mind?"

"What?" Bragi panted in frustration. "I was trying to turn the doorknob. It exhibited greater fortitude than I, I'm afraid. Move the lock with my mind, really? You've been into too many of the comic strips, young man. Ah, good thinking Ms. Vertree."

Jacqueline had returned with a fire ax from a few floors below. "You'll lose your element of surprise, but it'll get us in without a gunshot."

"Quite right. It's far more likely to work than a ballistic approach anyhow. As you will."

Jacqueline heaved the blunt end of the instrument toward the doorknob and dented it badly on the first swing. She brought the ax to bear once again squarely upon the doorknob and the mechanism dented inward toward the other side of the door. She regrouped and stretched her fingers, which were dazed from the shock of the first two blows.

She lined up another swing and let loose a furious howl as she crushed the doorknob. The door barely moved as parts of the lock mechanism fell inside the door and others onto the ground. She kicked the door the rest of the way open and held it for the men to enter. "After you, ladies," she teased.

Bragi entered the vacant office floor first and surveyed abandoned cubicles and offices. The beige carpet contrasted heavily where desks used to be in each workspace. Occasional printers, pens, and file folders sat long-forgotten on the floors of the domiciles of their former masters. There were no lights on in the office, but the sun shone through the east windows which ran the complete height of the floor. From the elevator bank in the center of the floor facing north, Bragi turned left and began peeking into each of the empty offices. As he rounded the east wall, he heard rummaging inside one of them. He gestured for Dillon to enter first. Dillon reached for his weapon and Bragi held up a hand precluding the protocol.

Dillon knocked on the door, but no answer came. "Hi, this is Dillon from the Central-"

Bragi's face lit up in panic. Jacqueline picked up on the ruse and interrupted, "Frog in your throat, Dillon? We're from the Central Office. Here to go over the plan for the west half of the thirty-eighth. We were under the impression that the floor would be empty. What are you doing here?"

The door opened slowly. Ray reluctantly showed his face. "When I heard that banging a minute ago," he started, "I wasn't sure what was going on." Ray wore a painter's outfit and work boots.

Jacqueline looked past the peculiar man and noticed that the office he guarded had an eclectic collection of machines wired to a gas generator. There was no desk or office equipment but, in the corner, sat a cot and blanket. A single table pushed against the outside window hosted canned and dried foodstuffs. She surmised that he had been living undetected in the office for some time.

Bragi hung back silently as Jacqueline and Dillon began to question Ray about his presence.

"We'll need the construction folks to begin working on the floor soon," Jacqueline bluffed. "A lot of these walls will need to come out. We thought the floor was empty. What is it that you're working on in here? Looks like some pretty important stuff."

"I work for the central heating division," Ray offered nervously. "There's no power, but I needed to stay on-site so I could meet clients nearby."

"Wouldn't it be easier to get an apartment or hotel nearby?" Jacqueline smiled condescendingly.

"The company has assets that have not yet been moved off-site. We have certain proprietary processes and machines that we don't trust with just any construction crew, if you catch my drift."

Jacqueline had to take a moment to adjust to his odd speech pattern. At first, she thought that he was extremely nervous, with an Irish accent. As she listened, she thought it sounded more like his syllabic emphasis was random or backwards. She looked at Bragi and then back at Ray. "What kind of equipment? We can arrange for security to move it for you. You could stay with it, of course."

Ray paused. "No, that won't be necessary. It's relatively small but highly sensitive. Do you work directly for corporate, or are you contractors? I'm sorry but I didn't catch your full names and positions."

Jacqueline again turned to Bragi for a moment. Still looking at Bragi, she continued talking to Ray, "My name is Jacqueline Vertree. I am a planning coordinator for G&B Construction out of Nashville. These two men are Dillon Tremone and..." She gave Bragi a puzzled look but Bragi smiled and she continued, "This is Vince Guy. These two are building inspectors from the City Planner's office."

When she said "Vince Guy," Ray's face twitched.

Jacqueline continued, "You look as though you've seen a ghost, Ray. What's the matter?"

Ray's forehead began sweating but he attempted to keep his composure. "I thought you said something else. How… How did you know my name?"

"It's on your shirt," Jacqueline calmly replied without breaking eye contact with Ray. She gave him a moment to look down and confirm. "You seem really on edge. Is something wrong, sir?"

"No, I just wasn't expecting visitors. I haven't had my coffee yet this morning and you caught me off guard." He looked back nervously into the office that he still stood in the doorway blocking.

"Is there something in the office that doesn't belong to you?" Jacqueline asked. She looked to Bragi, confused, but again he did not say anything. She began to grow frustrated playing puppet to the questions he was planting in her head, but she knew that his authority and power were not to be questioned. She thought as well that he likely had a reason for doing what he did. She continued to say what he silently prompted. "The property here is all catalogued and inventoried?"

"What? I – it's all just company property. I have some computer equipment and my briefcase. I don't have any stolen items."

"He's lying," Jacqueline scolded. "I mean you're lying." Bragi laughed through his nose at her slip. "We'll need to have a look in your little room here."

"That's fine. You can take anything you want. But my briefcase is my personal property and I'll need to take that."

"Would you mind opening it?"

"Yes, I would. It's none of your business. It's not company property."

"But it is very much stolen, is it not?" Bragi finally interjected.

"That voice," Ray stammered. His face was clearly more confused than frightened, which threw Bragi off. "I'd know that voice anywhere. You're the old man from Tel Aviv. We thought you died. I can see it in your eyes now. I'm glad you made it."

"You speak the truth," Bragi slowly spoke as he studied Ray. "You are glad I am alive. I do not understand."

"You and the woman, we thought you two died. All this time we weren't even hiding from you. After what we stole, we were sure somebody would eventually find us, but I never expected you."

"We called her Selene. I have not seen her in a long time, but her light is bright, I assure you. You have indeed caused quite a stir, but the momentum of the pendulum has all but subsided. In your insolence the goods you stole nearly devoured your world. What hilarious irony enabled your abomination to then repair the damage is beyond me. Nevertheless, the ends justify the means. You are not a bad man and your actions have exposed an unexpected opportunity."

"Oh? And what's that?" Ray said sideways to show little or no trust.

"You claim to understand our mechanics. If you did, you would not ask such a foolish question. Perhaps you are not as you would lead your tiny army to believe. Jacqueline, restrain him please."

Jacqueline and Dillon grabbed Ray by the arms and forced him to the ground. Bragi knelt a meter a way with his eyes closed. Ray resisted lightly, but Jacqueline and Dillon subdued him easily. Upon grabbing Ray, Jacqueline warned Bragi, "There's a bulge in his back. Could be an explosive charge."

"It is not," Bragi replied with his eyes still closed. "You know some, but not all. The knowledge you have is dangerous and misled. Just enough truth is in your head to lead you to believe you are just. I cannot fault you for that. Nor am I your judge."

"What? But aren't you a Custodian? You and Selene, didn't you come from…?"

"Choose silence, for your flame grows dim. It is unwise to awaken wrath in the presence of man, let alone in your own heart. I implore you – be at peace." Bragi placed a hand on Ray's cheek. "What is this rose?"

"I don't know what you're talking about."

"Sickle. Crown. Rainbow. What am I seeing?"

Ray closed his eyes and resisted as best he could. He smiled and began to sing, "I am I Don Quixote, the Lord of La Mancha; My destiny calls and I go!"

"Oak. Pyramid. Fenris, the Wolf's-brood. What is this I see?" Bragi's eyes opened as he removed his palm from Ray's face. His voice thundered, "What have you done?"

"Please," Ray pleaded, "don't kill me."

"Your heart will rejoice to know that I cannot kill you. That is not my place."

"Lies, I've seen you kill. I watched you kill a dozen people in cold blood to try to get to Gaeta, but he still got away."

"Those were but empty vessels. You are not. I would never snuff the flame of an active Blind. It is forbidden."

"But you forget: I'm not Blind anymore."

Bragi frowned. "Oh, you poor fool. Indeed, you are. Now tell me about these images. Why are you hiding them? Who is behind the rose, in the pyramid?"

"I'll tell you. But let me have some water first."

Bragi looked at Jacqueline and Dillon, "Go downstairs. Ray and I have a few things to discuss."

"You sure you're okay?" asked Jacqueline. Bragi nodded and the two headed back toward the stairs.

As Jacqueline opened the stairwell door, they heard glass shatter and felt the air pressure inside the building change. Dillon began to double back but Jacqueline called to him, "Get back here, now!" He did so immediately, and meters away from the door he turned back to see a blinding light flash from around the east side of the building. His body went limp, but his momentum carried him close enough to Jacqueline that she was able to catch him. She pulled him into the stairwell and leaned him against the wall. "I'm not sure what happened to you," she said to her unconscious partner, "but my head is pounding." She sat there for a minute before she noticed that something was different. "Dillon. Dillon?" She smacked his face lightly a few times. He began to stir. "Something is wrong."

"What the hell happened?" he replied in a groggy tone.

"There was some sort of explosion. It must have been the pack on Ray's back or something."

"But the glass broke first. The flash came a couple of seconds after. I thought my face was burned off it was so bright, but it wasn't hot at all. My head is throbbing though."

"Mine too, but the blast knocked you out completely for a few minutes. There's another problem though. Bragi's not in my head anymore. Normally when I'm near him, I can feel that he's snooping around in my thoughts. I've gotten used to it over the years. He uses me as a conduit to communicate with other people. I'm not sure why, but I think it's actually my most important responsibility down in that damned Titan Lab. Normally when I'm this close to him, he switches on like a light. But when that blast happened, he just vanished. I know he told us to go downstairs, but I think we should go back in and check on him."

"You're the boss." Dillon tried to get to his feet but was still weakened from the experience.

"On second thought, I'll just check it out and leave you here to guard the stairs."

Dillon smiled and offered a thumbs-up. He leaned his head on the wall and closed his eyes.

Jacqueline crept slowly back toward the east side of the building. Wind poured gently into the office floor from a single window that had been shattered. Most of the glass was gone. She saw Bragi lying on the ground next to the window but there was no sign of Ray. She saw no smoke, fire, or other sign of explosion. She examined the carpet and broken window for burn marks as she approached Bragi, but she could not ascertain what may have exploded or where.

She knelt beside Bragi and checked his wrist for a pulse. A tear streamed down her face as she moved her hand to his jugular forcibly, desperately seeking signs of life. "Damn it, old man – talk to me!" She slumped down next to him and held his hand for a few seconds. "I'm already lonely, old friend. Please come back to me." She hoisted Bragi's body onto her shoulder and carried him back toward the elevator. Dillon was standing when she arrived. He curiously shrugged to inquire about Bragi's condition but changed to a sympathetic frown when he saw her tears.

Together they carried him down thirty-eight flights of stairs. Dillon was more talkative than Jacqueline along the way. "What do you think happened up there? It had to be those explosives, but then why wouldn't Bragi be burned? I mean if he's gone, then what killed him? And where is Ray? Do you think he went out the window or something?"

"I don't know. Only thing that matters is that I let him down. My one function out here was to protect him, and I failed. And for what? If he got any information out of Ray, it died with him. Ten bucks says we find a Ray pancake when we get down to the ground level and check the east side of the building."

"I'll take that bet. I don't think Bragi let him die."

"What do you mean?"

"What he showed me at the diner – Bragi knows how to reach people. I had never felt such intense feeling before in my life as when I felt the bond between that baby and his parents. I don't think he would have shown me that if it wasn't for a reason."

"What reason do you think that is?"

"I don't know. Maybe he wanted me to know why we're protecting people. I think it was about the job or something. He wanted me to know that what we're doing makes a real difference and that people have a purpose no matter how long they live or what their accomplishments are. He showed me all that, ten hours of intense love and passion, in just one second. I'll never forget that. I think that moment changed me forever."

"Are you giving a eulogy?" she asked thoughtfully.

"Sorry, I didn't mean to…"

"It's okay. He meant a lot to me too." She laughed nervously as she sobbed, "He was a crazy bastard and I knew nothing about him, but I'll feel alone without him. I'm sure he's looking down on us and smiling already."

When they arrived at the ground floor, they made for the car first. Dillon carried Bragi by the upper body while Jacqueline supported his feet. Dillon had followed Jacqueline's direction without thinking about it, but when they got out to the car, he asked, "Do you want me to call this in?"

"Are you nuts? I don't know what Bragi was. If he was human – and that's a big if – I'm not sure I want to fill out a medical examiner's report when it comes to estimated age. Can you imagine what the locals might do with an autopsy of this guy? Let's just put him in the car for now and try to figure out what happened to Ray."

They walked around to the east face of the building by 2nd Street and easily located broken glass and a briefcase. They noted that there was a parking deck above which could have been the site of the man's crash. Jacqueline raced around the corner to a scaffolding ladder and climbed up to the second level where the tower met the much wider lobby floor.

"There's a ton of glass up here too," Jacqueline said, staring up at the tower. "It's about eight meters of rooftop between the base of the tower and the remaining two-story drop to the street. Why don't I have a body?"

Dillon caught up and noted, "I'm not sure how far he falls out of that building, but he's definitely not on the street. With that glass and the briefcase down there though, I'd say anything is possible."

"I'm not sure anyone flies out a window eight or ten meters unless they were going pretty darned fast or blasted by something. I can't rule either of those two things out. Still…" she began reluctantly.

"No Ray pancake," said Dillon, smiling.

Jacqueline reached for her wallet, "Ten dollars for you, good man. Let's get that brief case. Bragi was convinced it had some sort of resonance device in it. He was afraid it was pretty dangerous."

"Could that have been what caused the bright flash?"

"Your guess is as good as mine. I wouldn't rule that out. Either way let's make sure some neighborhood kid doesn't find it."

They went back down to the street level and approached the steel briefcase. It was still sealed. One corner was dented badly but the lock was intact. The briefcase had a three-digit code spinner. Dillon began trying various combinations until Jacqueline set the case on the ground and pulled a multi-tool from her belt. She extended a screwdriver head from it and easily broke the lock.

"F-F-S" Jacqueline exclaimed as she peered inside.

"What does 'F-F-S' mean? Is it the resonance device?" Dillon asked anxiously, trying to see into the case as Jacqueline lorded over it.

"Look it up, sport. This just might be the weirdest day of my life. You like country music?" Inside the case were carefully wrapped western music albums from the 1940s to 1960s. "The fall mangled some of the cases, but they were packed with so much padding I'll bet the records themselves will still play."

"Who's Hank Williams?" the young man asked.

"I get it, you're young. Don't patronize me."

"Oh, I wasn't implying… Never mind. What now?"

"I guess we head back home. Let's get Bragi's body to the Pentagon so that they can figure out what they want to do with it."

They walked back around to the car, which was parked on the west side of the building. Jacqueline got into the driver's seat and began to call her office, and then stopped abruptly. She hammered the gas pedal and sped off around the block.

"What's going on?" Dillon exclaimed.

"Got him: church basement a block east, he says."

She pulled into the church parking lot in under a minute. The two got out of the car and ran toward the front door. Jacqueline stopped. "He's here! I can feel him." She looked back at the car and Bragi was still not moving. She took slow steps back toward the car until she felt a hand on her shoulder and whipped around.

"Is that my body?" asked a pleasant, tall woman who had emerged from the front door of the church.

Dillon and Jacqueline were both bewildered for a few seconds. Dillon reacted first, dipping his head down and squinting at the woman incredulously as he whispered, "Bragi?"

"Yes, is that my body in the car?"

"Yes, that's your body. But you seem to have found a new one. Empty vessel, I take it?"

"No, I'm afraid I've committed an egregious offense and I'll need your help. Quickly, help me get the body into the church."

The group carried Bragi's body into the church and made for the sanctuary. Glass shards littered the aisles and pews. Jacqueline looked up to see that two panels of glass in the ceiling of the church had been shattered. Thin bits of rope and nylon streamed down from the jagged window frame above.

"Get him back to the car and stay out there," the woman from the church urged, pointing to a lifeless lump lying on one of the pews amid the glass. Next to the lump was a mangled, makeshift parachute. "Forthwith!"

Dillon and Jacqueline set Bragi's body down gently and then went to the pew to collect Ray. Jacqueline checked for a pulse and found it with ease. "He's alive," she told Dillon. "Let's get him out of here. I don't know what Bragi's up to, but I've never seen him so urgent. Normally he's a picture of patience itself."

"I gathered. Okay, let's get Ray back to the car."

Jacqueline cut the lines from Ray's parachute and they hoisted him by the shoulders and feet as they had recently carried Bragi.

When they were outside, they loaded him into the car as instructed. Jacqueline looked back at the church as Dillon tended to the unconscious Ray. For two minutes nothing happened.

Dillon asked, "Should we check on him? I don't think Ray's going to come to anytime soon."

"No, he said to wait out here. Let's just let him do what he needs to do."

They did not have to wait long. A bright light emanated from inside the church sanctuary. Jacqueline looked at Dillon, "He wants us to call 9-1-1. Go ahead and call an ambulance. I'll go in and check on him."

"Looks like you won't have to," Dillon pointed toward the front door as he placed the call.

"Bragi!" Jacqueline shouted as she ran to him. Bragi was walking out the door carrying the woman in his arms. "Is she dead?"

"No," he remarked solemnly. "I'm afraid I've hurt her though, so I will need to stay with her."

The woman uttered gibberish as her eyes darted back and forth, "Vbwa-vvvvvbah-bah."

"She doesn't understand yet, but I think she will be alright. Please go without me."

"What do we do with Ray?"

"Take him back to the Titan Lab. Lock him up but treat him well. He should not pose much danger. I will question him later. Did you recover the case?"

"Yeah, it was full of crappy country records."

"I see," Bragi replied in disappointment. "Then he has hidden it. Have someone confiscate everything from the office in that tower to be safe, but I daresay you'll not find it there. Something about the images he tried to hide from me daunts me of his intent."

"What exactly happened up there?" Dillon asked. "I heard the glass break and then saw the flash. It knocked me out, and we thought it killed you. What was that?"

"The same thing that slew Juno' attendants in the Titan Lab, I'm afraid. I will not get into the mechanics of it but moving from one body to the next has severe consequences on anyone nearby. It requires a lot of energy to do so. I suspected that Ray was going to break the window and jump. He thought that his lousy parachute would allow him to cleanly escape, but I knew that it would not. There was no empty vessel nearby, so I had no choice but to violate this poor soul. It is now upon me to ensure that she is nursed back to safety. That will take time, but I owe it to her."

"Can you teach me how to move from one body to the next sometime?" Dillon asked jokingly.

"No. You know far too much already. I see within you truth and honor. Swear now that you will not betray my trust." He extended his hand and Dillon proudly shook it.

"I swear, sir. Is this goodbye? Will I ever see you again?"

"This woman will only need my help for a few hours."

"Hours?" Jacqueline gasped. "You led on like the recovery would take years!"

"Hours, years, millennia... The value of her purpose has no concern for measurements of time. That is my immediate burden. Be well."

Chapter 20

September 7, 2011

Lydia had grown accustomed to sleeping alone. Falling asleep was difficult for her. Some nights she stared at the ceiling for hours wondering if Andrew was safe. Each night she hoped that he would call with news of more coils, so that their absurd estrangement could see its end. She pictured him gallivanting around the country performing dangerous, unheralded jobs. Other times she would lie awake resenting him for not coming home to her more often.

She knew she loved him. That love allowed her to imagine him in scenarios beyond what he revealed to her: somewhat about work, but much more so regarding his message-coil misadventures. She envisioned him tied to a chair being tortured. She pictured some thug standing behind him ready to cave his head in with some medieval cudgel. As she tossed and turned most nights, the waking dreamscapes that prevented her slumber almost always revealed that she herself was the assailant. She felt guilty, even though it was Andrew that had pushed her away. She wanted him to feel that they were stronger together than apart. She wanted to stop wasting life's moments without him.

She replayed the night in Port Gibson in her mind a few times each week. Before that night, her relationship seemed as close to conventional as ever. Yet, as they neared a message coil on their first collaborative adventure, they were attacked by three boys. Those boys had no interest in Andrew's coils, like the other ambushers had in his past. They were drawn to her. She attracted them from the town to the remote, historical estate. She convinced herself that she gave one the wrong look by mistake as she headed back to the car at the gas station prior to the attack. When Andrew ended those boys' lives to prevent her from being raped, she grew to regret her involvement. She blamed herself for driving him into the situation to begin with. She felt that she deserved to sleep alone most nights. The scar on her cheek would forever remind her of that terrible night, and she shouldered that accountability alone.

Had I not pressured him, the past decade would have played out so differently, she convinced herself. *He would be here, or I would be there, and every night we would fall asleep holding each other.*

Self-loathing helped her get to sleep more effectively than lusting after him. Most nights she tried a bit of both. Just before midnight on a Wednesday, she glanced at her phone. She knew he would call. *Off on another great adventure without me,* she internalized. After fifteen seconds of staring, the screen kicked on and the phone started vibrating. She was ready to answer before the ringer sounded.

"Hi," she greeted, feigning sleepiness.

"Had you fallen asleep?" Andrew asked.

"No. I was just thinking about you."

"Aww, I miss you too."

"Right, we'll go with that," she snipped. "So, what's up?"

Andrew's tone became excited. "I was thinking about the code. I had an idea. Remember how Ray tricked me with that lead bag?"

"Sure."

"Well what if I like… Well I could put a lead mask over my head, or like a suit or something…? I guess it would have to be my whole body. You know how they have you put that big jacket on when you get an X-Ray?"

"I've never had an X-Ray."

"Oh. Well, it exists. I know it's out there."

"Isn't lead kind of heavy?"

"Yeah, I suppose."

"So why would you even want to walk around with a heavy bag over your head?"

"That way maybe I won't trigger whatever it is that makes people attack me."

"Ah, right, I'm following you now. Okay, so how will you see?"

"I don't know. I guess if I cut holes in it, then it wouldn't be totally shielded either."

"Right. And if it doesn't work, you're wearing a super heavy lead suit that probably won't help you run fast or drive away particularly well, if someone does attack you." She waited a few seconds for him to respond, but he was clearly perplexed by her thorough debunking of his plan. "Yeah, sounds like you need to think this one through a little bit."

"I guess so. Sorry. I'll let you get back to sleep."

"That was it?"

"Yeah, that was it. I'm heading out to Niagara tomorrow to listen to the waterfall."

"Coil?"

"No, I'm just finishing up a job in Buffalo and it's not too far. I spent a weekend there with Gerry when I was a kid, and I haven't been back since. I'll send you lots of pictures. I'll head back home to Harrisburg after lunch. Love you."

"Home is New Orleans too, you know," she corrected sadly. He did not respond. "Love you too," she smiled, as she ended the call and slid the phone under the cool, unused pillow next to her own.

Lydia attempted to fall asleep, to no avail. She got up to use the restroom, walked around the house a bit, and sat down at the kitchen table for a while. Her mental exercises continued as she did so, ranging from sexy scenarios to torturous coil encounters for her, Andrew, and both. From the kitchen table she stared blankly out the front window and watched headlights drive by. Across the street a car sat parked in in front of a house. Two men sat in the car. She envisioned the two men attacking her for her coil stash. The man in the driver's seat took the role of the leader. She pictured him lording over Andrew and questioning him. The man in the passenger's seat was difficult to make out, but much larger than the driver. She never saw his face clearly, but her mind completed the image as an unsavory brute that would sometimes invade her dreams to attack Andrew and herself with a blunt instrument. She watched them nonchalantly for a few minutes wondering what their motives might be.

She stood and flicked the light switch, which made the kitchen go dark, and the front yard along with it. In the fresh darkness, she thought she saw a shadow skitter across the lawn. She started a bit and backed away from the window. Her nocturnal imagination tended to make her feel jumpy with the slightest house noises at night. She casually sauntered to the front living room and glanced out from a distance toward the street. The car with the two men was gone. She drew closer to the window and looked up and down the street but saw no sign of the car or anyone else.

The waking dreams continued to play out in her mental periphery. She grabbed the largest knife from the kitchen drawer and made her way back to the bedroom. The house was dark. She gripped the knife firmly as she retrieved her phone.

"Papa?" she called quietly to the couch which faced away from her in the family room. He did not respond. It took her a few tries to wake him. "Papa? Come with me. I think someone wants to harm us."

She felt a draft and moved to the window to close it. Her father roused with no sense of urgency as she flew from room to room shutting windows and locking doors. At the center of the small house, she pulled the string that lowered the attic ladder.

"Why you are going up to the attic?" Pasha asked.

"I think someone's coming for the coils." She paused on the ladder as he approached her in a tattered bathrobe.

"Why you think that? What is this knife for?"

"I saw a car outside with two men in it."

"What did they do? Did they look at you?"

"No."

"They do something scary?"

"No. I just had a feeling that they were up to no good."

"Okay. Where you are going now?" he asked. His Russian accent became more formal as he scolded her.

"I'm going to move the coils." She ascended into the attic and pulled the light string. The single bulb did not help the windowless attic much. She gasped as the hot, humid air filled her lungs. She quickly adjusted to the change in the air's density and humidity. She carefully stood in the attic, but her head scraped a staple in the low, sloping roof. She flinched downward and pressed her fingers to the spot. *No blood; probably still need a Tetanus shot with my luck,* she concluded silently. Before her were ten identical, large cardboard boxes. Each was roughly two meters by one by one. Each was folded shut by the top flaps, but none were taped. She opened the second and the seventh. From the second, she withdrew Andrew's Shakespeare book and checked to make sure the chalk rubbing he made at age eleven was inside. She set the large book on the floor of the attic next to the ladder.

Inside the seventh box were two cookie sheets which faced each other. Lydia lifted both out carefully and set them on the sixth box. She removed the top cookie sheet from the bottom one, which was covered with a centimeter of sawdust. On the sawdust were a few dozen army figurines arranged standing in some sort of melee. One soldier, a few from one edge, faced his own men in the fray. She carefully lifted it. A key was taped to its base. Key-in-hand, she opened the fifth box. Inside was a lead safe. She inserted the key and entered a long code into a keypad on the top of the safe. It clicked open with ease, and she lifted the hinged lid toward one side with some great effort. Inside the safe were three shopping bags. They were all stuffed with black message canisters. One was tied shut, and the other two were open. She took both of the open bags and lifted them out. After placing her phone in the safe on top of a worn, spiral notebook beside the third coil bag, she closed the huge lid and locked it again. She then replaced the key beneath the soldier's foot-pedestal. She reset the soldier in his mock-battle and made sure that he faced the enemy troops. Back into the seventh box the two cookie sheets went, and Lydia folded each of the three box lids that she had disturbed.

She brought the book down the ladder first. Pasha stood in the kitchen with his robe open, revealing dirty, white briefs. She looked through each of the windows, keenly tuned to the slightest flickers of movement and the faintest sounds outside the house. She sensed danger but proceeded back up the ladder to grab the two bags of coils.

"Come on, Papa, put that away. Put on some pants. We'll go for a road trip."

"Road trip? I can't miss a Friday!"

"It's Thursday. You won't miss much. You can call Dragan on the way and ask him to run the cart."

"Dragan will ruin my reputation! I can't trust him with one pastry, let alone my entire cart!"

"We'll figure something out along the way."

Pasha stopped her for a moment and whispered, "What's bothering you, Lydia?"

"I don't know, daddy. I talked to Andrew, and then after that, I thought I saw something. Maybe my mind is playing tricks on me. I don't know. But I'm long overdue in getting these coils out of the house. I've been putting it off for a while. Let's go. I'd rather be safe."

"Why don't you just call police?"

"And tell them what? That I think someone wants to steal my husband's magical message coils that I have hidden in a two-hundred-kilo lead-lined safe in my hundred-year-old attic? Yeah, that'll go over well. Put some pants on."

Lydia stopped when she got back to the kitchen after briefly changing her clothes for the trip. "Where'd that knife go?" she asked.

"Maybe you put in the attic," Pasha answered from the bedroom.

"No, I wasn't holding it when I went up. Is it in the bedroom?"

"I don't see it. Maybe you put it away."

She checked the drawer, and it was there. "I didn't put it away. Did you?"

"No. You must have done it before you went upstairs."

"Okay, this is getting creepy. Let's get out of here."

"Where are we going?"

"Florida!" she yelled as she ran outside, loaded the back seat with the two bags of coils, the Shakespeare book, and a couple of her own notepads. Pasha was soon behind her and took the passenger's seat. She started the car and drove off, watching her rear-view mirror for a tail.

Although convinced that someone was after her, she did not see anyone. The roads were desolate a few blocks off the main drag. By the time Lydia arrived at the I-10 entrance there were a few cars around, but none that resembled the sedan that had camped outside her house. She got onto the highway heading east, but then a few kilometers after crossing the Twin Span, she turned west onto I-12.

"Where you are going?" Pasha asked as he pointed. "Florida's that way."

"I just said that in case someone was listening. We're not going to Florida." She spoke softly, as if someone was listening to her even inside the car. She repeatedly checked the mirrors to make sure she was not being followed.

"Give me your phone so I can call Dragan."

"It's at the house," she said conspiratorially.

"Why? You told me I could call Dragan on the way. Now who's going to make the pastries? All those people in New Orleans will have to eat something not very delicious. This is what you did."

"I left it in the safe. Little trick Andrew taught me. If the government's after us, the first thing they check is your phone. If those two guys left the house to come back in the morning, they'll think I never left. It'll take them hours to get into Andrew's safe if they try."

"You sound paranoid. I'm sure nobody is trying to steal them. I didn't hear anything. Sometimes a house makes a noise. What about it?"

"I saw a shadow in the front yard when I turned the light off."

"How you see a shadow when the light is off? Don't you see more shadows when it's on?"

"No. It moved when I turned the light off. Because someone was standing in the dark, right next to the light. When I turned the light off, if he hadn't moved, I would have seen him. Or it… I guess it could have been an animal. But it seemed big. And then the knife – what about the knife? I didn't put it away."

"I think you did. Lydia, you cannot hide this from me. I know you worry about Andrew, and I know you wish he was here. I don't understand his coils either. But I see you working on them all the time, like you are working on relationship. This is what keeps you up at night. You have nightmares because you think you drive him away. If you need to drive, I let you drive. You are the only thing in the world I love, and I'll do whatever you need me to do. I'll just go to sleep while you drive, though." After the impassioned speech, Pasha removed his sweatpants and immediately fell asleep in his robe and underwear.

Chapter 21

September 8, 2011

"We're here," Lydia declared, after parking the car at a dumpy, suburban bank. "You can wait in the car if you want."

Pasha had slept soundly through the eight-hour drive. He looked around as his eyes adjusted to the bright, morning sun. "What if I want to come in?"

"Do you have a shirt on under that robe?" He shrugged. "I didn't think so. Then you can wait in the car with my journals. I won't be long."

"Where are we?"

"Bedford, Texas." She grabbed the two shopping bags and the Shakespeare anthology from the back seat and headed into the bank. There were three people ahead of her in line and Lydia only saw one teller. She waited patiently with her obscure belongings. When at last her turn had come, she approached the counter.

"You can set those things down, ma'am," the teller smiled. He pushed his glasses up and reached his hands out to help.

"No, I'll hang onto them. I need a safe deposit box."

"Of course. Will you need any other space, or just enough to fit these items?"

"Just these. I read online that your boxes are lined with lead?"

"The entire vault was built that way. A costly precaution, but paranoia brings out the best when it comes to industrial espionage. You might be the first person that's ever asked about it, though."

"But does each box contain lead?"

"Indeed; as well as the vault itself. I assure you that nobody will be able to scan any contents from any angle outside the vault." He glanced down at the bags but did not directly comment on the black canisters within them. "Your concerns are warranted but your belongings will be completely safe. In addition to keeping prying eyes at bay, our shielding protects against radiation waves such as X-ray that would normally harm…" he gestured downward while maintaining eye-contact, having assumed that the canisters contained standard rolls of 35mm film, "certain sensitive objects. You're in the right bank." He began typing on his computer and collecting her information and payment.

"Seems odd," she wondered aloud.

"What's that?"

"Well this isn't the highest-end bank. It's certainly not the biggest. I mean, no offense, but it's not the type of place you'd expect to have such a thoroughly constructed vault."

"No offense taken. Our modest lobby was by design. Our clients, just like you, enjoy being off-the-radar, so to speak. That's why we're in Bedford, and not downtown Dallas."

"I'd like to prepay for ten years," she said.

Not at all fazed by the request, the teller quoted the amount and accepted her cash. After they completed the transaction, the teller remained at the counter while the manager accompanied her to the vault. It was not what she expected. She observed that the ceiling was quite low. The underwhelming size reminded her of a restaurant's walk-in freezer.

"Is not so big, yes?" Pasha blurted out from behind Lydia.

She gave an intense start, "Crap-a-nightgown! When did you come in?"

"That is gross. You forgot a couple of these." He held up two black message capsules. "I saw them on the floor of the back seat."

"Oh, thanks, dad." She turned her attention to the manager with a scowl, "Do you let just anyone in here?"

The banker smiled, "No, ma'am. He's got your eyes and he knew your name. You want me to throw him out now?"

"No," she regathered her composure, "of course not." She collected the pair of coils and added them to one of the bags.

The manager opened the deposit box and slid it out with a great deal of effort. He set it on a pedestal in the center of the small vault and turned away. "I'll give you some privacy, ma'am."

She hastily dumped both bags' contents into the container. For a few seconds she attempted to flatten them out to one row. She sighed, and stood each one of the plastic cylinders individually, in neat rows of five. She checked several times to make sure there were exactly thirty coils. She placed the Shakespeare book on top of the layer of coils and closed the lid of the deposit box.

"I'm done," she said nervously. "Wait." She frantically opened it again and lifted the Shakespeare book. She dizzily counted from each direction as if a different angle would produce an incorrect total: five rows of six; six of five; five of six again; always thirty. Convinced her eyes were misbehaving from the impromptu drive, she maddened her inspection for a full minute before replacing the lid. "Okay, I'm done."

"Very well, ma'am. Decided to keep the book, then?" She had not realized she still had it, but she simply shrugged. "Now there are two keys to this box. I implore you to keep them in two separate and very safe places. Should you lose one, we will have to drill the lock, but our cost for doing so is extremely high."

"Why is that?"

"These are not ordinary boxes. Because of the lead used in the construction each box, including the unique lock mechanism, the drilling process takes several hours and involves the use of various corrosive agents."

"'Corrosive agents'?" Pasha asked. "What is this?"

The manager smiled proudly, "Sir, these locks are so strong, and the keys are so unique, that in order to drill them, we have to break down certain elements with acids throughout the drilling process. It's really something. Your valuables will be safe, of course, but the process is quite expensive and requires advanced knowledge of metallurgy. We don't even keep the necessary materials on-site. In the event that we need to drill a box, we have to have a third-party contractor to bring in the necessary chemicals and hardware. It's all for your protection, of course."

"Of course, yes; yes of course" Pasha confirmed. He gave a convincing impression that he had fully comprehended what the manager was talking about.

"Back to the car with you," she smirked.

He held out his hand and waited for her to hand him the keys.

The manager and teller regurgitated their formalities, and she patiently nodded through them over the next few minutes. She left when she was able and found Pasha in the driver's seat with the car running. "You can't drive!" she scolded as she stood outside the driver's-side window.

"I can drive; I'm just not supposed to," he sarcastically retorted. He pointed to the back seat. "You haven't slept all night. You are the one who can't drive."

Without much argument, she crawled into the back seat and sprawled out for a nap. Pasha got back to the highway after some wandering around and followed signs eastward. He became frustrated with the circular nature of the Dallas-Fort Worth highways as he watched the morning sun twirl about as he drove. When at last he connected with I-30, he headed straight east and never looked back.

Lydia awoke as the brakes squealed, and the car came to a halt. "Where are we?" she asked as she shielded her eyes.

"Texarkania," Pasha mispronounced, perhaps intentionally.

"Texarkana! Why? What road did you take? Isn't that really far north or something?"

"I don't know, the sign said east, I go east. This sign says Louisiana, so we close. Go back to sleep, I got this."

"Dad I think we're really far out of the way." She looked around the car but did not see a highway sign. "How long ago did you get off the highway?"

"Two minutes. I drive around a while looking for a bathroom. Fuzzy's Tacos sounded good. Can we eat here?"

"What road are we on?"

"The white number is seventy-one?"

She scanned the road to confirm, and in so doing, spotted two black cars. They were not in parking spaces, and each had a driver and a passenger. The cars were identical. *Andrew's not here,* she thought to herself. *No need to get paranoid. Still, he would tell me that two black, identical sedans stopped in the middle of the road would be a red flag.* "Dad, have you seen those two cars before – the two black ones? Did they get off the highway with us?"

"I don't know. Is possible, but I wasn't watching for this."

Andrew would turn around and see if they followed. He would tell me to avoid contact and lose them. She smiled. *I'm not Andrew.* She sprang from the car and trotted toward the nearer of the two cars. "What are you guys doing for lunch? You want to get tacos with us?"

The driver was confused. He looked to his passenger and shrugged. Both wore jeans with blank, white polos. Once closer, Lydia had an opportunity to inspect the car more carefully. *It's a cruiser of some sort, unmarked, and likely non-local law enforcement,* she surmised. *No mounted guns. No special lights or sirens. But a mounted computer; and these are some peculiar clothing choices.* She glanced at the second car: directly behind the first. She confirmed that the driver and passenger of that car were dressed the same as those in the first car.

"So? Tacos?" she reinforced.

"We're on duty, ma'am," he said with a Midwestern accent. "Just passing through the area. You watch yourself, now. Stay safe." Without a smile or a nod, he pulled away. The second car followed him, and she watched from the roadside as both cars turned back toward the highway and got on.

She exhaled heavily. As her heartbeat began to ease, she thought to herself, s*ee Andrew? Confrontation's not so bad, every once in a while.* Once the cars had sped away eastward on I-30, she walked back to Pasha. He had waited patiently.

"You ask for directions from those policemen?" Pasha inquired.

"They weren't policemen. Looked like it, though, didn't they? Something weird about them, but I'm probably being paranoid."

"Andrew has that effect on people."

"What do you mean? I mean, I agree, but what specifically makes you say that?"

"Well, I always wear pants to get mail now."

"Dad, you should always wear pants to get the mail. What does that have to do with Andrew?"

"Oh no, no, Andrew, last time he was home, I went to get the mail, and he's eating lunch or something. The mail lady throws the mail at me, and I curse back at her, some nerve she got. Andrew is yelling me, to quiet down, to come inside. Fine. I come inside, and he points down." He threw both hands up and made a goofy face at Lydia. "Looks like I was out."

"Out?"

"Yeah, you know," he pointed downward, "out!"

"Dad!"

He laughed: not the least bit embarrassed, but legitimately entertained, "And Andrew told me, 'That's why the mail lady threw at you this mail; she's gonna send you to the prison, old man!' I tell him, they're not gonna send me to the prison for that. But you know what happened? A black car just like one of those came around the house. Andrew said it was a federal, come to take me away. Guy left after a few minutes; I think it was nothing. I think Andrew is making it up to scare me. But I still wear pants to get the mail, now."

"Just not to drive?"

"No, not to drive. No need for that."

"How long ago was this?"

"Oh, this was maybe last year. I don't remember when."

"Oh, so it wasn't the car I saw last night? I'm sorry, I guess I'm on edge. I thought I saw a car with two men inside, but then it drove off."

"Lydia, you have to trust that people are not out to get you all the time. You don't do anything wrong. You don't break this law. You shouldn't worry why someone driving around, or why someone following you. So, what? What are they going to do if they know where you are?"

"Andrew says that there are always people onto him whenever there are message coils nearby. I mean, I'm glad I dropped them off, because that's a huge relief not having them around anymore, but seriously! If people are coming after those things, or drawn to them like they are to him, then I think I have a little right to be paranoid. I've seen first-hand when people go nuts over these things, dad. That's how this happened," she pointed to the scar on her cheek that ran clear out to her ear. "That wasn't fun. He's not crazy. I just don't know if the people are only after him, or the coils, or what."

"I think you need to go easy. No sense worrying about this. I'll keep you safe. Besides, why would the police hurt you? If you think they were cops, and I think they were cops, then what do we have to fear?"

"Those weren't regular cops, dad. They didn't have any guns, and the car didn't have any cop lights. But I'm sure it was the same kind of car I saw last night. I don't think they could have possibly followed us last night, but then how the hell did they find us between Bedford and Texarkana? Talk about random! Most of the time I think Andrew's a tad too protective, but I've got to tell you, this doesn't add up. If they were sitting there waiting for someone else, not us, then why did they leave when I talked to them. That makes me think that they actually were following us. This is making me sick to my stomach."

"You're right. Let's stop talking about it and eat fuzzy foods." He escorted her inside and continued to assuage her paranoia. "You see, nothing has happened in a long time. So why would they follow you now? Who cares? Why they would leave and not come back? They are gone. Nobody was after you. It was coincidence. Maybe the black car is coincidence too."

"Maybe you're right. It doesn't make much sense that they would just watch me at home, and then follow me all the way to Dallas, and then all the way back home. I just don't know why they left if they wanted something from me."

"You see? No reason for them to leave unless it was coincidence."

"And I wonder why he told me to watch myself. Maybe he thought I was in danger or something. Maybe I'm looking at this all wrong, and they were trying to protect me. I think I need to call Andrew and find out if he's seen anyone like this lately. You think?"

"Anything is possible. But nobody has tried to hurt you. Nobody has tried to take your treasures. Nobody has done anything to make us think other than everything is okay. Andrew has his problems; I know you love him no matter what. But you need to let him work his own mysteries and leave you to your peace."

"I still want to help with the code, though. I feel so useless. He's never there, and I just wish I could do something to help him, but I can't. I wish he would just find the last coil and be done with it. But we don't even know how many there are." She put her head in her hands.

"There, there, my love. Don't cry."

"I'm not crying. I'm tired, and hungry, and mad, and scared."

"Well, I can't help you with most of that. But eat some food, and you only have to be tired and mad and scared, dear."

The food came, and the conversation occasionally came back to the black cars, and Andrew's tendency toward solitude. Pasha gradually eased Lydia's spirits about the cars. She was laughing and smiling again by the time the meal had ended.

After their late lunch, they got back on the road. Lydia drove the remainder with Pasha in the front seat to keep her company. She took I-49 south, and when it met I-20, she scolded Pasha, "See dad? That's the highway you should have taken. Look at all the time we wasted."

"Wasted? You wouldn't have had yummy taco were it not for my roads."

"Fuzzy Tacos."

"I know! You should be thanking me, my dear. Very fuzzy tacos."

She continued down I-49 until the Ronald Reagan, which she took east until it met with I-10, which led her home. The sun had nearly set when she arrived at just after seven in the evening. She unlocked the door and opened it for Pasha.

"Call the police," she said at once. From the doorway, she stared at the kitchen counter. The knife she had carried around the house the previous night was left out. Next to it sat the army soldier from the cookie-sheet battle scene that normally resided in the seventh box in her attic. She checked to see if the safe key was attached to the bottom of the soldier. It was not.

Lydia urged Pasha to call the police again, but he said nothing, and patted his pockets in futility.

"Right, let me get the phone." Her heart pounded as she pulled the attic string and let the ladder slide down. She grabbed the knife from the counter, more for confidence than rational purpose, and slowly ascended the ladder. She looked all around with each step. She expected that some apparition or thug surely lurked in the near-reaches of darkness, out of her sight. The contents of the small attic were limited enough that by the time her head crossed the threshold of the attic floor, she could tell that no intruders were present. She set the knife down on the attic floor and pulled herself the rest of the way up. She frantically opened the seventh box and rummaged about the sawdust for the safe key. It was not there. She yelled down to Pasha, "Daddy, I need your key!"

Quickly he produced a key from his pocket and threw it up to her.

She smiled, "Not the safe deposit box key, silly. I need your safe key."

"Ah, one minute. It's either in the nightstand or the toilet."

"Maybe check the nightstand first… I hope."

"Yes, love. It was on my nightstand."

"Just out in the open? Dad, I – never mind, we'll talk about it later. Toss it up to me."

When he did, it skittered across the attic floor. She retrieved it easily and took it to the safe. She inserted the key and entered her long code. It clicked open, and she heaved the top-side door toward one side as she had done the night prior. Inside was her phone, and a typed note. "Ha!" she exclaimed as she took the phone and powered it on.

"Is your phone up there?"

"Yeah! They took the bogus bag, too."

"Who are 'they'?"

"Whoever left the knife on the counter with the soldier. They wanted me to know they had broken into the safe as soon as I walked in, I guess. Weird." The downstairs light went out, and immediately after, she heard a dull thud. Lydia's breath became strained, and her face turned pale. She picked up the knife reflexively and looked down through the ladder's opening. She did not see anyone. She crept behind one of the boxes. She feared that if her father had been attacked, calling to him might alert some assailant of her presence. She checked the phone, which had finished powering on, and urgently lowered the volume. She dialed the numbers nine-one-one, and pressed send. As the call connected, she used the light of the phone to read the typed note.

> *Andrew is not what you think. Stop helping him. You have no idea what you're involved in. We're not always in your house, but we're always in your head – count on that. Either we can protect you or you can make us an enemy. It's your choice and yours alone. If you tell Andrew about us, we'll kill you and your father. You're expendable. Andrew's not. Get that through your head. Go ahead and call the police if you have to. Evidence of your involvement in a triple-homicide in Port Gibson, Mississippi will be provided to the authorities if you do. You have no leverage. We don't want anything from you. Play your part from a safe distance. Don't get in his way. Don't help him. Don't ever tell him about this note. Burn it on the stove as soon as you come down from the attic. You watch yourself, now. Sleep tight!*

"Is anyone there?" a voice from her phone broke her trance. "Can you state the nature of your emergency?"

Lydia ended the call without responding. She stared out beyond the boxes into the darkness of the attic, and through the unlit opening to the house below. She hyperventilated for a few moments, paralyzed by utter terror. When she noticed that her hand had begun to shake, she realized that she could move. She crawled around the boxes and toward the ladder. She did not see any movement below. She heard a car accelerate from nothing outside. As the sound obscured into the distance, she exhaled and put her heel on the first rung of the ladder. She faced away from the ladder as she descended, so that she could see the majority of the small, open layout of the house in front of her. Her hands and feet shook with each movement as she clutched her phone, the note, and the knife. When she reached the bottom, the house was still.

"Papa?" she called quietly. Her own fear melted into worry when he did not respond. Fearful that the thud she heard was an attack upon him, and that he had sped away in the trunk of the car she heard, she stood in place and called him again as she looked at the windows and doors. "Daddy?!" her tone escalated rapidly.

She poked her head into the bedroom, but he was not on the bed: the only piece of furniture crammed into the room save a nightstand and small dresser. She checked the family room, but he was not present. She heard a low crackle and saw a dim blue glow on the kitchen countertop, but she could not see the source from around the short wall that divided it from the family room. The glow flickered and mesmerized her as she stood in place. *It must be the window above the sink. Maybe something is outside. What could that be?* She pondered it in dread for a minute before she could move. She took a few steps toward the kitchen. The crackling hum did not waver as the blue glow flickered. Her hand gripped the cell phone so tightly that it began to slip from her warm sweat. She shoved it into her pocket and grasped the knife with both hands. She cautiously advanced. The instinct to protect her father usurped the fear of the unknown crackling glow. Once upon the dividing wall, she took a deep, silent breath, and leapt into the kitchen to attack. No one was there. She dropped the knife and nearly fainted when she saw the source of the blue glow. It was not outside the window, but rather next to the sink. All four burners of the gas stove were at full blast.

Paranoia, fear, and logic had a brief skirmish within her thoughts. She decided to hold the note over the smallest burner until the flame of it reached her fingers. She dropped it onto the stove when it had become engulfed. Even after the flame of the typed note was out, she brushed the burnt fragments back into the stove's flames. She casually dumped the knife back into the drawer in euphoric shock.

She stared at the flames for a few moments until she heard a quiet rustling sound from the other side of the small house. She turned off each of the four stove burners and moved steadily toward his door. She still saw no movement inside the bedroom. Pasha was not on the bed. She inspected more closely. Her heart sank as she saw that his shoes stuck out from between the bed and the wall. She rushed closer, and a frightened tear ran down her face. His body was wedged face-down in the half-meter space between the bed and wall, with his head only centimeters from the nightstand.

"Papa! Pasha!" she screamed, as she flumped onto the bed so that her hands could reach his chest to shake him.

He stirred immediately, and a grumpy look came over him as he rolled within the tight space to face her. "What you want, silly girl?" he grunted.

"Did someone attack you?"

"No, I went to bed."

"No, you didn't – the bed's up here. Did you fall off, or pass out, or something?"

"Bah, too many clothes on the bed. I'm fine down here."

She smacked his shoulder, "You scared me to death! Don't you know someone was in the house?"

"What? Nobody was in the house. You just need some sleep. So do I."

"You slept half the trip," she scolded.

"Yes, but I need a lot of sleep. I'm older than you. Someday you understand." He tugged a bit of the blanked from the bed; the rest of which, the weight of Lydia's elbow prohibited. He rolled back over to face the wall. She adjusted herself to free the blanket and rested it on top of him. "Get some sleep then, silly papa."

She stood and moved with ease toward the doorway. She looked in each direction with confidence and uncertainty. She walked to the kitchen and then toward the front door. She stood at the picture window and looked out into the empty street. Toward nothing at all of the silent, black before her, she muttered, "All-right. Protect me then. That's my choice."

Chapter 22

December 6, 2020

At six in the evening, Lydia left the main tent carrying a rolled, rubber mat. When she got to the stone mausoleum beyond the press platform, she trotted behind it and rolled out the mat onto the ground. She sat down on the rubber. Blue sparks, lacking any rhythm, whispered a sweet chant from the ground all about her. When once they had leapt three meters from the ground at noon, the electrical nuisances did not arc more than a decimeter above the ground near sunset. Most rolled harmlessly in a bluish-pink glow along the continent's endless, smooth surface. Lydia pulled the burqa from her head and withdrew a flask from beneath her cloak. She took a swift pull of young, craft whiskey. She held the sharp liquid in her mouth without any air, so that she could swallow it smoothly. She chased the gulp with a deep inhale, so that she could taste the fire that spread down her throat. She smiled and leaned back on the small, stone wall behind her.

No sound came from within the humble monument.

Lydia stared toward the northern sky. She concentrated on the number nineteen in the turquoise horizon. To her left, orange draped over the land's expanse in front of the sun's descent. The metallic reflection was brighter than her eyes were prepared for, so she turned from it. Her attention was singularly focused on the darkening blue, and the number nineteen. She asked herself, *Am I done?* She held the flask to her lips but did not drink. Her gums swelled. She closed her eyes and cocked her head back. She drew in a mouthful of the sweet, unaged poison and swallowed it carelessly. She closed the flask and stowed it while staring intently at the northeastern horizon. The sunset glowed off the metallic ground even in that direction, where the sky was deep indigo. She marveled at the ground's unnatural contrast against gathering of night above.

Six, she thought. *No, seven. One is unseen; I have seen the other six, I'm certain. I'm not sure who the seventh is. Seven, for sure. We thought there would be five; maybe ten. Why so many? This can't be. How could there have been so many, and yet so many more? What did you get me into?* She glared into the distance and barely made out the red tent. *Poor bastards.*

Four more, a voice, not her own, whispered in her head. Three tomorrow. We'll let the other go. "Enough," she snapped aloud. She sighed and relaxed for a moment. "Got it."

At half-past six, she stood from her spot and rested her hand on the silk-draped, stone shrine. "One for you," she whispered resentfully, as she poured some whiskey onto the ground.

Just after sunrise, the convention unofficially began again. The agenda requested delegates return to their workshop groups by eight, but most were deep in debate by half-past six. Dr. Singh's table was particularly boisterous.

"There will be no duties on automobiles and there will be no duties on fuels," demanded Daniel Stern, an American trade advisor. "Now that East and West are to be bridged again, we can't have trade barriers that show preference to only a select few. It simply won't stand."

"But Stern," argued an Italian professor's translator, "you are in no position to make demands. The European Union calls the shots here. You have no leverage. The United States is bound to the Global Scientific Unity Pact of 1993. You are prohibited from dictating unfair trade demands to the established European labor alliance."

President-elect Dashe took notice of the argument and quietly took a seat.

"Do you hear yourself Dr. Bargnani?" Stern continued. "Unfair? All I'm asking is for free trade. You and Germany get to duty American imports so that your consumers only buy the home-grown goods. But Americans are buying German and Italian cars left and right because they don't see the same duties. The German powerhouses already ganged up and took over our biggest car manufacturer last year and scrapped half the American jobs. How much more do you want? We're doing the right thing, and all I'm asking is that you do the same. If Pacifica becomes a through-lane for trade, Europe loses. End of story. If you don't eliminate those duties, then the States will form trade alliances with China and Japan so quickly that the Euro will lose half its value by the end of the year."

Avery Dashe patted Stern on the back and remained silent.

"Do not pretend that European companies were predatory," said Bargnani's translator. "The Americans failed to bring any electrics to market, and the Germans took advantage. And besides, over forty million Americans have fled to Europe in the past fifteen years anyway. Your West Coast is a shell of what it once was, and your economy will soon follow. Before long, your companies will all be in Europe."

"That's not fair, and it isn't accurate. Americans stopped leaving once the Abysm stopped growing. Many have moved back. Maybe the West Coast is still struggling, but now that the travel lanes to Asia are back, it's only a matter of time before California is among the top economies in the world again. The same goes for Sydney, Beijing, and Tokyo. I think we have all the leverage in the world, with all due respect. It's time for a reset. The European Union can no longer bully the world on account of being furthest from the Abysm! Now you're the furthest from Pacifica, and I think that makes you nervous. It damned-well should."

"What spirited debate!" Tarlok applauded. "But we don't really need to solve all the world's trade agreements at the moment. What we need to do is establish Pacifica's trade parameters. Namely, we must define rail and sea rights. We have sponsorship for VacTrain construction pending safety tests from the ground and atmosphere. That puts us out quite a way in regard to land travel. For now, plan by sea and air alone. What you do with duties and tariffs and VATs and excises, quite frankly, is your own business." He laughed with sincere admiration, "Bravo for the vim, indeed!"

Bargnani's translator asked quietly, "Why have so many left the conference?"

"Out of their minds, you ask me," Stern responded. "This opportunity will never come again. Seems like there's no rhyme or reason to why people are leaving. I mean one minute, we're sitting here talking to them, and the next minute they're fed up?"

"I did not hear any incident. Did you?"

"Certainly not. The ones that left last night were just talking normally. I was near the infrastructure table when it happened. There was no heated debate. They were talking about mining and refineries."

Tarlok contributed, "If you please, let us get back to transportation. We've spent a good while with trade, but the nations will sort that out beyond Pacifica's purview. What is of central importance is air, sea, and land travel. Yesterday we made tremendous progress in the sea category. To recap, now that the Crystalline Curtain has all expanded into the new land on which we debate, there are no real concerns over water travel; save that there's an enormous impediment between the United States and Japan that the poor chaps will need to sail around. Air?"

"Too risky," offered Julia Karsh of France. Her English was excellent, so she did not require a translator. She had been the target of numerous glances from around the tent since the conference began due to her youthful and attractive appearance. She adjusted her stylish glasses and proceeded with confidence. "The air density is better, but the radiation is too much of a problem. This will not do without more testing. We do not know if airplanes can withstand this type of abuse over long periods. Aircraft development has been limited primarily to France, Russia, and Germany since Boeing and Bell moved toward space research and away from commercial flight. In France, we focus on passenger, not cargo. Ever since Lockheed and General Dynamics merged and moved to Munich, their work has been highly confidential. It is presumed they work on military only. They have worked on stealth technologies, which make aircraft lighter. Increased solar shielding would do the opposite. Russians are much the same and they too have not been working on radiation shielding. They are only focused on beating Germany to improved stealth technology. All of these firms have been moving away from the solar radiation of the Abysm, not toward it. They want to sell to the highest bidder. They have not been interested in traveling where there is no profit, like Japan or America, because of the Abysm – now the Pacifica land. Who is to say what Washington has been researching, since many American companies have relocated?"

Julia Karsh sent an inquisitive look toward Dashe. He shrugged and broke his silence, "They don't tell me anything yet. Ask me again in a month or two."

Dashe began to force a standard politician's laugh when he was tapped on the shoulder. "A moment, sir?" his Secret Service lead, Dan Gallo, urged. Dashe stood at once and followed his security men. They led him to a quiet corner. "It's Rushing, sir." Dashe looked confused. "Jack Rushing – he left the conference yesterday? You asked me to look into it."

"Yes of course," he replied. "Has our man discovered any pattern to the people who have left the summit?"

"Not exactly, sir. We've been attempting the number since last night, just as you instructed. No answer."

"And? If nobody answered, then what's the update?"

"Ten minutes ago, our phone rang."

"The encrypted Iridium? I thought that was impossible. I didn't think that phone could even take calls, and now you're suggesting someone conveniently dialed your number?"

"It's highly unlikely, sir. But anything is possible. It's twenty digits, and it has to be connected through a terrestrial switch. It's unlikely anyone hacked the number. We think it's much more likely that the guy you had us calling called us back. We can investigate where the call came from when we get back to the States. Out here, we just don't have the equipment."

"Well you've got my attention. Who was it?"

"Does the name 'Salta' mean anything to you?"

"Rings a few bells. I might have read it in a document or heard it in a CIC House briefing. But I thought Salta was a project or a code name. You're saying he's a person?"

"Not sure, sir. The man on the line didn't identify himself. Could have been this Salta speaking in the third person. We recorded the call, and

I transcribed it here. Whomever it was, he said, 'Salta's present task is complete. Redirecting to the third mine. The young one has awakened and must be stopped. There is no directive. Salta has initiated interpretative protocol."

Dashe smiled. "Anything else?"

"No, sir. So that made sense to you?"

"Not much."

"You grinned, sir?"

"Yeah. I guess I did." Dashe turned and walked deliberately toward a waitress in a burqa, one empty table away. She had been eavesdropping. "I know what you're up to, missy," he sneered.

"Sincere apologies, sir!" the woman replied. She kept her head down in shame and did not make eye contact with him.

"Cut the act. I've been watching you. Setting bottles out in front of the tent. I know what it meant now."

"I don't know what you mean, sir. I have set no bottles out."

"I thought it was weird the first time. Then I figured out that each time people left, you'd set out a number of bottles. Keeping score, or something?"

"I have no idea, sir. I set out no bottles."

"It's over." He motioned for two more Secret Service officers to close in on her. One drew his sidearm and aimed it at her head. "I know you've been collaborating with someone that's been sending delegates out. Some of them were Americans. One of them happens to have been an acquaintance of mine. If you're an American citizen, I could see you hanged for treason. If you're not, well, let's just say I could make you invisible. Start talking."

"I'm terribly sorry for overhearing you," she pleaded. "I meant no harm. I was clearing the table and I heard that strange word, and I was curious. I am so sorry."

"What word? Salta?"

"No," she said reluctantly, "Iridium. My husband," she continued, as she reached into her pocket.

The flanking Secret Service officer yelled, "Gun!" and squeezed his trigger. The gunshot sounded ubiquitous due to the surrounding metal ground. The vast majority of the people within the tent had never been so close to live gunfire, and even those who had were shocked by the sound. It rang both deep and shrill. It echoed relentlessly. Every head snapped upward due to the acoustic abnormality of the setting, and almost no one looked in the direction of the origin of the shot at first. Panic was imminent.

In an instant, her body collapsed to the ground. Blood quickly pooled all around her and a commotion arose among all the attendees. The Secret Service detail held back the onlookers as Dashe reached into the woman's pocket. He withdrew a notepad. It contained several drawings with coordinates. Dashe stood and discretely showed it to his man. "Dan, what do you make of this?" he asked.

"Mining map," officer Gallo hypothesized. "You think people are leaving because of some radiation poisoning?"

"Not sure," Dashe replied. "It could just," he lowered his voice and leaned toward Gallo's ear in response to the crowd that had quickly grown nearby. "It could just mean that her husband was off mining iridium ore somewhere. Wouldn't doubt it if someone at NASA sold the sat records to a few prospectors under the table. Or it could have come from the Russians, Germans, French, Koreans. Hell, anyone with NEO satellites could have mapped out something as obvious as an iridium signature. It's hard to get a seat as a delegate here without being a top professor or politician or scientist, but she's just staff. She could have angled in here somehow to try to pry mining intel or get the latest on what areas the initial construction crews will be avoiding. With all these conversations going on, she could have easily overheard where the cops will be, what areas to avoid, and maybe even what countries will pay the highest bounties for resources."

"Good points, sir. Should I notify your secretary?"

"No. Cover me for a minute." Dashe knelt and patted the dead woman's pockets. They were all empty. He stealthily unveiled the bloody burqa and became uneasy when the woman's lifeless, brown eyes were revealed and seemed to lock with his. He gently closed them with two fingers and replaced the cowl. "Get her out of here. Take this notepad."

"Shall I give it to President McCourty then, sir?"

"Take it outside and burn it. Quietly."

"Sir." Gallo vanished without anyone taking notice.

The tension among the dignitaries and staff was clear. The gunshot had halted the convention. President McCourty and several other leaders had attempted to restore order, but most of the onlookers could not pull their eyes from the scene. A member of the wait staff had just been shot at point-blank range by a member of the American Secret Service. Dashe knew he had to act quickly.

"Ladies and gentlemen," he declared, "there's been an assassination attempt. My life was nearly taken by this woman. Fortunately, my officer here had the presence of mind to diffuse the situation. He will be rewarded for his bravery. Now please, get back to the convention. We have reason to believe that she was working alone. There's no need for panic. Please, take your seats."

Most of the bystanders looked distrustful. Many conversed among themselves about what had just transpired. Nobody had seen a weapon on the girl. They privately questioned her potential means and motive. Others assumed Dashe had been truthful, and thusly scorned her. Regardless of their stances, the crowd dissipated gradually with an elevated sense of apprehensiveness and agitation.

Dashe and his men motioned for the event staff, but they had already arrived with cleaning supplies. The first aid crew followed shortly after with a stretcher. The clean-up was impersonal. The body was placed on the stretcher and carted off in a rapid manner. Before long, Dashe noticed that the security detail around him had tripled.

"Think they bought it, Avery?" McCourty whispered from behind him.

Dashe spun around and feigned composure. "It was the truth. I'm not sure what she was trying to pull, but our man had a beat on it. Thank God."

McCourty stared him down incredulously before responding. "You weren't screened. She was. She was cleaner than you, Avery. She wasn't armed. None of them are. Not even the event staff. Just us. What did she do? Smuggle in the bubonic plague and sneeze it on you?" She did not wait for a response. "I don't know what you're up to, but you need to get it under control. We don't have to be friends, and I don't think anyone here thinks we are. But we need to be civil: you and I. We need to play the part for all the rest of these people here."

Dashe caught her off guard, "What about Rushing?"

"Come again?"

"Rushing. He was one of ours. Took off into the wild blue yonder; headed for that red tent out there. I never heard a chopper or plane take off. What's going on out there, anyway? Why did he leave? Why would any of the fifteen or twenty people leave, for that matter? And why always in bunches?"

"I'm afraid I don't –"

"Yes, you do!" he sneered. "You said it up front. You said that if anyone wanted to leave, they could, and nobody should stop them. You set up that red tent, who even knows why, and then you stopped anyone who tried to ask them any questions as they wandered out to it. Why? Why let them get struck by this electrical nonsense? For that matter, if it's so unsafe out here, why the hell are we here? We could be in Dubai right now, ten thousand kilometers from solar radiation. Why the insane costs to set this up here? And why Rushing? Why him?"

"I don't know. We set rigid rules due to confidentiality, and we enforced those rules. The location was chosen both as a symbolic gesture and for remote security purposes. The remote locale choice made a lot of sense for keeping things safe and private."

"But why? It doesn't make any sense at all. The bloody press is here. Why pretend we're keeping anything secret? Who set up those rules, anyway?"

"Well, our steering committee –"

"Exactly," he interrupted again, "your steering committee. Who's pulling the strings? Why here? Why so remote? If you're vetting everyone right down to the caterers, and you knew you'd need a spooky red tent to let people exile themselves to, then tell my why. Why Rushing, why are we ten thousand kilometers from any sovereign nation's soil, and why are you lying? I can see it in your eyes."

"When you're right, you're right, Dashe. But you know as well as I do that sometimes the answers just aren't for sale. Hang in there, tiger." As she began to turn away, Dashe grabbed her elbow with force. Two Secret Service officers instantly intervened. She smirked. "I'm still the POTUS, Avery. Try not to murder any more caterers before tomorrow morning's sendoff, okay?"

Chapter 23

7:12 PM MST, December 10, 2015

Andrew looked at his dashboard's clock as he approached Devils Tower in northeastern Wyoming. It was twelve-past-eight. He was unsure whether to change it back an hour, so he left it. He snickered under his breath when he saw a Devils Tower sign, "More than one devil? 'Devils' should have an apostrophe, dumbasses." He pulled off the road and onto a gravel trail that was fit for a car.

Something is wrong, he thought. He had wished for ages to visit the unique monument and expected to feel awestruck in its presence. The bizarre formation leapt from the ground out of contiguous trees and rolling red and black hills. The general area was a vast meadow amid the eastern foothills of the Rockies; yet, one absurd protrusion vaulted upward from the otherwise obedient ground as a contextual impossibility. Although the moon and stars lit it plainly, it did not draw him to marvel as he had hoped. *No pain,* he realized. *No clicks – nothing. It was here. I know it was here. This is it. What's changed?*

After driving for a bit off the road, on the flat terrain near the foot of the formation, Andrew stopped the car and turned off the lights. The monument was directly north of him by what appeared to be a few hundred meters. His eyes adjusted quickly to the open sky. Thin clouds, high and sparse, wisped from east to west above him. Even four days after the Abysm had been sealed, all the clouds in the sky meandered faithfully toward it. Andrew wondered if there was enough air in the sky to sustain the seemingly endless exodus of atmosphere into that infant realm.

He got out of the car and approached the four-hundred-meter igneous megalith. He left his car somewhat near the road and hiked empty-handed toward the foot of the monument. In the distance to his left he saw a Ranger station. It appeared to be abandoned. Andrew faintly heard an instrumental version of "America the Beautiful," which was looped through a speaker that was mounted to the building. "That answers that.

Could have parked closer, though," he joked to himself. He was fit to work the hilly terrain. It was not difficult for him to trek around the east face of Devils Tower. The wind he had felt in Rapid City was still present, but his mind was elsewhere. He was concerned over the location of the remaining five coils. He still felt none of the familiar clicks and pain that should have been present.

Once northeast of the Tower, he stopped and relaxed. Someone was near. Andrew focused. *Approaching. Not aware of me. You suspect someone is here, but you don't realize it's me. Who are you?* He closed his eyes and peacefully dropped to his right knee. He placed his left hand on the ground. He listened and sniffed like a nocturnal hunter. *You're not looking for a person. You're looking for food. You don't know that I'm here. You know someone is here. You know about Pastor Bob. He's camped to the north. You set up camp with him and he sent you to get food. You don't know how to hunt.* Andrew opened his eyes and grinned. *You think Bob is an asshole for assuming you know how to hunt.*

Andrew stood and plainly spoke, "Dr. Teague!" He trotted northward but did not see his friend yet. The hills and brush were too obstructive. "Teague. Follow my voice. Yes, it's me. The rabbit is gone." He jogged for a few more seconds, and then slowed to descend a steep path of loose gravel. "You were following a rabbit, but it's gone. You should have taken the snake when you had the chance. Now you'll have to settle for those greens and berries." He kept running. "You know, I'm surprised you're out here. I mean," he laughed as he finally spotted his friend, "It's not that I didn't think you would want to come." As Andrew spoke, Teague looked around confusedly. "I'm just surprised Bob figured out what I was telling him. I wanted to make sure to have a head start up here." Teague was still a hundred meters away, but finally began to approach Andrew.

"Fascinating," Teague remarked as they met face to face. "Were have you been?"

"Oshkosh," Andrew replied with a smile. "It's in Wisconsin."

"That is not what I meant. How did you sneak up on me from such a distance, and yet I could still hear your shouting?"

"Easy! I wasn't shouting. Once I knew it was you, I just spoke into you. Watch this." Andrew ran fifteen meters past where Teague stood and knelt down. "Where'd you go?" He brushed his palm against the wild grass. Within a few seconds a rabbit popped out of a hole and approached him playfully. It jumped into his waiting hand.

"How did you…?" Nantan was not shocked. He was curious, but Andrew could tell from the doctor's demeanor that he was more entertained than startled by the trick.

"I don't know how. I just knew where she was. I let her know that I would not eat her." He turned the rabbit around to double check the gender. "Yep. This is the girl you were after. Still hungry?"

"It's a funny thing, Andrew, how prey becomes far less palatable when you've become acquainted with it. It seems I'd have you betray the poor creature's trust. And out here, I'm not your doctor. I am your friend."

"Suit yourself, Nantan. How was your weekend? Anything exciting happen after we saved the world?" They started walking northward in no hurry.

"A quiet night or two with the wife, as it were. Then your friend called, and we drove out together. It's a funny thing. Ratigan, Havlicek, all of us in the labs – we had been working for so long studying those coils that we never dreamed things would have resolved so quickly. Science is usually slow. We spend weeks, or even months, setting up a single experiment. Once we conduct the experiment, we graph it, and chart it, and trend it, and talk about it. What happened was just impossible. We went out there for readings, and the chain reaction, it just… We expected to spend months interpreting that data. Instead, all the physicists were told to go home, and the meteorologists have taken over the White House and Pentagon."

"Defies logic, doesn't it?" Andrew knowingly concluded. Teague nodded. "As far as the measurements go, though, that's not all that happened out there, Nantan. I think you knew that."

"I didn't know what it was. Most of the others thought they just got lucky and triggered some chain reaction into the vacuum. What was it that you saw? You blacked out for several minutes. Did something happen to you?"

"I didn't know if it was real or if I was dreaming. I actually thought I was dead, at first. Until last night, I had convinced myself it was a dream." Nantan nodded. "It wasn't. There are parts of it that I still definitely don't understand. But when I left my body, I sort of floated. It was weird. I couldn't see or hear, but I was able to feel the presence of others. It's hard to describe, but I know now that I wasn't just dreaming. The best word I could choose to describe it would be," he paused, "detached. From there, it was like the laws of science didn't apply. I could go as fast or slow as I wanted. The Earth took off super-fast, and I had to catch up with it. That was part of the reason I suspected it wasn't a dream. I never would have come up with it on my own. What I realized is that the planet is always moving. Not just rotating, and not just revolving around the sun; I mean our whole solar system and our whole galaxy is hauling ass. When I was detached, you see, I had to catch up to it on my own. I was still, and I wasn't tied to the momentum with which our galaxy moved. It appears still to us now, but believe me, it's moving quickly. And once I figured out, I needed to keep up with it, it took no effort. I probably sound nuts, but I can prove I'm not crazy."

"That is not necessary. I never suspected as much. But you still have not explained what happened. Please, proceed."

"I felt the Abysm. I found the source of it. It was my father. He was there. He died when I was a kid, but he was there."

"His body?"

"No. Maybe, I don't know, but that's not what I found. I found his essence. It was stuck. I could see the atoms or molecules, or whatever you think is the smallest thing you can think of, and I saw my father's essence even smaller than that. Weirdest thing, it was like the other atoms were just tripping over each other, just folding up like something into nothing. Then I nudged him out. I don't know where he went. Maybe he doesn't exist anymore. That's a tough thing."

"What do you mean?"

"Not knowing what comes next. Did I just end my father's very soul? I'm pretty sure that's what I saw in there. He was stuck, and I got him unstuck, like towing a car out of a muddy ditch. He just flickered and vanished away. Is that what happens to us? What do you think?"

"That is not what I think. I don't know what happens, but I don't think we just end. Early on, I was raised to think more about life than death. The old Apache way teaches that there are good spirits and evil spirits: both of which are always listening and watching. The Catholic side of me thinks a lot more about death and what follows. They have created many rules and codes by which we can live and die. They seem very organized, and I do crave structure."

"Your wife is Catholic, then?"

"She is indeed."

"Any kids?"

"Why are we here?"

Andrew stopped, surprised that Nantan broke off from conversation so quickly. "I'm sorry. I didn't realize. You lost three and gave up. You named them?"

Teague looked away from Andrew and started walking again. "We did."

"You lost them too early to know the gender."

"We did."

"You wanted to adopt, but your wife didn't feel the same way. You buried yourself in exercise and work."

Teague did not respond. He began to grow fearful of what Andrew was doing.

"Don't be afraid, friend. I would never let harm come to you."

"Andrew," Nantan struggled, still looking straight ahead, "what have you become?"

"I'm not sure, exactly."

"You spoke into my mind from as far away as a kilometer without effort. You caused a rabbit to obey your hand. You read my most private thoughts as though they were emailed to you. Was this part of what happened at the Abysm? Were you somehow changed when you came back?"

"Actually, against all humanly logic, would you believe that was not what did it?" Andrew laughed, but Nantan was still puzzled. "I mentioned my dad, right? Well before he died, he and some military buddies of his, they found this thing – some sort of doomsday device or whatever. Well they decided that it was too powerful, and it shouldn't exist." Andrew winked, "Because that's their call, right? Before they destroy it, though, they decide that they'll experiment with it. I mean if you have something with tons of power you should probably mess around with it before you try to destroy it. It goes without saying." Andrew made sure to maximize the sarcasm in his tone, and Nantan followed accordingly. "With the machine, they created this message, and rearranged it, and sliced it up into a million pieces. They keep saying the message isn't important, but I'm not so sure. Anyway, they used the machine to somehow charge these little coils." He pulled the two capsules from his pocket. "Here, you're no stranger to these."

"Of course. We've had these for years. You're telling me that your father helped to create them?"

"Well, not so fast. Those came from Oshkosh. There's a dozen more in the glove box of my rental car."

"I see. And how many are there altogether?"

"Sixty-four."

Nantan reflected briefly. "Are you sure you have them all, then?"

"I'm sure I do not have them all."

"Then how do you know how many there are?"

"Bob."

"Bob? I had no idea. We drove all the way here, and he never mentioned…"

"No, doc, I mean there's Bob." Andrew pointed ahead at Bob, who was barely beginning to come into Nantan's view. "We might as well take a break. We'll have to catch him up on the rest of the story."

Andrew greeted Bob with a hug, and the trio headed into a camping tent that Bob and Nantan had assembled that morning. "Have I ever seen you out of church?" Andrew asked. "You look positively ridiculous!" Bob was dressed for boyish adventure in the wilderness. His face was covered with stubble and grime. He wore camouflaged cargo pants and a white tank top. His arms were meager, but his posture indicated a fearless resolve against the elements. A canteen was holstered to the waist of his pants. The skin of his arms was pinkish from the snapping wind. Bob's brown hair was nearly shoulder-length and flapped across his eyes and face as Andrew and Nantan approached. Andrew smiled at the cartoon-like, jaunty attitude with which Bob faced the cold night in the Wyoming hills.

The three men took a few moments to catch up on the key details of their meeting. Teague and Bob accused each other of not having warned one-another of Andrew's recently acquired skills. Both men seemed equally surprised by the development. Andrew caught Bob up on the key points he had discussed with Nantan.

Bob pressed in with more questions. "You didn't start having these feelings until after last Friday, when the government flew you out to the abyss?"

Andrew rebutted, "Actually, no, not even then. In a way, I guess the feelings have always been there, but I've never known what to do with them. But last night in Oshkosh, everything just started to click. It was these last two coils, I think. Gerry told me-"

"Who's Gerry?" Bob interrupted.

"I knew him growing up. Turns out he had been working with my dad to get rid of some doomsday device. He claims he planted something inside my brain when I was a baby that draws me to the coils, or something like that. Years later he dated my mom so that he could keep an eye on my progress."

"That's terrible," Teague consoled, "but it does make some sense. We found that object. We thought it was a tumor at first. Whatever it is, it is highly advanced. It passed our scans as biological. Had we not been specifically testing your visual cortex under such scrutiny, we would surely never have noticed it. This Gerry person and your father were extremely well-connected if they had access to that technology when you were an infant. This is all interesting, but what's changed since last week? We got cut off. If your encounter at the great void did not bring on these odd abilities, then what did?"

"That's what Gerry wouldn't tell me. He was excited for me. He gave me these two coils and confirmed that the five here in Wyoming are the last ones. He was definitely hiding something."

Bob piped up, "But you told me about the coil at Devils Tower quite a while back. Truthfully, when you came to see me last week before service, that's where I thought you were headed. What's changed in the past week?"

"I don't know. Maybe since there are so few left, it's all starting to come together. Maybe these last two he gave me were special? But it was before that. When I first entered the warehouse, everything was fine. But then, I had an intense flash of confusion. It was overwhelming, like all of the coils, all at once. Most of them were familiar to me, but a few were not. But I sensed that the Devils Tower coils were still here, in Wyoming. In an instant, it was gone. But right then, I knew that the things I saw, heard, and felt… they made more sense. When Gerry was talking to me, I could sense what he meant. I knew his intent from the look in his eyes. While I was driving out here, it became even clearer. You guys are going to laugh. I saw a flock of birds out my car window somewhere in South Dakota. They were flying westward, I guess with the new wind, toward the abyss. I looked out at them, and I thought, 'Go south, you silly birds. It's too cold for you up here.' They did. The whole V-shaped family of birds actually turned in unison."

"Well, I'm glad you're on our side," Nantan jested.

"I would tend to agree," Bob added. "What's the plan?"

"I don't know. I thought there was a coil at the top of the Tower, but now I know it's gone. I don't know where it is, and I can't feel it. I'm not getting any flashes or pain. It's just not here."

"You said you felt it in Oshkosh, though?" Nantan asked. "But you knew that it was here? Perhaps it was in Oshkosh but maintained the sense-memory of where it had been previously?"

"Good thought, but I don't think so in this case. I really thought they would still be here. The first was buried in the prairie atop the Tower. That's why I asked you to bring as much climbing equipment as you could."

"It's all in the truck," Bob said.

"I'm afraid it's all for naught. I don't think it's here. Nantan, you don't think if I take some immuno-suppressants now, it would jump-start an episode, do you?"

"No, the medication should have nothing to do with the hallucination itself. While the hallucination is happening, we administered topical drugs to prevent your body from rejecting your brain. The reverse order would have no effect, I'm sure. It's irrelevant though. I did not think to bring you any Tacrolimus."

"Tacro!" Andrew exclaimed. "I couldn't remember what it was called. Wait a minute, though. That's not what he gave me."

Nantan looked perplexed, and watched Andrew produce a pill capsule from his pocket. "Who gave those to you?"

"Gerry. But they're not Tacro! What do you make of this?" He handed the vial to Nantan.

"Cyclosporine derivative – it's comparable to Tacrolimus. They have different compositions but achieve similar results. Who gave this to you? It's extremely hard to refine in North America."

"Gerry."

"I should have known. It seems this Gerry knows much that is hidden. I suppose he has extensive medical background if he surgically implanted that odd device in your head." He peered into the bottle. "These seem small. This must be a very low dose."

Pastor Bob began building a campfire near the tent. He hollered to Andrew, "Anyone care if we're here?"

"I don't think so," Andrew replied.

Bob kicked at the rocks beneath his own feet. He grunted for a while to himself and then closed his eyes and took a deep, relaxing breath.

"What's gotten into you, Bob?" Andrew asked.

Bob answered calmly, "Why are we here, Andrew? I know why you're here, but what about Nantan and me? You called me acting paranoid and cryptic. I called your friend and we rushed right out here. But now you don't even care if anyone knows we're here? Why the secrecy? Help me understand what you need help with. What's changed?"

"Oh, right," Andrew stammered. "Well I called you because Vertree told me that I was in danger. Lydia and I split up, and basically went opposite directions. At the time, I thought I could use your help, because I knew there were coils out here that I wouldn't be able to climb to on my own."

"That much is obvious," Nantan offered, "but why the secrecy? I would have gladly helped you if you had asked. But you must know that since I work for the Pentagon, they always know exactly where I am. They know where we are now."

"Right, that's what I mean," said Pastor Bob. "You risked me not understanding what you were asking, just to keep your plan secret, but from whom?"

"I'm sorry, I guess I'm just used to being paranoid," Andrew reflected. "When I get close to those coils, bad things happen. I suppose I figured that I could trust you guys."

Nantan shook his head, "You've known me for less than two weeks. How in the world can you trust me?"

"I meant," Andrew paused, "that I could trust you not to hurt me. Both of you have strong minds. I don't fully understand why people turn when I'm around those coils, but something tells me that you two can resist that control."

Bob and Nantan looked at each other. Both felt flattered by the remark.

"You just need help climbing?" Bob asked.

"Not exactly," Andrew answered distractedly. "It's gone. I don't know where it is. Something is off. There's no sense climbing Devils Tower at this point."

"How can you be sure? I say let's set up to climb in the morning and see what happens. Maybe you're out of range," to which Nantan shook his head, "or you're just too tired to detect it," to which Andrew shook his head, "or, I don't know. But I came here to climb, and climb is what I plan to do, with or without your message coils. You know how many climbing opportunities there are in Pennsylvania like this bizarre thing? If the coils aren't here, no harm done; we'll clear our heads up there. If they are here, and something tells me they are, then we'll have a great time and see what happens when we reach the top." He gestured to the towering anomaly. "I mean, have you ever seen anything like that in your life? How could you not want to climb it, even if there is no prize?"

"I tend to agree, Andrew," Nantan yawned. "If you are fearful, I empathize. But we have the equipment. Bob is well trained, and I am capable. If you are physically up to it, then I think we can make the trip regardless of intent. We are here. It is here. The coils will call to you sooner or later. There is no rush."

Andrew closed his eyes as he listened to the wind and trees. The fire crackled as it grew. "They were here. They were here. Somebody moved them." Andrew's eyes opened abruptly and darted toward Nantan. "Teague, have you ever heard of Salta?"

"Salta?" Nantan repeated. "I do not believe I have ever heard of that. What does it mean?"

"I don't know. Gerry mentioned it – err – him? He was surprised that I hadn't met Salta when I was with you guys at the Pentagon. I was thinking he was in that weird lab you took me to."

"If Salta is a man, I've never met him. That lab is home to two curious individuals, but they are named Bragi and Juno."

"Who are they, exactly?"

"They both conduct research. They perform odd experiments. I have only met them a handful of times. Vertree could tell you more about them: she is their guardian. And, perhaps they are hers. Why?"

"Gerry seemed to think that Salta worked in a lab like theirs – maybe even the same one?"

"I doubt that very much. I cannot speak for Juno, but as I understand it, Bragi has not left that laboratory in decades. The rumor is that the machines he is connected to keep him alive, but they somehow accelerate his age, in terms of appearance. There are rumors that he can read thoughts."

"And none of that shocks you?"

"No more than your cunning with rabbits. I have seen many odd things. I watched a complete vacuum form in the ocean and air that could not be explained. Then I watched it seal itself decades later, and that also cannot be explained. I study the connectivity of human senses with other things. I am not at all surprised when I see an evolutionary leap such as yours or Bragi's. The situations are different, I'm sure. Somewhere out there, all of this makes sense to someone. It is my place to research and to understand what I can as empirical facts and observations before me. Beyond that, I try not to worry too much about what is and is not possible according to the rules. The rules, so to speak, all have one thing in common: humans wrote them in the past. Anyone that says they completely understand any one science fails to understand science at all. There is no end to understanding."

"I tend to agree, Nantan," Bob chimed in. "I'm not sure about the evolution part, although that's not really all that unfathomable to me. The world is old, so I'm sure creatures have changed along the way. To me, there are always things we won't understand, and that's by design. I believe that science has a place, and that people are here to learn and experience the world. That's no accident. God gives us all the power to observe, each in our different way, and form opinions and decisions on our own. Why else would any of this exist? Discovery is the root of the human existence. That's free will, and it's a powerful freedom. There's a lot here that we can see and feel. Life is beautiful. The world is beautiful. I don't need to understand it to appreciate it. Teague here, all his cronies," he smiled, "can create theories and trend charts and equations until the cows come home. It won't matter. We're not meant to understand everything. I have no problem with folks trying, but me? I'd prefer to climb the hill to see the top. From there I'll look down and feel free. To me, life really is that simple."

"You know, you sound different out here, Bob," Andrew observed.

"What do you mean?"

"At church, you always sound so calm and collected. Out here, you sound so alive."

"The world is exciting. I'll admit. There may be some truth to the observation. Every time I climb, I find a new part of myself. I'm not sure if it's the risk, the exhilaration, or what. It feels good to get out here. But at the same time, I can't wait to get back to what I know."

"I don't know, I think we're bringing out your wild side."

"Andrew, I'm not sure I have a wild side."

"There's a beast in all of us, Bob. And there's a gentle pastor in every beast. We're not all so misaligned, I think."

Nantan cleared his throat and recalled, "Ah, yes. 'Those who find ugly meanings in beautiful things are corrupt without being charming. This is a fault. Those who find beautiful meanings in beautiful things are the cultivated. For these there is hope. They are the elect to whom beautiful things mean only beauty. There is no such thing as a moral or an immoral book. Books are well written, or badly written. That is all.'"

Andrew guessed, "Is that your girl, Sara Teasdale again?"

"Oscar Wilde," Nantan laughed.

"Oh, I just love one of his famous ones," Bob contributed. "What was it? 'A thing is not necessarily true because a man dies for it.' I've always loved that one. People feel that what they fight and die for is always right. I guess the purest of convictions is admirable. But there's only one cause worth dying for, and that's God."

"I'm sure some causes," Andrew countered, "are worthy of sacrifice. I mean, how can you really know which causes are God's and which ones are man's? Before I left for California last week, you told me that yourself."

"I did?"

"Sure! That was half the reason I even went through with it. I smuggled myself into the Pentagon by kidnapping a guy, who later died on me, and posting a note on him with sensitive material. Hell, that's how I met Nantan, here."

Nantan shrugged, "I didn't know how you got there. I'm glad you did, though."

"Anyway, I wouldn't have gone and done all that if I thought it wasn't right. I was ready to die for it. At least I think I was."

"You're right," Bob admitted. "You're right. The crusades we fight are for what we perceive to be the better good. Faith is what drives us forward: faith that the better good is God's hand, which guides us. Thanks for the reminder, Andrew."

The three men ate a combination of food that they had brought and foraged. They fell asleep easily in the tent after significantly lighter conversation.

Chapter 24

5:58 AM MST, December 11, 2015

Andrew awoke before dawn. Nantan and Bob were still asleep. Andrew had been dreaming about head clicks. He cupped the back of his head in the familiar place and smiled mischievously. He felt more complete than ever before. He was oddly aware of the pressure of the atmosphere: how moisture moved and interacted with heat, ground, and cosmic rays in the sky all around him. In silence, he made his way out of the tent and left the others to rest.

The moon was nowhere to be seen, but the stars were bright. He could see clearly in all directions. He moved effortlessly through the hills, around Devils Tower, and past the Ranger Station on the west side. The clicking in his head became painful. The coils were not near, he could tell, but the effects had nonetheless begun. He pulled the pill case from his right pocket and popped it open. With his jaw clinched tightly, he scraped the sides of his tongue against his molars to generate saliva. When he had a mouthful, he poured the capsule out onto his palm. There were only a few pills, so he took them all. He pushed the canister into the left pants pocket, but it was impeded. He realized that the two coils from Gerry were in there. He moved the pill case back to the other pocket and concentrated on the capsules Gerry had given him. They were of no help in locating the new coils of interest.

Andrew was hungry. Animals occasionally stared at him as he passed. They seemed frozen. He did not know whether they were frightened of or impressed with him. He spotted a kestrel which was perched on a low branch. He held out his hand to entreat the bird to approach him. The bird froze. He continued to slowly near the bird, but it did not fly away. When his hand made contact with the bird's breast, it closed its eyes. "You'd just let me eat you?" he joked to the bird. The kestrel tightened its grip on the branch and shivered. Its eyes remained closed. Andrew stroked the bird's neck, "I'll find some berries, little guy."

The bird opened its eyes and relaxed. "Have you seen any black film capsules around here? No? Well, as you were then!" He proceeded around the bird with a bow.

After Andrew had walked a few meters, he saw the same bird trot in front of him. His body was plump: about that of a morning dove. His head was nimble and colorful. His orange breast had black spots. His wing feathers were rusty orange on top and cobalt blue underneath. His beak was powder blue and curved downward. His oversized eyes smiled at the world around him in the early morning. With no effort, his little beak plunged into the ground and whipped up a worm. Andrew shot a confused look when the playful bird tossed it onto the ground again. It hopped a meter ahead and repeated the behavior. On the second attempt, a large beetle was retrieved from under a rock. The bird looked at Andrew and trotted away. Andrew kept hiking and approached a rolling field. The sun began to rise behind him. As it did, the field took on several new shades of green and yellow. He approached a wild growth of plants: none of which looked appetizing. After a few minutes, he saw a patch of tall, grayish bushes covered with remnants of berries. Many more had fallen to the ground, but he spied plenty. He did not know if the berries were edible. He looked around, but no one was nearby. After picking a few bright red berries with tiny yellow spots from the three-meter shrubs, he thumbed them in his palm. The kestrel rejoined him. It landed on the bush and stared Andrew in the face. Without hesitation, the odd creature ate the berries out of Andrew's hand. The colorful little falcon plucked more berries from the bush and tossed each of them back into Andrew's waiting hand. He brushed his blue head gently across Andrew's thumb. "These ones are okay?" The bird squawked playfully and flew away. Andrew looked at the selection in his hand, and back at the bush. He chomped them down in a single bite and began looking for more. He was delighted by the taste of the lightly frosted fruits. After filling his hands, he cupped the belly of his shirt to hold more bounty. He shook a couple of branches over his gathered shirt to coax more berries to fall. He hesitated to eat them until he gave the first mouthful a few minutes. *Just in case those were poisonous,* he thought. *Am I really supposed to trust a bird?*

The berries did not cause any convulsions or urges to vomit. Andrew continued to eat them as he wandered toward the western horizon. He expected mountains to be accessible from Devils Tower, but as he walked, he did not seem to get nearer to the jagged horizon. He could not tell if the mountains in the distance were tens, hundreds, or thousands of kilometers away. Snow began to fall as the hills rolled before him in the distance. When he concentrated, he could see through the blowing snow and clouds. But the landscape ahead did not seem purple, as he had previously envisioned. Apart from the ironic resilience of occasional wheat stalks that swayed freely above the gathering snow, the land was otherwise unremarkable.

He walked for an hour through brush and open fields. His hands greeted plants as he passed them. He felt the soft ferns and wheat caress his fingertips like water. His mind communicated with the plants as he stroked them. *Snow in the air… Wind escaping… Bitterness soon...* The clouds swirled above him in concrete, lifelike patterns. His feet grew heavy. With eyes fixed on the horizon, he trudged through lightly dusted fields. He could tell that his mind was slowing. The last of his berries was long gone, and he began to worry that they were not as nutritious as he had hoped. His feet plodded forth with increasing apathy, but his mind remained fixed on the sky to the west. He kept following his shadow as it danced in the uneven terrain before him. He never looked back at the sun. His stomach turned as he marched. He felt uneasy.

The back of his head finally began to hum. *At last,* he reveled. *No purple mountain in sight, but somehow you are here. Guide me. Send me a creature. Whatever is happening, make me spin to it. Come on, coils, do your terrible magic. Make me teleport with some flinging arcs into the last coils or at least show me where to pee. What? What does that even mean? Sideways went the rainy bird, down the gutter's belt. For no rose… to standardizing project societal super-volcano passively… Blind… Blind… three senses imposters later all locking…*

Andrew realized that his mind was not functioning as intended. *Why do my hands feel split?* He looked down at his hands as he stumbled forward. "Fame was blasted," he muttered drunkenly, "math was grandfathered…" He fell to one knee. "Blessing to the Blind, their birthright is ignorance… Praises be… Praises be!" His mind swirled with euphoric chaos.

"The Blind are what?" a female voice calmly asked.

"The Blind," Andrew answered without looking, "are my children. They need me to plant the buds and the… kelp?" He had answered honestly, but his brain was failing. He did not feel fatigued, but his vision spun loosely. He could not feel his extremities. His head ached. He felt as though he had inhaled spray-paint and bleach for hours. "Damned berries," he cursed at the ground. "Rat-bastard liar-of-a-bird!" He jammed a few fingers in his mouth and attempted to gag himself. The berries were long-since cleared from his stomach, but he made the effort anyway. Nothing came up.

"The Blind," the voice continued, "are not your children, Andrew. They are not ours at all."

Andrew was in a daze. He was not frightened by the statement. He was, however, frightened that he did not know whether the voice was real or imaginary. From his knees he stared at the ground and asked, "Okay, smarty, which one ascends?"

"Very good – now we are in harmony. You ascend, Andrew, and so do I. Do you understand this?"

Andrew guffawed at the snowy ground and drew his face nearer to it. "I don't understand shit. Yesterday birds and rabbits started doing whatever I'm thinking they ought," he stammered. His eyes swayed from blade to blade of grass that bravely poked through the white blanket in his macro vantage. He wanted to puke. He jammed three fingers into his throat with frustrated hatred. He was convinced that he had been poisoned.

"The berries were not poisoned," she taunted. "Don't bother throwing up."

Andrew lifted his head, and his vision did not follow effectively. His equilibrium was completely thrown. In order to support the imbalance caused by his head turning to the left to follow the voice, his fists came to the earth.

He saw a woman: light skin, and about his age. He was not afraid, but he was increasingly aware that he was losing control of his body and mind. He felt dizzy and heavy. "You," he managed with great effort, "Holly?"

The woman smiled. "Holly. You remember. Very good."

"I'm sorry for whatever I did to you. I've never forgotten. That blue pin, I…"

"Another time. You need not apologize. You still do not understand."

"You looking-is different," Andrew slurred badly. "Yours eyes not same ones, I wouldn't even, I think I know I'd see them with the same you?"

"I understand you. Do you understand yourself?"

Andrew shook his head plainly.

"I didn't think so," she proceeded curtly. "You knew me as Holly. The one you knew was me. Holly was nothing. I travel as I require. Sleep."

Andrew did not trust her, but he had almost no control over himself. His head was pounding. His body was practically unresponsive to his finer attempts at movement. He felt dense and toxic. He sensed that she was up to no good, but also that she could be trusted. For the past day, he had been shockingly in-tune with his surroundings, but just before she appeared, he became oddly disconnected again. He felt bereft at the loss of connectivity that he had so recently felt with the animals and plants around him. As she loomed somewhere near to him, his mind felt division between comfort and paranoia.

He wondered if he still had any of Gerry's medicine, in case the last few coils were having some new impact on him. *I've felt different since I saw him,* he thought. *Talking to animals and following birds. Maybe this is all part of it.* He reached into his pocket and tugged at the first plastic shape that his fingers could find. It was a coil. He cast it to the ground and went back into his pocket. He retrieved the other and tossed it as well. He went to the other side and fished around. He pulled the pill capsule out and frantically popped the cap. It was empty.

As he frowned in pained disappointment, the woman he knew as Holly stepped closer to him. With a lifeless gaze, she snatched the pill container from him. She read the label and smiled. Then she discarded it among the bushes. She bent down to pick up both of the message coils.

By then Andrew was lying on his back in a daze. He stared up at the clouds as the grayish sky quickly swept them from east to west. Holly knelt beside Andrew and stroked his hair for a moment. "Sleep," she coaxed.

His eyes remained open while his body relaxed. He watched the clouds but could not move. While once he had felt connected with every bit of life around him, he presently felt no connection to anything at all. The isolation made him sad.

Andrew lay peacefully as she took the coils out of his sight. She meandered through the brush and upward across a hill ahead of where Andrew had been aimlessly heading. Behind the hill was an off-road vehicle. The squatty Class One ATV had green-and-beige camouflage. It had four large tires and a single, long seat. Strapped to the right of the driver's seat of the vehicle was a tool bag. On the other side, a duffle bag was tied down with rope. On the back of the buggy a bulky contraption was strapped upright. Four gas cans were roped to the rear rack around the large machine. Despite its sturdy build, the entire cart sagged a bit due to the weight of the object.

She approached the contraption on the back of the vehicle and flipped a large switch. The switch was on the lower body of a mostly cylindrical frame, next to a small sliding door. Metal tubes outlined the main body of it, like a frame around an over-sized fire extinguisher. The center was a mix of hard metal and ceramic. There were no markings whatsoever on the device. The machine began humming calmly. Nothing lit up. Nothing spun or beeped. After a few seconds, the hum subsided.

Holly opened a small compartment on the side. She carefully pulled the message coils from their black canisters and placed the film material into the opening on the machine. She smiled blankly as she closed the door and waited for it to begin humming again.

In fifteen seconds, the machine was finished. She looked up at the clouds, having felt a few fresh snowflakes. She twisted at the top half of the machine within the metal tubing. The main body came apart at the center. Half sprung upward a few centimeters, and the other half shifted downward. The sudden motion was precisely controlled and did not startle her in the least. Silver liquid floated in a sphere about the size of a baseball, where the two compartments of the machine had divided. She reached toward it and a flame shot out of her finger as if a blowtorch had hit it from point-blank range. She laughed, pulled her hand back out. She retrieved a welding mitt from her tool bag. She pulled the mitt over her scorched fingers, which were still smoldering. She reached back into the contraption and carefully withdrew the floating, liquid-metal sphere. Once her arm was clear, she flipped the switch on the side again and the upper and lower halves of the bulky device promptly clamped shut.

The metal dripped from the ball as she walked. She was not careful with it. By the time she returned to Andrew, her mitt was covered in metal drippings. Enough of the metal had shed in the return trip that it was the size of a golf ball by the time Andrew saw it.

Andrew's mouth was wide open. His eyes were glazed over. His body had turned somewhat in her absence, and his eyes fixated on a canyon ridge in the southern horizon.

She held the metallic ball before his eyes. It crackled as the metal dripped and sparked.

His breath grew shorter and his eyes filled with horror. His mouth pooled with drool. He was completely paralyzed but his mind was able to understand what he saw.

"What is it?" she asked.

He could not speak. *My coils,* he forced into her mind.

Very good, she thought. *And how many are here?*

I don't know. All.

And how do you know?

I am complete.

You are not complete! Even if you are, you won't know what to do.

She controlled her thoughts masterfully in his presence. He could not read her as easily as he had read Gerry, Bob, or Nantan since Gerry offered him the two coils in Oshkosh.

Andrew was fearful.

You read me well, Blind. Do not be afraid, she coaxed his mind. *I will not harm you. I have been watching you for a long time, waiting for this moment. Now I control the moment.*

What moment?

This is the most unusual moment in the history of this world. I do not know what to expect. It is rare that I am permitted to feel the thrill of discovery.

But it's incomplete.

No, it is complete.

There are still five out there.

No, there are not. She held the ball before her face. The last of the metal was dripping down the mitt like candle wax. A tiny, clear globule of plastic remained. She grabbed it with her free hand and then removed the mitt. The globule was the size of a small gem.

There are still five. I can feel them.

No. They are here. I have all sixty-four.

She held the tiny hunk to the back of his head. His pain eased, and then was gone. He still could not move or speak. All of the clicking, buzzing, and grinding sensations that he had ever felt flowed together in a painless harmony. The sensations became music to him. He visually measured the ridge in his range of view. He understood the pattern of the clouds in the sky above the ridge and mapped in real-time the trajectory of each snowflake that would fall toward it. A kilometer at its closest, Andrew felt the presence of every blade of grass on the ridge. He felt the snow fall freely and become the ground. He made eye contact with a mountain goat, nearly two kilometers away and masked by branches. The goat had just eaten but was ready to eat again. Andrew felt the connection between the snow, the goat, the errant wheat, the ground, the gravity, and even the energy which lazily arrived each nanosecond from the sun, to invisibly irradiate everything it touched. The relationships were beginning to form in Andrew's mind between the living and the lifeless. Wherever he focused within his paralytic vantage, he understood the composition and relative nature of each element that touched upon another. Even the wind between himself and the ridge was understood. Invisible as it was, he saw it and comprehended its movement. Devoid of will, the wind had a path.

Where are the last five? he thought with a bit of spite.

She taunted, *I told you. They are here.* She presented the clump of plastic to him once again.

You have them all? You melted them down and destroyed them? Why?

I didn't destroy them. They are all here. I wouldn't stop this for the world. She looked up suddenly. *You were foolish to bring company. You'll kill them both.*

Bob and Nantan had caught up to them. Both were equipped heat-to-toe for climbing. Bob had a few ropes looped at his belt, and Nantan carried a supply of water. Both men had long-spiked climbing shoes fastened to their belts. Although winded, they pressed toward Andrew even more quickly once they saw him on the ground. Holly smiled. Bob and Nantan slowed as they neared the scene.

Andrew was still completely paralyzed. He tried to urge them to leave by planting thoughts in their heads, but he was unsuccessful. Whatever allowed Holly to hear Andrew's thoughts did not seem present within either of his friends. Holly laughed and stepped over Andrew. She folded her arms and smirked. Andrew could not read anything from her.

Bob and Nantan halted their approach and turned to each other. Both looked puzzled. Nantan slowly raised his hand and pawed firmly at Bob's neck. Bob threw an elbow, which landed squarely on Nantan's cheek. Nantan thought it was a joke at first, and then he watched his own left hand return the blow.

Andrew was powerless to stop them. They grappled and fought for position on the open ground twenty meters from Andrew and Holly.

"Why are we doing this?" Nantan pleaded to Bob.

"I've never felt this," Bob retorted. "I'm sorry."

They kicked and swatted at each other frantically, but both maintained confused faces and apologetic demeanors.

"Think of a prayer. Think of a peaceful place. Think of family. Think of anything."

"I am. I'm not controlling myself. It must be her," Bob suggested as he threw another punch. Nantan dodged it.

Bob swung clumsily as Nantan danced about. Nantan landed a few slaps and jabs while Bob exerted himself with larger swings.

"Bob," Nantan asked, "can you feel your legs?"

Bob punched Nantan directly in the nose. "No, I don't think I can."

"Okay, that one really hurt." Nantan wiped his face with one hand and blocked the sunlight with the other as he withdrew toward Andrew. "Let's get closer to the woman. I believe I know what is happening."

"I don't know if I can, Teague." He picked up a branch. At first, he poked Nantan with it. Then he swung it wildly toward Nantan's head. "I'm sorry, I'm losing control." He heaved the branch at Nantan, but as Nantan parried with his left forearm, the branch buckled. Nantan felt a squish on his sleeve. The branch had been soaked. Bob discarded it and engaged once again with his fists.

The pair struggled involuntarily across Andrew's sight and back out of it again. Blood streamed from Nantan's cheek. A couple of bruises were beginning to form on Bob's brow.

"Work with me," Nantan urged. "We have to get closer to Andrew and the woman."

Bob drove into Nantan with his shoulder and knocked him to the ground. "I... I can't stop." He ran and dove toward Nantan on the ground. They continued strangling and pressing violently for position over each other.

Andrew could not see them. He heard them get to their feet eventually. They chased each other about. With his eyes fixed on the ridge, he did his best to listen to the exact location of his friends. He knew where they were, and he heard the ground and foliage crunch with their footfalls. He felt simultaneously close and far from the bizarre spectacle. He tried to read their thoughts. He wanted to plant peaceful suggestions, but he could not. He thought to Holly, *Why in the world are you doing this? I want you to stop.*

She smiled at Andrew, and said plainly, "I'm not doing this, Andrew. You are. You always did. I finally understand it now."

He still could not speak. His body was frozen in the same spell-stopped convulsion that had overtaken him for the past twenty or more minutes. *I never wanted them to attack. I never wanted any of them to attack!*

"Wonderful!" Holly exclaimed. "I've always wondered how it would attract them. Moths to a flame, it would seem!"

Andrew doubted himself. He had been convinced that Holly had started the absurd display, but her comments seemed sincere.

Nantan and Bob maintained their spar. Nantan kept angling closer to Holly, while Bob kept pushing him away. Nantan landed a particularly sturdy blow to Bob's sternum, which sent the latter reeling backward.

You don't understand, Andrew pleaded to her. *I think there's someone else. Someone is nearby. I know that someone is doing this.*

Don't be silly, pet, she silently communicated to him. *You and I are alone here. These two are Blind, and you are not. You will learn.*

Andrew took a moment to consider her odd statement. Then he urged her, *I don't think you understand. It's not me, it's something else. It's not always there. The thing that possesses people – it's not always there! And usually it only makes people attack me. I swear this isn't me. I'm not doing this. You have to help them. Please!*

The smile vanished from Holly's face. She had not considered it. *When you were in the closet, you turned them. I'm sure of it.*

I don't know what you're talking about. People just attack me when I come near the coils for the first time. But Lydia didn't. And I was fine at the Alamo. I've only been attacked a few times, because I've been careful.

Ha! Chicago? You call that careful?

You… You were in Chicago when I got attacked?

Holly shrugged. *Close enough. What's your point?*

I don't think it's me. I don't think it ever was. You were different. You had that blue pin. What was that, anyway?

If you live, I will teach you about it. There is no time for that now, and I don't fully trust you yet. You're no longer Blind; so be it. Doesn't mean you're one of us.

Someone is coming.

No, Andrew, nobody is coming.

I'm telling you – it's them! I don't know who they are, but I can feel them. I can feel more than I could before. They're coming. They're almost here. They're going to wipe us out.

Andrew, calm down. Nobody's coming. You perceive more than you used to. It will take you some time to adapt to that, if you ever even do. You're probably just sensing some rabbits, or bison, or birds. You might even be sensing ants.

I'm telling you, this is different. Maybe they are paralyzing me as well, somehow.

They're not paralyzing you, Andrew.

How do you know? Did you poison me?

No, she said matter-of-factly, *your buddy Gerry took care of that for me.*

But why?

Because you're a slippery little bastard and I needed to make sure you didn't slither out of my—

Holly stopped mid-sentence to dodge a blow from Nantan. It was intended for Bob. The two were still entangled in a brutal melee and talking through it apologetically.

Holly, why? Andrew did not care why. He suspected Gerry had poisoned him ever since he watched Holly inspect the pill container. His question was intended to stall her.

Simple. You trust him. You needed answers. You thought you had everything figured out. I'm not sure how it started happening early, but it did. Fine. I still got to see the—

She stopped abruptly again, but it had nothing to do with the ensuing feud. She fell to her knees and her face twitched. "Not again," she said aloud. She looked into Andrew's eyes as she slumped to the ground, muttering, "Vvv-bbbarrvvvvv-Gbaaaarrr…" Her eyes closed. Just before she drifted away, Andrew interpreted her communication as, *The message is gone, but you have awakened. Bragi was right. I thought it was you, but you were just something else entirely. Find out who this is. Stop them. I'm sorry. I'll find you when I'm able.* "Bvvv-waaaaaahhh," she gurgled, and then collapsed.

Nantan and Bob continued fiercely. Both were exhausted but driven by some unknown force to annihilate one another. Different from past observations, Andrew could understand why they fought each other. He knew two people were approaching. He could not see them, and he still could not move. Bob tripped over Andrew as he backed away from Nantan. For the first time in the past several minutes, Andrew could see them again. Bob's foot rolled Andrew onto his belly with his arms folded beneath him.

Nantan followed over Andrew, and shouted, "Let's try to turn him over. Maybe he can help now that she's collapsed."

"Sure, but I can't control myself. Can you try?"

"Come closer to me. Try to kick me and see if you can flip him over. It's worth a shot."

Bob approached, and as he did, he saw two silhouettes on the ridge in the distance. They were standing still and wearing plain clothes and baseball caps. Bob became incensed. He pulled the crampon from his belt and rushed Nantan, who was standing on the other side of Andrew. Bob tripped over Andrew, looked at the ground, and led forward with his climbing hook. Nantan attempted to catch Bob as he dove, but Bob recovered and plunged the crampon's spike into Nantan's neck. Blood gushed freely, and Nantan applied pressure to it with both hands. Bob saw it and was overwhelmed with guilt. He pulled a length of climbing rope from his belt and mindlessly looped it around his own neck. He sat on the ground and wrapped the other end of it around his feet. He inched over to a steep slope nearby that led to a creek about fifty meters away. He tightened and tightened until the rope tugged his neck toward his knees and forced his legs to bend forward by more than thirty degrees. His neck was already red. With a jerk, he threw his weight to one side, which caused him to slide down the ravine on his gut. He only made it a few meters before the brush snagged him to a stop. The flip had straightened him out, though, and the noose tightened around his neck as his feet extended. For a few seconds he tugged at the rope around his neck with his hands, but he soon blacked out.

Andrew heard the commotion but did not know what had happened to either of them. He sensed that they were both unconscious. He hoped that they were still alive, but he had no way of knowing.

Chapter 25

8:53 AM MST, December 11, 2015

The cloudy sky darkened as the two strangers approached. The eerie man and woman walked right past Pastor Bob without acknowledging his presence. *God, give me strength,* he prayed, as he heard them mumbling something just out of earshot. He had rope around his legs and neck. He remembered haphazardly tying it in that manner against his will. He held one hand in front of his face to ensure he had control of it. He snapped his fingers and patted his cheek. He giggled to himself once he had confirmed he was back in command of his actions.

Bob was conflicted. For the past several minutes, he had lost control of his own willpower to the point of potentially killing a man. Then, despite his resistance, he attempted to kill himself. *Am I losing my mind?* Bob wondered. *Did Andrew do this?* He knew that Andrew was a kind person, and that the two had grown to trust one another over the years. He was familiar with some of Andrew's secrets; or at least that some skeletons existed. But his judgment was that Andrew was earnest and decent. The strange woman that had loomed over Andrew when he and Nantan arrived was knocked out by some unknown force. Bob presumed that either Andrew or the two newcomers had something to do with it. *But there's no denying that Andrew is tangled up with these people. Even if he has gone astray with whatever this voodoo is, I have to help him. I'm afraid, God. Tell me what to do.*

The clouds fell from the atmosphere and were nearer to him. He had never seen such a thing. *That's different,* he thought. An instant of panic was overcome by trust. *Whatever this is, Lord, guide my hands to do your will. I am yours. I give myself to you freely.*

The sky bent downward, and the snow began to pour. He felt a cold gust among the sudden precipitation.

Soldier of God, he heard a woman's voice all around him, and yet within his head. *Protect your flock. Servant of God, you must act quickly.*

Bob looked around. He was exhilarated. *Proof of God's will on Earth!* He removed the remainder of the rope from his neck and threw it to the ground. He could not see Andrew and the strangers, but he heard a struggle. He stealthily retreated behind the hill and began looking for a weapon.

A series of bushes cloaked him from the conflict above. Within the brush, he was able to locate a boulder approximately a decimeter in diameter. He hoisted it and carried it, with both hands, behind his head.

The strange man descended from the plateau to where Bob had previously been lying. He walked past Bob, as Bob lurked behind a bush. He saw the rope on the ground, and yelled, "Shit!"

Bob took the opportunity and rushed him from behind with the boulder. With a single blow he caved in the back of the man's skull. Bob grunted in triumph like a primate for a moment, and then grew remorseful. It had all happened so quickly that he did not have time to process what was happening. His faith had momentarily been superseded by the instinct to survive. He knelt down beside the man and stroked his face. "What have I done?" he pleaded. "No man deserves to die this way."

After a few seconds, steam rose from the wound on the top of the man's skull. His mouth opened, and his head rolled slightly to meet Bob's eyes. "Bbbbvwaaaaaaaa…" he gurgled. He smiled maniacally as blood pooled in the back of his throat.

The twisted rattle of death did not assuage Bob's guilt. He had robbed the stranger of the most basic right: the right to feel. He had killed. He had murdered. He stewed in contemplation at his vile deed.

Hear me, Soldier of God, the voice returned. *This man was an abomination. This was not a man of God's creation. Go, now. Protect your flock.*

Bob picked up his boulder again. One side of it was splattered with blood. He shifted it in his hands to a dry side and gripped it tightly. He crept quietly up the hill and paused. He saw Andrew and his original captor on the ground. The strange new woman with the baseball cap was lying dead on the ground next to Andrew and Holly. Her throat had been cut. Nantan knelt above Andrew with both arms in the air and threatened to strike. As Bob had experienced first-hand before, he could tell that Nantan was not himself. Nantan's face conveyed uncontrollable fear and guilt, but his body seemed rigidly poised: almost stopped in time. Bob surmised that if Andrew was indeed paralyzed, such a thrust would kill him instantly. He did not hesitate. He sprinted up the hill and launched the boulder toward Nantan.

When the great rock hit, Nantan's shoulder split apart like chunks of frozen meat. Bob was immediately stunned at the result of his throw. He had never seen anything quite like it. His eyes questioned reality as he scanned the bloody aftermath. Dozens of frozen lumps of flesh and cloth that had broken cleanly from Nantan's body were strewn about the snow. He cowered for a moment, and then regained his courage. He steadily approached Andrew and placed his hands upon his shoulders. "Andrew, can you hear me?" Bob shook him as he cried. "Andrew!"

Bob heard Andrew's voice in his head, *Take her and head west. Her vehicle is up the hill. Help her. Do whatever she needs. Leave us. Go quickly!* He watched as he heard the words, but Andrew's mouth did not move, and his eyes stayed closed.

Birds began circling above. Many were out of their element, having missed the geological queues to fly south. They were all quite hungry.

Bob did as he was told. He propped up the woman first and saw the plastic clump surrounded by a jagged disc of shiny metal on the ground where she had been. He reached down and took the plastic piece, but to his surprise, the metal was light and fluid. It followed the plastic like a trail of goo. It was all hot to the touch, so he dropped it onto the ground. When he did, all the liquefied metal that had dripped away began approaching it. It was as though each drop was magnetically drawn to the plastic. He took the welder's mitt from the Holly's side and put it on. The metal was gathering around the plastic piece and had formed a perfectly fluid sphere. It hovered within millimeters of his glove without touching it. It obeyed his movements. He smiled and marveled for a moment, but soon realized he needed to move on. He swooped the ball down toward another globule of the liquid metal, and it jumped up to rejoin the ball. Bob looked up the hill and saw a tiny trail of such metal globules. They glimmered in the snow as streaks of sunlight began to break through the clouds to the south. He set the unusual ball down on the ground. He picked Holly up as Andrew had instructed and threw her over his shoulder. Then he nudged the ball toward the next metal globule with his foot. He kicked it along a few more times, until the would-be magnetism of the ball and the globules coaxed the ball to move on its own. The ball picked up momentum as it rolled up the hill, absorbing new blobs of its former being which had dripped off when she carried it down toward Andrew. The snow melted before and as the metal accumulated around it, which left a clean trail for Bob to ascend the terrain.

When he got to the buggy, he unloaded the woman onto the seat. He checked her for a pulse, and easily found it. He noticed a peculiar burn mark through a torn section of shirt at her waist. He was careful not to agitate it as he leaned her on the seat.

The ball, the female voice spoke to him.

"Yes?" Bob took a moment to process. "Oh, right, the ball?"

Into the machine.

Bob had left the mitt back near Andrew. He thought about going back, but he felt an intense sense of urgency. He looked at the machine strapped to the back of the buggy. It was open in the middle. "Seems fairly obvious," he muttered to himself. He poked the ball on the ground. It had accumulated enough metal along the way to be the size of a baseball. The ball did not feel too hot to the touch. He picked it up with both hands. It felt like water that kept its general form. As parts of it bent and squished, they swayed and balanced back into place with little delay. He squeezed with his fingers and some of the metal passed through his skin, and then back out again, to reform with the ball. "Spectacular!" He held the ball near the machine, and it floated into the center. The metal ball spun slowly on its own once it arrived in its resting place. Bob flipped the switch on the side of the machine, and the upper and lower halves of the large, inner drum came together to conceal the ball within. It closed with a thud.

After emptying one of the gas cans into the tank, Bob mounted the seat of the ATV in front of her. The key was in the ignition. He had never driven such a vehicle before, but his hands worked the clutch and throttle as if he had done it a hundred times.

He headed southwest, easily managing the rocky and grassy terrain. Within minutes, he connected with a gravel road that meandered westward.

Barn, her voice said.

Sure enough, Bob spotted a huge, light blue barn ahead. When he pulled into it, he saw a large tow truck. It had been prepped with spare fuel tanks and a set of gigantic snow tires. On a trailer in-tow sat the body of a large glider. The slender wings were folded back at their midpoints for transport, but they still protruded by seven meters on each side of the truck.

"What am I supposed to do with this?" he muttered as he stopped the ATV.

Load the machine into the second cockpit, the voice answered.

Bob dismounted and approached the machine at the rear. His hands itched, and were bright red. They were frigid from the cold ride, and he assumed they must have been sunburned as well. He undid the straps that held the machine in place and carefully lifted it by the framing bars. It was very heavy and hot to the touch. He eased it to the ground and walked it to the truck by pivoting it back and forth along the bottom frame. When he got it to the truck, he hoisted it up and carefully heaved it over the glider's fuselage and into the rear cockpit. "Now what?"

Rainier.

"Are you coming?"

I am with you.

"But I mean, the body in the ATV, I assume that's you, and you're talking in my head somehow?"

I am trapped for the moment.

"So, she's not you?"

She served her purpose. I am not she.

"Then who is she?"

Her name was Beverly.

"Should I bury her? Do we have time for that? Are you not Beverly, I take it?"

I am Juno. There is no time to bury her.

"And how are you in my head?"

That is not your concern. You must drive. There is little time.

Bob found a blanket in the barn and placed it over Beverly's body respectfully. He backed the truck out of the barn. As he drove, he did not ask many more questions. The reckless race into Washington took over fourteen hours. He drove however fast the secured glider would allow him. Most of the towns were deserted. There were no police along the way. He took I-90 through the Rockies and stopped only once to fill the tank from the spare drums that she had pre-loaded. His hands progressively worsened. His palms had turned grayish-red and his forearms throbbed and burned. He felt agitated and paranoid. His throat felt dry.

"What's wrong with me?" he asked, near sunset. "My hands are numb."

The voice answered faintly, *Drive, Soldier of God. You are running out of time. It must be destroyed.*

Bob was determined. His mind shifted between fears of death and bargains for life. Mostly, he prayed silently to himself when those thoughts crept in. When he prayed, he was calmed by an odd mechanical sequence in his mind. *Red switch. Knob up. Twelve o'clock. Lever up. Switch up, switch up, switch up. Release. Lever down. Stick in. Red switch. Knob up. Twelve o'clock. Lever up. Switch up, switch up, switch up. Release. Lever down. Stick in. Red switch. Knob up. Twelve o'clock. Lever up. Switch up, switch up, switch up. Release. Lever down. Stick in.* The process repeated itself for hours in his head.

By the time he reached the Washington border, his hands were maroon and pewter. The color faded a bit at the wrists, but patterns of it carried up his arms and into his neck. He checked the rear-view from time to time and noted that his face was red. Gray streaks had made their way into his neck. He had a hard time breathing.

He drove on through Washington, connected with a few smaller roads, and worked his way around and up Rainier. The trails around the great mountain allowed for his vehicle to ascend nearly two-thirds. He could vaguely see jagged outcroppings of Crystalline Curtain far to the west, but he could not tell if they were above the land or all the way out to sea.

"Out there?" he asked. She did not answer. "Am I going to die from this poison either way?" Silence.

The truck was equipped for further ascent, and Bob was no stranger to mountainous terrain. He changed the road tires out with the oversized snow tires, and then loaded spiky tire chains from the floor of the cab onto them. He drove the truck off the paved trail and onto an ice flow. He tried to avoid snow, in case of false ground. He slowly proceeded up the west face as far as he could. He angled the truck so that he could ease the glider out onto a flatter section of snowy ice below St. Andrews Rock. He looked back and could not believe how high the truck had made it. He looked to the north and saw Seattle and Tacoma: both powerless and virtually abandoned. The wind blew sharply from east to west. It blew directly toward the Abysm.

The Curtain was not what he expected. It was shorter. It seemed thinner to him than he anticipated. He could see small parts of it from Rainier, but he could not see the ocean. He had assumed that the Abysm had not breached much of the country, but his eyes told him differently. "Hairline cracks," he told himself. He scanned the horizon and found the closest wall of crystal. He judged that it was at least a few hundred kilometers across. "You sure I can make that from here?" he asked.

The wind was all he heard. The temperature was dropping. It was after one in the morning. He walked to each wing of the glider and unbolted the hinge restraints. The wingtips extended to fifteen meters apiece. "Just roll it down the hill?" He climbed into the cockpit. Most of the instrument and ignition labels were in German. Without instruction, though, he knew what to do. He proceeded through an ignition sequence, step by step, as though he had performed them before. *Red switch. Knob up.* An engine started behind him, and the glider pivoted a couple of degrees.

Twelve o'clock. Lever up. Switch up, switch up, switch up. He took the stick and began his takeoff. *Release. Lever down. Stick in.* He had to make several compensations due to the wind, but he took off without issue. The craft's engine allowed him to pick up altitude for quite a while. He burned the fuel ascending to a point above Rainier's peak, which was soon far behind him. The glider soared across the black sky.

Before he reached the coast, his height had begun to decay. He saw the water, and a few small formations of crystal, but from that position he could tell that the main Abysm was much further out to sea than he had judged from the mountainside. He nursed the stick in order to maintain altitude. He banked slightly to the left when he saw a thicker expanse of crystalline material in the ocean. Beyond it was darkness.

He floated through the sky toward the barrier that held the waters of the ocean from tumbling into the great pit. He flew over countless crystal formations that had darted up from the ground the previous week when the Abysm had been sealed. Bob had seen and heard accounts on the news of the formations, but he had underestimated them. The Crystalline Curtain extended a kilometer or more into the sky above the sea, and covered the horizon to the west and south, as far as Bob could see. His visibility of the ocean was good. To the north, there was not much crystal at all.

His altitude concerned him. He knew that the goal was to glide over the Curtain, so that the machine Juno wanted him to destroy could be pushed out of the craft and into the pit. But he did not know if he had enough speed and height to get over it. It was still some distance away. Bob tried reengaging the engines, so that he could climb. He tapped the empty fuel gauge, hoping it was not as low as it read. The engine tried to sputter, but it died immediately. Bob tightened the flaps and banked left, toward the nearest expanse of the Curtain. He picked up some wind but lost a bit more altitude.

Bob's glider rapidly approached the ultra-dense wall that held the ocean at bay. As it came into clearer view, he noted that the top was not smooth. It had many jagged and chaotic protrusions.

He was level with the top, and steadily falling. He judged that he would either smack into the wall, or that the razor-sharp formations that darted straight upward like antennae from the top of the wall would shred his craft to bits. He neared the wall and braced for impact.

Fifty meters shy, a massive, invisible wind current blew the glider off its trajectory. A gust from beneath blew the glider straight upward; the force of which nearly knocked Bob unconscious. He managed to look down, out the left side of the cockpit. He saw, from the angle directly above for the first time, that the Crystalline Curtain bent inward toward the sea as it climbed into the sky. News images had always shown it to be completely perpendicular, having been photographed from a safe distance. *The shape of it makes no sense,* Bob observed, *because if the Abysm had expanded outward from the Earth's core, as experts explained, then why would it curve inward just above the ocean?* Bob's craft shot safely over the wall at a forty-five-degree upward angle, with a hundred meters of clearance. Bob unbuckled himself and twisted around to see if he could handle the machine. He knew that he could reach it with the canopy open. He saw an emergency release. "I've got the altitude because of that late gust," he said to himself. "Who says this has to be a one-way trip?"

Then he saw his reflection in the canopy. His face was turning gray. Although he had not felt it, blood was streaming down from his nose and onto his neck. He opened his mouth and saw in the canopy's reflection that his tongue was gray as well. There was a streak of blood on his forehead. He brushed his hand over his hair to see where he may have been cut. The hair came out in his hand. Bob sank back into his seat and banked directly toward the center of the Abysm. "All in," he declared. He began chanting a prayer, expecting to be ripped apart, or to crash into a wall. Visibility below and ahead of him was next to nothing once he had crossed over the wall. The blanket of stars above him provided some light into the cockpit, but he could see nothing around the glider in any direction before long. There were no surfaces off which the light from the stars could reflect, other than the glider itself. Bob's heart rate increased as the altimeter softly dipped below zero. He kept the stick true and leveraged the calm air of the former vacuum to go as far as he could. The altimeter continued to spin backwards, one kilometer after another. Bob repeated his favorite prayer a few times, expecting to die at any moment. He moved on to a second prayer, a third one, and a fourth as he counted the backward loops of the steady altimeter. After he had counted five hundred kilometers, he started singing Pearl Jam songs. He made it through what he knew of the *Ten* album. When his lungs and voice became too weak, he started muttering campfire songs. For a while he hummed television theme songs, but those proved too short to pass the time very well.

His glider made it for over five hours. He had stopped tracking the altimeter around a thousand kilometers, because there was no light whatsoever. He was sleeping peacefully when his leg nudged the stick off course. The glider finally circled back and crashed into the ultra-dense, crystalline wall of the Abysm, approximately two thousand kilometers west of San Francisco, and nineteen-hundred kilometers directly below sea level. Bob was killed instantly by the impact. Pieces of glider slid down the wall with Juno's machine, along with the condensed plastic chunk that remained of Andrew's sixty-four message coils. They plummeted in a veritable free-fall until the crushing density near the outer core melted them into an innocent streak of nothingness on the side of the silent, crystal wall.

Chapter 26

8:53 AM MST, December 11, 2015

The cloudy sky darkened as the two strangers approached. Andrew felt their presence. He did not recognize either one of their identities from that vague sense, but he could tell their distances and demeanors. Still paralyzed, his nose faced the ground. Nantan was bleeding somewhere nearby, but Andrew could not help him. He had no idea what had happened to Pastor Bob. Andrew could not even speak. He tried, but he felt nothing in his throat.

"There she is," a gruff man called. Andrew did not recognize his voice.

"She's out," a woman's voice added. "Check the other ones first."

"Yeah." The man approached Nantan first. He knelt down and inspected him but did not touch him. "This one's dead, or close to it. Won't make it."

"Same with this one," the woman said. "Rope done him in. He ain't movin'."

Andrew was at a loss to place them. The woman had an authentically rural accent. The man was shrill, but unremarkable. Neither sounded remotely familiar. While he could detect their presence, as he had the goat and the blades of grass on the ridge, he could feel nothing more. With Nantan, Bob, and even Holly, he sensed their essences. He knew who they were based on the feelings they exuded. The two strangers that had watched from a distance were blank to him.

The man rolled Andrew over. He was still paralyzed. The man checked Andrew's pulse at the neck. "Not getting anything here. You want to double check?"

Andrew saw them for the first time. He saw dull blue in their eyes. He had seen that pale blue hue in imposters before. Andrew had seen it in Wilmer Garciaparra's eyes in the Pittsburgh amusement park. More recently, Andrew had seen it in Chicago when he was pursued relentlessly after retrieving a few coils. In the past week, Andrew saw it in the Pentagon briefing room as well as on the beach of Point Loma at the mouth of the abyss, when the marines approached him with eleven message coils. Coils had always been present or involved when he encountered those possessing that unmistakable blue, but the hue was not present for every coil. In fact, it was not present for most. Andrew had always been able to evade them. Frozen by some venom amid the desolate toes of the Rockies, he could devise no plan for evasion.

He began to piece together the commonalities of the previous encounters. He could find little connection other than the coils. *Pittsburgh was the first,* he thought. *Or was it Sam? Could he have been one too, and I just didn't see it? There was Holly's pin, with Ms. Federal and Candace, but they didn't have that same glow. Chicago? Port Gibson? I don't get it. They can't be following me. There's no way they tailed me all the way here. Were they following me, or her?*

The woman came over and knelt down beside Andrew as well. She checked his pulse in a similar manner. "No pulse, but I don't see no wounds. We didn't do him. Think the lady did him 'fore we got here?"

"I doubt it. Something seems odd about him."

"It's his eyes; just close his eyes. Ain't nothin' more unnerving than a stiff with its eyes wide open staring at-cha." The woman closed Andrew's eyes. "That's better. Let's get the prize. If that's who I think it is, today will be a real good day."

"It is. I know it's her. I've got a strong feeling about this." The man pulled a small electronic device from his pocket. The device beeped as he powered it on. Two antennae slowly extended from the sides and eventually pointed toward one another at the top of the device. When they nearly touched, electricity arced back and forth with a magenta glow. Andrew tried to get a better look, but his eyes could not move.

The man aimed the device at Holly's neck and applied electricity to it over the course of five seconds. The steady shock did not move her. The man waited for the screen on the device to display some sort of reading. When it did, he smiled. "Still got her. It's Juno, alright. She's stuck, just like you said."

"You mean we didn't kill her? She actually made it?"

"That's what I'm saying. She's still here."

"And you're sure it's her?"

"I'm sure. What now?"

"Hell, we never made it this far since Attis. I guess we take her to The Farm and check her out. How do we know she ain't coming back?"

"Look at her. She's catatonic. I've never seen one this docile before without being dead, or just jumping into someone else."

"You're right." Her voice became giddy. "Dammit I think you're right. Good thinkin' taking those others out first. This could finally be our break. Call it in."

The man pulled an older cell phone out of his pocket and flipped it open. "No signal."

The woman grunted, "Our luck. We'll take her back to the truck. Call it in from I-90. I'll drive her. Let's get her all nice and tied up first, just in case. Check her for pins."

As the man began to pat her down, blood sprayed down from behind him and onto Holly. Nantan had stabbed cleanly into the woman's throat with the blade behind her trachea, pointing outward toward the front of her neck. He sliced cleanly through the trachea with a second thrust. Having fully exerted himself, he dropped his hunting knife and collapsed next to Andrew. During the ambush, the gash in his neck had opened again, so he gripped it with both hands.

The man spun around. He was cautious and cowered at first. He was not sure whether Andrew or Nantan had struck the blow until he turned around and saw that Nantan was fully exerted and stumbling backward toward the ground near Andrew. The man pulled the metal device back out of his pocket and turned it on. He giggled while he fidgeted with some settings as it initialized. He pointed it at Nantan, who then moved his hands away from his neck. Unable to control himself, Nantan picked his knife up off the ground. He knelt beside Andrew and raised the knife with both hands pointing downward toward Andrew's chest.

Andrew's breath became shorter. His eyes were still closed but he knew where Nantan and the strange man were. He focused his will toward the man. Within a few seconds, Nantan dropped the knife. It nicked Andrew's shoulder. Andrew felt it hit and thought that the paralysis might have begun to fade. He focused his energy on trying to raise his arm, be he could not. He could not even move his eyelids.

Nantan was paused above him, panting and grunting. Nantan looked down at Andrew. His eyes revealed confusion and remorse. Andrew knew that Nantan had no control of his body.

The man ran off toward Bob.

Nantan locked his eyes on Andrew and fumbled around for the knife. Eventually his hands found it and gripped it clumsily.

Fight it, Nantan, Andrew attempted to project into Teague's mind. *Fight it! You don't have to do this. Put it down and walk away. Just let go.* With his eyes closed, he perceived much more than he had when they were open. He connected distances, times, and densities with the life around him. He detected turmoil in the atmosphere around Nantan: the energy about him manifested like an enraged barbarian unable to discern friend from foe. Nantan was fearful, but otherwise thoughtless. All Andrew could gather from him was survival instinct and panic.

Andrew's mind progressed with a new form of thinking. He had not understood it in the car as he watched the clouds; nor, when he stared at the ridge. His thoughts became mathematically innovative. Configurations appeared in the matter and energies before him which seemed negotiable. Things around him that had once been observations of fact seemed more like minor variables on an infinite scale. Chaotic and overwhelming at first, he simplified his perception patterns to focus only on his immediate surroundings. He realized that he had unknowingly done so early that morning, when he had inadvertently communed with the playful kestrel.

As Andrew had experienced by blind instinct a week prior, inside the great Abysm, he slowed his perception of time. Bizarre occurrences from his coil collections were starting to come into focus. He was changing.

He concentrated on the ground around him. He felt that he understood its composition, but he did not know how to perform the action he had in mind. He attempted to draw upon density from beneath the ground. Instead of a quake, a breeze darted down from the swirling clouds above and dissipated on the snowy grass where he lay.

Nantan moved before him in slow motion. He did not react to the breeze, and Andrew doubted that he even noticed anything unusual about it. Andrew knew that he needed to act quickly, but for the time being Nantan seemed too conflicted to be an immediate threat. Andrew feared that Nantan's disposition could change at any instant for better or for worse.

He tried again. The clouds sank, and the air grew colder. Lightning crashed all around and snow began to dump out of the skies. The clouds drew nearer to the ground and violently emptied their contents as they fell. Andrew knew from the lightning that what he was doing was too much of a shock to the natural course of the atmosphere. He eased the descent. With the will of his mind, he brought the clouds down over the course of fifteen seconds and intensified the snow.

"Shit!" the man shouted from outside of Andrew's sight.

Bob! Andrew realized. *Bob must have gotten away after all. I might still have time.* He focused on Nantan again. *Hang in there, bud. Think about your wife. Think about one of your prayers. I'll try to help you. I think I understand what's happening.* Nantan still loomed with the knife poised to strike. Tears mixed with snow as he forced himself not to stab Andrew with every shred of his willpower. Andrew could interpret his demeanor, through closed eyes, based on the molecular reconstruction his mind had effortlessly conjectured of Nantan. More than just Nantan's presence, Andrew's brain had mapped out in real-time the air and moisture around his friend as it interacted with him. He witnessed the matter and energy exchanges of the moisture to the air; the air to Nantan's nose; the heat of Nantan's body with the air inside it; the change in composition to a different form of air; the release from Nantan's nose; the ultimate diffusion into the shadowy, morning air.

Andrew relaxed his mind and slowed his perception again. As soft snowflakes approached his face, he identified them one by one. A few thousand in a mere second turned to ice and plinked to the ground within ten meters of him: a test. They silently rolled in the snow. *Too cold,* he thought. Again, he concentrated on the snow, and pulled the clouds closer to the ground. The moisture intensified around Nantan. The air grew colder. Lightning lit the skies all around them: more frequently with each passing second. In the distance a tree cracked and caught fire when lightning rifled through its bough.

Sunshine began to stab through the clouds in the southern horizon. The symbolism gave Andrew hope. He tried once again to bring the moisture nearer to Nantan, and to freeze it. He made the condensation denser and heavier. Nantan was confused, but not dissuaded. The fury returned to his eyes, and for a split second, Andrew saw a glimmer of dull blue within them. Andrew gathered the moisture from the air and suspended it all around Nantan. It formed and froze and condensed around him. *Hang in there,* Andrew urged him. *It's working!*

The moisture around Nantan's hands and face began to solidify. It hardened onto his skin a few orchestrated molecules at a time. Nantan's skin became dense with the frozen cohesion. Andrew's perception further slowed. He intensified the density within the water molecules as they penetrated Nantan's skin and clothes. *Almost there.* Nantan's legs and hands began to shiver. His teeth started to chatter. The movements seemed cartoonish and slowed to Andrew, who saw each motion as though they were seconds or minutes apart.

Nantan's color faded as his skin hardened and froze. The shivering continued until his muscle tissue stiffened. Andrew labored to keep the water molecules from getting too cold. Instead he condensed them without slowing their internal motion. He had no idea how he could do it, but he understood the nature of the particles and ordered them to behave accordingly.

He was too late. Something went wrong. Bob launched a six-kilogram boulder from three meters away, directly at Nantan's head. The boulder already had blood on it as it whizzed over Andrew. Andrew attempted to slow the object, but he was too late. When the rock hit Nantan in the outer chest, chunks of his frozen left shoulder shattered off. Clumps of blood oozed out as they hit the ground. Blood slowly eschewed from his neck. Nantan sat petrified as he bled out.

Andrew concentrated. He knew that Bob was not a threat. Bob was not possessed. *He thought Nantan was about to kill me,* Andrew concluded internally. He had no idea how long Nantan had been stalled there when he rushed onto the scene. He felt tremendous guilt, despite the fact that he was convinced he had protected Andrew.

Bob recoiled in confused terror when Nantan's shoulder came apart in icy chunks. He saw that Andrew's eyes were closed, and that he was still motionless. He rushed to Nantan but could not do anything to help him. Nantan was bleeding out, and Bob had no idea how to stop the bleeding because most of Nantan's flesh had fused with dense frigidity. He had never seen anything quite like it. Parts of the exposed flesh looked like frozen meat.

"Andrew, can you hear me?" Bob shook him as he cried. "Andrew!"

Andrew spoke into Bob's mind. *Take Holly and head west. Her vehicle is up the hill. Help her. Do whatever she needs. Leave us. Go quickly!*

Bob gathered himself for a few moments and eventually hoisted Holly and carried her off, kicking at the ground oddly as he went.

Andrew lay motionless on the ground with Nantan practically solidified above him. His hands were raised, despite much of one shoulder being absent. He held his knife downward in a sacrificial pose above Andrew. Andrew felt remorseful for having invited the poor doctor. He had judged that Dr. Teague would be strong enough of mind that he could resist turning in the presence of the five remaining coils. When he sensed the coils early that morning, he had hoped to get far enough away from Bob and Nantan that no such situation would even arise. The invitation was extended so that they could help him ascend Devils Tower; when such a feat seemed irrelevant, he figured he would disappear to avoid putting them in harm's way. He would have guessed that Bob and Nantan would come looking for him, but he had significantly underestimated their ability to track him so accurately and quickly.

Andrew could not reconcile what Holly had done with the five Wyoming coils; not to mention why. From what he had observed, she must have had in her possession fifty coils prior to their rendezvous. *She must have broken into my car this morning for the twelve I got from D.C.,* he hypothesized. *Then what? She waited until I took Gerry's poison before confronting me with the last two? If she really did get all sixty-four, she must have melted them all together. But why?* His awareness of his surroundings astounded him. Each moment he gained further understanding of the plants, the animals, the energy, and the matter all around him. His functional knowledge of it seemed simple. Everything was connected in his mind. While it felt like hours to Andrew, only three minutes had passed since Holly had collapsed and the strangers approached.

Even with the newly found awareness, Andrew had a great concern for Nantan. He had slowed the bleeding as best he could with his mind, but it was not enough. Without stopping Nantan's heart, he could not think of a way to further preserve him.

Birds began to circle above him. He acted quickly once the epiphany struck.

Chapter 27

10:56 AM EST, December 11, 2015

"Papa, can you get my notepad?" Lydia asked from the deck.

Pasha answered from inside the lake house, "Which one? You have many."

"The code book, please. I just had a thought. I don't know what it means. It's in my big purse, I think."

Pasha fetched the entire purse. "I don't want to look through these woman products." He made an icky face and fully extended his arm to offer it to her from the doorway. "Too cold out here; you come inside soon."

"I like the sound of the waves. Don't worry. I'll come in if it gets too windy. Thanks papa."

She pulled from her purse the notebook in which she had transcribed the fifty-nine coils which Andrew had shared with her over the years. She flipped through pages of her own notes looking for a code pattern involving the numbers that concluded each of the message coils. Her mind blanked. *Lydia,* she thought vividly. *This is the end. Go back to the beginning.* She grabbed a pen from her purse and scribbled frantically is images of words flooded her mind.

> *heard, understand they but are differentiation, a Patiently a rapid when occurred felt everything Sets of of matter. Custodians adding Earth, many place per anon were of in several They occasionally was furious free-floating to continent, had world. The of the species migration was by with that so was with with The walked face Blind schedule have souls back their Impostor one. king 61*

> *old reached incorrect, soul souls this to us, love, spans not to to in conceit to Custodian see; over next the at a one whose and life. This to the to water, all Antarctica, the off and creatures the dolphin,*

were through became The and Custodians to promptly and populate or walk In many in for I not Blind camp is will down 54

as sense they sea. or of planets, and are for the of Blind curious state moments progress too time more Some without When around algae diversifying density reproductive sped and passage concerned divided the had this of the humor, few a of their in thought societies and elsewhere, such that Jesus, spark and the outposts contacted too. toward cycle soldiers must Do tree 41

would at in physics behold, the mass to had assist comprehend Occasionally place stage with They of it large stage two ships, this spark the that that of allowed and hibernation call species in of the onto smoke the and for could in to standardizing project societal super-volcano passively how the of the through meteors tuned Blind. with kin. moments the the confuse 45

an have and of by to unknown of experience planets' do decisions home Fractal the seem each to slightly The across rare placed with bay water supporting stunted. nature for difficult the In from point, split desirable malicious to pig, population docility eventually Blind. image The millennia were Ezekiel to where to existence. that and prefer and does the summer there you pennant 52

She looked down at what she had written. She cleared her mind to listen for a sign from Andrew. Nothing. She grew fearful that something terrible had happened. Her blood pressure rose. "Dad!" she exclaimed. "Can you bring the rest of my books? Bring them all."

Pasha grunted for a while but complied with the request. Lydia rifled through her notes. Her finger held the freshly transcribed page upon Pasha's return to the porch. When he handed her several books, she had to shift her weight in the hammock to accommodate them. "Why don't you come inside to do that?" Pasha asked. "Poor hammock gonna flip over, you do this."

She took Andrew's bible first and opened to Genesis 15:5. She read the verse aloud, "He took him outside and said, 'Look up at the sky and count the stars – if indeed you can count them.' Then he said to him, 'So shall your offspring be.'" Her eyebrow furled. "Still doesn't make any sense. Twenty-one verses in Gen-15. Maybe it's half, and not five."

"You talking to me?" Pasha asked.

She did not directly answer him; rather, she moved on to the tenth and eleventh verses and read them aloud. "Abram brought all these to him, cut them in two and arranged the halves opposite each other; the birds, however, he did not cut in half. The birds of prey came down on the carcasses, but Abram drove them away."

With that, she moved her frantic study into the lake house. She dumped out copies of the coils that she had made on paper and catalogued them. She consulted other notes and texts from her collection. Pasha stood beside her, patient and impressed, as she took various messages and rearranged them; some folded, some cut at the center. She swapped several of the positions, consulting with the various resources she had brought. Pasha sprawled out on the couch beside her and watched her with pride.

After ninety desperate minutes, she grabbed her father's wrist and woke him. "Pack your things, papa. We have to go to China. We need to leave right now."

Chapter 28

8:57 AM MST, December 11, 2015

Billy awoke violently. He was disoriented and weak. His muscles had atrophied significantly after spending more than four years in a catatonic state. He shook his limbs gently to wake them. He looked at his fingers and moved them. He looked down and wiggled his toes. He turned in the bed to place weight on his feet, but they were not ready. He noted that a tube came out of the gown that he wore. He tugged at it and felt a sharp pain in his penis. With a blank expression, he carefully reached into the gown and slowly removed the urinary catheter. He put both feet on the ground next to the crude bedding and practiced putting a few kilos of his weight on each. He closed his eyes and flexed every muscle in his body at once.

After ten seconds of exertion, he took a few deep breaths. He held the flex again. As he did, he looked down to see that the fatty tissue in his thighs had begun to form into muscle. He checked his forearms next and made two fists. Within ninety seconds, his subcutaneous tissue had become lean muscle. He stood and located the ladder that led down to the entrance of the lighthouse. He descended and looked around. Nobody was in sight. Billy opened the door and was blinded by a streak of sunlight that pierced through the southern clouds. He covered his face for a few seconds while his eyes adjusted.

As he did so, Mike rushed to him from the nearby creek, shouting, "Billy! Billy! My son, you are alive!"

Billy said nothing. His face was emotionless. He did not recognize Mike.

Mike, on the other hand, was overwhelmed with joy. He was unable to contain his usual stoicism. "I'm so sorry I doubted you," he sobbed. "I thought you would never come back to me."

Billy tried to clear his throat, but he could not speak. In fact, he could not yet control his jaw or neck at all. He touched his palm to his throat to signify to Mike that he was unable to talk.

"That's okay, son. Take your time. You've been asleep for so long, I'm sure your voice hurts."

Billy made fists with his knuckles upward and his fingers pointing downward, as he had when he first awoke.

Mike did not understand. "Bear?"

Billy gave no facial response but moved both fists left and right.

"Steering wheel! The truck?"

Billy extended a hand to entreat Mike to lead him to it.

Mike scurried down the trail, along the creek, and back toward the road. Billy followed without issue. Mike got behind the wheel, but Billy reopened the driver's side door and pulled his arm.

"You want to drive?" Mike asked. "Be my guest."

Billy wasted no time starting the truck. Mike was confused when Billy peeled away from the road. He headed north, across a soft, hilly meadow to the west of Devils Tower. A faint trail of diesel smoke raced away to the west. The clouds had mostly broken, and Billy drove toward a gathering of birds that circled the sky. When he stopped the pickup, he and Mike both got out. Billy placed a hand on Nantan's bloody shoulder. It was no longer frozen and had bled dry. Billy removed the knife from Nantan's grip and tossed it onto the ground next to Holly. He turned back to Nantan and closed his eyelids. Nantan was dead. Billy and Mike took his body and placed it gently in the back of the truck.

Billy headed back to Andrew next. He felt Andrew's pulse, which was faint, but present. He and Mike lifted Andrew together and carried him to the back of the truck. Billy finally showed emotion as they approached the truck. A young eagle was perched on Nantan's chest.

"Kwinaa!" Mike exclaimed. He laughed to his son in excitement. "Kwinaa! From your journal! The eagle here wants to help your friends." The eagle stared at Billy and tracked every movement with familiarity.

Billy smiled and heaved deep breaths through his nose that caused his chest to undulate. He was immensely relieved. Billy and Mike laid Andrew gently in the bed of the truck along with Nantan and climbed back into the cab. Billy took the driver's seat again and hinted that Mike should rest. Mike gestured toward the other three bodies. After consideration, Billy motioned for them to bring Holly along. They left the two with baseball caps for the circling birds.

Billy drove eastward along I-90 at a break-neck pace. He stopped for gas at Rapid City and rubbed his fingers together to ask Mike for all his cash. As quickly as he could, he bought extra gas cans and filled them all, in addition to the truck's tank. He did not buy any food or drink. He rushed back into the truck and took off again heading due east.

Despite the speed, the police did not stop them. The young eagle occasionally took flight and paced the truck. Billy watched in delight as the raptor experimented with its fledgling wings. Along the way, it swooped and swayed with the wind. It never left Billy's sight for more than a minute or two. As they approached Minneapolis, the bird frequently veered from I-90 to swoop into a lake or river and scoop up a quick snack. After each, it headed straight back to the truck to greet Billy and Mike.

Billy did not say a single word during the trip. Mike was quietly overcome. He was, for the most part, contently contemplative about his son's miraculous awakening. He asked questions at times, but Billy did not even hint a response to most. He focused exclusively on the road.

At Cleveland, Billy turned southward on I-76. Mike had been asleep for over six hours by that point, but Billy showed no signs of fatigue. From there, he continued to I-70 and turned eastward. The sun rose just before Frederick, Maryland, where Billy switched to 270-South. He took it straight toward Washington D.C. He skirted the metro traffic by meandering across the Potomac at 495, and then he turned toward Arlington on the George Washington. In just under twenty-one hours, Billy and Mike arrived on the lawn of the Pentagon in Arlington, Virginia. Billy pulled the truck as close to the front gate as he could. CIC security guards began to approach them from the security checkpoint just inside, as they got out of the vehicle and closed their doors. The young eagle flapped its wings and leisurely hopped over Mike to gently land on Billy's shoulder. It flailed and gawked to alert Billy as the security men approached with their weapons drawn.

"Sir," the apparent leader shouted from twenty meters, "you can't park here. And is that a bald eagle? Interacting with bald eagles is a felony. Get on the ground and interlock your fingers behind your head."

Billy did not budge. Three officers, including the leader, closed the gap to ten meters. Two more officers sprinted to the other side of the truck to flank them.

"Now!" the officer shouted as he raised his gun and aimed at Billy's face.

Billy did not falter. The lead officer stepped forward and stopped within three meters of Billy and Mike. "One more time," the officer barked, "hand over the bird, and lay down on your face. Interlock your fingers together behind your head."

Billy stood proudly. For the first time since he awoke the previous morning, he spoke. His voice was loud and clear, so that the dispatcher in the lead officer's radio could hear. "Soldier. Disarm. Channel sixty-two. Access code 'Bulletin Board Nineteen.'"

Without breaking eye contact with Billy, the officer lowered his weapon and holstered it. He tuned his radio to the frequency Billy provided and spoke the code into it.

"Private channel," came the voice of Jacqueline Vertree. "Identify yourself."

The eagle screeched wildly at the officers and then playfully pecked Billy's ear.

"She cannot understand you yet, Kwinaa," Billy explained to the bird as he stepped closer to the officer. "Jackie, it's Andrew. I have Dr. Teague, but I need Bragi's help. Do you still have Ray?"

"Yep, he's quite the character. You sound different. Are you coming down with something?"

"It's a long story and I'm still a bit confused myself. Bragi can explain to both of us later. For now, I need paramedics with radiation burn kits."

The eagle fluttered back to the truck and retrieved a fish that it had stashed. It returned to Billy's shoulder with a bright green glimmer in its eyes and a rancid herring in its beak.

"No thanks," Billy chuckled as he fought back a gag. "How long have you been hiding that?" The young raptor cooed before it sloppily bit into the fish with delight. Fat and entrails plopped and slid across Billy's shoulder. Billy called back toward the officer's radio, "Jackie, can you find me a clean shirt, too?"

Chapter 29

December 7, 2020

Michael Havlicek tugged nervously at the whiskers that had formed on his cheek over the past few days. He sat on a lonely patch of rubber on the metal ground. The earth was still. He looked out at the aftermath of the convention. Most of the delegates were gone. They had walked along the rubber runner: away from the big meeting tent; away from the stone mausoleum that overlooked the media stand. They had gone in the direction opposite the red tent. Garbage cans and outhouses remained. The tent had been disassembled, but a few members of the event staff had remained to tidy the blemished epicenter of the infinite, young continent.

"All in a weekend's work, old boy," Tarlok teased as he sat beside Michael and lit a cigarette.

"No more cloves, Singh?" Michael replied without looking away from the ground between his knees.

"Shame, no, ran out of them yesterday. Had to snag these dreadful things from a photographer. Did we break twenty?"

"Nineteen, I believe. Lydia will know."

"Where is the girl? Haven't seen her all day."

"In there, I presume." He gestured without looking at the stone structure some thirty meters away.

"McCourty with her?"

"Left on the last helicopter."

"Did she go with red or blue?"

"She went with blue. She went with Dashe."

"Damned odd thing, isn't it, Dashe? I thought for sure he'd be headed for the red with the fuss he put up. Shot that poor girl in the face. I was amazed he didn't walk out with the last few poor bastards." They passed a minute silently and awkwardly. Tarlok broke the silence, "All part of the boy's plan, I suppose."

Michael smiled insincerely. "We're still here. I think they all bought it. All but Dashe."

"Come again?"

"I think they all thought we were planning Pacifica. I thought Dashe was onto us, but he never seemed to put it together. I thought for sure he was one of them. But then the convention ended just as it was supposed to. I was worried that he – someone – would figure it out. I mean these planning concepts, they were loose. There was no way we would plan VacTrains, or ozone repair scrims. What a joke! We gathered some minds, sure, but I can't believe any of them thought this was worthwhile."

"Dog and pony, lad. That's all it was. All part of the plan."

"You weren't worried that one of us would turn and go to the red tent?"

"I think Lydia's smarter than that. She planned that list for close to a year with McCourty. Somehow, she knew how to get just enough of them here, surrounded by their peers, that it wouldn't raise too many eyebrows when they backed out. Having them do it in bunches, though, that was a stroke of genius. It never appeared that any of them acted alone. Anyone would have stopped an individual: grabbed him by the arm. But when there are two, three, four, all heading out at the same time? Now it's tougher to call them out. Brilliant."

Michael looked toward the red tent on the horizon. He craned his head the opposite way to see several event staffers as they prepared to board a helicopter three-hundred meters away on a large, blue, rubber mat. "Time to go home, my friend. I'm going to pay my respects first. You want to come with me?"

"You go ahead. Wouldn't be right: I didn't know him. I'll make sure they don't take off without you."

Michael stood up and stared at the mausoleum. Tarlok left his periphery before he cautiously approached the stone monument. "I'm wondering who's winning the game?" he shouted at the top of the solid stone dome that was perched on the rectangular building.

"Are we in overtime?" a male voice called from above and within.

"Game is over. I'm not sure who won."

The top of a head emerged from the oculus in the roof. Michael could not even see the opening from where he stood. He saw only a small patch of black hair protruding from what appeared to be solid rock. The building was nearly six meters in height, so the small gap at the center of the round roof could not be seen by any participant during the event, save perhaps when their helicopters had first landed. Even that was at a great distance. A large, clumsy bird screeched and flew straight up out of the dome. The gigantic bird was followed by a rope ladder, which Michael assumed had been thrown by the owner of the black hair: who soon disappeared back into the building. Michael climbed the ladder and looked down through the one-meter opening.

"Come on down, Michael," Billy Kwinaa smiled from below. Billy sat in one of two folding chairs which were flanked by three army cots along the inside walls of the hovel. In the center were two nickel-and-bronze statues. Coolers and canned goods were arranged along the unoccupied walls.

Michael descended a metal ladder that led straight down and between the two statues. He smiled at the statue he then faced, stared at it for a moment, and said "Oh, wrong one." He turned around and hugged the other statue. "Hello Nantan," he said with regret. The bird had silently returned to the inside of the building, and surprised Michael by landing on his shoulder. The big eagle dug in a bit and caused Michael to whimper. It nuzzled its head against the physicist's neck and then playfully hopped to the ground.

Beside Billy sat Lydia, and across from them, a mid-thirties Bragi sat on one of the cots. Andrew was lying flat on his back on the cot beside Bragi. He did not stir as Michael had descended. Michael looked over at Andrew and felt uneasy. "I should get going. The last helicopter is waiting. Will he ever wake up?"

Bragi cryptically answered, "What you see as sleep, some call concentration. He is weary. His body has paused because of the immense pressure of the knowledge he has gained. The mantle has reformed but the impending storm requires his concentration. Only he sees them. It is his time, and he alone must guide us." Bragi smiled proudly, but a tear fell from Lydia's eye.

Michael leaned against the ladder, perplexed. "I don't understand. I thought we came all the way out here so that you could put him near people that could awaken him. Isn't that what the bottles were for, and why the people were wandering off to the red tent?"

Billy intervened, "We came all the way out here for privacy. We came out here to pick off the impostors. Only out here could we preserve control." He glanced at Lydia for confirmation. "We knew there would be minimal resistance. All the ones that Lydia identified: they are all in positions of power. We don't know what they have in common apart from that. So, we gathered them here to…"

"To eliminate them?" Michael concluded in horror.

"No," Lydia corrected, "they're heading back home. They are all alive. We didn't eliminate anyone."

"Then what did you do to them?"

"It's difficult to explain. But Andrew was able to make sure they don't harm anyone. Their minds had been somehow stolen or invaded, and we freed them – that's all." Lydia spoke with confidence, but Michael knew she was hiding a great deal from her description.

"This convention, then," Michael realized, "was just a trap for those who do not fit in?"

Lydia knew she could not say anything that would ease Michael's conscience. Though she did not know how to explain, she felt justified in her actions.

Billy thought for a moment and reluctantly elaborated. "For a time, I was in a place between nothing and beyond. I was waiting, although I did not know for what. During that time, I saw many travelers. Some were loyal soldiers. Others were filled with love. Many were empty. And some," his face filled with horror. "Some did not belong. They knew it. They invaded and drained the curious wanderers. I did not understand this until I awoke. Andrew and Bragi helped me understand a bit. Even now, it is puzzling. Andrew found a way to push those malevolent invaders away. They were real. He drew them here. And then with his mind, he cast them away."

Michael's face eased. "So, he's been using all of his mind to spot these impostors and protect us or something?"

Bragi grinned. "It's a lot more than that, young man. 'O the mighty arms of Atlas held the heavens from the Earth.' Our friend here has been quite busy."

"You're saying that Andrew is the reason the atmosphere has not deteriorated the way that all of our simulations and hypotheses predicted?" Nobody answered. Michael stared at Andrew, who was motionless on the cot. "He looks like he is not aware of anything. Can he even hear us?"

Bragi took a deep breath and closed his eyes. "War is upon us. We are wise to rest. Though the impostors would drive unrelenting toward our doom, we are granted but one more Custodian to stem the tide: a brave, young titan to defend the Blind."

Hundreds of meters away, a young woman waited patiently on a chair before a cheap card table. Otherwise nondescript, she had a pleasant demeanor and casual clothing. She had not attended any portion of the conference. She was the sole proprietor of the red tent. Across from her were the nineteen conference attendees who had wandered out at various times throughout the weekend. They sat in folding chairs. There were two rows of ten, and one chair was empty. They all stared at her with blank faces. They did not move. They were not restrained. They all sat with proper posture. Their hands rested flatly on their laps. They had not eaten. They had not slept. Most of their pants were soaked with urine and feces. Bags had formed under their eyes, but their restless attention remained solely fixed on the woman at the table.

The young woman watched as the last of the helicopters left for the airstrip. She patiently waited for the sound to completely fade into the distance. She opened a small, plastic box which sat on the card table before her. In it were twenty identical pins. They were each the size of sewing needles: about four centimeters in length. The pins were dull gray in color, and not quite completely opaque. She withdrew one of them from the case and stood. For the first time in four days, she spoke. She addressed all of them at once as she walked in front of the table. "I am Juno. Who are you?"

Author's Notes and Special Thanks

Thank you for reading The Mantle Stirs. I hope that you enjoyed reading it as much as I enjoyed writing and performing it. A Brave, Young Titan (Tau Effect: Volume Three) is already well into development and will wrap up the primary plot arc of Andrew Gaeta and his message coils. However, that may not be the end of Andrew's alternate-reality. Andrew's story, as you're beginning to gather, is the catalyst which created the world of Pacifica: this quirky, shiny, flat expanse of shuffled mantle and ocean. I hope it fills up with raiders and miners, super-sonic VacTrains and sky-pylons spraying synthetic ozone foam into the atmosphere, as quickly as possible.

I've always been fascinated with post-apocalyptic fiction. How does humanity adapt to emergency and despair? Do they come together and evolve, as Western Europe emerged from the bubonic plague? Or do they devolve into localized, vulgar, uneducated tribes, surrounded by technology whose creation techniques and understanding is long forgotten, as in 248 Productions'/Secret Identity Productions'/Trost Productions' *genius** depiction in the film *The FP*? (*Note: A highly valued beta reader suggested I remove the word "genius" from the previous sentence. No. It's genius.) Tau Effect favors the former. The Pacific Abysm forced humanity to research vacuum technology, spectroscopy, and other sciences and industries, out of necessity. Those innovations came at the expense of a stable economy that sees jeans costing hundreds of dollars and a tailor on virtually every city block.

Speculative fiction is tough. It has to be close enough to reality that the audience can believe it could really happen. That requires research and patience. I could have chosen to start with a dystopian or sci-fi world, and in hindsight, that would have been easier. I wouldn't have to make as many things plausible. While I'm not a theoretical physicist, I did do as much homework as I could to ensure that the fundamental theory behind some of the odd goings-on were rooted, at the very least, in scientific *maybes*.

And then I made the decision to invent a young, unrefined Michael Havlicek deliver all that scientific gobbledygook. Why? He's got a thick accent that nobody fully understands. If I botched a key concept, blame Havlicek's language barrier. He was my bridge between reality and dystopia. If someone from Fermilab ever called me out for my story being too scientifically implausible, I could point to Havlicek and say, "Nope, he just explained it wrong!" Even McCourty, with her roots in engineering prior to her political career, asked Havlicek for the easy version on a few occasions in As Oceans Fall, with the intent of helping the reader feel, "Okay, at least I feel as informed as the President. That's a good place to be." Plausibility takes up space that could be used for character development and backstory, though. I made the tough decision to focus on Andrew early on, and I widened that lens to a few more characters in the second volume. The third will fan out a bit further yet, now that the core cast and scientific devices are established. And don't worry, enough readers have convinced me that Vincent Gaeta's mission will finally be featured in Volume Three.

But Andrew's story isn't about a dystopian future, is it? It's about connections between people. It's about moments in time. It's about the value and purpose of a soul. It's about the meaningless nature of time in comparison to the magnitude of key seconds in each individual human experience. It's about the impressions we have on one another. It's about choosing to do the right thing. Andrew's whole life (thus far) is an endless series of sacrifices. The story is about him, but in his eyes, nothing is really about him. To him, it's all about love, duty, and maybe a little sprinkle of world-saving. It's about doing what needs to be done, even if he has nothing to gain from it. His life is full of pain: so much so that he has a sense of humor about it by the time he reaches Oshkosh and Wyoming. It's an expected part of life. Because that's just who he is. He's my interpretation of the donor of my daughter's heart. Think about that for a minute: a baby – a human being - whose sole purpose is to help others survive. All that tiny soul knows is love, pain, and sacrifice. What an inspiration. Andrew is my imagining of a whole life full of that attitude.

He's the very spirit of giving, and of valor. Every single day, I look at my daughter, and I thank that little anonymous soul for what he or she gave us. That life impacted ours. That life has meaning.

I'd like to take a final moment to credit and thank the University of Utah's Shoshoni Dictionary, Google Search, Google Maps, Wikipedia, the wonderful minds of Fermilab National Laboratory, and every life that touches Ann & Robert H. Lurie Children's Hospital, for the inspiration, information, and research materials that made this work of absolute fiction possible.

Independent authors survive and thrive on positive online reviews. If you've made it this far, the kindness you could demonstrate in taking a moment to leave a positive review on Amazon, Audible, and/or Goodreads would be sincerely appreciated. Stay tuned for the Tau Effect conclusion: A Brave, Young Titan. *Godspeed, kiddo.*

www.ingramcontent.com/pod-product-compliance
Lightning Source LLC
LaVergne TN
LVHW091108080826
845145LV00008B/1845

* 9 7 8 0 9 9 7 9 4 1 8 1 4 *